SHERLOCK HOLMES

Jaico Sherlock Holmes Series

The GOLDEN YEARS

SHERLOCK HOLMES

Jaico Sherlock Holmes Series

The GOLDEN YEARS

KIM H. KRISCO

JAICO PUBLISHING HOUSE

Ahmedabad Bangalore Chennai
Delhi Hyderabad Kolkata Mumbai

Published by Jaico Publishing House
A-2 Jash Chambers, 7-A Sir Phirozshah Mehta Road
Fort, Mumbai - 400 001
jaicopub@jaicobooks.com
www.jaicobooks.com

Published in arrangement with
MX Publishing Ltd
335 Princess Park Manor
London, N11 3GX

SHERLOCK HOLMES
THE GOLDEN YEARS
ISBN 978-81-8495-709-9

First Jaico Impression: 2015

Page design and layout: SÜRYA, New Delhi

Printed by
Repro India Limited, Mumbai

ACKNOWLEDGEMENTS

IF YOU COULD, in reality, see what lies beneath the author's name on the cover, you might see many names, stretching back to my second grade teacher, Sister Mary Frances, who awarded me a Rudolph the Red-Nosed Reindeer snow globe for a Christmas story I wrote sixty-one years ago. However, let me focus my gratitude on those people who *directly* contributed to the writing of this book:

Sir Arthur Conan Doyle – the consummate storyteller. I hope that you will see his inspiration in these stories.

Dan Andriacco – whose books I sought when I needed "more Holmes." When I reached out to him as a fellow author, he was available, helpful and encouraging.

Steve Emecz – whose love for Sherlock Holmes ripples out to an international audience of Holmes aficionados, through his works, and via authors like me, whom he supports, encourages, and publishes.

Bob Gibson – a talented artist who designed and rendered a cover that captures the "spirit" of this collection.

Joe Revill – a talented author, who generously gave his time and talents to make this a better book. His editorial guidance would make Holmes proud.

Sara Rose – who consistently reminds me to *taste* life – not just write about it.

And *you* – who complete the human connection that writing, and all art, is about. Thank you.

CONTENTS

PREFACE

THESE FIVE, TOTALLY new, Sherlock Holmes adventures take place after Holmes and Watson *believe* they have gone into retirement. Of course, you and I know, such a notion is irrealizable for either of them. Indeed, some of their most remarkable, and dangerous, adventures await them.

While each story is a separate adventure, the five tales within this collection follow one another chronologically. Some characters move from one story to the next as well. Therefore, it is suggested that you read each of the stories in the order in which they appear in this book.

While it is not necessary to be familiar with Doyle's Sherlock Holmes stories in order to enjoy this collection, it would definitely enhance your reading experience. Certainly, if you are not already a Sherlock Holmes fan, it is hoped that these stories will encourage you to indulge in the original canon, as well as the many excellent stories and books that are keeping the spirit of Holmes and Watson alive in the world.

Finally, this collection is only the first of the "golden years adventures." You can look forward to more.

1
THE BONNIE BAG OF BONES

Mythical monsters, and the woman, hunt Holmes.

THE GOLDEN YEARS, as they are called, were becoming colourless for me. Holmes had long since moved from London to Sussex Downs to play the part of a gentrified English gentleman. As he predicted prior to his relocation, "I am ready to leave my profession, however I fear retirement will elude me."

Since our separation, our meetings had become more and more infrequent. So, I was much surprised to receive his telegram in April of the year 1912:

WATSON

KNOWING HOW OUR TURBULENT WORLD NEEDS REASON MORE THAN EVER AM MYSTIFIED AT YOUR LATEST OFFERING TO GULLIBLE MASSES.

YOU ARE PANDERING TO SUPERSTITION.

HOLMES

This brusque missive, no doubt, alluded to my latest series of articles for *The Strand Magazine* chronicling the mythology of the British Isles. I will admit to some small poetic licence as I retold folk stories that are as much a part of our culture as roast beef and Yorkshire pudding. However, Holmes's assessment chaffed me. It was an affront to my character, and I intended to tell him to his face.

It took no small effort to find my way to his cottage. His modest dwelling sat adjacent to the Eastbourne to Brighton Road less than a mile from salt water. Unlike the craggy cliffs to the north, green hillocks rose from the channel, undulating ever higher to his modest estate. This verdant setting offered protection for his precious bees.

I arrived at a traditional thatched roof stone cottage. It was larger than I had imagined, with its huge pitched roof no doubt housing two or more bedrooms. The overgrown walkway led to a white plank door flanked symmetrically by two windows with questionable glazing. It was hard to imagine my cosmopolitan friend resting in this bucolic locale.

The anticipation of seeing my dear comrade again was barely contained. *Get a hold, you old fool,* I told myself. I took a moment to catch my breath before I knocked. When the second knock failed, I walked to the back of his lodgings and spied him across the laurel-clumped lawn, deep within a neglected garden, hunched over one of his hive boxes. As I approached, he spoke without turning to me.

"Honey is very precious, Watson. I estimate it takes the year-long toil of many hundreds of bees to produce one pound of honey."

"Interesting, Holmes, but I did not make this trip to talk of bees."

Ignoring me, Holmes continued.

"Honey is a natural healing potion, Watson. Alexander the Great was embalmed with it."

Before I could intervene, he turned and looked at me sheepishly.

"No doubt my telegram brought you, my friend," he said, as he removed his gloves and protective head-dress.

"Indeed, Holmes, you are insufferable at times."

"My dear fellow," said he, in an unusually effusive manner, "I apologize for causing offence, but your latest installment in the *Strand*, you must admit, falls into the realm of ghosts and goblins. The Grey Man of Ben MacDhui… really!"

"I might ask what you know about it, Holmes."

My huffing seemed to bring a smile to his lips as he added, "I have missed you, my friend."

He took my arm to walk us back toward his lodgings. However, he would not allow us to bask in sentimentality for long.

"Ben MacDhui, I believe, is the second highest peak in Britain. It's situated among the Cairngorms, which I have always thought are Britain's grandest range." He paused. "As for this Grey Man creature, you must know that it is but shadows in the gloom – a figment of imaginations soggy with usquebaugh."

"It's funny you should mention that, Holmes," I noted. "My first encounter with the Grey Man tale was at the Days of Yore inn in Aviemore. I had received a telegram from the innkeeper, who, evidently, had been reading my collection of stories. Bones were discovered upon Ben MacDhui, and he invited me to see them."

Holmes and I walked through the open back door into the kitchen. He scrambled across the brick floor to the stove and began stoking the coals as well as his own curiosity. As he set the kettle on, he quipped, "No doubt, these were the bones of the Grey Man."

"On the contrary. They were human bones."

Holmes remained motionless at the stove, his back to me still.

"Really, Watson." He turned to me with raised eyebrows, and a familiar glint in his eyes. "Pray, tell me more."

"As I said, I received a telegram from a Mr. Duncan Munro at the Days of Yore asking that I come as his guest to examine the bones, which he felt may be those of the Grey Man," I recollected. "So, I decided to take a bit of a walking holiday and visit the inn."

"And, what, precisely, did you find there, Watson?"

"The premises seemed to be in disrepair and offered the barest of accommodations. The tavern was dark and fusty, and there was but one gentleman sitting at the bar. When I approached, Munro popped up from behind the counter and greeted me. He was a huge man with a face as craggy as the local foothills. When I made my introduction to Mr. Munro, his entire countenance lighted up. He thanked me for coming, offered me a drink, and began his tale."

"You would say then, that the inn was a less than successful enterprise, Watson?"

"I would say so."

"Did he show you the bones?"

"Only after recounting the strange reckonings of this grim creature he referred to as Fear Liath Mòr," I said. "It seems that strange sightings and experiences, over the last several centuries, have amalgamated into a popular image of a huge, ape-like creature that has the malign power to send people into a blind panic down Ben MacDhui Mountain. Some have said that the creature attempted to push them over the steep cliffs of Lurcher's Crag."

"Blind superstition, Watson. The bones… tell me about the bones."

"Eventually, Munro hauled a musty sack from under the bar and placed it in front of me. As he did, a friendless gentleman at the bar leaned closer. I pulled the bones out of the bag one at a time."

"And…"

"There was a human skull – actually, part of a skull; the jawbone with several teeth in it, and most of the facial frame. There was a hole in the top of the skull, and the area around it was cracked."

"Do you suspect foul play?"

"Possibly," I said. "It could have been caused by a blow… or from a fall."

Holmes left the kettle upon the stove and sat down at my side.

"And the skull was human you say."

"Most assuredly. One can tell from the large cranial cavity. And, a subsequent look at the remaining bones confirms this assessment. There was a femur, tibia and most of a pelvic girdle. Also some smaller bones, most likely metatarsals."

"But, no Grey Man," Holmes said, with a little smile. "No doubt your assessment proved disappointing to Mr. Munro."

I chuckled.

"Only momentarily. He is convinced that this person, whose bones were scattered on the bar, was a sad victim of the creature."

Holmes shook his head, "I have no doubt that there are some wild men wondering among the Cairngorm Plateaux, but they are much less hairy than the average ape, and more inclined to be popping up in the Days of Yore tavern."

The kettle was boiling, and Holmes turned to the stove. He took two cups from the shelf above the dry sink and set them on the table. As he went about making tea, I could feel his great mind grinding steadily faster like a bicyclist pumping uphill.

Holmes brought the teapot to the table and set it down. "Where are the bones now?"

"They are in my apartment in the city. Mr. Munro was reluctant to part with them, but I wanted a closer inspection before writing my story."

Holmes raised his eyebrows in wonder. "And, what of the local authorities?"

"I stopped by the local constabulary before leaving Aviemore. Rumours of the bones had already reached the station. As it turns out, there was some interest, because a man went missing in that area some time back. Evidently, I had preempted the sergeant's call on Mr. Munro."

"And, they allowed you to keep the bones?"

"My credentials were of help here," I noted. "I promised to provide my expert assessment and, of course, return the bones in due course."

"I would inspect the bones at some point," Holmes said. "I am certain they have much to tell."

Holmes silently poured the tea. He sat down and raised his cup as in a toast. "The evil that men do lives after them. The good is oft interred with their bones.' And, you and I, my dear Watson, will find the evil left behind. That is, if you are disposed to joining me for another visit to Ben MacDhui Mountain."

"Holmes, nothing would give me more pleasure. However, I came ill prepared for such a journey."

"Nonsense, my friend," Holmes said, reaching out to grab my arm. "Leave that to me. You shall bide here tonight, and I will provide all that is needed. You have no commitments in London. Come along, let us prepare your room."

It was sad for me to note that he was right. There would be no need for a telegram to London. No one was expecting me. And, for a moment, my mind turned to my dear Mary. However, my mood brightened because I could see that the lust of the chase was, once again, upon my good friend.

As Holmes climbed the stairs to the loft he remarked, "Like old times, is it not?"

When I entered the gabled loft, Holmes had spread a new blanket on the bed and was setting out a nightshirt. He began bustling around gathering items for my toilet when a knock came at the door.

"Get that if you please," Holmes said. "It's Mrs. Thornton, my housekeeper."

Mrs. Thornton began preparing fisherman's pie for us, a maritime version of shepherd's pie. As she worked her culinary magic in the kitchen, I perused the parlour. As in our old Baker Street lodgings, his Bohemian nature was evident. Books and papers were scattered among the tables; glass jars, with wilted flowers and dead insects, were lined along one windowsill. His latest book sat next to his old Morris chair – *Practical Handbook of Bee Culture with Some Observations Upon Segregation of the Queen*.

I ran my fingers over the leather spine and wondered: *Segregation of the queen, indeed.*

Just then, Holmes entered the room with two glasses of brandy. "I see you have happened upon my latest offering."

"Quite so. I must admit to not having purchased my own copy as of yet."

"Then you shall have that one. The most fascinating creatures on this earth, I would venture to say. Magnificent creatures. If the noble bee disappeared from our earth, I fear mankind's years would be numbered. It is the cornerstone of our agriculture. I've observed these creatures pollinating carrots, broccoli, apples, cherries, pumpkins, sunflowers – indeed the vast majority of flowers rely upon the bee."

"Fascinating Holmes," I replied, as I hefted the book in my hands. "I look forward to learning more. What did you learn about the queen – the segregated queen?"

"Ah, that is the most fascinating thing of all," Holmes said, as he sprang to life. "The entire hive lives and works in service to the queen. She mates only once in her life, with many drones, over a two or three day period. She stores their essence away and uses it to fertilize the hundreds of eggs she lays."

His eyes turned into the distance as he continued. "When she is removed, or segregated, the entire colony falls into disarray. They buzz around madly without purpose. It seems that producing into the needs of the queen is their *raison d'êtr*."

"I suspect that may be true of many species," I reflected aloud.

Holmes was silent.

The next day we set out for Aviemore, changing trains in London and Glasgow. When we arrived at the Days of Yore inn, I was astounded to find it bustling with patrons. As our valises were being brought in from the cart, Mr. Munro was dashing out of the kitchen with two plates of sandwiches. His broad florid face was sweaty. His bushy brows lifted as he spied us.

"Oh, hello Doctor!" Munro exclaimed. "I'm delighted to hav' ye ca again." He raised one finger as a signal to wait, and went into the dining room with the sandwiches. A moment later, he returned, empty-handed. "A while since we've had such'a full hoose."

"I say... I trust you can make room for me and my companion. This is Mr. Sherlock Holmes."

He wiped his hand on his soiled apron and extended it toward Holmes. "My, my – most honoured, sir. Your reputation precedes ye."

Holmes took his hand with a little reticence and remarked, "It seems your lot is much improved."

"Indeed, sir. It is, and largely thanks to this gentleman," the innkeeper said, setting his huge hand upon my shoulder. "Your article in the *Strand*, and recent reports in the *Daily Record* and *The Herald*, have been a bonny boon." He pointed to the clippings above the desk next to us.

"Gentlemen," Munro went on, "I'll need a wee bit o' time to prepare your rooms. You, no doubt, wish to wet your whistle after a long journey." He motioned toward the bar.

"I could use a draft, Holmes. What do you say?" I enquired.

"Splendid idea, Watson."

We settled into our modest accommodations, and later enjoyed a country dinner. The "inky-pinky" was average, but I cannot say when I enjoyed a better pudding. As the dining room cleared out, Holmes motioned with his head toward the bar at the other end of the room, where Duncan Munro was wiping the counter.

Holmes walked to the bar, with me in tow.

"Did your dinner suit ye?" Munro enquired.

"Yes, more than adequate," Holmes replied. "Would you have some time for a brief conversation?"

"I am at your service, sir."

"It seems the bones that you discovered have created a wonderful notoriety," Holmes said.

"Mebbe, aye. It's bogle work indeed. I ken Fear Liath

Mòr as returned to Ben MacDhui," the innkeeper replied in an ominous tone. "But, it were not *I* that discovered the bones."

"Is that so. Who did then?" Holmes responded, with a disgruntled eye toward me.

I hid my embarrassment in my notes as I jotted down the latest memoranda.

"A lass," Munro said. "She was on a walkin' tour of the Cairngorms; and upon her descent from Ben MacDhui, she discovered 'em and brought them back to me."

"How remarkable," I said. "You say a young lass brought you the bones?"

"Well, sir," Munro replied, "We might call her young, but I suspect her age be about twenty. It's difficult for me to say, as she was wearing a hiking costume and a lad's cap."

"And, she brought these bones to *you*, Mr. Munro?" Holmes repeated.

"Well, what's a lass to do with old bones?"

"She might have taken them to the local authorities," I ventured.

"And constable McMann made no small point of that, Dr. Watson," Munro grunted. "Shortly after your departure, I was chastised properly for not report'n the find. Your visit at the station has given McMann some reassurance, however." Munro paused, and looked sheepishly at me. "Might I ask if you have the bones with you today, Dr. Watson?"

"I am afraid not," I replied. "They are presently ensconced in my London home. This trip was hastily planned. However, Mr. Munro, I regret to tell you that I have promised to return them to the authorities."

"Of course, sir. I understand. And, I do have this wee fella here," Munro said, as he took a small bone from his vest pocket. "It must have fallen from the bag. I will keep it as a remembrance."

Holmes smiled. "Would it be possible for me to find this young woman, who discovered the bones, listed in your register?"

"Aye, sir. I am most particular about that. Nary a guest passes through my portals without putting their name in my book. I dare say I've registers that date to when the Days of Yore opened its doors in the year 1867."

"Then, you might give us a look at this woman's registration?" I asked.

"Do ye wish to see it now – at this hour?"

"I think it can wait until morning," Holmes said. "It has been a long day. We will see you after breakfast then, Mr. Munro."

"Aye, on the mor'n. You've not eaten fish until you've enjoyed fresh trout from County Moray gentlemen."

As we got to our rooms, I could see Holmes was caught up in an inner reverie.

"Goodnight, Holmes," I said, hoping to gain his attention. "Interesting case, no?"

He put on a smile and looked up. "This case certainly presents some singular features. Tomorrow will tell us much, I venture."

As I retired, I wondered if I would be able to sleep amid the clatter of the wheels now turning in my friend's head. It was clear that he suspected the innkeeper of instigating the story in the hope of gaining public attention for his enterprise. But, the sudden materialization of a young woman had widened our field of inquiry.

~

The day was just breaking when I awoke to the smell of charcoal wafting through my window. I glanced out to see the cook buttering trout and placing them on a large grill. It was then I noticed Holmes on the edge of a nearby field. He was standing motionless, his eyes no doubt taking in the misty splendor of Ben MacDhui in the distance.

How many times had I watched Holmes in thoughtful repose? After a gap of five years, I am once again chronicling his travels. And, although he often pokes jibes at my scribblings, he understands that, in the end, we all disappear into someone else's story.

I dressed and went down to join Holmes in the dining room. A cup of tea rested upon the plank table in front of him, and his pipe was clenched in his mouth. The aroma of his Dutch shag stirred pleasant memories, and I wondered what had become of the Persian slipper that often sat on the mantle at 221B.

"Good morning, Holmes," I said, as I took my place across from him. "The trout smells superb."

"We must have a hardy breakfast before we trek into the Cairngorms."

"I presumed we were looking at the register?"

"That will take but a little time," Holmes noted. "I am growing anxious to meet the Grey Man of Ben MacDhui!"

"Holmes, you amaze me. You lambaste me for my tales in the *Strand* and here you sit, pretty as you please, hoping to make the acquaintance of the legendary creature."

"Lambaste is a bit strong, I would say. It appears you are still upset about my telegram?"

"I don't pander to the gullible masses, Holmes."

"Ah, but we all pander to the masses, Watson, each in our own way. I use my reputation, one that you have helped to craft, to gain entry to the hidden rooms in people's lives. Nonetheless, you and I will tell the true tale of the bones of Ben MacDhui."

"Very well, Holmes. I would be happy to chronicle our current venture, if you believe it merits such attention."

"Yes, you might well recommence your narrative, Watson."

And, despite our best efforts, neither of us could fully contain our mounting joy.

After we took breakfast, I started off in search of the innkeeper. I found Mr. Munro chatting to a member of the constabulary near the door to the inn. When their conversation concluded, I approached. "Mr. Munro, I must say, I enjoyed the breakfast. Nothing like trout fresh from the stream."

"Aye, Dr. Watson. Did ah nae tell ye," Munro said, puffing out his chest with the appearance of some little pride.

"Mr. Holmes and I would like to see your register if you have a moment."

"Surely sir," he replied. "It appears the interest in that auld bag of bones is growin'. I've just been informed that I might have a visit from Scotland Yard on the morrow. It's pertaining to the gentleman who went missing two years ago."

As I walked with the innkeeper to his desk, Holmes joined us. Duncan Munro turned the leather-bound register around and thumbed back several pages. "Aye," said he, pointing to a name in the register. "Here's the lass I told ye abit."

Holmes picked up the large, dusty volume and walked to the window with it. He peered down intensely for a long while. Then, he asked me to make note of the name and address – Adaline Odinsvogel, 644 High Road, North Finchley, London.

"German. It appears the lass was German, Mr. Munro," Holmes noted.

"Well sir at ma be, but she spoke the King's English, right enough. And she were a braw lass – a real stotter, so she was."

"Beautiful, you say? Thank you, Mr. Munro, for your assistance. And, if I could impose a little further," Holmes said, as he leaned closer and whispered, "I would like to inspect that souvenir of yours."

Munro went to the bar and walked around behind. With furtive glances to each side, he brought forth a scrap of cloth. As if he were unveiling the crown jewels, he slowly unwrapped a tiny solitary bone – obviously a metatarsal.

Holmes pulled his glass from his coat pocket and began to look over the bone. At one point, he requested a small knife. Munro reached under the bar and handed him a rusty blade. Holmes began scraping the bone, which greatly alarmed the innkeeper.

"I beg you, Mr. Holmes," Munro said, "I... I..."

"You needn't fear, Mr. Munro," Holmes said. "I will not cut it. I just wish to see what lies below the surface." And, after a pause, "H'm, and there is indeed *much* that lies below the surface here."

"What do you deduce, Holmes?"

"A bone – I see what might appear to be an old bone."

"Mr. Munro," Holmes enquired, "did Adaline Odinsvogel happen to say where she found the bones?"

"Now that you mention it, she did. She made a point of it, as I recollect."

Holmes waited in silence as the innkeeper's eyes squinted and flashed side to side in an attempt to dredge up his conversation with the lass who brought him the bones.

"As I reca, she said 'twas just off the trail three miles from Coire Cas. That's at the base of Ben MacDhui. The trail is well marked. But, if ye ur planin' to go there, best be prepared. Tis dreich weather on that old mountain this time o'year. More than one poor soul has lost his life or limb up there. And then, of course, thar's th' creature."

I can tell you, I was having my doubts about mounting an expedition on such short notice, but Holmes was undeterred.

"We will dress warmly and take whatever good sense might suggest, Mr. Munro," Holmes said. "If you could please lend us a sturdy lantern and prepare a picnic, Watson and I will gather our things and be off, before any more of this day is lost."

We returned to our rooms to don warmer clothing. When I descended the stairs, Holmes was waiting, and Munro by his side with a substantial dinner sack and an old, brass anchor lantern.

"This lantern's a wee bit heavy, but it can bear up to the elements," Munro said. "It served the British navy fur many years before it found its way here."

Holmes hired a trap to take us the two miles across the desolate plain to the Cairngorm where the trail up Ben MacDhui Mountain began. The weakening sun slid behind grey clouds, and the wind whistled, as we began our ascent. The cold was already penetrating the staunch tweed sweater I sported under my pea jacket. The rugged beauty tantalized my senses and numbed my common sense that told me this would be more than a country walk.

Holmes silently trudged onward with the lantern, I behind with the picnic bag. His pace quickened as his eagerness carried us along the track.

"What do you expect to find, Holmes?"

"I'm not sure, Watson. If you can forestall further conversation, it will help me to measure our distance. There are approximately 1,760 paces in a mile you know."

I began counting along to myself until I heard Holmes's voice again. "One mile."

"Do you propose that the German lass knew *precisely* how many miles she marched from the bones?"

"I do, Watson. Munro's report was most illuminating. The fact that she shared an *exact* number of miles with Munro is remarkable, since most people would only offer an estimate, not a precise number."

"I say, I believe you're right, Holmes. Very interesting."

"Indeed."

The mist grew thicker and swirled around us. At times, I could barely see Holmes, who was moving just out ahead of me. He walked at such a pace that my sedentary life began to tell on me. I puffed and scrambled so as not to fall behind.

The fading sun created an eerie glow all around us. The cold bracing atmosphere penetrated to the marrow. We marched on silently two, three miles before Holmes spoke again. By then, the fog and mist had cast a shroud over us.

"Watson, come here, and help me to light this lantern."

I obliged, and was surprised by the bright light emanating from the lamp. "By Jove," I said. "You wouldn't think a lantern in the daylight would make a difference."

"The mist dampens the sunlight a great deal, Watson. We must move keenly from here on. Watch your step."

We began counting paces once again until Holmes beckoned just beyond a heather-tufted mound.

"Look here, Watson."

He had found a cap just off to the side of the trail and was inspecting it.

"Hold this lantern, if you will."

He pulled the glass from his jacket pocket and began to examine the inner band. He stopped and pinched a hair between his forefinger and thumb. He held up a long coppery strand to the lantern.

"Auburn," he said. "Munro did say the lass was wearing a gentleman's cap, did he not?"

"As I recall, he did. Is that the cap then?"

"Right you are. Miss Odinsvogel was kind enough to leave this memento."

"I say, Holmes, jolly good luck."

"I suspect luck has little to do with it."

He jammed the cap into his pocket and caught up the lantern. He then knelt down by the edge of the trail and began moving away from the path on his knees in a systematic survey of the brush, his free hand sweeping lightly across the mottled grass.

"What's this?" Holmes said, as he picked up a small bone. He brought it closer to the lantern for a look and then handed it back to me. I bent closer to the light and examined it.

"I would say this is a hand-bone," I declared.

"Precisely, Watson. One of the twenty-seven bones in the hand – a finger bone. I would venture it is a proximal phalange."

"It could be," I said, taking a closer look. "Maybe a middle phalange. Difficult to say without the remainder of the hand bones."

Holmes returned to his knees and began to sweep his hand over the gravel and grass more rapidly. His face was about a foot from the ground; the lantern, in his left hand, was held just behind his ear. Suddenly his right hand stopped. "Hello, what have we here?"

Holmes carefully reached into a clump of bracken. Draped on one of the stems was a chain with a round disk hanging from it. He clenched the trinket tightly in his fist. As he rose and turned, he opened his hand to reveal the new find.

"A watch chain?" I ventured.

"Very good, Watson. A bit of a watch chain, and something more."

The small round medallion was encrusted with dirt, but we could make out that it bore an etching of a small tower upon a hill, with the letter H below it.

"Come, Watson," Holmes said. "We have obediently discovered what Fräulein Odinsvogel left for us."

"Left for us, Holmes?" I gasped. "You believe that the woman intended for us to find these things?"

"I do indeed."

His cheeks were flushed with the exhilaration of a master weaver before his loom, holding all the threads in hand.

The late afternoon temperatures were falling and the mist was thickening and swirling in the wind. A light sleet stung my face. The path grew indistinct, as the unnatural grey daylight washed over us.

"Holmes, I think we ought to return to the inn before the weather gets the best of us."

As we turned to leave, an apparition suddenly appeared in the far-off haze: silhouetted in the distant glare were two gigantic ape-like creatures! They stood erect, silently staring us. I was paralyzed with fear.

"Holmes," I whispered, "I trust you observe those figures upon the far hill?"

As the fog swirled around us, the creatures grew more distinct. A bright halo appeared around them with the red and yellow rays radiating in all directions, making it difficult to see their features. My heart was racing. I had an overwhelming impulse to flee. Holmes must have sensed this, because he caught me by the arm to still me. My mind flashed to my revolver sitting in my desk drawer, over four hundred miles away. We were ill equipped to deal with these creatures in their dim and secret world.

Suddenly, Holmes, with his mouth half-open, ever so carefully, began to wave his left arm up as if in greeting.

"Holmes, please! We are quite defenseless at the moment."

"Watson, Watson," he said, as he tugged my sleeve to prevent retreat. "Watson, stop. Look again at our two companions."

I was amazed to see that... yes, indeed, one of the creatures was waving back. As I turned to retreat again, I heard Holmes chuckle. Then, in a loud voice he said, "So, that's the Grey Man of Ben MacDhui. Wave your arms Watson – say hello to our mountain brothers."

"I fail to see the humour, Holmes," I cried over my shoulder. "We must flee."

"Wave your arms, Watson."

As I reluctantly did so, I saw that the shadowy creatures were swaying and waving back. "They are our own shadows Holmes. But how?"

"It's a refractory illusion. When the sun is behind us, our shadows are cast on the mist in the distance. I encountered a similar phenomenon in the Harz Mountains in Germany. This, together with a mild panic people feel when they cannot navigate clearly, would seem to explain the old tales. I venture Mr. Munro will be delighted to know that there are two Grey Men – or possibly a Grey Man and Grey woman." Holmes began to laugh heartily.

We made our way down the mountain. It was no small relief for me when we reached the road. The sleet and wind were diminishing. My limbs were weary and stiff.

"We have a long walk ahead, Holmes. What do you say if we stop for a rest, and partake of the supper Munro prepared for us?"

"Very well, Watson," Holmes said, as he doused the

lantern and began walking with a new energy down the road toward the Days of Yore.

We found a dry area under an old oak and I peered into the supper bag.

"Holmes, it is said a Scottish picnic is a pint of ale and pickle, but Munro has prepared a small feast for us." There was cold trout, several cheeses, hearty oat bread, and some savory fruit tarts.

After our supper, we were well prepared for the long walk back to the inn. We arrived just as the sunset was painting the mossy stone inn in broad strokes of red and amber. As we entered the inn, we saw Munro sitting in the dining room with two tweed-suited fellows. We were about to head up to our rooms to wash up when the innkeeper hailed us.

"Mister Holmes – Doctor Watson – if ye will, come here a moment please. I've someone I want ye to meet."

The two gentlemen at the table turned. Munro continued, as we approached:

"These gentlemen are from Scotland Yard. Mr. Holmes and Dr. Watson meet Inspector Slader and Constable Rafferty."

A mature rotund gentleman, with a bulbous nose, rose and presented his hand to Holmes, "Detective Inspector James Slader, Mr. Holmes. Pleased to meet you. Your reputation precedes you, of course." He then turned to me with an outstretched hand. "James Slader."

The other fellow was much younger, with a rutty complexion and side-whiskers. His shaggy hair covered his eyes, and he smiled warmly as he rose and stood behind Slader, a pipe clenched in his mouth. He slowly extended his hand and made his introduction with but two words, "Rafferty here." He smelled of a pungent tobacco.

"If I may be so bold, Mr. Holmes," Slader said, "may I enquire as to what brings you to these parts?"

"The same thing, I suspect, that brought you," Holmes replied. "Bones."

"Bones, indeed," the large inspector remarked. "Did you know that a man went missing in these parts near two years ago?"

Holmes nodded, "I think I did hear something of the sort. I suspect the missing gentleman was of some prominence to merit the attention of the force."

"You might say so," Slader replied. "Though, it was his more celebrated wife who was able to rattle the doors at the Yard."

"Rafferty leaned forward. "I was wondering if you might know the gentleman in question?" Rafferty asked, in a matter of fact tone. "His name is Godfrey Norton."

A paroxysm swept over Holmes momentarily, then his demeanour, just as quickly, grew calm. "Norton... Norton," he said, in a languid fashion, "I fear I will be little help there." And, after a pause, "If you gentlemen will excuse me, Watson and I have just returned from a rather long trek, and we would like to refresh ourselves."

"Certainly," Slader said. "Would you mind if we talked more later?"

"I'm at your service," Holmes said, with a slight bow of the head. "Until later then, Inspector Slader... Constable Rafferty."

As Holmes turned away his face grew ashen. He walked to the bar. Trailing behind, I sat down next to him without a word. Some minutes passed before he spoke.

"I trust you recognized the name, Watson," said he, fumbling with a coin on his watch chain.

"I believe I do, Holmes." And, with those words, the events from one of our earliest adventures swept over me, along with the possibility that "the woman" was, once again, in Holmes's life.

It had been twenty-three years since he encountered Irene Adler, or Mrs. Godfrey Norton as she became. She was one of the only human beings to get the better of him. I had always wondered if his feelings for her were affection or professional admiration – although the two are not mutually exclusive. Though seldom spoken of, I could sense her lurking in the background of our lives ever since her singular departure so long ago.

Holmes had unwittingly become a witness at her wedding to Norton in the church of Saint Monica. That was as close to the altar as Holmes had ever come. She presented him with a gold sovereign that he has, ever since, worn upon his watch chain – the only bit of sentimentality that my friend ever allowed into his life.

"Watson," he said in a low tone, "you must help me keep this secret of ours." His face was waxen.

"Certainly, Holmes."

Munro walked around behind the bar.

"I say, Mr. Holmes," Munro said. "It looks like you could use a drop of my best."

He took out two glasses and filled them with a golden scotch. He went on: "Drink up! From th' looks ay ya, you might hae seen a ghost."

"Indeed," I said, "an old ghost, Mr. Munro."

Holmes took a drink and then turned to the innkeeper, "Mr. Munro, I neglected to ask you how it was that you came to call upon my dear friend here when the bones first turned up."

"Well, sir," he said, "to be completely honest wi ye, I'd have to say that it was th' lass that pit the idea in mah heed. She had a copy of *The Strand Magazine,* and pointed out that Dr. Watson here was writin' abit British folktales, an' he might be interested in the bones of th' Grey Man."

"Thank you."

Holmes turned away and shook his head from side to side. "I feel like a fly dancing upon the edge of a web."

"And the spider?"

Holmes looked into my eyes. "Possibly, an old acquaintance of ours, Watson. In many cases we seek to know *who,* but this case derives its interest not so much from *Who?* but *Why?*" Holmes finished his drink and pushed the empty glass toward the innkeeper.

Duncan Munro filled it again. "Dinner this evening, gentlemen?" he asked.

"You wouldn't have some more of those trout would you?" I enquired.

"Aye, more came in tae our scullery this afternoon," Munro said, rubbing his hands together.

"You enjoy your dinner, Watson. I think I shall retire early this evening."

Holmes sat drooped over the bar, his brows drawn tight, peering into the amber liquid in the glass.

I was accustomed to the swings of his nature, but this was something different. When he rose from his stool, Holmes ambled slowly out of the room in a trance. His mind had turned inward and, in his pensive mood, he did not notice the two Scotland Yarders as they nodded their good evenings.

The next morning, after dressing, I knocked upon the door of Holmes's room. When there was no answer, I went downstairs to the dining room with the intention of awaiting him. However, I arrived to find him on a bench in front of the inn taking a pipe with Constable Rafferty. Their foul smoke circled above as they chatted.

"I can certainly see the convenience of a twist," Holmes said, "but I'm afraid I am keen on my shag."

"Good morning, Holmes," I said. "And, a good morning to you as well, Constable Rafferty."

Their heads thrust forward and turned to me as I stood out a ways in front of them both.

"I thought maybe you'd take up the habit in retirement," Holmes said, holding up his pipe.

"Can't believe it does much good for the human body."

"I don't suppose it does," he said. "But, it's not for the body, Watson, it's for the mind. Wouldn't you say so, Rafferty?"

"I might agree with you there, Mr. Holmes," the policeman answered. And then, after a pause: "My colleague and I will be leaving this afternoon and we were hoping to have a brief conversation with the two of you, if you can spare us the time."

I waited for Holmes to reply.

"I am not sure there is much we can offer, but... by all means, if you wish," Holmes said dryly.

Rafferty got up. "Then, after breakfast, gentlemen," he said, before departing.

"What are you going to tell them, Holmes?"

"I have little I wish to share with Scotland Yard, Watson. However, there may be much they can tell us. I would appreciate it if you would take the lead. I wish to stand apart."

"I will do my best," I said.

I was happy to see Holmes had recovered from his shock. At least it seemed so, as his appetite had returned. When the breakfast dishes were cleared Slader and Rafferty, who were sitting at another table, joined us.

"Thank you for your time, gentlemen," Rafferty said.

Holmes nodded and began fingering the coin on his chain. Slader started the enquiry.

"Dr. Watson, Mr. Munro said that you examined the bones discovered on Ben MacDhui."

"Aye."

"Would you concur that they were human remains?" Slader asked.

"Most assuredly, Inspector.

"Male?"

"From what I recollect from the pelvic girdle, I would say so."

Rafferty leaned in closer, "Can you tell us anything more about the bones?" he asked.

I shook my head in the negative.

"Inspector Slader," Holmes interrupted. "This Godfrey Norton fellow you mentioned last night – why might you suspect these bones are his?"

Slader cocked his head to the side as if sizing up my companion. "Well, as you are a friend of Scotland Yard, I suppose I can tell you what little we know. In May of 1910, Godfrey Norton took a walking tour that brought him to this very inn. The morning after he arrived, as you and your colleague did yesterday, he trekked to Ben MacDhui. He never returned."

"What does his family say about his disappearance?" I asked.

"His wife seemed distraught, as you might expect," Rafferty said. "It seems the local constabulary did not meet her standards, and she used her notoriety to bring us into the investigation. Despite countless interviews with relatives, friends, and associates, we are unable to ascertain the whereabouts of Mr. Norton; nor do we have any idea as to what might have happened to him."

It felt strange to be managing the interview, but I continued on, as Holmes had requested.

"So, neither his wife, nor anyone in his family, has shed any light upon his disappearance?"

"Not really," Slader replied. "I interviewed his wife,

and family members, several times. No one could offer any explanation. We did learn, however, that Mr. Norton and his wife did take walking holidays, and to this very inn, on several occasions early in their marriage. However, Mrs. Norton said it had been a dozen years since they had frequented this establishment. She could not account for why he might choose to visit Aviemore again."

"So, Mr. Norton's wife did not accompany him upon his last trip?" I noted.

"No," Rafferty said, "his name alone is in the register upon the day of his last visit here. Although, there may be reason to believe…" Rafferty stuttered and looked at Slader.

Inspector Slader grimaced. "What Rafferty is trying not to say is that Norton was seen here on previous occasions in the company of a person. We were unable to ascertain the exact identify of this… person."

I quickly followed-up: "This individual who was seen with Norton… a man or woman?"

"A woman," Slader replied.

Holmes remained silent. I tried to anticipate the questions he might ask in this situation. As he smiled and leaned back in his chair, I did suspect him of enjoying my discomfort too much.

"Do you have any reason to expect foul play?" I asked.

"There are the bones," Slader said. "And, as Munro reported, Doctor, the skull was smashed in."

"There could be many explanations for that cracked skull," I said.

"Quite so, Doctor Watson, I venture there are, and one of those explanations is murder."

"Any suspects?" Holmes asked.

All heads turned in his direction.

"Just the usual ones, Mr. Holmes," Slader said, coolly.

"As you know, murder is often perpetrated by someone close to the victim."

The tension between Holmes and Slader was palpable. The two men stared into one another's eyes. However, Holmes's calm nature prevailed.

Rafferty suddenly intervened. "You know, Mrs. Norton is a celebrity of a kind," he said, "a famous singer who has traveled the world. Her professional name is Adler... Irene Adler. You might know of her," Rafferty said to Holmes.

"I know her by reputation, of course," Holmes replied, "but I have never had the good fortune to see her... see her on the stage."

"Neither have I," Rafferty said. "But I can tell you, though on in years, she is still a beautiful woman."

Wanting to take back the conversation, I enquired: "Can I ask if you told her about the discovery of the bones here on Ben MacDhui?"

"As Mrs. Norton was so adamant about a thorough investigation, we felt she should be kept informed of any new events related to the case. You understand, I'm sure."

I was about to ask another question when Holmes bolted up from his chair. "If there is nothing else gentlemen, my friend and I are anxious to see more of this majestic countryside," Holmes pronounced. "I bid you good day."

Slader and Rafferty rose and nodded to us both.

As we climbed upstairs, Holmes turned to me. "Watson, you did an admirable job there."

"What next?"

"I suggest we wait until the inspectors are on their way before we proceed. They are already too suspicious about our presence. If you don't mind, I am going to have a smoke, and take a short walk. I will join you later."

I passed the morning with three patrons in the bar – old soldiers, as it turned out, from the York & Lancs' Regiments of Foot. We shared our Asian war stories and drank to the King's health.

Shortly after the two Scotland Yarders started off for the station, I joined Holmes, who was sitting behind the inn staring out over the landscape at the grey-green mountain. In this moment, he looked like a very ordinary man.

"Here you are, Holmes," I said, pulling him from his mental abstractions. "So, what do you propose?"

"I think we should see if our good innkeeper is as fastidious with the inn's registers as he asserts."

We walked back through the kitchen and into the tavern where Munro spent most of his time. He was rolling an empty keg out from behind the bar. Holmes waited for Munro to notice us.

"Is there somethin' ah can get fur ye, gentlemen?" the innkeeper asked.

"Indeed there is, Mr. Munro," Holmes began, "I was wondering if we might have access to your registers for a short while?"

"It's yonder on the desk," said he, "You may..."

Holmes interrupted. "Thank you, and we would like to see those registers dating back for the last twenty or so years as well, if that is possible."

"My, my, twenty years," he replied. "Those would be in the cellar. They may be a bit fusty, you understand, but ye are welcome to em."

"May I help you retrieve them?" I asked.

"Thank ye," Munro said, "Ah shall appreciate yer help. I have to take this keg doon and ye can go wi' me, Dr. Watson."

As we approached the cellar door, Munro set the keg

down and picked up the old anchor oil lamp he had loaned us earlier. "If ye would be sa kind, Dr. Watson," he said, as he handed the lamp to me, and lit it.

He opened the door and motioned for me to proceed. I went down a few steps and waited for him to grab the keg and start down. Holding the lantern high, we made our way down. The air was damp and rank.

When I reached the dirt floor below, I turned to give the light to Munro who walked to the outside entrance of the cellar. He set the keg atop of another nearby and turned back my way. As he took the lantern from me, he remarked:

"It has bin some years since Ah hav' had to retrieve these old records. As Ah say, they go back to when the Days of Yore first opened its doors… nigh on fifty years since."

He rummaged through buckets and boards in the untidy cellar, and carefully moved an old chandelier on top of a pile of crates. The dust swirled and I began to sneeze. I covered my nose with a handkerchief and followed a few steps behind. He finally reached a wall of shelves covered with bottles and other trash.

Munro turned up the lantern and peered to and fro. "Aye," he sighed, as he reached toward a squarish pile with an oilcloth over it. He handed the lantern to me; and yanked the cloth away and shook the dust from it. I stepped away in a vain attempt to avoid the mouldy assault.

"Here they ur Doctor," the innkeeper said. "I think we best take all of 'em, as Ah am nae certain they ur in the proper order."

It took two trips for us to get all the registers upstairs through the kitchen and into the back garden. Munro asked one of the maids to dust the old volumes. I returned to find Holmes.

When I entered the tavern, Holmes's face opened wide with a smile. "I say, Watson. I took you for a chimney sweep."

"Really, Holmes! I do not appreciate your humour one bit. The dust has done me in. I can barely breathe."

"My dear fellow," Holmes said, "let us go outside, where I might be able to return some of this dirt to its rightful place."

We went out in back. Holding his handkerchief at arms length, Holmes began to flick it at me in a futile attempt to dislocate the dust from my clothing. Munro charitably intervened.

"Dinna fash yerself. I'll prepare a bath in your room, Doctor, and you change out of these dirty clothes, which Morag will clean fur ye. By the way, the registers are on da bench ov'r there, such as they are."

"I never want to see those blasted ledgers again," I mumbled, as I trotted off to my room.

After my bath, I reemerged downstairs to find Holmes hunched over the registers in the far corner of the dining room.

"Come here, Watson, with your notebook," Holmes beckoned. "Our friend, Mr. Munro, is a man of his word. There is, indeed, a record of guests that stretch back for decades."

"Then you found something of interest, Holmes?"

"It seems Mr. Norton frequented this place on many occasions during the last twenty-three years," Holmes noted, "and, there is a curious pattern in his visits."

I began making notes, as Holmes shared what these aging volumes were telling him.

"The first visit by the Norton's I can find is in June of 1890 – and again they returned in the fall of that same year. This was the pattern, more or less, for the next decade. They took accommodation at the Days of Yore inn at least once a year from 1890 until 1899. Then their visits stopped completely until the May of 1909. What do you make of that?"

I shrugged my shoulders. "They may have been out of the country, or simply took their holidays in another place."

"Very true, Watson, but I can not help but note that, after a ten year respite, their visits began *again* just sixteen months before Norton's disappearance."

"Were you able to find Norton's last visit in the record?"

"Yes," Holmes assured me. "As the inspectors noted, he signed in on May 10, 1910 – alone it would seem. But, lying in the folds of that page I found an interesting letter addressed to Godfrey Norton."

Holmes held the envelope between his thumb and forefinger, twisting it to-and-fro in the air.

"This envelope had not been opened. It was not delivered. This special-delivery letter was addressed to Godfrey Norton in care of the Days of Yore inn. I can tell from the postal date stamp that it likely arrived the very day he disappeared. I suspect Mr. Munro was planning to give it to him upon his return from his hike and he stuck it in the register, as a reminder. However, as we know, Norton never returned."

"Very curious, Holmes," I said. "What do you make of it all?"

"Well, I wasn't sure what to make of it, until I opened the letter."

I shook my head, "I am not sure that is proper, but I suppose…"

"Propriety be damned! This tiny note has provided an important clue."

I examined the paper upon which the written words were fastened and read the missive:

Darling,
So sorry - arriving late.
Love always, X

"A simple message. From his wife possibly?"

"If that is so, she would have signed it. No indeed, Watson, this letter did not come from Mrs. Norton."

"How can you be so sure?"

"The stamp, Watson," he replied. "When a person prepares to glue a stamp to a letter, they must hold the corner of it with their finger tips. A right-handed individual usually holds the upper right hand corner. A left-handed individual holds the upper left-hand corner. As a result that particular corner does not adhere. Note this stamp here," Holmes exclaimed, throwing the envelope upon the table in front of me. "This letter was sent by a right-handed person. Irene Ad... Mrs. Norton, you may recollect, is left handed."

I sat in quiet admiration of his subtle methods. This was a striking confirmation that his deductive powers had not waned. "So, it may have been a liaison with another woman that brought him here."

"It appears likely."

"So, there was something to what Slader and Rafferty inferred about his tryst with a woman?" I said, looking through my notes.

"There is always a smidgen of truth within any rumour, Watson. And, in search of that smidgen, I offer this letter in evidence. A lone woman did not appear in the register; however, that does not mean that one was not present when he disappeared. It is probable," Holmes continued, "that it was this same woman who accompanied him in

May of 1909, and again in September of that year. You might recall that Inspector Slader said that Mrs. Norton reported that it had been more than twelve years since the couple had visited the Days of Yore inn. The pieces seem to be falling into place, Watson."

"But, we do not know if the bones are Norton's or not?"

"It is safe to say that they are not his bones. I will explain on our way back to London. There is a 4.15 leaving for Glasgow and we should be on it. There is much for us to do in London."

"London! Very well, then I shall be able to return your hospitality. Do you miss the old city?"

"I do, Watson, but during my last visit I was put off by what appears to be an unsavory European influence. The pubs were ablaze with talk of war in the east. Casinos are sprouting up in open view, women are being courted in dance halls, and hideous slums are spilling over into our once grand thoroughfares. I fear London is crossing the threshold into what can only be seen as a darker age."

We paid for our board and made our farewells to Mr. Munro, thanking him for his time and generosity. As the trap pulled up in front of the inn, Holmes turned to Munro.

"Mr. Munro, can you recollect if, after Mr. Norton's disappearance, some personal items may have remained in his room?"

"Aye, there was some clothin', a watch an' other personal items," Munro noted. "The local coppers looked them over and asked me tae send them on tae his wife – which I did, a'coorse."

"Very good, Mr. Munro," Holmes said, as he placed a half-crown in the innkeeper's hand.

On the train home, I noticed Holmes again fingering

the gold sovereign on his watch chain as he watched the shadow filled landscape flit by. I decided to catch up on the *Times*, and leave my friend to his thoughts. I opened the paper to a hideous tragedy.

"My God, Holmes," I gasped. "Hundreds of people lost!

"What are you babbling about, Watson?"

"Holmes, the *Titanic* has sunk."

We sat in silent disbelief as we entered Waterloo Station. As we exited our compartment, we could see that a quiet sorrow had descended over the city. The usual hustle and bustle seemed muted, and people moved in sombre fashion. The carriage driver on Cab Road merely nodded as we approached with our luggage.

A pall hung over London, and an abiding sadness penetrated citizens to the marrow, like a cold, damp winter fog. A bit of Britain died along with the poor souls that lost their lives in the frigid North Atlantic. Our business of missing bones, and mythical beasts, seemed trivial by comparison.

The neighbourhoods seemed devoid of human voice. As we rattled through the endless labyrinth of streets, the hollow beat of the horse's hoofs, and the dull rumble of carriage wheels, echoed in my aching breast.

I made Holmes comfortable in my apartment and, over breakfast, picked up the threads from our expedition to Aviemore. "Holmes, why is it that you believe the bones are not those of Norton? You have not yet examined them."

"Aside from the fact that we seem to have been baited and led to the bones, they belie their true nature. If the ones in that bag on your desk are like Munro's wee memento, they are not old bones at all, Watson. They have been stained, I suspect with tea or other such agent, to appear aged. When I scraped Munro's bone with a blade, it was plain to see that their russet patina did not penetrate the outer surface. However, when I inspected the cracked ends of the bone, the stain had furrowed deeper within. The sponge-like nature of the interior drew the staining agent within. If these were truly two-year old buried bones the colouring would have been more uniform throughout."

"After all these years, you still amaze. But, why would someone go though all of that trouble?"

"Why indeed, Watson? I suspect we have several mysteries here, the bones being but a part of one."

"Are we going to see it through then?"

"I would say that curiosity has the best of me, Watson. If I can rely upon your assistance, I think we shall return to the problem.

"Where do you propose we begin then?"

"We have three pathways to pursue: the bones, Fräulein Odinsvogel, and the letter left in the register. Where might a person obtain human bones, Watson?"

"Let me see," I pondered. "Crypts, museums and the like, I suppose."

"Yes, many possibilities there – too many at the moment. What about the fair Adaline Odinsvogel at... where was it, Watson?"

I paged through my notes. "644 High Road, North Finchley. Do you believe the address to be genuine?"

"I am certain of it," Holmes said. "Miss Odinsvogel – or whatever her name – wants us to find her. And then, we have this," he said, taking the special delivery letter from his jacket pocket.

"I would appreciate it if you would pay a visit to Miss

Odinsvogel, Watson. When you do, pray return this bit of watch chain and what I believe is a medallion from Mr. Norton's university chorale. I will see where this letter takes us. Please be diligent if you are fortunate enough to interview the woman. I will meet you here around supper time."

I made my way to 644 High Road and perused the rather stately three-story Georgian home before I went to the door. I pulled the doorbell. A moment later a young maid answered.

"I am seeking a Miss Adaline Odinsvogel," I said.

"Odenvolger?" the maid attempted to parrot, in a perplexed manner. "I'm sorry sir, but no one by…"

Just then, a voice shot from the hallway. "Becky, I will take this call. You can be about your business." A tall young woman with long, strawberry-blonde hair, and the most astonishingly beautiful countenance, gracefully stepped forward. She opened the door wider and asked:

"Would you like to come in, Dr. Watson?"

I was flummoxed. "How did you know?"

"I had every confidence you would find your way to me," she said. "I had hoped your companion, Mr. Holmes, might accompany you as well."

I was at an uncomfortable disadvantage and not certain as to how to proceed.

"Pray come in, Dr. Watson," the woman begged.

"Thank you, Miss Odinsvogel."

"My name is Dart. Mrs. Adaline Dart," she replied. "Although, Odinsvogel may be more appropriate."

I was uncertain as to her meaning, but I let it pass and stepped inside. She led me to the parlour.

"Tea, Dr. Watson?"

"Yes, thank you, Mrs. Dart."

She rang for the maid and took a seat adjacent to me. I decided to get to the heart of the matter.

"Mrs. Dart, I am here because we found your address in the register of the Days of Yore inn. The innkeeper had told us that you discovered some bones on your walk."

"That is true, Dr. Watson."

"Did you suspect that the bones where those of that fantastic creature on Ben MacDhui?" I asked.

Just then, the maid Becky, entered with the tea. Mrs. Dart directed her to a nearby table. Together they set out the tea-things, plates, and biscuits. As they did so, I arose and walked around the parlour. I noticed a photograph of Mrs. Dart, posing along with a man, resting on the mantelpiece.

"That is my husband, Dr. Watson. Raymond and you have something in common. He is a student of the human body as well. He is an anatomist, and presently enrolled at the University of London. He assists Dr. Arthur Keith at the Hunterian Museum."

"Well," I replied. "My old *alma mater*. Keith has assembled one of the finest records of anatomical and embryological history in the world, I dare say. Your husband is fortunate to have such a distinguished colleague."

"Quite so," she replied softly.

"Would you mind if I made some notes?"

"As you will," she said, and with a gesture invited me to sit for tea. "I believe you asked if I thought the bones belonged to the Grey Man. I must confess that I am certain that they did not. I *borrowed* them, if I might use that term. I am afraid that my actions may reflect poorly upon my husband, so I beg your discretion with regards to the bones in question."

"Very well, Mrs. Dart, but the bones themselves aside, it appears that you have created a rather elaborate ruse, it would seem, to make my acquaintance – and that of my colleague, Mr. Holmes."

"I apologize for the charade, Dr. Watson," she replied. "It was my mother's idea actually."

"Your mother?"

"I believe you and Mr. Holmes made her acquaintance two decades ago," she said. "My mother is Irene Adler."

My jaw dropped at this revelation. I could instantly perceive the extraordinary resemblance. I was uncertain as to how to continue. Holmes was, once again, accurate in his earlier assessment. I too, now felt like a fly tangled in an attractive web.

"I suppose you may wonder why we chose this manner of bringing you into our lives."

"Yes. You had but to call or send a telegram to..."

"I understand," she interrupted. "My mother very much admires Mr. Holmes and, somewhat nostalgically, wanted to recall, and (I suppose) rekindle, what she described as a 'playful battle of wits' between herself and Mr. Holmes.

She leaned closer to me. "If you will keep a confidence, the matter for which my mother seeks your aid is both upsetting and embarrassing for her."

"I suspect for you as well – if I may assume this matter has something to do with the crushing misfortune that accompanied your father's disappearance."

With my words, Mrs. Dart's head dropped low.

"If you only knew, Dr. Watson! The saddest part of this dark business is the incessant gossip, and the shadow cast by the vague suspicions of Scotland Yard. They have compounded my mother's grief. She is a strong woman, but her heart is breaking bit by bit."

I wanted to comfort this unhappy lady, but I kept myself in the chair, and my feelings to myself.

"I must confess," I finally said, "I am not certain as to how to best be of service."

The lady regained her composure and gazed into my eyes. "My mother seeks the aid of Mr. Sherlock Holmes and, as she describes it, his singular powers. I will give you her address and ask that you carry with you my own heartfelt plea that Mr. Holmes come to her aid."

She wrote an address upon the back of a card and passed it to me.

"I will do as you request, young lady, but I can offer no guarantee regarding the outcome. There is much that lies beneath your mother's dealings with Mr. Holmes."

"I quite understand, Dr. Watson."

With that, I produced the bit of watch chain with the attached gold pendant, and tendered them toward her. Adaline held her hand out, and I placed the property in her palm without a word. She simply nodded.

My head was whirling as I made my way back to my apartment. I feared my report might unnerve my dear friend. I was grateful that he was staying with me. Such news might otherwise cause him to seek refuge in his careless addictions.

When I arrived home, Holmes was not there. As I waited, the concern I had for my friend was diminishing as my appetite grew. The tea and biscuits, I had earlier, did little to abate my hunger. I went to my cupboard in search of sustenance. I found a tin of short bread, but little more.

Holmes arrived back just before dark. "I apologize for my tardiness, Watson. I had an extraordinary afternoon."

"Then that is something we share, Holmes. I am anxious to hear your tales, and to share my own; and, it is my hope we can do so over dinner."

"I can see by the crumbs on your vest that you have made a start on your dessert," Holmes quipped. "Shortbread, I believe."

"I will ignore your jests, Holmes. But, since it appears we each had a singular afternoon, I suggest we reward ourselves with a meal at Rules."

"In Covent Garden?" Holmes recalled. "Right you are! As I recollect, they offer an exceptional pheasant."

"Indeed, and the Galloway beef is extraordinary."

We made our way to the heart of Covent Garden and enjoyed a delicious meal without once speaking of bones or mythical creatures. But, as the table was cleared, and the brandy served, Holmes pulled out his pipe.

"So, Watson, you found Adaline Odinsvogel, I presume."

"Mrs. Dart, and before that Miss Adler."

Holmes just shook his head in confirmation. "Odinsvogel," he spoke aloud. "Of course... I should have noticed. Odin's bird, Watson. Odin's bird!"

"Odin's bird, Holmes?" I parroted.

"In German, Odinsvogel means Odin's bird – in the German tradition Odin often took the form of an eagle – *adler*."

"Then, you are not surprised to learn that Adaline Odinsvogel is Adaline Adler?"

"Her daughter," he whispered softly. His mind seemed to be grasping at vague shadows. It's at rare times such as this that you can almost see Holmes wrestling with his emotions. I'm convinced he is actually deciding how he should feel.

I produced my notes and began to recount my visit with Mrs. Dart.

"You say Mrs. Dart is married to a prominent anatomist, Watson. That accounts for the bones then."

"Indeed. More to the point, Mr. Dart is in the employ of Dr. Arthur Keith who is conservator of the Hunterian Museum at the Royal Academy of Surgeons, which boasts an extraordinary historical collection of human bones."

"Dr. Keith's reputation, of course, comes before him," Holmes replied. "I have followed his copious writings over the years including his most recent work, *Ancient Types of Man*. Mr. Dart, it seems, is in excellent professional company."

"Yes, it would seem so, and Mrs. Dart fears that she may have jeopardized her husband's relationship with Dr. Keith by 'borrowing' the bones she placed on Ben MacDhui."

"Then, you didn't tell her that the bones are in your possession?"

"I was tempted, but then thought the better of it," I replied. "I was thinking we might help to set things right for Mr. and Mrs. Dart."

"Your generosity of spirit is, as always, most admirable," Holmes remarked. "We will do what we can, of course. I look forward to meeting Arthur Keith and hopefully gaining a closer look at his remarkable collection."

I continued my report to Holmes, ending with the note card Mrs. Dart gave me bearing her mother's address. I held it out; but, when he did not take it, I set the card down upon the table between us.

Holmes mused upon the belated request.

"Tell me again how Mrs. Dart described her motivation, Watson."

"I believe she said that they wanted to recapture what she termed the 'playful battle of wits' between you and her mother. I suppose you might chalk up this flamboyant masquerade to her theatrical nature."

"There is no explaining the feminine mind! Did she believe that sending us on a ridiculous journey would garner my appreciation?"

"Well, Holmes, you must admit to having extracted

some joy from the last several days. The Sherlock Holmes I know so well has risen from his bucolic refuge and is, once again, unraveling a mystery that has baffled Scotland Yard."

"What you are implying is ridiculous."

"As I see it, she has offered a gift she knew you would enjoy above all others: a mystery."

I could see the great wheels in his mind turning in a vain effort to grasp and analyze this assertion. He wore a vacant look. I expect he was in that private place we all keep just to ourselves. I let him rest there a moment before I continued.

"So, Holmes, you haven't shared your afternoon. I am curious about where that wayward letter took you."

He immediately sprang to life, shaking off his dull demeanour.

"Quite so, Watson. Where do I begin?" He pulled the envelope from his coat pocket and held it in his fingers. "Fortunately, one of my old collaborators at Royal Mail was still in harness, and I was able to trace the special delivery letter to its author. You see, a record is kept of all such letters to protect against any liability."

"And the author?"

"A woman," he said, "as we suspected, a delightful and beautiful young woman I might add. It seems we have both been blessed by encounters with the *belle femme,* Watson."

"What did you learn?"

"I can tell you that Miss Arabella Kenna did not appreciate my inquires. She, of course, denied any association with this matter. I regretted having to confront her with the facts that we unearthed at the Days of Yore. I may have implied that we knew more than we do. She was shaken to the marrow. Indeed, the mere mention of

Aviemore nearly caused her to swoon. When I mentioned Godfrey Norton she did her best to disavow any knowledge of him."

"Unsuccessfully?"

"No. She made no confession, but her behaviour belied her involvement."

"So, where does that leave us?

"I had hoped that my visit might cause Miss Kenna to bolt and lead us in some new direction, but alas the woman remained in her quarters on Curzon Street for some time. However," said he, with a raised index finger, "my interview did tell me that a gentleman had been in the very parlour where we chatted, not too long before my arrival."

"What did you see, Holmes?"

"Not see, Watson: smell. My olfactory senses picked up on a singular male cologne wafting in the air. A redolent aroma that is familiar to me."

"And where, if I may ask, does *that* take us?"

"This scent, while I am not familiar with its particulars, emanates from a family of Chypre colognes," Holmes explained. "On the morrow we go shopping, Watson."

~

The next day Holmes was up early and had already, by the time I was dressed, made a list of establishments we should visit.

"I can't see how you expect to find a unique scent among the hundreds that sit upon the shelves of the many shops on your list."

"The nose's memory is long and resilient. Smells are deeply imbedded in our brains. The smell of sweet yeast not only conjures up baking bread, but images of home, mother, and Sunday picnics long ago. The nose is an olfactory time machine, Watson, and this ancient old-fashioned scent is one I will always remember."

"Where does it transport you, if I may ask?"

Holmes peered out beyond the walls of the room, "It is similar to the scent my grandfather would wear on special occasions… like Christmas."

After breakfast, we set out. The first shop on Holmes's list was Penhaligon's in the Burlington Arcade. The counters sported bottle after bottle of scents. Holmes went straight to the men's section and enquired about offerings in the Chypre collection, but there were none.

Next, we went to Floris Estates on Jermyn Street. Better luck there with Holmes sampling something called Vetivar from a scent box. On to J. D. Harris, a tonsorial parlour, with it's rich mahogany walls and private rooms. No luck there; however, that changed when we walked into the George F. Trumper establishment. Holmes's nose immediately picked up on something that told him we might find our scent here. The proprietor approached.

"Good morning, sir. May I be of service?"

Holmes took on a foppish demeanour. "I have always loved fragrance," Holmes exclaimed, "and your shop verily abounds with possibilities."

"I believe it is not boastful to say that George F. Trumper offers the most rare and unique colognes in Britain, and the continent."

Holmes gushed on, "Cologne is my one indulgence. My skin chemistry is particular, and, as well, my nose. I am hoping you might have an ancient scent that I have not been able to find in all of London. It is in the Chypre family."

"Ah, Chypre," the proprietor said, "from Cyprus in French. I can see you are a discriminating olfactory *connoisseur*. While everyone is rushing to the florals, a chosen few prefer the darker, mysterious aroma of the woods."

"So, you have something to offer me then?" Holmes asked.

"Indeed," the proprietor said, "Let me show you something from the collection of Francois Coty," he said, reaching under the counter to reveal a small glass bottle filled with an amber liquid. "Please, put this to the test."

Holmes picked up the small bottle and lifted the stopper. He then waved the bottle slowly back and forth just below his chin several times.

The proprietor broke in on Holmes's apparent reverie. "It is called Mistero."

"Very nice indeed," Holmes declared, "but I was looking for something even darker, if you understand."

"I do sir, I do! I believe I have just what you are looking for."

He produced a large round bottle with a cork stopper topped with the silver letter T. He tilted the bottle so that it wet the stopper and then presented it to Holmes.

Holmes held it in front of him and, using the stopper as a kind of wand, slowly waved it in small circles in front of him. Then, he lowered the stopper to the counter, and leaned his face forward to capture the scent.

"Yes," Holmes said, with his eyes flashing. "Warm, liquory, very unconventional. I love it."

"We call it *Tobac Blonde,*" the proprietor said. "It is our very own fragrance. There are but a few gentlemen *connoisseurs* such as yourself, who can appreciate this rare fragrance."

"Then you do not sell much *Tobac Blonde*?" Holmes enquired.

"It is popular on the continent, sir, but I have few customers in London."

"Oh, and I can guess one of them," Holmes exclaimed, as he turned to me. "Mister... Mister... you know, Watson. The gentleman we recently met who lives on Curzon Street... in Mayfair."

Holmes caught me off guard. I blinked and furrowed my brows not quite knowing what to say. Fortunately, the proprietor came to my rescue.

"You must be speaking of Mr. Norville," the proprietor said.

"Quite so," Holmes said, "that's the name. Forty-three Curzon if I am not mistaken."

"Indeed, sir. Then, you are acquainted? It has been only fortnight since we made our last delivery to him."

"Oh dear," Holmes said. "If I were to wear *Tobac Blonde* my colleague might take offence. I hadn't contemplated that. But, perhaps a gift? Very well. I'd like to purchase two ounces."

The storekeeper returned, after a few minutes, with a wrapped package.

As we departed, I remarked: "Holmes, you are a wonder! I trust you are not thinking of wearing that dreadful concoction."

"I rather enjoyed it, Watson," Holmes replied, "but I fear, I already possess too many bad habits. No, Watson, I intend to use this 'dreadful concoction' to bait the gentleman who is frequenting the apartment of Miss Arabella Kenna."

"You mean this Norville fellow?"

"Norville?" Holmes said, quizzically. "Norville is an old Anglo-Norman word meaning 'north town.' The anglicized version is Northham or Norton – family names that go back for three hundred years."

"Then you believe we have found Mr. Norton? What shall we do now?"

Holmes stopped in mid-stride and peered into the distance. "I find it strange that I do not have a ready answer to your question. It may be that our best choice is to stop here."

"I'm perplexed," I said softly. "I've never known you to abandon the chase."

"I never have. You are quite right, my friend," he agreed. "However, I am not sure what I am chasing anymore... or why I persist in the hunt."

I gave no reply. I found my dear colleague embroiled in a vague place that was, no doubt, alien to him. If there were but one characteristic that would distinguish Holmes from others, it would be the certainty that lies beneath his actions. But that was missing now, and its exodus seemed to have taken his confident spirit with it.

We walked side-by-side in silence for some time before Holmes spoke:

"Indeed" he murmured, and then he turned to me with a brighter countenance. I venture my apprehension was upon my face, for he remarked, "Be of good cheer, my friend! The game will continue a bit longer."

We took dinner in my apartment. After the dishes were cleared, he took his pipe and sat puffing away until I joined him. "*Apis mellifera,*" he said.

"Holmes?"

"*Apis mellifera*, Watson," he repeated. "The honey-bee. They are the hardest working creatures on earth, I believe."

"They do seem to be constantly buzzing around to this flower and that."

"Indeed. I have observed a single bee go to fifty or more flowers in less than sixty minutes... perhaps a thousand flowers a day. Day after day they go until they die."

He took the pipe from his mouth and pointed it at me. "Do you know how long a honeybee lives, Watson?"

"Well, I can't say that I do. A blasted short time, I venture."

"Quite so," Holmes said. "A blasted short time – six weeks on average. And during their entire life they produce less than a teaspoon of honey."

I chuckled. "I shall remember that the next time I sweeten my tea."

"Indeed, my friend," Holmes replied. "They bring a sweetness to our lives that we seldom recognize or appreciate."

I noticed he was rubbing the gold sovereign that served as a fob upon his watch chain. We were no longer speaking of bees.

Once again Holmes was up and dressed when I first glimpsed the sun peeking through my bedchamber curtains.

"I have a favour to ask of you," Holmes said.

"Certainly, what do you require?"

"I need you to make a delivery," he said, holding the wrapped package containing the *Tobac Blonde* he had purchased the day before.

"Then, I am off to Mayfair and Curzon Street?"

"Indeed, Watson. Take my card and present our gift to Miss Arabella Kenna along with my regards. I have taken the liberty of adding your address on my card. Do you mind?"

"Not at all. Nothing more?"

"My friend," Holmes said, with a furtive smile, "I suspect our gift will communicate more than any words might relate. If you do not mind, when you return, we will deliver the wayward bag of bones to its proper owner."

"What of my promise to the authorities in Aviemore?"

"I am sure all parties involved will be pleased to know that the bones are in the hands of their rightful owner. I must beg you to hurry, for we have a grand day before us."

While hurried is not typically a term an Englishman would use to describe breakfast, I found myself gobbling up two rashers of bacon and toast in record time. I was off to Mayfair, with package in hand.

When Arabella Kenna answered my knock, I simply tipped my hat and, with an apology for my intrusion, extended the package toward her. She was alarmed. "Please madam," I said. "Accept this gift with the compliments of Mr. Sherlock Holmes."

I placed his card on top of the package.

Slowly and reluctantly, she reached out for the package. As she took it in hand, I tipped my hat again, and scampered down the steps without looking back.

When I retuned, Holmes was pacing on the hearthrug with a poker in his hand. He was alive with nervous energy – a decidedly different man than the pallid country beekeeper in Sussex Downs.

"Are you in need of a few coals?" I asked.

"No, my friend." He set the poker down against the hearth. "I take it the delivery went as planned?"

"I have always been amused by how the mere mention of your name can unnerve some people."

"You are speaking of Miss Kenna, I assume?"

"Indeed."

"She should know, as women do, that a sweet scent can bait a trap."

"Do you think Mr. Norville – or Norton – will acquiesce?"

"We shall know soon. If he does pay us a visit, would you think it rude if I were to ask to see him alone?"

"Not at all," I responded. "I understand that this has become a personal matter for you… a matter of the heart."

He turned away from me. "Please, Watson, your sentimentality astounds me." Quick to change the subject, Holmes went on: "Are you willing to accompany me to the Hunterian Museum, or are you in need of a cup of tea?"

"The tea can wait, Holmes. It has been some time since I have frequented the infamous edifice of the Royal College of Surgeons."

Holmes grabbed the bag of bones and we started off.

It was only a matter of minutes before the brougham brought us to Lincoln's Inn Fields and the Hunterian Museum. The curator's offices had recently relocated near the entrance and we were fortunate that Dr. Arthur Keith was currently in residence.

Keith arose from his desk as the secretary ushered us into his office. "Mr. Sherlock Holmes." Dr. Keith welcomed us, as we approached. He was tall and thin with aquiline features and searching eyes. Keith spoke with a soft piping voice and subtle Scottish burr. "And, Dr. Watson. It is a pleasure to meet ye both. Is it possible, judging from that sack you carry, that you offer something of interest to this collection?"

"I am certain it is of interest, as I believe they originated in your collection," Holmes replied, as he carried the bag to the desk. "May I?"

Holmes retrieved the skull first and set it upon Keith's desk. Dr. Keith bent lower for a close look.

"Ah, for a moment I didn't recognize it," Keith remarked. "Now I see that this skull, and these bones are the ones that have gone missing – a bit worse for the wear. Might I ask how they came into your hands?"

"I need to keep a confidence," Holmes said, without apology. "I am acting as a simple intermediary."

"Do ye know how they got into this dreadful condition?" Keith asked, as he peered down for a closer look.

"No," Holmes replied. "It appears to me that they were stained, possibly with tea or other fluids."

"While there is much about your story that is unsatisfactory, I am delighted to have them back. I might not have known they were missing except that some colleagues and I are preparing for a presentation at the upcoming Eugenics Conference in July. Men of reason and science, like you both, might find this momentous gathering interesting, to say the least. Major Leonard Darwin will preside."

Holmes grimaced. "I have been monitoring the work of Leonard Darwin for some time. My opinion is not fully formed, but I am disturbed by the fact that my own society is supporting a notion that seems to feel human beings need to be bred like livestock."

Dr. Keith turned sharply toward us. "Look, sir, like many others, you are reducing social Darwinism to a sensational catchphrase. I urge you to enlighten yourselves. Some of the greatest minds in Britain will be at the Cecil Hotel on July 24 – Mr. Balfour, H. G. Wells, Winston Churchill, George Shaw, to name but a few."

Holmes's jaw was clenched, but he remained silent. I broke the stalemate.

"It seems strange to me that the son of Charles Darwin would take human evolution out of Nature's hands," I said frankly.

Arthur Keith squared off with me. "I might agree with you, Doctor, if Nature's way were permitted to function in our society. However, recent civilization has brought with it the notion that we, as a people, must protect the weak. This very notion is at odds with natural selection.

Indeed, we, in the eugenics movement, only seek to support the process of natural selection and prevent this reversion toward mediocrity."

Holmes could contain himself no longer. "It seems to me that you are attempting to create a new morality – one clearly designed to secure your rank, power and status," Holmes stated. "I find myself on the side of G. K. Chesterton who has pointed out that eugenics is based upon a flawed notion – namely that mental and physical health is a quality such that, if you marry two healthy and intelligent people, the result will be a healthy intelligent child. However, I think that physical and mental health is but a *proportion* of qualities that contribute to a better human being. I fear we need not look far to see that, even the most superlative couple, can produce an imbecile!"

Holmes spoke with an uncommon force that bordered on anger. I was struck dumb for several moments, as was Arthur Keith. However, Keith turned away and began to gather up the pile of bones on his desk. With his back still to us, he spoke:

"I fear your good intentions in bringing me these bones are being held hostage to our intellectual disagreements." He turned around and offered his hand to Holmes. "Please except my most sincere thanks for the return of these artifacts."

Holmes took his hand. "I'm afraid that I find the age that has fallen upon us in Britain disturbing. As you can appreciate, I am rooted in a different time. I will take consolation in the thought that we both desire to nurture what is best in people, and in our beloved country, though we seek to achieve that goal in different ways."

"Well said, sir," Dr. Keith remarked. "But please consider attending the conference in July – as my guests, of course."

And, with that, we departed and returned to my apartment. Holmes was anxious to get back because he was anticipating a special visitor.

⁓

We arrived home as the lamps were being lighted. I put the kettle on. When I brought the tea into the parlour, Holmes was lighting his pipe.

"So, you expect Mr. Norton will call?"

"Indeed, Watson, he has already arrived. Did you not notice the gentleman across the street as we came to your door?"

"Not particularly."

Holmes came to my side. "Does it concern you that I prefer to see our imminent guest alone?"

Before I could respond there was an agitated knock at the door.

"Hello," Holmes said, and nodded to me. I took refuge in my bedroom and closed my door. As Holmes made his way to answer the knock, he unlatched my door and opened it ever so slightly. I retrieved my notebook and chair, and sat down with my ear to the adjoining room.

The knocks continued, yet Holmes did not immediately answer. After an interminable time I heard the door open.

"Mr. Holmes, I presume!"

"Mr. Norville," Holmes replied. "Pray, come in."

"We don't have to continue the masquerade, do we, Mr. Holmes?"

"I assure you, sir, that you need not do so for my benefit," Holmes shot back. "But, it obviously benefits you, does it not?"

"I detect a sharp edge to your words, Mr. Holmes, and I must confess that I am not sure how my identity, or anything about me, is of any concern of yours."

I heard Holmes retreat into the parlour. "I might agree with you, but I am not certain that your daughter or wife would feel the same."

Norton stomped into the room. "My daughter and wife?" he said, with artificial restraint. "And, pray tell me, sir, what relationship do you have with my family?"

"Ah," Holmes snipped. "Then you claim Adaline and Irene as your family. How do you support that claim?"

After a pause, Mr. Norton responded. "You have me at a great disadvantage, sir. Your obvious disgust, I assure you, is no greater than that I feel for myself. I find myself caught between honour and love. I ask, what choice would you have me make?"

"If honour appears as a choice sir, then you have already lost it."

"It's so easy for you then. Have you ever loved a woman – I mean loved a woman beyond all reason – totally and completely?"

"I suspect I have not," Holmes replied. "And, your reprehensible behaviour might cause me to give thanks for my situation. For, while I can most assuredly imagine living without the love of a woman, I cannot imagine living without honour."

"Ah, the stoic English gentleman! Proud, honourable, loyal, and – if I might offer an observation – a little lonely," Norton said. "Where does love fit into your philosophy?"

"After honour sir; that's where love belongs."

"Is there a heart that beats in your chest, or is that a drum beating a cadence to yesterday's ideals?" Norton asked. "Do you march in lockstep to tradition, even if it leads you to a lonely, solitary existence? What is life without love?"

"What is love without honour?" Holmes answered.

"And so, we have come full circle, my dear sir," Norton

noted. "You would create a dilemma: honour without love, or love without honour."

"At times, one needs to walk the line between both honour and love?"

"I must believe you are an intelligent man, Mr. Holmes. I can tell you that there are circumstances, when walking the line between honour and love may *promise* the possibility of both… but the reality is, that you have neither."

An eerie silence closed over the chamber, and I could hear nothing but the sounds from the street. Finally, Norton spoke. "So, what would you have me do, Mr. Holmes? Why have you brought me here?"

"I brought you here to ask that you to do the right thing… the honourable thing," Holmes said. "However, your moral compass seems to be out of order."

"So, that is what lies beneath your vest: a compass! What happened to your heart? Where did you lose it?"

I wanted to come to the aid of my friend, when I heard him stand and walk to the door. "Thank you for coming, Mr. Norton."

"May I ask what you plan to do with the information you have?" Norton asked, as he strolled toward the hall.

"To be quite honest, I am not certain. My hope is that I need not take *any* action. Good-evening, Mr. Norton."

Holmes's abrupt manner showed that the interview was at an end.

When I heard the door close on Mr. Norton, I returned to the parlour with my notebook in hand.

"If I might make an observation," I said, "this is a singular tale. Our stories typically end when the mystery is solved, but I have the strongest feeling this adventure is not yet concluded."

The next morning Holmes rose early. He greeted me with a statement that took me by surprise:

"I think it is best if I return to Sussex Downs today, Watson."

"I understand that you would be more comfortable in your country abode; but, as I remarked yesterday, this story has not found its end."

"On the contrary. The Grey Man of Ben MacDhui is alive and well in our British mythology, the bones are returned to their rightful owner; and we have done what is necessary to take the watchful eye of Scotland Yard from Mrs. Norton and her daughter. Most importantly, the wheels are set in motion that will allow these two gracious ladies to get on with their lives."

"Then, you have no plans to see Irene Adler-Norton?"

"I see no need. Do you, Watson?"

"Then you think Godfrey Norton will come forward?"

"I strongly suspect he will," Holmes said. "However, their affairs are their own. I think I have done as much as I can to honour the request young Adaline made of me. Do you not agree?"

"You have done as much as you *care* to do, is more to the point," I remarked.

Later that afternoon, we made our way to Waterloo Station with promises and plans to spend more time together, and possibly to attend the Eugenics Conference in July. It had all the markings of a rather jolly farewell, but I was left with deep melancholy, as I watched Holmes's train pull out.

Some five days after Holmes departed, I was only just falling back into the monotony of my daily existence, when a knock came to my door. Mrs. Dart stood there.

"Dr. Watson," she explained, after entering. "I have come to thank you and Mr. Holmes."

"I'm afraid my good friend has returned to his country cottage," I reported.

"Then, you must give him the good news," she went on. "My father has returned, though I suspect you know as much. While relieved, my mother has been caught up in deeper emotions. But, just today, she asked me to come to you and Mr. Holmes. We are immensely indebted to you. We wish to express our sincere appreciation and to ask how we might compensate you for your services."

"I assure you, it was an honour to be of service to two gracious ladies such as yourselves. And, it was a personal delight for me to, once again, be at the side of my good companion – in the hunt again, you see. No further compensation is required."

"You are most generous, sir. But, if I can impose upon you a bit longer, I have a delicate matter of importance I would like to discuss."

I took her wrap and settled her down at the tea-table in the corner of my parlour. I offered tea, but she demurred and sat for a moment caught up in her thoughts.

"As you can discern," she said, "It is a delicate point. However, I feel I can confide in you because you are a man of honour and discretion. I think the scheme my mother and I created – the bones and all – had a two-fold purpose." She paused. "We did indeed require the superior deductive powers of Mr. Holmes and… and… I believe she had hoped to become reacquainted with Mr. Holmes in the process."

She blushed and covered her mouth as the last words escaped.

"How shall I say this?" I said. "I believe my friend and I were aware of both motivations."

"I see. I see." There was a brief pause. "Then, I suppose there is no more to be said, but to, once again, express my deepest gratitude, and that of my mother."

"It was our pleasure, most assuredly."

"One more thing, Dr. Watson," Adaline added. "If you would be so kind as to give me Mr. Holmes's address, I should like to send a personal note of thanks."

I wrote Holmes's address upon the back of my card and presented it to the lady. She left, and I sat quietly with the scent of her perfume still lingering, thinking how wonderful it felt to have a woman in my home again.

The next morning, I sent a telegram to Holmes to let him know that his expectations for Godfrey Norton had played out. I did not share the particulars of my conversation with Mrs. Adaline Dart, but only added that I hoped he would soon return for a visit.

My invitation was answered some weeks later. A telegram was waiting for me upon my return from dinner one evening.

WATSON

BELATEDLY ACCEPTED DR KEITH'S INVITATION. PLEASE JOIN ME AT THE CONFERENCE. ARRIVING WELL AHEAD THIS SUNDAY 3.15.

HOLMES

I supposed that the eugenics movement, which was growing in prominence and popularity, had rightly ruffled his feathers, but I wondered if there were other reasons for his visit as well.

Holmes had no sooner arrived than he invited me to sup, once again, at Rules. During dinner, we chatted about his latest apiary experiments, the mounting tensions created by the suffragettes who had taken to the streets, and the flurry of recent newspaper articles touting the British eugenics movement. It was only after brandy was served that Holmes retrieved a letter from his coat.

"I received a delightful letter from Mrs. Adaline Dart thanking us for our help," he said, laying the letter on the side of the table. "She observed, as an afterthought, that she felt our collaboration brought some small measure of joy into our solitary lives."

I bristled a bit.

"It was a jolly time. Taking up residence together… on the scent like a couple of old hounds again… but, did she use *those* words: joy into our solitary lives?"

"Indeed, she did," Holmes remarked, tapping the letter on the table.

"My life is quite full – as is yours. We are solitary fellows to be sure, but certainly not without joy."

"I quite agree, Watson," he replied. "But, I wanted you to know that I much enjoyed our little adventure as well; and, accordingly, I am resolved to see more of you, beginning with the First International Eugenics Conference."

"I will drink to that!"

He did drink, and took a leisurely stroll back to my apartment. As we reached my lodgings Holmes retrieved his pipe from his pocket.

"I think I might enjoy a smoke, Watson, and linger a bit longer in the balmy evening air."

I went to my room and glanced out of the window at my friend puffing on his calabash. The smoldering amber tobacco set a glow upon his face. Holmes was absorbed in an introspective reverie that was not diminished by the occasional passing carriage.

After a bit, he tapped his pipe upon the stair rail lightly to shake out the ashes. As he reached for the door latch, a slender youth in an ulster and tweed trilby hurried by with a passing greeting:

"Good-evening, Mister Sherlock Holmes."

Holmes remained frozen in place. An enigmatical smile came to his lips. His face turned down the street as he watched the "youth" disappear into the shadows.

The path upon which my bemused friend had now found himself was unfamiliar. He stood in a place where reason alone would suffice.

2

THE CURSE OF THE BLACK FEATHER

A new diabolical adversary threatens Sherlock.

ONE WHO DID not know better might suppose that Holmes originated from our smallest colony, Gibraltar – that universal symbol of the unalterable, unbroken, and unchanging. Yet, recently, I had begun to discern changes in my friend's static existence. So, our encounter before breakfast, on the morning of June 28, 1912, did not entirely surprise me.

"Invitations seemingly abound, Watson," he said, twisting a card in his fingers. "First, Dr. Keith's invitation to attend the Eugenics Conference three weeks hence, and now this!"

"An invitation, you say. You seem to be considering it, or it would be already burning on the grate. Who sent it?"

"I'm sure that you'll be amused."

I sat in quiet expectation.

"The invitation is from Mr. and Mrs. Dart. We've been invited to attend the Henley Regatta next weekend," Holmes said, placing the card next to my plate, and sipping from his cup.

"If you are asking for my opinion, we should accept. I

understand that your college's eight-man is in the running for the Grand Challenge Cup."

Holmes shrugged his shoulders.

"What comes to mind when you consider this invitation, Watson?"

I could barely contain a chuckle.

"So, you suspect Mrs. Dart and her mother of playing games once more. But, you love games, my friend. Indeed, you are the chess master."

"Or the pawn, more like."

I let the matter rest as I watched my friend descend into a closeted part of himself. If Holmes's inner world is shared, it is primarily through his moods, which are wide-ranging; and, at times such as this, unfathomable.

~

The next day, I heard tetchy mumbling in the next room. I peered in to see Holmes rummaging through his trunk.

"I had packed in anticipation of attending a conference, Watson, not a picnic. What does one wear to a regatta?"

"A taped-edge blazer seems to be the fashion, and a straw 'boater.' A pity you left yours at home!"

"Your witticisms are appreciated, of course, but I was hoping for some sensible assistance."

"I apologize, my friend. It appears that we are attending the Royal Regatta, then. What tipped the scales?"

"My *alma mater*," he replied. "Or, more accurately, *utilis mater*. Cambridge offered me a wonderful laboratory, but I missed the frivolity that echoed in the hallowed halls of Oxford. However, it may be time to cheer the old place on. As you say, our eight-man is a contender for the Grand Challenge Cup."

"Shall I seek accommodation for us?"

"No need, Watson. A room is awaiting us at

Bremingham Farm at Henley-on-Thames. It is on the Berkshire bank, with an excellent view of the race. However, you might look to our transportation. We are expected for dinner on the fourth."

Interest in the Royal Regatta might have consumed much of Holmes's immediate attention. However, mounting anticipations were interrupted by a loud knock at my apartment door, which came as I was putting a kettle on.

A regal mountain of a man, weighing something like twenty stone, stood on the threshold. He removed his crumpled homburg and, taking a cigar from his lips, spoke:

"G. K. Chesterton to see Mr. Sherlock Holmes."

Indeed, he needed to add nothing more. Somewhat taken aback, I escorted him into the parlour and motioned toward a chair.

"I was just putting the kettle on," I said. "Might I offer you a cup?"

He held up a hand.

"No, thank you, Dr. Watson."

"Very well then, let me summon Holmes," I said, turning toward the adjoining room.

When I announced Chesterton to Holmes, his startled look quickly twisted into a smile. He put on his smoking-jacket hurriedly, and, placing a hand on my shoulder, said: "Let us not keep the gentleman waiting."

When we entered the parlour, I saw that our guest had removed his cape, and was already seated on the edge of a red leather wing-back, with both hands resting on a mahogany stick sandwiched between his legs. Holmes approached; I stayed behind to better take in the moment in which these two great minds were to meet.

"Mr. Chesterton, you honour us," Holmes said, offering his hand.

Our guest stood and shook Holmes's hand.

"The pleasure is mine, I assure you, sir. We share so many interests, the criminal mind being but one!"

"I quite agree; although my interest has been primarily focused on removing the criminal mind from our society."

"My visit, you'll be happy to hear, is driven by the same desire." Then, with probing hesitation, Chesterton added: "Then… you do not accept the popular doctrine of criminal rehabilitation?"

"I have not met many criminals who wanted to be rehabilitated. I believe that is a prerequisite."

"Mr. Holmes, I completely agree with your philosophy," the large man said, pounding his stick on the floor like a three-dimensional exclamation mark. "Free will, and the role of human choice, applies to both the law-abiding and criminals alike, does it not? There are few joys that compare to engaging with another first-rate mind. I have followed your endeavours closely, not so much as a journalist, but as a student of human genius."

"You are very gracious," Holmes replied, "and I can more than return your appreciation. Your criticisms of Dickens have an honoured place in my library."

"Most kind! Have you, perchance, read my Father Brown stories? You might be interested to know that your methods were the inspiration for my hero."

"Are you speaking of my rational methods, or less rational inspiration?" Holmes asked, with a half-smile.

"For me the rational and irrational come together in one ideal, which I think we share," Chesterton said: "that we care for our fellow man, and wish to safeguard our society from evil."

Our guest's remark was terminated by a pregnant pause that offered me an opportunity to engage in the conversation.

"You said earlier, Mr. Chesterton, that you had come here because you wished to remove a particular criminal mind from our society."

I pulled up a chair next to the two men, and we all sat down.

"A criminal mind – yes, Doctor, and a criminal enterprise, too. One that, in my opinion, ranks with the worst blights upon our country."

With a sweep of his open hand, Holmes encouraged our guest to continue.

"There are different names," Chesterton said, "for this enterprise of which I speak, the common word is 'baby-farming.' To be honest, I have, in the past, devoted little attention to the matter; but our housekeeper – former housekeeper, I should say! – recently brought the foul practice to the attention of Mrs. Chesterton and myself."

"As you might suppose," I interjected, "I have come across baby-farming in my practice as a doctor, although infrequently. I thought the Child Act had put a stop to the more immoral methods and practices."

"No doubt, it simply drove the villains deeper into the shadows," Holmes remarked.

"That is true, to be sure," Chesterton replied. "Rather than dying out, baby-farming, or some new form of it, seems to be enjoying a resurgence that I cannot explain."

"And, why have you come to me?" Holmes asked.

"Because, I suspect that this practice, which has plagued our nation for more than half a century, seems to be taking on the form of a well calculated, and well financed, criminal enterprise, the roots of which are buried so deeply within our society that conventional approaches to justice are not likely to prove efficacious."

"So, you seek an unconventional approach," Holmes said.

Our guest, with head bent downward, awkwardly glanced up.

"I'm afraid that my investigative abilities are limited. Also, as I will disclose, there appears to be some danger associated with the investigation. I wish to endanger neither my family, nor my household. In short, sir, I am fearful."

"Fear often brings clients to our door," said Holmes. "However, I can promise only to look into the matter, and test your assertions. From there, we must let the facts take us where they may."

"You seem, sir," I said, "to have some special insight into this subject. What has led you to believe that there is a criminal organization behind this resurgence in baby-farming?"

"As you may be aware, Dr. Watson, I am employed by the *Illustrated London News*. Recent events concerning our housekeeper led me to discover that my own newspaper had printed an advertisement offering the service. I have the notice here."

The huge man stretched back in his chair to gain access to his waistcoat. He took a few scraps of newsprint from his pocket and held one of them out to Holmes, who snatched it up, unfolded it, and read it aloud:

> NURSE CHILD WANTED TO ADOPT
> Lying-in home and re-homing available.
> Widow with family and allowance would be glad to receive the charge of a young child. Will adopt, if under two months, for the small sum of twelve pounds.
> East Finchley
> Box N, Illustrated London News.

"A respectable district," I said.

"And that is what piqued my curiosity," our guest

replied. "I made enquiries to discover who had placed the advertisement, and so revealed some curious details."

"Of course, you discovered that payment had been made in cash," Holmes stated, matter-of-factly.

"Indeed. And our clerk noted that payment was made by, as he put it, 'a fine gentleman' who would not give his name."

"What does that tell us?" I asked. "This enterprise, as you call it, is a business, is it not?"

"Yes," said Holmes, "but baby-farming contracts involve only small sums of money, relatively speaking. Isn't that right, sir?"

Chesterton nodded.

"They can vary from ten to twenty-five pounds, I've been told: a substantial sum for the young women involved, but one that is hardly able to support a grand lifestyle. And, most of the baby-farmers are small businesswomen, who have no other means of support."

"Curious," remarked Holmes, "but there could be many explanations."

"There is more," Chesterton added. "Maud had left our employ more than three months ago. She stated her reason simply as 'a family emergency.' Of course, now we know better. She was with child and, as it turned out, had experiences with the very lying-in and baby-farming service advertised in my newspaper. Her experience was not a good one, to say the least. Her child was born with a defect, dwarfism I believe."

I felt a tug at my heart. "Achondroplasia is a malady whereby the child's bone and cartilage formation is not complete, causing abnormal body proportions. The results range from the mild to the horrific."

"Maud described the child as 'mostly normal,' except for shortened legs and a flatter than usual nose." There was a catch in Chesterton's voice. He reached for his cigar, which had gone out. "Frances and I have now taken Maud under our wing, and back into our household. The young woman is distraught in the extreme." He paused for additional composure. "As I said, her child, which she named Treasure, was put up for nursing and adoption. Then, only a week later, she discovered that the child's life might have come to a horrible end."

Holmes did not reply, but sat straight up with his eyes closed. Finally, he said: "Details, please."

Chesterton put his cigar down in order to retrieve the other newspaper clipping, and something else, from his coat pocket. He offered the clipping. Holmes remained motionless, eyes closed. I took the bit of newsprint, opened it, and read it.

"Watson?" Holmes appealed. I read aloud:

June 12

The metropolitan police reported that a small babe was retrieved from the Thames River last evening near Kew Bridge. Foul play is suspected as the girl child, less than one month old, had deformities including short legs. Authorities are requesting information from any party.

A heavy hush hung in the air, like a suffocating fog.

"Despite great embarrassment, reluctantly, and belatedly, Maud contacted the authorities. However, by the time she had come forward, the babe had been buried. She guided officers to the East Finchley address, but none of the persons living there matched her description. Furthermore, the residents nearby denied any knowledge of a lying-in home, and the police could not find evidence of such – even as they searched the area."

"One might have expected," I said, "that the authorities would have pursued the matter further."

"I believe they initially attributed their lack of success to Maud's condition. She was, after all, in labour at the time she went to the lying-in home. Later on, due to her great distress, she did not… shall we say… present herself well. Of course, when she came to us, more than a week later, I followed up on the investigation. I was disheartened, and angered, at the lack of attention being given to the crime. After questioning several of those in command, it became clear to me that some senior officer was likely discouraging the investigation. Statements such as, 'my hands are tied,' and 'there is a limit to what we can do,' were frequently heard during my interviews. And then, I discovered something else…"

"So," Holmes said, "you have more information for us, Mr. Chesterton. Does it, perchance, have some connexion with that feather which you are twirling in your fingers?"

"Indeed, Mr. Holmes. When it became clear to me that the police were either powerless or incompetent, I decided to investigate Box N. myself. I reconfirmed the information with Maud, and I myself called at the East Finchley address."

"With unsatisfactory results, presumably."

"Yes, and I might have desisted from further efforts, thinking, as the police maintained, that Maud was confused or mistaken. However, I came to learn that my inquiries were noticed, and most unwelcome."

"The black feather," Holmes said.

Chesterton nodded.

"I returned home one evening to find a letter for me, that had been delivered by hand."

He retrieved an envelope from his inside pocket, and handed it out to us. I opened it, and saw one line scrawled:

Curiosity and ignorance is a dangerous blend.

"This black feather was enclosed. I took it as a threat."

"As well you might!" Holmes said. "May I?" Taking the five-inch black feather from our guest, Holmes held it up to the light and ran his finger over the edge.

"From a large bird to be sure, most likely a raven; clearly a flight feather from the wing or tail."

Turning back to Chesterton, Holmes asked: "Is it possible for us to speak with Maud?"

"Then, you will take my case?"

"We may well discover that this incident is nothing more than another unholy tragedy, like that of Sachs-Walters; but, rest assured sir, Treasure's death will not pass unnoticed."

Holmes and I made an appointment to visit Chesterton's former housekeeper, Maud, on the afternoon of the following day. She was staying at the Chesterton's home in Buckinghamshire, west of London.

We also asked Chesterton if he would introduce me to the clerk at the *Illustrated London News* later this morning – the fellow who had taken payment on Box N. We hoped there was more to be gleaned from him than our client had been able to gather.

Shortly after Mr. Chesterton left, I was preparing to depart for the Strand when Holmes called to me. My companion was sucking on his pipe and writing on a tablet placed upon his knees.

"Watson, in your visit to the *Illustrated London News* I should like you to deliver this placement request."

"A placement? To whom?"

"I suggest that you deliver it to whomsoever is at the front desk, and ask that it be given to the advertisements office, rather than taking it yourself."

I waited while he placed the note in an envelope and addressed it. Handing to me, he remarked: "I suspect a little bait is called for as we begin to craft a trap."

As I turned to go, he continued, "And, Watson, do not dawdle. I'm looking forward to a hearty lunch, as we seem to have foregone our breakfast."

"Quite so. What would you say to lunching at Simpson's in the Strand – around one?" Unable to resist a jibe, I added, "Mulburry's is near-by you may recall; it might be just the place for that blazer which you'll be needing for the Regatta." I didn't wait for his reply, but hustled off to my tasks.

The streets of the financial district were bustling. Near the centre of it lay the offices of that bastion of British journalism, the *Illustrated London News*.

I delivered Holmes's letter to a young man at the door, and followed him to ensure that he carried the missive to the third floor. I then made my way to the editorial offices to speak with Mr. Chesterton.

He was, of course, expecting me, and arose from his desk in welcome. "Dr. Watson, what type of introduction would best serve your purpose?"

"I believe the less said the better. A callow youth will undoubtedly bend to a simple request from a distinguished senior member of the staff."

We climbed the stairs to the third-floor office. There, standing behind a caged counter, was the clerk in question – a wholly freckled lad of about eighteen years, with spectacles that doubled the size of his eyes. He bore a constantly anxious expression.

"Hello, my boy," Chesterton said, approaching. "I am in need of your help again, and your extraordinary memory. Our client here requires information about the gentleman who placed an advertisement a month ago – Box N. Do you recall the man?"

"I am at your service, sir," the youth replied, as he nodded to me.

Chesterton smiled broadly. "You are now in good hands," he said to me, and thanked the lad. As he departed, I began my interview.

"So, you recall the gentleman to whom Mr. Chesterton referred – he of Box N.?"

"It's been some time sir… but, well enough, I suppose."

"Please tell me everything that you recall."

"Well sir, he was a dapper gentleman. Finely dressed," the young man began, with his eyes flashing upwards in recollection. "He wore a fine frock-coat with a fancy waistcoat. I do not recall his trousers."

I took notes as the lad continued to dredge up additional details.

"He had a top hat, and grey gloves, as I recall. Set them down on the counter here as he retrieved his wallet. A walking stick as well; he hung it on the edge of the counter."

"His features?"

"He was an older man, maybe in his fifties, with a moustache – finely trimmed, black, salted with grey, and hair to match," the lad noted. "As I say, a fine gentleman."

"British? From London?"

"British to be sure," the clerk said. "From London… possibly. His accent had something of the West."

"Cornish?"

"Possibly, sir. I'm not skilled in such matters."

"Was there anything unusual about this gentleman?"

"He did have a large pin on his tie," the boy said. "A swan, the body made of a white pearl – a large one, the size of an aggie. He was a man of means, I should say, and his wallet bore that out."

"How so?"

"His advertisement cost far less than a pound, but he gave me a fiver in payment. I had to go to the head cashier to get the change," the lad noted. "I could see, when he paid me, that his wallet was very plump indeed."

"Thank you, young man," I said. "You've been most helpful."

As I turned to depart, the lad piped up again. "One more thing: a little thing, sir!"

I turned.

"He had a slight limp. The cane was more than decorative. Does that help sir?"

"Indeed." I said, making one last entry in my notebook. "You are a most observant young man."

"Accountancy necessitates it."

My watch showed 12.25 as I walked out of the building.

As I passed Mulburry's, I caught a glimpse of my colleague entering the establishment. *My, my,* I thought, *this is also one for my notebook.*

I went on ahead to Simpson's and secured a table for Holmes and myself. I was reviewing my notes when he arrived, just ahead of the waiter.

"Watson, I trust you have not been waiting long?" he enquired, in a curiously cheerful tone.

"No, indeed."

"Did your visit to the *Illustrated London News* prove fruitful? Anything that might support our client's suspicions?"

I shared the information I had received from the clerk, point by point. Holmes listened in his usual impassive manner. He gazed off into a distant corner of the room, unblinking and completely still. Others often find his lack of eye contact unsettling; but I have long understood that his great intellect is always hard at work behind the mask-like face.

"Most enlightening," he said, at last. "To our knowledge, the baby-farming business is not a lucrative one. Yet, we have a moneyed individual, presumably from a class which we might not associate with baby-farming, apparently in charge of such an enterprise."

"Investing money in it," I added.

"Yes, Watson. Money is the grease that keeps the engines of the world grinding on – and those of the underworld, as well. Yes, I am beginning to believe something sinister is stirring here. Our enquiries may soon take us into some dark places."

"That would not be unfamiliar territory."

"Yes; but we may well be hunting a new kind of criminal and, consequently, have need of some special scouts to guide us."

"The irregulars, you mean?"

"No, Watson, we shall require the services of someone who can travel unseen in the underworld: someone who might mix in."

"Do you have someone in mind?"

"Possibly, if she is presently gracing our city. I know just the woman – the lovely Cinka."

At that moment our waiter appeared. I shall spare my readers any account of the menu and meal, much of which was passed in silence, or in simple conversation. However, as we concluded our luncheon, I risked a question.

"Did you, perchance, happen to visit Mulburry's?"

"Watson, you know I abhor gamesmanship. I saw you pass, and observed you gazing at me as I entered the establishment. I will not gratify your mock inquiry. Suffice it to say that I will fit into the *milieu* of the Royal Regatta." And after a pause, "I trust you will find your wardrobe adequate?"

His comment catapulted my mind into the dim reaches of my armoire. "Most certainly, more than adequate I would say," I replied, imagining my waistcoat tightly stretched across my belly.

A knock came on our door early the next morning. It was a newsboy. Before I could address the lad, he blurted out: "Dr. Watson, sir?" I barely had time to nod my head before he'd thrust a note into my hand and darted off.

The brief note was addressed to Mr. Sherlock Holmes and Dr. Watson:

> *Maud has agreed to meet with you this afternoon. I will be engaged, but Frances will be expecting you about 2.00 pm.*
>
> *Gratefully,*
> *G.K.C.*

Knowing my duties, I consulted the railway timetable, which showed a train leaving Marylebone at 1.14.

When I approached Holmes, he was ankle-deep in a pile of old newspapers. He had torn out several advertisement pages and laid them over the arm of his chair.

"I assume that was a message from Chesterton," he said, without looking up.

"Yes, we're expected at two. The train leaves Marylebone at 1.14. Breakfast is ready."

The Chesterton residence was rather grand. Centred between two wings was a mediæval tower with a crenulated parapet. A gothic alcove in the lower part of the tower framed a pair of ancient oak doors dotted with hobnails.

The bell brought Mrs. Chesterton to greet us.

"Mr. Holmes and Dr. Watson – so good of you to come! Gilbert and I are so grateful for your assistance."

She was a tall, slender woman with chestnut-coloured hair arranged upon the top of her head. She wore a plain white apron over a grey dress, and held a glass of water.

A maid came scampering behind her, and rushed to take our hats and coats. Before the maid departed, Mrs. Chesterton handed her the glass of water, and nodded toward the stairway. The maid darted away.

Holmes was anxious to talk with Maud, but we accepted an offer of tea. When we were settled in the spacious parlour, Holmes said: "Mrs. Chesterton, may I enquire as to Maud's condition? Is she in a... fit state to see us?"

"Gentlemen, Maud is troubled. Physically, she seems fit enough, although she is not eating well. Emotionally, she displays huge swings in temperament and mood. One moment, she is melancholy and sedentary, the next angry and raving. This experience has broken the poor woman. I feel so useless."

I collected my notebook to assist Holmes as he recounted the information which we had gleaned from her husband, and then asked: "Is there anything more you can add that may be of help to us in this investigation?"

Frances started to speak, and then stopped. "I have gathered some little information from Maud. But, am I correct in assuming that you would prefer to hear it in her own words?"

"Quite so," Holmes replied.

"She knows that you are coming, and is prepared to see you. However, let me go on ahead to settle her. Please enjoy your tea. I will send for you shortly."

It was less than five minutes before the maid fetched

us upstairs. We followed Frances's voice to a room at the far end of the hallway. Mrs. Chesterton was sitting next to the bed where Maud was propped up. She wore plain white bedclothes and had a bright yellow robe about her shoulders. The large pillows, that supported her, dwarfed the tiny woman. Her eyes were murky, and her complexion pallid. Francis introduced us and brought another chair to the bed for me.

"We are here to help you," I said. "Mr. Holmes and I will need as many details as you can offer regarding your experience with the lying-in home in East Finchley." At this, Maud's eyes became wet. Mrs. Chesterton, who was standing behind us, reached in with a handkerchief.

Maud tried to speak between sobs. "I don't know… what can I say… or remember…"

Holmes interrupted. "Perhaps, Maud, it may be easier if we were to ask some questions."

She nodded, and he continued. "Was the lying-in home in East Finchley?"

Maud nodded, but then shook her head. "I enquired at East Finchley, but was taken, by carriage, to another location within the city. I'm not certain where. I think it was near St. Giles."

Holmes nodded. "More in keeping with my expectations," he said to me. "Maud, please tell me what you can of this lying-in house, and the people within."

The young woman did not impart many new details. This can be attributed to the fact that she was in the first stages of labour when she came to the lying-in home. She described a dank, windowless room where she resided throughout the birthing. An older woman who, it seems, had little to distinguish her, other than possessing large hands, attended her. We asked Maud if she recalled a dapper gentleman, possible one with a large pearl tiepin.

"I saw no one but the woman. But, there were visitors from time to time. I could hear their voices below."

"Could you make out anything of those conversations?" I asked. "Anything which you can recall may be helpful."

Maud sat quietly for a time twisting her mouth and lips. Her eyes shot back and forth searching in recollection. "There was one time, just after the birth of Treasure, several visitors – men came. Treasure was taken from me and shown to them. At first, I did not hear their words, but voices were raised at one point. I heard the keeper woman insisting upon more money. She said that this... 'this dark bit of work'... that's what she called it, 'this dark bit of work'... would cost the gentlemen more."

Maud paused. Her hands began to tremble. Tears streamed down her cheeks. "That was the afternoon before I left. I never saw Treas...

Mrs. Chesterton swept in to comfort Maud and turned to us. "Gentlemen, I believe Maud needs her rest now."

Holmes and I found our way downstairs and were escorted to the door and our waiting carriage. As we drove back to the station, I felt a melancholy which I had not experienced since my first wife died. I glanced over at Holmes, who was in a trance-like state.

"This venture is a heartrending affair," I said. "It's quite overwhelming. I'm not sure I will be good company this evening."

"As for me," Holmes remarked, "the sadness you speak of runs deeper than Maud's tale, for there are many others like that poor child. We live within a web of convention that is doing violence to our womenfolk. You and I, Watson, have the ability to navigate the entire spectrum of our society. We operate within a region between the entitled and the disenfranchised. We must remember, when we are picnicking on the Thames two days hence, that our ability to help the 'Mauds of the world' depends, in part, on our acceptance within the supposedly nobler classes."

The words "Henley Royal Regatta" conjures up all that is British – eight lean men, rowing on glass-like water at high speed, growing tanned in the pursuit of victory. With the Olympics just ahead, success at Henley would be seen as a harbinger of British victories yet to come.

We caught the train at Paddington for Twyford, where our hosts had arranged for transport to Bremingham Farm in Henley. I spent most of the train ride buried in the *Times*, while Holmes, deep in reflection, gazed somewhere beyond the blurred countryside streaking by his window.

When we arrived at Twyford, we found an open carriage waiting with two other guests aboard. A gentleman and lady were chatting as we approached.

The driver jumped down to open the carriage door. He made short work of our introduction. "Mr. and Mrs. Craig – Dr. Watson and Mr. Holmes." He immediately stowed our suitcases, hopped into his seat, and was off.

"Mr. Holmes," Mr. Craig said, "Mary and I are looking forward to making your acquaintance. Your reputation, and that of Dr. Watson, comes before you, of course."

James Craig was stiff-backed, impeccably dressed, and sporting a proper English moustache spider-webbed in white. He methodically strummed the top of a hat cradled in his lap. His wife was a small woman in a pink and grey crinolined dress, and bearing a huge straw bonnet with pin ribbons that touched her shoulders. She wore a forced smile.

"May I ask gentlemen," Mary enquired, "is it your custom to attend the Henley Royal Regatta?"

"No," I replied. "However, I enjoy many sporting events. In school, I took up the single skull. And you?"

"The Royal Regatta has become an annual event for James and me," Mary Craig said. "However, this is the first year that we have been guests of Mr. and Mrs. Dart."

"Likewise, Mrs. Craig," I replied, "We too have only recently become acquainted with the Darts."

Mr. Craig ceased drumming his hat, and straightened up. "Gentlemen, would I be correct in assuming that your relationship with Mr. Dart is scientific in nature?"

I waited for Holmes to respond.

"You might say so. We will soon be guests at the Eugenics Conference. As you are an MP, Mr. Craig, I am curious to hear from you how our government esteems the idea of eugenics."

Mr. Craig became pensive. His lower lip protruded as if his mind were weighing Holmes's question.

"Of course, His Majesty's government has taken no official position, you understand. Yet, obviously, many MPs see that eugenics might offer a way for us to address many of our country's ills."

Holmes pressed on, with an edge to his voice. "Do I understand, then, that you are an advocate of the idea?"

"Let me say that I can see great potential, if the concepts can be put into practice. Wouldn't you agree?"

"I can see some potential for good, and great potential for evil, depending on how these beliefs are manifest," Holmes answered.

Craig bristled a bit, and his wife squirmed in her seat. She turned to the driver behind her. "May I enquire as to the distance to Bremingham Farm?"

The driver's reply was quick and sharp. "About another three miles, ma'am. Are you quite comfortable?"

"Yes, thank you," she replied. And then, turning back to me: "I am so looking forward to this holiday. John's work often precludes outings such as this. I feel it is good for all of us to get away from our routines and meet interesting new people like yourself and Mr. Holmes."

Aiding Mary Craig in the relentless British effort to stave off embarrassment, I replied: "I quite agree, Mrs. Craig. I look forward to better making your acquaintance, and that of our fellow guests."

Mrs. Craig leaned in toward Holmes and me. "I understand Mrs. Dart's mother is involved in a very nasty divorce."

"And what, exactly, do *you* know of it, madam?" Holmes retorted.

That comment put a large full stop at the end of our conversation. We travelled on in silence until we reached the farm.

When we arrived, we found other guests sitting on the lawn surrounding a large white-shuttered, two-story, stone home. I saw Adaline Dart walking across the lawn toward our carriage even before it slowed down.

Adaline's reddish-blonde hair was loosely tied behind her head. Her white dress rustled as she hastened to greet us. "My dears, Raymond and I are so pleased that you could join us!" She instructed the footman regarding our luggage, and we stepped out of the carriage onto the lush green grass to shake off the dust from the road. The Craigs asked to be excused and followed their bags into the house.

Adaline approached us with arms wide. Her winning smile widened, and her grey-green eyes flashed. "Thank you both for accepting our invitation." She grabbed my left arm and looked straight into my eyes. "You see, I have learned my lesson, Dr. Watson." Then, reaching for

Holmes's right arm, she explained: "A clear and direct invitation is the proper way to summon two gallant gentlemen."

Adaline strolled us both toward the others on the lawn. No doubt, Holmes saw Irene Adler before me. She was engaged with two other women on the croquet lawn. Her white dress fell in several tiers from her waist, and a wide green collar framed her face. As she turned toward us, her eyes widened and she flung her long red hair, curtained with a white beaded headband, behind her shoulders and waited.

Adaline called out: "Look who just arrived, mother!"

"Miss Adler – so very good of you to invite us!" I said in greeting. "You look lovely."

"Indeed," Holmes added, "I hardly recognize you without your ulster and trilby."

At that, Irene Adler's smile transformed into a chuckle. "Mr. Holmes, you have found me out, I fear. It seems as though neither of us needs to masquerade. A sign of maturity – would you agree?"

Holmes was slow in reply, "Hmm, 'maturity,' you say. Possibly, but I might also say 'self-respect.'"

Adaline intervened. "This conversation is far too confusing and serious. Come, Dr. Watson, let me find a drink for you, and introduce you to some of our other guests."

As we walked away, I glanced back at Holmes and Miss Adler, reflecting on how uncommonly strange it was to see Holmes engaged in conversation with the woman who, until today, had primarily existed for him as a photograph kept in his top desk drawer, and a gold coin on his watch-chain.

Adaline introduced me to an eclectic bunch. There was an artist, a business-woman, and a lady who was undoubtedly in the political arena – though her exact position was not immediately clear to me. I quickly came to learn that these guests were but vague acquaintances of Adaline and her mother. Indeed, several in the party expressed a mounting curiosity about Mr. Dart, who had not yet appeared. The couple, it seemed, had convened a multifarious gathering.

I mingled and chatted with several of the entourage, and struck up an acquaintance with a rather strange young artist-writer – Austin Osman Spare, from Snow Hill. Mr. Spare, a young man in his twenties, was tall, and possessed a clear, clean face topped with abundant chestnut hair. I recalled, some time ago, reading that he was the youngest artist to have ever entered the Royal Academy summer exhibition. However, when I pursued that line of enquiry, he seemed almost uninterested in art. He asked if I had read *Earth Inferno* or *The Book of Pleasure*. Of course, I had not… and it was unlikely that I should, from the sound of them. However, I found his youthful energy delightful. Austin Spare stood as a symbol of a new age, making me aware that I was a rigid icon of a bygone one.

Holmes, however, was showing some animation; his sitting and talking with *the woman* could only be seen as evidence of a new era indeed. My curiosity about their conversation was tempting me to rejoin them. But, no sooner had I taken a few steps in their direction, than Adaline snatched me by the arm.

"Dr. Watson, I want to introduce you to my husband Raymond."

Mr. Dart's youth surprised me. His demeanour was winning. He was a slender man, clean-shaven, wearing a loose white shirt with the sleeves rolled up. He was Australian, which may account for his informality.

"Doctor," Mr. Dart began, "Adaline and I owe you a great debt. Your intercession with Dr. Keith saved me from, not only great embarrassment, but also, most probably, the loss of my prospects."

"Holmes and I were more than happy to assist."

"Mr. Holmes, yes," he went on, "I must shake his hand as well. Where is that gentleman?"

I nodded in the direction of a large tree that shaded two chairs upon which Irene and Sherlock were still seated.

"So, the historic meeting is taking place!" Raymond exclaimed.

Adaline poked him in the ribs and smiled like a Cheshire Cat.

"Forgive me, Dr. Watson," Mr. Dart said, timidly. "I'm afraid that I have embarrassed my darling wife, so let me change the subject by saying that I look forward to gleaning advice and counsel that might serve me in my medical studies."

As the sun began to paint the landscape in a golden hue, guests began to move off toward the house. Dinner was at eight.

Holmes and Miss Adler approached me at a casual gait.

"Miss Irene Adler, allow me to formally introduce the finest friend and companion anyone could have, Doctor John Watson."

Miss Adler stepped forward, taking my extended hand in both of hers. A wonderful floral scent enveloped me. I was struggling to place it... clematis... morning glory... no, forget-me-not. She had a way of tilting her head and widening her green eyes that charmed me.

"Miss Adler," I said, "I must say that I never expected this day would come, but I'm most pleased that it has."

Just then, Mr. Dart formally announced the

approaching dinnertime. This evoked a stampede toward the farmhouse, as people, no doubt, were aware that shared bathrooms would complicate their dressing for dinner.

When I arrived at the farmhouse, Mr. Dart showed me to the upstairs room which Holmes and I would share. Our bags were already there, on the end of our beds. Holmes trailed closely behind after taking leave of Miss Adler.

"A lovely lady," I remarked, as I opened my suitcase.

"Yes, Watson. More importantly, she has a sound head on her shoulders. I shared with her a little of our recent enquiry into lying-in homes and the like, and she took an unusually keen interest in the subject... although disquieted by it."

"I should think so. A lady of her breeding would find the entire notion of baby-farming repugnant."

"Indeed, Watson. Nonetheless, she offered us her assistance."

"Are you contemplating a partnership of some kind?"

"You needn't be coy, Watson. I simply wish to learn as much as I can about Irene – you see, my decision to attend this *soirée* is a professional one."

"Professional, you say?"

"Watson, I'm a realist. You know that I have developed some... some attachment to the *idea* of Miss Adler. It began as a expression of respect, but, over the years, has grown into something other."

"Other?"

"A fantasy, I'm afraid – a dangerous fantasy. My mind is, at times, clouded by imaginings."

"I think some people might call that..."

"Watson!" he said, reprovingly. "Even the most disciplined mind may be subject to assault by fantastic notions. In most cases, these pass quickly." He paused, thoughtfully. "The best course of action is to expose these delusions to the cold light of reality, whereupon they will probably wither away."

"Well, Holmes, no one is likely to call you a romantic; yet, such a speech does conjure up modest suspicions."

"Suspicions?" he questioned.

"With apologies to The Bard and Queen Gertrude," I said, *"The gentleman doth protest too much, methinks."*

Holmes was put off by my playful taunt. He dressed silently for dinner, and went on without me.

Most of the guests were gathered by the time I made my way downstairs – assembled in the parlour, where Champagne was being served. The Craigs were there, of course, as was my new acquaintance, Mr. Spare. Holmes situated himself just outside a circle of guests. He did not acknowledge my entrance, but I was certain that he had noticed it.

Our hosts seemed to be absent, but then I spied Adaline talking to a parlour maid who had just entered with another tray of bubbling wine. The only individuals who I had not yet met, were a foreign-looking lady in a close-fitting bronze-coloured sequined dress, and next to her, a stately woman with abundant auburn hair. When the "foreign lady" noticed me glancing, her broad brows lifted, she smiled, and approached. She had a swagger in her walk that was exaggerated by the long strides she took. Her blonde hair was cut short in the new fashion, the so-called *style Jeanne d'Arc*. Unusually long lashes accentuated the darkness of her eyes, and her too-red lips were wrapped around the end of a mother-of-pearl cigarette holder.

She came uncomfortably close, blew some smoke from the side of her mouth, and remarked: "You must be Dr.

Watson. Austin mentioned that you and your friend, Mr. Holmes, were among the members of our little party."

I extended my hand, which she took with just three fingers of her left hand. "You are well informed," I replied. "But, I'm afraid Mr. Spare did not mention you."

She offered a polite laugh, "Oh, it's nothing like that, doctor." She paused abruptly. "Doctor sounds so formal, would you mind if we were on first-name terms? My name is Freda… Freda Strindberg."

"John."

"John," she repeated. "You are most handsome, if I may be so forward – for a doctor, I mean! You make a lady wish she had a malady."

"Heavens!" I cried, finding myself at a loss for words. "Miss Strindberg… Freda, do you hail from the city?"

"Indeed, John, I have an establishment on Heddon Street. For some reason, I doubt that you know of it."

"I often find myself in Mayfair."

She opened a black beaded bag that hung on her right wrist, and took out a card that she held out for me.

Taking the bright red card in my fingers I endeavoured to read the black engraving. There was a silhouetted cow in the upper left corner. The legend read: *The Golden Calf*, with an address below.

As I caught Freda's eye she added, with a small flourish of her cigarette holder: "It's a cabaret."

"How –" I paused. "How wonderful! A little piece of the continent here in our very own metropolis."

Just then our host entered the room, and made his way to me. As he did, Freda pulled away, saying: "Later, John!"

Raymond Dart watched Freda walk back to the group, and then turned to me.

"Dr. Watson, dinner is about to be served, and I wonder if you would not mind escorting one of our ladies."

"Certainly," I replied, glancing at Freda, who had just turned back to smile at me.

Dart went on: "I should like to introduce you to Mrs. Emmeline Pankhurst. Possibly you have heard of her?"

"Of course. She is –" I hesitated between *famous* and *notorious,* as the suffragettes had been front page news lately.

He sensed my discomfort. "Dr. Watson, I'm asking *only* that you to escort Mrs. Pankhurst to the table."

The dinner was mostly uneventful, despite the varied character of our assemblage, which might easily have given rise to arguments, if not to blows.

My dinner partner, Mrs. Pankhurst, was situated just across the table from Mr. Craig, who had recently made a speech in parliament denouncing her bellicose public demonstrations. On Mr. Craig's left, sat Frieda, the cabaret *chanteuse.*

Sensing the potential for disagreement, we all eventually took refuge in the least volatile topic – the regatta. Conversation aside, the meal itself was excellent.

The main course was star-gazy pie, with the heads of the pilchards bursting through a crispy brown crust; while, for the less adventurous, there was also lamb. By the time the savoury dish came, fruitcake served with Wensleydale cheese, the buttons on my (already challenged) waistcoat were worried indeed.

Holmes's dinner partner was, of course, Miss Adler. I could make out mere snippets of their conversation, which seemed to be focused on Holmes. Mr. Dart sat at their end of the table, and was also engaged with Holmes from time to time, once in a seemingly tense interchange. I was compelled to satisfy my curiosity when we later retired to our chambers that evening.

"A most interesting evening!" I remarked.

"Is interesting the right word, Watson? I found it, at times, rather taxing."

"How do you mean?"

"I was thinking of Raymond Dart," he said. "His benefactor, Dr. Arthur Keith, had shared with him the news that we had accepted an invitation to attend the Eugenics Conference."

"And, how is that taxing?"

"Mr. Dart assumed that we supported the eugenics movement. He was speaking of putting theoretical ideas into practice – such as a complete purge of our mental institutions. It was all I could do to retain a semblance of civility. Fortunately, Irene did not seem to share his convictions."

"Then your experience of Miss Adler was much less taxing?"

"Yes. She was unusually inquisitive, but I suppose that is an attribute of women." With a look of fond reminiscence, he continued: "She is highly intelligent and able to converse on a wide variety of subjects, including the sciences. Indeed, she has been quite taken up, recently, with the archaeological discoveries within our own country."

"So, the lady's interest in bones is quite extensive," I laughed.

"Yes," Holmes replied with a chuckle, "and, on that subject, she did apologize."

"Really?"

"Well, not exactly. Women have this way of apologizing without actually doing so."

"My late wife shared that quality. I have come to learn, though, that where there is affection, solemn apologies are seldom required."

I was aware, in that moment, of a tear running down my cheek.

While I might tell more of what transpired at the Henley Royal Regatta, the remaining events were of little relevance to the adventure that lay ahead. I would add, however, that the Australian eight-man, which won the main event by one and one-half lengths, at a time of seven minutes and six seconds, sadly beat the eight-man boat from New College, Oxford. The Grand Challenge Cup for 1912 would spend a year "down under."

When we returned from Henley, a message for Holmes was waiting under my front door. Having read it, he handed it to me, saying: "It appears that someone has taken our bait."

He explained that he had placed an advertisement for a lying-in home and baby-farming service in competition with Box N. He suggested that we go immediately to retrieve our message before the newspaper office closed, promising some supper in addition, as the trip from Twyford had been without nourishment.

Holmes waited outside the offices of the *Illustrated London News*, asking me to retrieve the message inside. Afterwards, we returned to Simpson's for a hasty repast. When the last bites were taken, Holmes asked me to read the message. It read as follows:

July 6

Box S,

I would be interested in learning more about your services. I have a proposition to our mutual best interests. I suggest we meet soon at the Hare and Hounds public house near St. Giles to discuss the matter further.

If you are interested, please reply to Box N and suggest a day and time to meet at the aforementioned establishment. Please wear a white feather.

Regards,
Box N

I caught Holmes smiling when I looked up. "A strange place to hold a meeting!"

"You do not recall the Hare and Hounds, Watson? A most remarkable rogue, 'Stunning' Joe Banks, is the proprietor. The former pugilist provides a valuable service, sitting as he does at the propitious portal to London's underworld. Yes, Watson. I believe Box S. has helped us to snare our prey."

"Now that you mention it, Holmes, I do recall the place. It lies within the Holy Lands, does it not?"

"Yes, Watson. It is the doorway to one of the darkest rookeries in London – lying between St. Giles and St. George's. There are certainly many there that need saving. I believe it's time to find the helpmeet I mentioned earlier. Come, let us see if we can locate the darling Cinka."

Cinka was a gipsie woman whom Holmes had engaged in years past on a variety of cases. The gipsies – or Romany, to give them their proper name – are a remarkable people who skirt the fringes of civil society, holding equal disdain for the law-abiding, and for the criminal element. They live and work within a tribal community, wherein few outsiders are welcome – save for those such as Holmes, who share the gipsies' regard for a justice which often stands apart from the law.

"How do you suggest that we find Miss Cinka?"

"Oh, Watson, we should never find her unless she wished to be found. No, we shall let her find us. With her knowledge of horses, she will not be far from a track. Could I interest you in a day at the races?"

~

We had decided that Alexandra Park course, at Muswell Hill, would be a good place to begin our quest. Just as we were entering the grounds, we spied a man in a wide-awake cap with a betting man's pouch on his belt. He wore a velveteen waistcoat studded with silver buttons and a small gold ring in his left ear.

Holmes pulled his wallet from his pocket and approached the man. "Who is the favourite?" he asked.

"I myself, like the horse that wins," the gipsie said, with a twinkle in his eyes. "Would you have a wager for me?"

Holmes caught the man's eye and tilted himself closer. *"Mande, I'll pen ya na, I rig a purs fur Cinka,"* he said, in the gipsie vernacular. Then, switching back to English: "Tell her that Sherlock Holmes seeks her help."

The man winked once and replied, *"Coliko, coliko sorlo me,"* he replied. And, with a smile added: "If she will come."

"Holmes, you astound me! I assume you asked for Cinka. What was his reply?"

"He said that he would arrange a meeting tomorrow morning – if she will come. The good news is that she appears to be nearby. As you know, the gipsies are not overly fond of *gorgio,* as they call us. However, Cinka and I have an understanding that goes back a long way. That understanding has not included you – until now."

~

The next day we returned to Alexandra Park, and there the Romany man stood in the exact same spot. Just behind him was a small boy dressed, from head to foot, in black. Holmes approached. The man put his hand on Holmes's shoulder and drew him closer until they were looking eye to eye. Suddenly, Holmes started. His right hand struck out violently to grab the lad's hand as it was entering his jacket pocket. A smile visited the lips of the gipsie tout. Holmes's hand relaxed, as the boy withdrew his empty hand and shrugged his shoulders.

"Seems like Nicko needs a bit more practice," the gipsie said. "But, he knows enough to bring you where you wish to go this morning." He nodded to the boy, who began to walk down the lane and, turning around, waited for us to follow.

The lad, without a word, took us, in a roundabout manner, through the city to a place just east and south of Friar's Mount – the "Nichol," as it came to be called from the local street name.

The fifteen or so acres of the "Nichol" were not so much a thieves' stronghold, as a breeding ground for future jail-birds. Dwelling therein were a multitude of irregular, casual, and low-skilled labourers. Along the damp, rubbish-filled lanes, the population was housed in two-and three-storey tenements that sagged onto the ill-drained streets and gutters. And, just as I was beginning to feel the dreary place closing in on us, we came suddenly into a square.

The young boy crossed to the opposite corner, where a public house was situated. Nicko stood at the doorway until he was sure we had seen him, and then darted inside.

Holmes and I found our way to the Bethnal Inn, as it was called, and paused for a moment outside. Holmes turned to me.

"Watson, I think it would be best if you were to remain

here for the time being. I will come, or send for you, if I can. For now, simply watch my back. The bench which we passed on the square gives you a good view of this doorway." I was about to protest, when he put his hand on my shoulder. "Please, Watson."

About three minutes after Holmes had entered the inn, I noticed our young guide reappear at the doorway, and casually lean against the jamb. Becoming curious, I left my bench and sauntered over toward him. As I approached the doorway, the youth popped straight up and shook his head to warn me off.

I was feeling more than helpless at this point, concerned for my friend, and yet not wishing to upset his clandestine meeting with Cinka – or whomsoever was inside the Bethnal Inn.

Someone must have summoned the lad, because his head suddenly snapped around, and he dashed inside again. I used the occasion to approach the inn and, peering through the open door, could make out only a darkened taproom. The windows were tightly curtained, and a few chairs were piled up against the far wall. The only light poured from a doorway at the far end of the bar.

The sparsely furnished room smelled of fetid tobacco smoke and sour ale. As I stepped inside, I was able to hear faint, indistinct voices emanating from an anteroom beyond. The character of the voices did not immediately suggest concern, but I was worried because I was not able to hear Holmes's voice among them. Then, as the voices became strident, I detected shadows moving on the floor just beyond the doorsill. I stood motionless against the wall as two silhouettes, male and female, became framed in the doorway. Thank God, one was Holmes.

"Watson," his voice shot out, "please, come and meet my good friend, Cinka."

I confidently walked toward them. As my eyes became more accustomed to the dim light, I noticed that an outsized man had been skulking in the corner. But, as I approached, he turned and walked out of the inn.

Cinka was dressed in a colourful red skirt encircled with a rainbow of silk scarves tucked along her black belt. A long yellow polka-dotted scarf was tied around her head, and trailed over her waist-length raven-black hair. Her face was deeply furrowed, and coarse black hairs sprouted from her upper lip. Her broad smile, and sparkling dark eyes, however, possessed a youthful twinkle.

"May I present Dr. John Watson. Cinka's been looking forward to meeting you!" Holmes exclaimed.

She extended a hand that had more rings than fingers. I took her hand in mine and made a small bow.

"I can assure you, madam, that there has been mutual curiosity."

At this Cinka laughed, and patted my cheek with her hand. Although done in the gentlest manner, her playful slap was deftly felt, because her heavy gold and silver rings created a gauntlet of sorts. As I glanced at her rings, she remarked: "Ah, you like Cinka's jewellery, eh?" She leaned close, and in a serious whisper, said: "Safe property is portal property."

Holmes spoke up then. "Cinka and her family are going to help us, Watson."

As we turned to leave, Holmes stopped and walked ahead toward the entry, where our young guide waited. As Holmes reached the doorway, he made an about-face and stood still, presenting his right pocket. The lad deftly reached into the pocket and retrieved a silver coin. Without acknowledging this in any manner, Holmes marched out of the inn. Cinka's laughter echoed down the street as we departed.

On our trip back to our quarters, Holmes shared the plan that he and Cinka had worked out. I had a limited role, as he and Cinka would rendezvous with Box N.

Since any hesitation might put off our quarry, Holmes immediately dispatched a note to Box N., suggesting a meeting on Friday next, leaving time for our message to be delivered in the intervening day. The meeting time was set for ten in the morning when there would be sufficient cover within the Hare and Hounds, but not so much that its rowdiness would be extreme.

Holmes prepared for the meeting on Friday by costuming himself in Romany garb. An azure jacket set off his billowing trousers, and he wrapped a red scarf around his neck. He wore a broad-brimmed black hat that dipped down over his face, which he had darkened with a concoction of coffee and palm oil. He carefully placed a large white feather in the band of the hat, which was to act as a signal.

As previously arranged, we met Cinka around the corner at St. Giles before the appointed time. Another man was waiting with her, whom she introduced as Lugar. Beyond introductions, few words were spoken. Holmes had already asked me to enter the establishment a few minutes ahead, in order to find a quiet corner from which I might monitor the proceedings.

The lintel was exceedingly low and the hinge screamed as I pushed the door open. Heads popped up and eyes glowered at me.

The notorious Hare and Hounds was large enough to host pugilistic events, possessing a large arena in the centre that was ringed with gas lamps sprouting from the floor. The arcade above the ring would undoubtedly fill with crowds gathered to view the matches below. Around the ring, tables and chairs were situated helter-skelter. I approached a long bar that stretched across the entire back wall. Above the bar were photographs of boxers including, no doubt, "Stunning" Joe Banks himself. I ordered ale and took a seat just as Cinka and Holmes were entering. Lugar was nowhere to be seen.

Holmes and Cinka entered, and sat at a table in the corner just opposite me. They waved away a woman who had approached for their order. Holmes removed his feathered hat, placed it in the centre of the table, and waited.

I had just begun to think our appointment would not be met, when the waitress approached again and handed Holmes a note, lingering while he read it. Rising to play their parts, he and Cinka stood. When Holmes attempted to put her back in her chair, Cinka slapped his face hard and quick. He raised a hand as if to return the blow, but stopped with his hand in the air. He shrugged his shoulders. Then, he and Cinka followed the waitress through a portal just behind the bar.

I waited for almost a quarter of an hour before I returned to the bar to order another mug of ale. As I crossed back to my stool, I noticed that Holmes had left his hat on the table, but the white feather was gone.

When another ten minutes had passed, my apprehension was roaring. Something had gone amiss. I walked to the other end of the bar, and began to peer around the end into the doorway through which Holmes and Cinka had been led. As I did so, a barrel-chested barman tapped me on the shoulder. "You've no business here – none!" he said, with a finger pointed an inch from my nose. Being a head shorter and three stone lighter than he, I felt that any challenge would prove fruitless.

"Just a bit of curiosity," I remarked.

"Curiosity can be dangerous," was his reply. This

phrase struck a deep chord in me, prompting me to seek another entrance to the inn's rear area. As I exited the front door, I found Lugar, leaning against the facade. He gave me a questioning look as I approached.

"I fear that something is amiss," I said, explaining what had happened, along with my intention to circle around to the rear of the public house.

Looking the odd pair, to be sure, Lugar and I walked down the adjoining alley, which – my nose told me – served as a latrine. As we trod on, we were startled by screeching noises, and the stench of putrefying blood, as we passed an underground slaughterhouse, where sheep were being tossed to an awaiting butcher's knife. The assault on my senses, and my mounting concern for Holmes and Cinka, fairly turned my stomach.

As it turned out, the Hare and Hounds did not have a back room, but simply a hallway that led to the alley. Lugar and I put our heads to the door in the hope of hearing something. It was then that I noticed the white feather from Holmes's hat lying outside the doorsill. He had been taken somewhere else from this doorway. I glanced at the cavernous slaughterhouse across the way, and noticed the ominous bloodstains on the cobbles.

Lugar and I, helpless and terror-stricken, rushed up and down the alleyway asking anyone if they had seen two gipsies coming or going. My inquiries became frantic as the minutes passed. I found myself going to the same doors, asking the same question, and receiving the same useless answer.

Lugar took me by the arm and motioned back toward the Bethnal Inn. I was reluctant to leave my search in this squalid circle of hell, but I went with him.

Just as we rounded the corner to the main thoroughfare, we saw Cinka racing toward the inn from across the square. We followed her inside and found her collapsed in a chair near the entrance. Her skirt was torn, and blood dotted her chin. She turned wide-eyed and, breathing hard, held out her arms to us.

"The men – Lugar, fetch the men!"

Immediately, he ran off.

Cinka turned to me. "Your friend is in danger. It may already be too late. They knew... they knew who he was."

"Where he is now?"

"We must hurry," she exclaimed, losing her balance as she rose. I steadied her. She wiped the blood from her lip and looked at it momentarily. As we moved toward the door, I spied a gang of eight or nine gipsie men racing across the square with a small horse and cart trailing behind. A large man in a long black frock-coat grabbed Cinka and lifted her up in an embrace.

"You are well?" he asked.

Cinka nodded. "We go now," was all she said, as she moved toward the cart. The large man lifted her into the seat and motioned for me to climb in the back.

Cinka directed us back toward the Holy Land. Just east of it lay a timber yard that had a hidden entry. She pointed to a small portal and two of the men put their shoulders to it. The jamb splintered, and the men pulled the door off its hinges.

There was a stairway that led to a floor above; the lower level opened into a long passageway formed by crumbling brick walls. This was the gateway into a hideaway deep in the bowels of the Holy Land.

Cinka held her arms out to halt us, and signalled for quiet by wagging her index finger above her head. The momentary silence was immediately shattered by a garbled, choking cry coming from a lodging at the end of the passageway. Cinka's hand shot out in a point, and the men raced forward. As I followed, she caught my arm to hold me back. Yanking my sleeve away, I arrived just as a kick sprung the door.

A ghastly scene presented itself.

Two men stood behind my friend, who was tied hand and foot to a chair. One of the men was forcing a leather funnel into Holmes's mouth. The other poured a milky liquid into the funnel.

Holmes was twisting in the chair, gagging and retching.

The brutes twisted their heads in alarm. But, before they could raise a hand, the gipsies were upon them, pummelling them mercilessly.

Despite the tumult, my world went silent. I saw Holmes, pinioned to an armchair, slumped over, motionless. *Please – no!* was all that I could think. I picked up the leather funnel that now lay at his feet, and knelt down at his side. Holmes was panting and delirious. His clothing was soaked and speckled with a snowy particulate. At Cinka's command, one of the men cut the ropes that bound him and, with the help of another, he was carried into the waiting cart.

"You go with him," Cinka said to me, as one of the men jumped into the driver's seat. "Go to the camp," she told the driver.

As we drove off, I could hear angry words behind me, followed by sharp yelps. The rescue party was interrogating the two thugs, as only gipsies can.

I ministered to Holmes as best I could in the cart. He lapsed into unconsciousness. Although he was bleeding from his lips, I did not detect wounds or broken bones. Copious amounts of saliva poured from the corners of his mouth. It was clear that Holmes had been forced to ingest something harmful – but what?

It took nearly an hour to get to the gipsie camp on the outskirts of the city, near the Mosley racetrack.

Most men and women live between four stationary walls, but the Romany carry their homes, indeed their entire community, with them as they wander. Colourful wagons and tents dotted a huge pasture in the distance, as we passed under a banner that proclaimed a show-ground that attracted local folk after the races. Booths were set up along a parade touting fortune-telling, lucky dips, and shies at which customers had to knock down prizes with balls. Passing quickly through this gauntlet of amusements, our cart arrived at a large tent in the centre of the compound.

As we arrived, a crowd of Romany gathered around our cart. The driver carried Holmes's slack body into the tent, and laid him on a cot. I quickly went to work loosening his collar, and removed his wet jacket and waistcoat. I leaned my ear to his chest and held my hand up for quiet. His breathing was shallow now, and his heart rate extremely low.

Two women held candles overhead to assist my examination. I ran my hands over his body more carefully now looking for wounds or injuries; and, again, found none. I pulled his jaw open and gazed into his mouth. The foaming saliva was restricting his breathing. I stuffed my coat under his head to prop it up. As I bent my ear to his chest again, I noticed a sickening metallic smell on his breath. A ghastly diagnosis found its way to my lips: *poison*.

My initial thought was that it might be arsenic poisoning, but the odour did not confirm that. I examined the light grey powder on his clothing and brought his waistcoat to my nose to smell it again. It was a metalloid of some kind.

Cinka and the rescuers returned with one of the thugs in tow. A burlap bag was fastened over his head and around his neck with a rope. His hands were bound behind him. He made no commotion. His comrade had evidently not been as lucky. As the large leader of the rescue party put it, when I enquired about the other assassin: "He wears a red smile."

I explained that I needed to know the poison used. The thug stood stoop-shouldered and sallow. His shirt had been torn off, and he wore greasy corduroys. As they removed his bindings and hood, an oilskin cap fell off his head, revealing a prison crop. Lugar held a knife to his neck.

The thug eagerly complied with my questions. He could not offer specifics about the poison, but produced an empty bottle from his trouser pocket. "I was told to put this-here in water and pour it down your man's gullet."

I snatched the bottle from his hand. There were no labels. However, the stopper had been coated with the poison. When I returned to Holmes's side, Cinka was on her knees wiping his brow and muttering: "Ben drabbed, ben drabbed." If I understood her properly, our diagnoses concurred.

"I need to fetch my bag and medicines," I explained, "but I'll be back directly."

Cinka, always a woman of action, was already bound for the canteen area. She put a kettle on a makeshift stove and began pulling bottles and jars from a crate.

"What are you proposing to do?" I asked her.

"Cinka does not 'propose' – Cinka does! We get the poison from his stomach."

My impulse was to object, but could not find cause, as I was sure that the poison was not acidic. Cinka's instincts were good.

Lugar drove me to my apartment and waited while I retrieved my bag, and several drugs. We stopped at a chemist's for a necessary extract on our way back.

When I arrived back at the camp, Holmes was still semi-conscious, but now he stank of vinegar and herbs – an emetic, no doubt. His eyes were closed, but I could see movements under the lids. Cinka had stripped him down to the waist and loosened his trousers. She had opened up his hands, and flattened them against his lower abdomen, keeping them in place with bandages wrapped around his torso.

I was mystified. When Cinka saw this, she explained: "The poison's already in the kidneys and liver. His energy needs go there." Holding out her open hand, she pointed to the centre of her palm. "This is the *loogan* point," she said. "Energy from there is needed to help his insides."

It seemed a lot of mumbo-jumbo to me; but, since I saw no real harm in Cinka's cure, I set about to augment it with a more rational treatment.

While the liver and kidneys were certainly impacted, I knew the more immediate danger was cardio-toxicity. I intravenously administered the adrenaline extract that we had purchased on our return trip. It had the immediate effect of increasing Holmes's heart rate. His breathing improved as well.

When it appeared that Holmes was out of immediate danger, I walked into the kitchen where Cinka and Lugar were waiting. She offered a cup of tea, which I gratefully accepted. It was only then that I noticed that the prisoner, who had been here earlier, was no longer to be seen. As I started to ask about him, I was cut off.

"Yes, he's gone," Cinka said, "that is all you need to know. You will be pleased to learn that we have *all* the information he possessed." I noted the accent on "all," and that Cinka had used the past tense.

"We did not fool the people," she said. "They knew it was Sherlock Holmes. They want him dead. He is in great danger."

"But, why poison?"

"He is the famous Sherlock Holmes. His disappearance, or foul play, would bring the police and enquiries. The poison would show as a natural death when his body was later found. You must take him to a safe place. They know he is here now, I am sure."

"I will take him to my apart...

"No!" Cinka said, taking my hand in hers. "They know where you live, and they will find him there. It must be a place where he has never been."

Finding such a place seemed difficult. But then, looking at my friend fighting for his life, I suddenly knew exactly where to go.

"I shall make arrangements," I said, nodding to Cinka and Lugar. "Bring Mr. Holmes to St. Paul's churchyard, near the bookseller's booths, in one hour. I shall take him the rest of the way."

I changed carriages twice *en route* to 644 High Road. My mind was a jumble, as I considered Holmes's condition, and how to make my appeal. However, any hesitation that I had in approaching the Darts for help disappeared the moment that I met Adaline at the front door.

My distress must have shown on my face, as she immediately led me into the parlour and sat me down. She asked the maid, Becky, to bring tea, and pulled up a chair.

"My dear Dr. Watson, you look dreadful. What is ailing you?"

"Not me – Holmes. We need your help."

"Then you shall have it," she said, without hesitation.

I briefly explained what had transpired, in less graphic form, and added: "There is danger in this for you. I shall do all I can to reduce it, but there is danger nonetheless. You must know this."

Adaline reached out to take both my hands in hers. "I understand. And, you must know that we are pleased to be able to repay the debt that mother and I owe to Mr. Holmes. He is welcome here."

The warmth I felt in that moment overwhelmed me and spilled over in a sob that shook my body. I glanced up at Adaline, "I am sorry for..."

"Please, you are among friends. You love him, and you are worried. Nothing more need be said. I will have a room prepared immediately. I will also send word to Raymond, who will be able to assist you in caring for Mr. Holmes."

Adaline's generosity of spirit, and unflinching response to my appeal, was more than I could have hoped for. I thanked her and set about bringing Holmes to this blessed refuge.

That evening, when Raymond Dart returned home, he found me at Holmes's side.

"Any improvement, Doctor?"

"Some, possibly, Mr. Dart; but, the poison has permeated his system and will take some time to work its way through." I said, with the uncomfortable coolness that doctors maintain in these situations.

Raymond enquired about the bandages that strapped Holmes's open hands to his sides. I had not removed the bizarre arrangement that Cinka had put there.

"It's a gipsie curative," I replied. "Probably a lot of hocus-pocus, but it can do no real harm."

"Indeed," Dart replied, "and possibly some good. The Orientals have a similar belief. As you know, Doctor, having served abroad, there is ancient knowledge that has yet to find its way into our civilized world."

The next day, I was startled awake in my chair by voices. Adaline held a pan of water. Another lady was using a towel to mop Holmes's brow. When she turned, I recognized the other at once. "The woman" might be dressed in a plain grey smock, with her red hair tossed up in a bunch on top of her head, but she still maintained the appearance of an enchanting lady.

In that moment, I felt a deep ambivalence. I recalled how my relationship with Holmes had narrowed when I was married, and wondered if that same thing might happen now – in reverse. At the same time, the better part of me wanted my dear friend to know the kind of affection that only a woman can offer.

Never did a man have more caring nurses. With Irene, Adaline, Raymond, and myself attending, Holmes continued to improve. Then, one morning, as I was changing his bedclothes, his eyes fluttered. He pulled his hands free of the bandages at his sides, and muttered a single word that melted my heart: "Watson."

Once Holmes was able to take solid food, I knew he was out of danger. I explained what had happened, and emphasised how extraordinarily hospitable the Darts and Miss Adler have been.

There had been little conversation between Holmes and the two ladies in waiting, but I could tell, as his condition improved, that he was becoming increasingly uncomfortable.

"I am better, Watson," he noted one evening. "I do not wish to impose any longer on the hospitality of the Darts."

"I understand, but you..."

"I am not unfamiliar with being incapacitated. However, I am unfamiliar – and uncomfortable – with having women attend me in an intimate manner. I wish to go with haste."

"Very well, but we cannot return to my apartment. My club might afford us accommodation."

"On the contrary," Holmes replied. "We must draw out our quarry if we are to remove the rotten core from this dangerous enterprise. We will go to your apartment. However, our snare will be skilfully set. There are more things than baby-farming afoot."

"Murder, for one."

"Yes, Watson. When one resorts to murder to thwart one's capture, the crime is most grievous."

We arrived at my apartment on Sheen Lane to find an envelope addressed to Holmes under the door. He held it up to the sunlight and a roguish smile twisted his lips. He handed it to me.

"It seems we are on the right trail, Watson."

Opening the envelope, I found a single black feather.

"A warning, Holmes. Notice the quill end," I added, handing the feather to him. The tip of the feather was coated in a reddish dye or ink.

Taking the feather from my hands, he remarked: "An attempt at signifying blood, I should assume."

"Your blood."

I could see that Holmes was still tired and weak. I helped him to settle in, and made a spot of tea. As I brought the tray into the parlour, I saw Holmes had laid his head back against the chair. His eyes were closed, and his breath laboured.

"You must take it slowly, my friend. You have been dangerously ill, and need rest."

"I am inclined to agree," he nodded. "The Conference is just two days hence and, if I might impose upon you further, I should ask you to make an appearance and offer my regrets to Dr. Keith on Wednesday. Indeed, it may be all for the best that you attend with your colleagues."

"Colleagues," I blustered, "only in the broadest sense of the word. I do not share their fascination with eugenics. However, I will make our apologies."

"Thank you, Watson. Before you go, I need you to summon what remains of the irregulars. I have a task for them. I have been away for some time, but I noticed Archie on the corner. I suggest you ask him to find Toby and the others."

The day of the First International Eugenics Conference had arrived and, as I dressed, I felt an odd mixture of curiosity and dread. Upon entering the kitchen to make tea, I found a pot already on the table, and Holmes sitting beside it.

"You must be feeling stronger, my friend," I said, pouring a cup, "since you are once again first in the kitchen."

"I suspect this may be a busy day for both of us. I hope to receive a full report on the conference over dinner tonight. Indeed, my appetite seems to be returning."

"That is the best of news," I said, "but I suspect it may not take all day to extend our apologies."

"No doubt; but, I am growing more curious about this burgeoning movement called eugenics, and I would greatly value your insight and opinion."

With that, I caught a hansom to the Cecil Hotel. Carriages and conference-goers jammed the entry. I found my way to the outer lobby, which was awash with luminaries. Among them were the former Prime Minister, Mr. Balfour, and the First Lord of the Admiralty, Mr. Winston Churchill.

As the delegates arrived, we slowly made our way into the hall where Major Leonard Darwin stood upon a raised platform. When the four hundred or more delegates had found their seats, the Major took to the lectern, and the rumbling voices diminish to a hush.

"Welcome, gentlemen and ladies," Major Darwin began. "We are on the brink of a new era in human civilization. My father gave the world a window from which we could see the one universal agency responsible for successful evolution: natural selection. Nature plays the part of the breeder, refusing to breed from inferior stocks.

"This forward movement has gone on since life first appeared on the earth... until recent times. Now, by social methods, everything possible has been done to prevent progress being made by Natural means.

"As we know in our very souls, there is danger in interfering with Nature's ways. We must proclaim aloud that to give any and all in distress aid, without considering the effects, is folly. Unthinking assistance, masquerading as charity, leads to the degradation of future generations.

"Our first efforts must be to establish such a moral code, as would ensure that the welfare of the unborn must be kept in view with regard to all the questions concerning both the marriage of the individual, and those organizations of the State that serve the distressed, diseased and decadent members of our society. We work toward the day that the twentieth century will be known, in the future, as the century when the eugenic ideal was accepted as part of the creed of civilization, and that we live in harmony with the incarnate laws of Nature."

Applause erupted and shook the room, along with cheering that lasted for several minutes. In the hush that followed, a vague apprehension and fear grew inside me.

This came, not so much from the words and ideas I had just heard, but from the fact that many of Britain's finest seemed to have wholly embraced an idea that flies in the face of all that has made us a great nation. And our American cousins seemed even more enraptured.

Before the exhibitions opened, the delegates heard from the American Breeders Association. A peculiar fellow, Noel Bleeker VanWagenen, described the American sterilization laws that propagated compulsory sterilization in order to, as he put it, "cut off the defective germ-plasm" in America.

Despite Holmes's request that I stay on, shaken to my core, I left the Cecil mid-day after making formal apologies to Dr. Keith at the luncheon. He expressed a mild disappointment, but did not seem surprised.

The carriage ride to my apartment was uneventful, but as I approached my door, I noticed a small Union Jack hanging vertically in my upstairs window. This was a signal that Holmes and I had used many times in the past to alert one another to potential danger. Although it had been many years since this warning signal had been used, I was not apt to forget, and I acted accordingly.

I reconnoitred the immediate area outside to ascertain if there might be someone lurking about. Seeing no one, I quietly made my way inside. I could hear muffled voices in the study above. On tiptoes, I made my way to the dining room cupboard and slid the bottom drawer open. There sat the oak case that held my service revolver. Upon opening it, I saw that my pistol was missing.

Knowing that my old stairway creaked sorely, I was hesitant to mount it. However, as the voices – those of Holmes and another man – became more strident and loud, I felt that I could safely approach.

Taking each step in turn, I waited and listened before I

took the next. The door to the study was closed, so I thought it best to enter the adjoining bedroom. When I entered, I was not surprised to find my bedroom door ajar, with a chair waiting nearby. Through our many years together, and now as an old couple, Holmes and I expressed our affection and respect for one another in small gestures unseen by others. As I sat down, with pencil in hand, a familiar affection filled my breast.

I extracted my notebook from my pocket, and bent my neck toward the door. I could not resist a quick glance inside, where I saw a tall, handsomely dressed, grey-haired gentleman standing. His nose was angular and jutted upward, supported by a huge black moustache. He had sunken brown eyes and a protruding chin that made him appear like a bird of prey. A *pince-nez* was dangling from his pocket. It was then that I noticed a small black feather pinned to his lapel. He was inclined toward Holmes, who was seated. A blanket rested on Holmes's lap.

"I know that you are an open-minded man of science, Mr. Holmes," the gentleman said. "You understand and respect the laws of Nature."

"I respect Nature," Holmes replied, "but, I am not so open-minded that I let my brains fall out. As you have said, the first law of Nature is survival of the fittest. Our very existence would seem to indicate that we human beings are fit, and improving with each generation."

The gentleman shook his head. "This is precisely our aim, sir. But, if the generations to follow are to become fitter, as you say..."

All of a sudden the man was overtaken by a spasm of coughing. He pulled a handkerchief from his sleeve and covered his mouth. His convulsions went on for some time before he regained his composure.

"Excuse me, sir, I am suffering from a bout of nasopharyngitis." He glanced at his handkerchief, and tucked it back into the sleeve of his jacket. "As I was saying… we must not interfere with Nature as our society is prone to do today."

"And so, you and your colleagues are doing just that: going about, as you say, seeking to 'cut off the inheritance lines of persons of unfit or meagre inheritance.' You use respectable terms and words to sooth yourselves, and those you wish to recruit. It seems as though plain words startle you. So, at the risk of doing so, I would describe your enterprise in a simple word: murder."

The gentleman's body recoiled at Holmes's assertion. Tapping the black feather on his lapel, he ranted: "Yes, we intend to pluck the black feather from the white swan. Call it what you will. Our species is jeopardized by the feeble-minded, pauperous, inebriate, criminal, epileptic, insane, and deformed. We… we operate as the right hand of Nature, which has been tied down by Church, state, and others that would succour them."

At this, Holmes' expression became one of amusement. "I fear I fall under the latter heading – 'others that would succour them.' And, as you cannot eliminate the Church or the state, you can do so with me, although I do not consider myself feeble-minded, nor insane."

"I would most heartily agree, Mr. Holmes. Your unwelcome interest in our endeavours has created a stir inside our little society, and the decision to bring a halt to your imprudent labours has posed a dilemma… for some."

"Those big words again! You did decide to murder me, am I not correct? Though in the manner of Pontius Pilate, you are washing your hands of the crime – unless you have come here to finish what you started in the Holy Land."

"I am not so crude, sir. So, if that is a weapon under that blanket on your lap, you may be at ease."

"I shall never again be at ease in our city knowing that you and your fiendish 'society' – as you call it – are stalking the streets and alleys. I will stop you, if it is in my power to do so."

"But, alas, sir, I fear it is not. And, if you intend to carry out your pledge, you will… eventually… meet your end. My hereto, meagre efforts, and those of my colleagues, will soon graduate to more effective measures. We must save our society and race."

"So then, why have you come here?"

"A promise made to some of my more tender-minded colleagues – a last effort to enlighten you. It is a promise that I made to gain their support. As you will come to learn, I keep my promises."

"So, killing innocent babies is good and necessary, but killing an adult man is not so simple?" Holmes took a deep breath and rose to his feet to look the gentleman in the eyes. He held my pistol in his hand. "The innocent love, and deserve justice, while the wicked naturally prefer mercy." Then, placing the pistol barrel under the man's chin: "However, I am not likely to grant you any mercy… and I expect none."

The man stood frozen for several moments. "As our conversation seems to have degraded into savage threats, I will take my leave."

At this, Holmes reached out and plucked the black feather from the gentleman's lapel and held it up.

"Your visit was not in vain, I assure you. I am enlightened. I do believe that the black feather is a curse on our country. It definitely needs to be plucked from the white swan." Handing the feather back to the man, he added, "It appears our differences lay in the confusion as to who, precisely, is the black feather, and who is the swan."

"The white swan is our beloved country, Mr. Holmes. Britain is drifting from its sacred destiny, and we must right the course." He turned slightly and walked toward the desk set in the nearby corner. He had his back to both of us, and was toying with some objects on the desk. Then, he turned suddenly. "This matter goes far beyond a handful of unfit babies. Your obstinacy puts you at odds with the divine destiny of our country. Good afternoon, Mr. Holmes."

The dark man then limped to my bedroom door. Tapping upon it, he added: "And, good afternoon to you also, Dr. Watson."

I did not reply, or move, until I heard his footsteps on the stairs, where upon I entered the room. "It seems his arrogance is unbounded, Holmes. Do we know who this person is?"

"Not as yet. But, his sense of invulnerability tells us that he is well placed in our society. The irregulars will be tracking him to his lair as he leaves. He has already proven that he is a dangerous person, but he is careful not to soil his own hands with foul deeds. Bringing his criminal enterprise to an end is, indeed, challenging."

"What do you plan to do next?" I asked.

"Wait."

Holmes handed me my revolver and walked to the corner desk. "Mizaru, Kikazaru and Iwazaru," he stated, obscurely.

"Whatever are you prattling about, Holmes?"

He turned, holding up a tiny brass casting of three seated monkeys in the palm of his hand. "The three wise monkeys, Watson. A last warning to us to see, hear and speak no more."

"The nerve of the gentleman is unbounded."

"I fear he may have forgotten the fourth monkey, Shizaru," Holmes said, crossing his arms across this chest. "Do no evil."

Holmes did not venture far from the study the next day. He took his meals there, read, and played his violin in the evening. His only visitor was Toby, the oldest of the irregulars, who brought him reports. At his admonition, my excursions into the city were limited as well.

"I would so much like to get a bit of air, Holmes. Do you still believe we must remain confined?"

"Just a precaution, but a prudent one. Let me change the subject though. No doubt you observed the rather violent coughing attack which our guest had yesterday. What do you make of it?"

"A bad cold, I should say."

"Indeed, that is what most people might say – a bad cold. However our man used the term nasopharyngitis."

"It's the same thing, really."

"Yes, but why use the medical term?"

"Ah, then you think he may be a doctor?"

"Possibly… though I doubt it. He is far too fastidious in his dress to be a physician."

"I think I might take offence at that, Holmes."

"You needn't, Watson. Although in semi-retirement, you still dress as a doctor in full practice, your choice of clothing being pragmatic, practical and altogether sensible – quite appropriate for the rigours of the physical activity once demanded of you. This gentleman's clothes were made for leather chairs and leisurely suppers."

"What do you make if it then, Holmes?"

"Nothing at the moment. Just a tit-bit to file away."

Early the next morning, a knock came to our front door. Holmes was already well down the stairway when I peered over the railing into the foyer. It was Toby, panting and excited.

"I think we got 'em sir!" Toby said. By the time I had retrieved my robe and started downstairs, the lad had made his report and was off again.

"Watson, get dressed. Our opportunity has come at last. I have sent Toby to fetch Inspector Walls and his crew."

I dressed quickly; and, one step behind Holmes, jumped into a waiting hansom. It was only then that I knew whither we were bound. "To Hanover Square, driver," Holmes commanded.

As we approached the parish of St. George, grand homes sprang up around us. As we came upon Hanover Square, Holmes rapped on the roof of the carriage. The small hatch above popped open. "To Fulham Road, with haste," Holmes ordered.

Within the next two blocks, the fine mansions melted into grey-brick tenements. A source of constant amazement to me was the proximity of fine neighbourhoods to the disease-ridden warrens within our city.

Fulham Road was a dead end, and waiting at the head was a wagon with a half-dozen policemen in it. Inspector Walls was waiting behind the wagon and nodded to us as we approached. Impeccably dressed, as always, Walls was clean-shaven and straight-laced. His brow seemed perpetually bent, as if he were scrutinizing everyone and everything. He was a recent acquaintance. Holmes had helped him with a case in which a fellow Inspector named Osborne had been murdered. Holmes used his tenuous connexions within the London underworld to point Walls in a direction that lead to a successful arrest and conviction.

When we jumped out of our hansom, Holmes asked the driver to await our return at Hanover Square, and we walked toward the inspector.

"Mr. Holmes," Walls began, "your message was a little confusing, but I owe you a debt that I will honour, if I may."

"Thank you, Inspector," Holmes replied. "The rogues that await you at number thirty-six are no doubt guilty of many past crimes, but I am not aware of any recent ones. However, I do know that they have been engaged to kill me."

"You understand, of course, that I cannot make an arrest," Walls noted plainly.

"I do not want you to arrest them – quite the opposite!" He then motioned to the Inspector to follow him some short distance from the wagon where they could have a more confidential chat. I am not certain what Holmes said, but Inspector Walls was initially startled. He shook his head silently as Holmes laid out his plan.

There was a long interval, after Holmes spoke, before Inspector Walls seemingly replied in the affirmative. The detective and Holmes walked back to the wagon of waiting policemen.

"Come, Watson, let us leave the inspector and his crew to do their work."

Walls ordered the men out of the wagon. They formed a circle around him. As he relayed his orders, Holmes and I retreated to an alcove a short distance away. As we took our place, the policemen, and Inspector Walls, made their way to number thirty-six and, on command, crashed open the door. A huge commotion ensued with one gun-shot being fired.

Within minutes, three brutes in handcuffs were led outside and lined up against the front wall. There the

Inspector interrogated the thugs, who seemed as though they were struck dumb. Then, Walls took up a position at the front door and ordered the entire crew of policemen to search the residence. One of the constables gave a shout. At this the Inspector poked his head inside, presumably to lend aid. Almost immediately, he was thrown against the door. He fell to the ground, and before he could stand, the three scoundrels took off – running toward us.

As I reached for my revolver, Holmes grabbed my arm and put his finger to his lips. The three men flew past and disappeared around the corner.

"No doubt there is a blank page or two in your notebook," Holmes said, as we settled back into our rooms on Sheen Lane.

"If I could surmise," I responded, "I believe I have most of the pieces. The missing element for me remains the identity of the black-feather fellow."

"Ciarán Malastier. One of his distant ancestors is buried in Westminster Abbey, Watson. However, it seems he is destined to leave a darker, and more twisted, legacy."

"This you learned from the irregulars?"

"Indeed, they tracked Malastier for several days. He led them to Brienheim Street, his residence. He was, just to-day, followed to Fulham Road, where he engaged the three hooligans you observed. Prior to this, he was seen making regular calls in Whitehall. This would obviously suggest a governmental relationship – although what, exactly, I have been unable to ascertain thus far. His position there might account for his feeling of invulnerability. However, I suspect Mr. Malastier's ability to act with impunity might soon come to an end."

"How so, Holmes?"

"I was able to convince Inspector Walls to assist. He bridled at the idea of letting the mercenary ruffians go, so I promised him that the irregulars would assist in retaking them, once they have served their purpose.

"You see, Watson, the hired assassins were led to believe that Malastier had sold them out to save his own skin – as, in a manner of speaking, he had. Whether or not this puts an end to Ciarán Malastier as a man, I do not know, but I suspect it will put an end to his sinister enterprise."

"And so, poor Treasure's sacrifice, and Maud's heartbreak, has served to save the lives of countless other babes. But, who is to know how eugenic ideals may manifest in the future."

"Your fears, I am sorry to say, are well founded, my friend. The foul seeds of eugenics have been scattered over the earth since time immemorial. This dark history is still being written today.

"Ciarán Malastier is merely a harbinger of greater evil yet to come."

3

THE MAESTRO OF MYSTERIES

A deadly chase in Undertown, far beneath London.

IN ALL MY years with Holmes, he had received no more than a handful of invitations from his older brother; so the special messenger, sent by Mycroft Holmes, was unexpected.

"Bad news," I ventured, as my friend sat in a well-worn Morris chair, the missive dangling from his fingers.

"My brother has summoned us, Watson," Holmes said, holding the monogrammed notepaper for me to read the message. Its brevity surprised me:

Sherlock,

Come at once.

Mycroft

"You see, we have upset him."

"You know that for a fact, eh?"

"There is a correlation between my brother's verbosity and his temperament. Now, if the message were simply 'Come,' I might do so, but only with *great* trepidation. But, three words – three words mean that we should expect only *moderate* unpleasantness."

His lips turned up slightly in a would-be smile.

We dressed formally and made our way to that long thoroughfare which stretches from Trafalgar Square to the Houses of Parliament, and upon which the Foreign Office stands. The skies threatened rain, and fog swirled around us in an effort to penetrate our heavy outerwear.

When we arrived at the Foreign Office, we were to find that Mycroft no longer had an office there, but recently relocated to the War Department nearby.

The five-story edifice of the War Department stood as a white knight in the centre of a bureaucratic battlefield, at the corner of Whitehall and Whitehall Place. This pallid building is guarded by turrets that top each corner – reminiscent of minarets from which prayers emanate each day, ensuring that God is with us, and especially in wartime.

When we enquired as to the location of Mycroft's office, we received no simple direction, but were asked to wait to be escorted to the fourth floor.

As we made our way, I noticed the sign above an ornately carved oak door that read: "Intelligence." We were ushered through a sitting area where two drab civil servants waited in dim lighting, files heaped upon their laps. The door was opened into a large office whose ceiling extended upward to the floor above. The two-storey gallery was lined with shelved books, and racks of newspapers and magazines. The primary light came from a huge stained-glass skylight in the centre of the room. It might have been resplendent when the sun shone, but on grey days, such as this, the day-light cast vague shadows across the room, as if to hide its secrets.

I immediately recognized Mycroft's bulky silhouette in the distance, standing against a large map of the world that was lit with harsh electric lighting. He stood as an inert grey mass, utterly still, with his back to us. When our escort departed, he turned.

"Sherlock – Dr. Watson – thank you for coming," he said, with arms rising slightly in a gesture of welcome.

"We are a little late because we did not know that you had moved," Holmes replied.

"I apologize. My work has been expanding and growing in new directions."

"So we may deduce from the sign over your door," Holmes quipped. "I must admit to being momentarily confused – that is, until I saw that this is a book repository."

Mycroft feigned a chuckle.

"I might make the same observation regarding your acumen. For, I never should have thought that there was a woman clever enough to make you feel that you are special, Sherlock. I fear, for that, and other reasons, that your mental faculties may be waning."

Holmes's body stiffened as he approached his older brother in deliberate steps. "Your intrusion into my personal life is as unwelcome as it is unexpected. You seldom proffer brotherly advice. Why now?"

"All that will change today. We have been observing you closely in recent weeks, because of your meddling investigations."

"I take it that Watson and I have stepped on some toes, and you are feeling the chafe. Might I venture a guess – Mr. Ciarán Malastier?"

"As is your wont, you have answered the question *Who,* but we have brought you here to tell you *Why*. And for that, a special meeting has been arranged. If you would be so good as to follow me down the hall..."

With that, Mycroft gathered us up and led us out through a side door in his office.

A narrow paneled passageway led to a door with a colourful insignia above it – a silvery human brain encompassed by the letter C in green. Atop the C sat a gold crown, and below it, in red, the words *Semper Occultus*.

As we reached the door, Mycroft turned to us. "I must ask you both to keep this meeting in *complete confidence*."

"You mean secret," Mycroft. "Could I suppose, then, that it might surprise you to know that I have been in this very office on *many* occasions," Holmes stated.

Mycroft's brows did, indeed, lift in surprise. Nonetheless, he gave a token rap on the door and entered, with us trailing behind. Seated behind a huge marble desk sat a man in starched naval dress, his captain's jacket was draped over the back of his chair. His black hair was plastered in place. The gold monocle he crimped in his right eye set off his round, florid face.

The officer rose as we approached. He marched to a large circular table in the centre of the room, and waited. As we took our places around the table, the captain came forward to offer his hand.

"Dr. Watson, I am Captain Mansfield Cumming… Mr. Holmes. Thank you for coming." This greeting seemed to confirm that Holmes and Cumming were, indeed, acquainted.

Holmes and I shook his hand in turn.

"I had heard that our country had been blessed with a secret intelligence bureau. I presume that is your domain," I said.

"Indeed," Cumming replied.

Mycroft looked askance at the captain. "Might I assume that my brother has some relationship with the service?"

"He does, but that is another matter altogether. The agenda today is, more or less, a domestic matter, it is not?" Cumming noted.

And then, turning to Holmes's brother: "Mycroft, would you be so kind as to ask Captain Kell to join us? He is waiting in the sitting area of the adjoining office."

"Yes, C.," Mycroft responded.

Holmes and I undertook to conceal our amazement as his brother waddled off obediently. At a slight gesture from our host, we took our seats at the table.

Cumming folded his tiny hands together in front of him, and began: "Mycroft sent this invitation, but he did so at the behest of Captain Kell and myself, gentlemen. When this matter came to my attention, I offered to broker this meeting in the hopes of bridging any potential gaps in understanding… shall we say.

"I want you to know that we, in the service, have the highest regard for you; and we are indebted to you for the services you perform for us on behalf of our country, Mr. Holmes. That goes without question," the Captain said. "However, you seem to have entangled yourselves in a matter that is causing distress for some of my colleagues."

"I take it we are speaking of our dealings with a certain Ciarán Malastier," said Holmes.

"I appreciate your directness, Mr. Holmes. Yes, this meeting is about Mr. Malastier, but ever so much more," the captain said, with all the sincerity which he could muster. In a hushed voice, he continued. "As you are aware, there are some dark forces at work in the world, and within our beloved country. You, your brother, myself, and many, many others… including Mr. Malastier, are fighting these forces."

Holmes smiled. "I must tell you, that I resent being counted within the same array of individuals that include Mr. Malastier. That is, unless these dark forces to which you refer include innocent babes that have been born into unfortunate circumstances, Captain."

Cumming stiffened in his seat; his brows lowered, and he tapped on the table with his index finger. He paused for a long time, no doubt for effect.

"We are aware of Mr. Malastier's 'out of school' activities, as one might call them, Mr. Holmes. And, I can assure you that his role in those matters has come to an end. However, we cannot afford to have Mr. Malastier come to an end."

"I would be curious as to Mr. Malastier's position and role in this department?" I asked.

Cumming opened his hands in front of him and raised his brow. "I can only say that he is in research relating to offensive and defensive efforts. You may surmise what you will from that information." Then, turning to Holmes, "As I am sure that you will."

The arrogance of the man was galling. "Sir, how can you align yourself with a person of such evil character, protect him, and put him in a place of trust within your enterprise? It does not bode well for your – your service, as you call it."

"Dr. Watson, I can appreciate that Malastier's activities, from some perspectives, may appear improper, but –"

"I should think from *anyone's* perceptive," I interrupted.

An awkward silence arose, broken only by the entrance of Mycroft with a man – obviously Captain Kell. He was not in uniform. Kell walked in slow, even steps. His body was thin, and his movements began with an almost imperceptible hesitation that made him appear awkward. He sported a compact mustache that did not dare protrude beyond the edges of this mouth. His brow was bent in a grim fashion.

Mycroft took his place at the table, sitting down without a word. His companion, Captain Kell, stood behind his chair, awaiting Cumming's formal introduction.

"Mr. Sherlock Holmes, and Dr. Watson, may I introduce Captain Vernon Kell, who heads up our Home Section," Captain Cumming continued: "Captain Kell is here to stress the importance of our rather perfunctory request to abstain from further efforts to pursue Mr. Malastier."

"I'm afraid that matter may already be out of our hands," Holmes replied.

"If you are referring to the hooligans whom you sent in pursuit of Mr. Malastier, you need not be concerned," Kell replied. "They are no longer an issue."

"But *we* are," I said, stating the obvious – for which I received no reply.

Cumming intervened. "Captain, if you please, remind us all of what is at stake here."

Captain Kell sat down and carefully folded his hands in front of him, mirroring Cumming. He turned his eyes upward toward the ceiling as if to call upon a higher power.

"Gentlemen, we here possess a special knowledge, awareness, and understanding. We appreciate that it is not simply in faerie tales that good and evil do battle. Such forces exist. They are in conflict every day." He lowered his eyes to focus on the two of us. "A great battle nears, which will call upon us all, in this nation, to fulfill what has been our sacred destiny since the time before history."

Holmes shook his head. "You need not reach so deep to find the devotion for our country that Dr. Watson and I share. We have, do, and will continue to serve Britain with honour. However, if Mr. Ciarán Malastier is counted among your ranks, then I would have to suggest that the 'evil' you so eloquently speak of, resides within the hallowed halls of Whitehall itself."

Before Kell could respond, Cumming interjected: "Mr. Holmes, at the risk of jeopardizing the good relationship we presently enjoy, I will simply say that, while Captain

Kell and I are not at liberty to share details regarding Mr. Malastier's work, or precise relationship with our offices, we are asking for your cooperation in this matter," Cumming said, restraining a deep irritation. "While I cannot insist upon your understanding, I *will* insist that you honour our request and cease your pursuit of Mr. Malastier."

Captain Kell seemed to be engulfed in a smoldering indignation that erupted: "Mr. Holmes, you seem to have a limited perspective on this battle with the malevolent forces around us – seeing them only as they reveal themselves within your simple investigations – that is what you call them, is it not... *investigations*? However, if you can elevate your perspective in order to see the larger battlefield upon which good and evil engage, then you will see that we are duty bound to engage and use *every* resource available to consummate this battle."

"What you are saying then," Holmes replied, "is that the end justifies the means."

"In this case, yes, that is so."

"I might agree if those making the choices have sufficient knowledge of both the ends and the means."

"I assure you that we are thorough and intelligent men," Kell stated, with a touch of indignation. "Our planning is impeccable. We want nothing less than to preserve our way of life and the cause of human freedom in the world."

Holmes leaned across the table. "You know what you want, but that is not the same as knowing, with any certainty, that your actions today will deliver what you seek. Life is not a chess game in which there is a final end. The real world does not stop with check-mate. What is more, simply because something ends well does not mean it is good and right."

"And, who is to be the judge of what is good and right, Mr. Holmes? You?" Kell cried. "Please cease and desist your pursuit of Mr. Malastier... immediately." Then, turning to Mycroft, "I believe that our meeting is concluded. Please show your brother and his friend out."

Mycroft stood and waved his hand toward the door through which we had entered earlier. Holmes rose in silence at first – then spoke in a soft tone: "The prospect of war seems to have given rise to an archaic Manichean perspective that, to me, seems to threaten the underpinnings of what has made us a great nation. I fear for my country – as I never have before."

"As well, you should," Kell added.

"Yes – well," Holmes remarked, "but what I fear is here in this room, not what may come later."

We were in Mycroft's den before he addressed us: "My brother, you have embarrassed yourself and me. And, while this is not an unfamiliar occurrence, my humiliation is particularly profound at this moment."

"My, my, Mycroft – your isolation within this dusty bureaucracy has you living entirely in a fantastical world of archaic beliefs and short-sighted actions!"

"Do you not see our fair country as a beacon of light on a horizon that grows darker every day?"

"I can see that you, and most likely, everyone in Whitehall, is caught up in the hysteria around the mounting tensions in the Balkans," Holmes said. "You propose banning the raising of carrier pigeons, and would have grandmothers perched on roof tops searching for zeppelins. You deliberately nurture a fear in the hearts of our countrymen that will likely be used to rally troops, fire canons and drop bombs. The light you, so eloquently, speak of may soon emanate from the funeral pyres of thousands of young Britons."

"Sherlock, you sought refuge on the Sussex seashore, where you only need fear the occasional sting of a bee," said Mycroft. "You have secluded yourself from reality, and now, when you venture out a little, you are unwilling to see beyond the dirty streets and alleys of this ancient city. Your ignorance has become dangerous. Go back to your bees."

Those hurtful words struck at my friend's heart. He stood quietly for a long time. I took him by the arm in an attempt to turn him to the door, but he stood transfixed and immoveable. Finally, he raised his head.

"I feel lost in my own country. Such a feeling comes with age. But, what I feel now goes beyond that. I feel that I have lost... my people."

We turned and left Mycroft's office and the War Department, walking in silence through Whitehall. We passed hundreds of bureaucrats racing to and fro, telling themselves they do not have enough time – a dull mantra too often sung by human beings.

When we arrived at my apartment, Holmes placed his coat and hat on the chair by the door, loosened his tie, and wandered into the sitting room. He collapsed on the settee by the fireplace.

I waited some time before approaching.

"Holmes, I share your concern that our country seems to be sinking in bureaucratic quicksand. I know your brother's part in this, and his callous words, have made these revelations all the more horrible."

There was no reply. Holmes leaned forward, and put his face in his hands.

"Holmes, these feelings will fade, and you will soon be able to put all of this business in its proper perspective."

Holmes looked up, wide-eyed and desolate. In a rasping whisper, he exclaimed: "I've heard enough. I've had enough!" He slumped down again, and stared blankly beyond the room.

"I think a spot of tea is called for."

"Please, leave me, Watson."

I turned toward the kitchen.

"Close the door," Holmes said, as I crossed the threshold. I did so.

I made tea and sat at the kitchen table for a while. I was expecting that my friend might come and share a cup, but after nearly half an hour, I retired.

As I lay in my bed that evening, I listened for sounds that would tell me Holmes was about, in the kitchen, or the adjoining bedroom. I heard nothing. Eventually, I drifted off to sleep.

The next morning, as is my custom, I went to put the kettle on before I dressed. I noticed that the door to the sitting room had remained closed. I opened it just enough to put my head inside. There, still on the settee, was my dear companion fully dressed in the previous day's morning coat.

I returned to the kitchen and put some bacon in a pan. If I could not get the attention of his mind, I would appeal to his stomach. Fried eggs were next. I had no mushrooms or beans, but I sliced some bread, and took out a jar of conserves.

I poked my head into the next room. "Holmes, breakfast is waiting."

There was no response. No movement. No words.

"Holmes, would you like me to serve?"

I arranged his hot breakfast on a tray, including a large cup of tea. I carried it into the sitting room and put it on a low table before him. "You must eat something."

Still, no rejoinder.

There was a mounting anger inside me that I did not

comprehend. I found myself shouting: "Holmes, you must stop this! Eat. You're being childish!"

He looked up. "Watson, I am not hungry. I am not childish. And, I am not in the mood for mothering. If you wish to help, you might offer me an escape that can best be offered at the end of a needle."

For our entire relationship, I had done what I could to prevent, and diminish, his use of cocaine. But now, for the first time, I was reconsidering that position. After all, I argued with myself, it is what any good physician might do for someone in pain. My friend was in pain.

I went to my bedroom and shuffled through my medical kit and I found myself holding a small vial in one hand, and my needle case in another.

I am always surprised, and grateful, how deeply engrained in me is the oath I took so many years ago – lying in wait until called upon. And so, the words from that vow again found their way into my awareness. *I will prescribe regimens for the good of my patients, according to my ability and my judgment, and never do harm to anyone.*

I knew Holmes had but to make a short trip to the high street to serve his addiction, but I could not be a party to such. I placed the bottle and case back into my kit and closed my closet. As I did so, an idea began to grow inside me. I retrieved my hat and coat, told Holmes I was going for a walk, and departed for 644 High Road.

I found my way to the splendid three-storey Georgian home of our newfound friends. I hesitated on the stoop, with my hand on the bell pull, wondering if I were doing the right thing. While still in my thoughts, the large red door swung open. There was the maid, Becky, in her starched white and black uniform, waiting. She opened the door wide and spoke: "Madam said that you're to come in at once, Dr. Watson."

As I entered, Becky took my hat and coat and motioned toward the parlour. For a brief moment, I recalled my first visit here in search of the elusive Miss Odinsvogel. As I entered, Adaline Dart and her mother stood up. Adaline wore a plaid dress-skirt and a white long-sleeved top. Miss Adler's dress fell in pink and white tiers from her waist. Her hair, tied with a white ribbon, fell over her left shoulder. Their faces were still, but their eyes smiled.

I was not sure how to begin. "My dear ladies, I have come, once again, with hat in hand, to ask your help. It seems that your good friend, and mine, is beyond my reach, and I am at a loss to know what might be done for him."

They motioned for me to sit and, as I did so, Irene sat next to me and took my hand in hers. "We are still in his debt, but more than this, we have come to count Mr. Holmes, and you, among our dearest friends. What has caused your distress?"

I related the story, with the knowledge that I was betraying a confidence. I rationalized that the atrocious behaviour we encountered in Mycroft's office had released me from any promises to him, and Holmes's dangerous state necessitated that I share details of a personal nature. I knew that, if I did not act, Holmes might well seek refuge in cocaine or opium, which lately has become the scourge of my country. Many times, I had seen Holmes sink into an addictive stupor out of boredom. This, however, was different. If he were to fall into the grasp of unnatural drugs now, I feared that he might never escape. However, I did not share these thoughts, or my associated fears.

"I don't know what it is that I expect you can do," I finally admitted. "I just didn't know where else I might turn."

"Thank you for coming, Doctor," Adaline replied. "I can tell you, from my own experience, that it is difficult to help those who are closest to us."

"Indeed," Irene concurred.

We explored various ideas and choices and finally, knowing how delicate Holmes's state was, adopted an indirect approach. The next day a letter of invitation would arrive in the post for Mr. Sherlock Holmes.

Holmes was in his bedroom when I returned. I heard him shuffling around during the night. The smoke from his pungent shag whiffed under my door. I thought this a good sign until I found him, the next morning, unshaven, sitting in the kitchen in crumpled bedclothes – something I had, hereto, never seen.

"Holmes, you're up," I said, stating the obvious. "I have had little time to stock our kitchen. What do you say we go out for breakfast?"

"Go. I suggest you go, Watson. That would be best." Rising and turning away he added, "You are not going to help me, are you?"

"If you are asking me to provide drugs for you, I can tell you that I will never agree to that."

"Ha – my dear doctor. You're above all that, aren't you? You're stronger, wiser. But, what do you know of it – really. You sit on the edges of people's pain and count yourself a saint."

He turned about, and swept out of the kitchen turning over a teacup on the table with his robe. It shattered on the floor.

I slumped into a chair, and prayed the post might come early today.

~

I was able to glimpse the postman as he climbed the stairs to my door. I waited until I heard the dull clank of the letter-box lid, and went down to fetch the mail. Holmes was in his bedroom, fiddling with his violin. From the sounds, it seemed as if he were striking the bow on the strings as though the instrument were a drum. After fetching the missive, I knocked on his door.

"Holmes, a letter has arrived."

"Go away, Watson," he said, continuing with this infernal noise making.

"I believe it is from Miss Adler."

A pause, but no answer.

"Shall I slide it under your door?"

"Blast it, throw it out for all I care!" was the sharp reply.

"Well, it is addressed to both of us, so I think I shall open it. I just thought that you might prefer to do so."

I went to the parlour and opened the letter:

Dear Sherlock and John,

Fritz Kreisler has honoured me by asking that I host a recital. I am inviting you both to a chamber performance and intimate dinner afterwards.

The event is on Friday evening at my daughter and son-in-laws's home, 644 High Road. Please come at seven.

I look forward to being in your company once again. Please reply at your earliest convenience.

Irene

I left the open letter on the desk, and went into the kitchen. I looked through the cupboards searching for a bite, and waited to see if Holmes would rise to the bait.

He did not – which was not altogether unexpected.

I went about my day as usual, including a brisk walk in nearby Mortlake Green. When I returned, I looked at the letter of invitation to see if it had been disturbed or moved. I saw no signs of such; but Holmes would be sly enough to prevent any such disclosure. I picked it up, and went, again, to Holmes's door.

"I say, Holmes, we have received a rare invitation from Miss Adler, regarding a private performance by Fritz Kreisler. I can still recall his debut performance more than a decade ago. I feel it is proper that we reply."

I was reaching for the knob when the door swung open.

"Please, be so good as to decline – graciously decline – for me," said Holmes, in a surprisingly serene manner, followed by a slight upward turn of the lips in a put-on smile. "*You* however should attend, most definitely."

"Very well." I departed without a further word.

Holmes continued his hermit-like behaviour, spending the remainder of the day in his room. Later, on rare occasions, when I engaged him in the kitchen or elsewhere, we nodded, but did not speak. Although he dressed, he remained in the apartment.

As Friday approached, I expected that Holmes might reconsider the invitation, but it became clear that he had decided not to attend Miss Adler's recital and dinner. And so, on Thursday morning, I sent a note to Miss Adler thanking her for the considerable effort that had gone into engaging her colleague, Fritz Kreisler, for the evening, and assured her that I planned to attend.

Later that day, I was returning from my afternoon stroll, when I noticed a carriage pulling up to my building. A man and a woman emerged. I immediately recognized the lady as Miss Adler. The gentleman was unfamiliar, but I deduced, from the case he was carrying, that he must be Fritz Kreisler. He was a tall, middle-aged man of swarthy complexion. He exhibited an economy of movement that testified to a careful precision in his character.

I hurried along to intercept them as they made their way to my door. "I say, my dear lady! I am so pleased – and surprised – to see you!"

"Dr. Watson, how opportune this is!" Miss Adler said. "May I introduce Maestro Fritz Kreisler?"

As I approached to take Mr. Kreisler's hand in greeting, the lady interrupted. "He is upstairs?" she asked, pointing in that direction.

"Yes, yes, I should think that a safe assumption."

"Take us to him, please." she said. And, I did so.

I seated our guests in the parlour. Miss Adler spoke, rather loudly, "Fritz was disappointed at not being able to meet Mr. Holmes, so I took it upon myself to arrange an informal meeting."

"I shall see if Holmes..."

"Please," the lady said, "let *me* bring our greetings to Mr. Holmes." I nodded toward Holmes's room. She marched to the door.

"Mr. Holmes – Sherlock – it is Irene. I have a wonderful surprise for you."

She followed with a gentle rap on the door, which cracked open, just enough for Holmes to answer.

"You have me at a disadvantage," Holmes said quietly. "I regret that I am unable to accommodate your *unannounced* visit, just now."

"Please, open the door, Sherlock," she said, softly, but firmly.

The door opened wide enough for the lady to enter. I heard muffled conversation and, as I moved closer to hear, became uncomfortably aware that my guest looked nervous and bemused.

"My apologies, Maestro Kreisler," I said. "I understand that you wished to meet my comrade, Sherlock Holmes?"

"I must confess to a certain curiosity, but I believe that it was Miss Adler who most desired us to meet."

"Quite so. She is a remarkable lady."

We chatted for some time, before I offered Fritz some tea.

"If I might be so bold," he answered, with an eye to our brandy on the nearby table, "do you have anything a little more stimulating?"

I poured two glasses of Armagnac, and we continued our *tête-à-tête*. Fritz was describing his last engagement at Wilton's Music Hall where shouts for an encore requested that he play Dvorak's *Humoresque*.

"I have never before experienced an audience that had selected its own encore," he noted with amusement.

"I wish that I might have been in that fortunate audience," I remarked. "Would it be an imposition to ask that you play that same encore, here and now?"

"Indeed, I came to play, Dr. Watson," the Maestro said, with a nod and a smile. With that, he plucked his violin from its case and began tuning it. I used this opportunity to approach Holmes's door, but only heard quiet whispers. As I re-entered the parlour, Kreisler pointed to the chair, motioning for me to sit. He began to play.

Light and lilting phrases of capricious character filled the room with Dvorak's popular melody. I was completely captivated and entranced. My head, bobbing to the rhythm, stilled only in those moments where brief melancholy interludes slowed time itself.

As the last note echoed in our chamber, I found myself applauding. And, it was then I heard other hands behind me. I turned to see them standing side-by-side. Holmes, for the first time in near a week, was smiling. When I caught Miss Adler's eye, she nodded at me. *What a remarkable woman!*

Holmes entered to thank Mr. Kreisler. I poured two more glasses of brandy.

"Maestro," Irene said, "I do not wish to take from tomorrow's program, but would you honour us with another selection?"

"Of course," Fritz said, "Possibly, I could persuade Mr. Holmes to join me in *Bach's Concerto for Two Violins*."

Holmes laughed. "A frightening proposition, Maestro. I am afraid the only audience who can tolerate my playing is my dearest friend here." He caught my eye and leaned closer, whispering: "You are a good doctor, and a *magnificent* friend."

We passed almost an hour listening and chatting. At last the Maestro begged his departure for a scheduled rehearsal. As he took Holmes's hand, he remarked: "I am sorry that we have not been able to coax your violin out of its case."

"In the shadow of such genius," Holmes said, "it would not dare leave its dusty bin."

"Genius comes in many forms, Mr. Holmes. It is incumbent upon us to exercise those gifts that we each possess. You, my dear sir, are the Maestro of mysteries." With that, he bowed, and took his leave.

Irene stayed behind and took charge of the conversation. "John, Sherlock has shared with me recent events intended to put you and him off the scent of Mr. Ciarán Malastier. Quite recently, I offered my help. I am not certain that I was taken seriously." She paused. "I assure you, I am serious, and I am capable of helping. Indeed, you may find that a woman has some singular abilities, which may not be at the disposal of a man."

Watching the face of my dear colleague at this moment,

I heartily agreed with her declaration. Holmes's total attention was on this woman – and not in his usual intensive manner. There was a softness in his look that was both rare, and welcome.

"It is no accident, I would add," Irene went on, "that I have made Mr. Malastier's acquaintance."

Holmes and I were jolted by this revelation.

"Ever since his attempt on your life, Sherlock, I have sought an opportunity to learn more about him. He runs in élite circles, you know. Rumour had it that he belongs to an unusual assembly or society. With a few casual enquiries, I was able to confirm this, identify the secret society, and apply for membership."

"Irene – Miss Adler – please, you are putting yourself in harm's way! Your gender will not protect you!" Holmes exclaimed.

"That is clear," she said, "I shall be relying on John and you for protection."

"Miss Adler..." I said.

"Please – *Irene,*" she insisted.

"Irene, Holmes is correct in his concern and opposition to your involving yourself in this affair. Malastier is diabolical, truly evil and..."

"And..." the lady countered, "we all share a responsibility to stand up to him and his kind. I thought it might be interesting to see exactly where he makes his nest."

"And, that is?" Sherlock enquired.

"The Order of the Golden Dawn."

There was cavernous silence as Holmes and I fully took in this revelation. This occult organization had first been heard of when William Westcott, then the London coroner, left some peculiar papers in a hansom cab. The scandal nearly led to his resignation; and, in the process, the fabled order had come into public awareness.

"Just how far have you gone down this path?" Holmes enquired.

"I have expressed an interest in spiritual development and theurgy, during recent social gatherings where Mr. Malastier was in attendance. After that, I simply waited for someone to approach."

"And?" Holmes urged.

"My efforts bore fruit. One evening Ciarán Malastier and Robbie Ross spent the better part of the evening, as they put it, 'exploring my natural interest in unseen aspects of our world."

"Robbie Ross?" I queried.

"An acquaintance of mine, from my days in the theatre. He was once part of Oscar Wilde's cadre."

"Did they actually mention the Golden Dawn?" I continued.

"No. Not then, but later I cornered Robbie, who was fully in his merrymaking. I asked him what he knew about the Golden Dawn. My question sobered him instantly. He winked and put his finger to the side of his nose and babbled, 'Double, double toil and trouble; Fire burn, and caldron bubble.' Then, with his characteristic grin, he added, 'You may get burned, milady.'"

Holmes became more intense. "He is right, you know. Mr. Malastier alluded to like-minded colleagues – a special 'society' to which he belongs. This might well be the Golden Dawn, or a group within it."

"I'm not naïve, Sherlock. Robbie is overly dramatic."

"If you are serious about engaging in this occultism," Holmes said, "you should be less casual about it, my dear lady. You may not take this clandestine collection of characters seriously, but I assure you they are serious – and possibly dangerous."

"Sherlock, I have a genuine curiosity about ancient

philosophies and practices – and, an even deeper curiosity about this faction's membership. Don't you?"

"As it is becoming alarmingly clear," Holmes said, "our own government is being influenced by some rather esoteric and ancient ideas…"

"Kell," I remarked.

"Kell," Holmes shouted, "and the whole ugly gang at Whitehall, including my own – my own brother!" He stopped. The anger lying beneath his recent depression burst forth – and subsided, just as quickly.

"Excuse my outburst, please. And, to your point Irene, I share your curiosity regarding the members of the Golden Dawn and…" Holmes paused, his head cocked to one side as if losing a slippery thought. "But, I have a sense of foreboding that I have not felt since Professor Moriarty was afoot."

"I know nothing of this Moriarty, but I have hold of a thread that may eventually bind Mr. Ciarán Malastier," the woman insisted. "I shall not pull hard, but rather, let him pull me to him."

With this final reassurance, Irene Adler joined our partnership.

The next day, Holmes and I prepared to attend the house concert and dinner party at the home of Irene's daughter and son-in-law in North Finchley. As I bustled about in my wardrobe, Holmes approached.

Dangling a tie from his fingers, he asked, "Watson, what do you think of this one – too audacious?"

"What do I think? I think that you have moved beyond a mere curiosity about the woman." I expected a sharp reply from Holmes, but received the contrary.

"I fear you may be correct, my friend." He dropped the tie on the table in an expression of resignation.

"In coming to know this phantom female from my distant past, I see that I have, for most of my life, disregarded women in certain ways."

"What ways?

"Numerous – but, one in particular." He put his hand on my shoulder. "I have always been well aware of how a woman might confine my life. However – I have never *seriously* considered what a woman might add to it."

"Really?"

He quickly grasped for composure. "That is all I care to say on the subject."

And, indeed, he need not say more.

While at Irene's *soirée*, Holmes was never far from her side. However, after dinner, as the ladies retired to the drawing room, he engaged me.

"Are you enjoying the evening, Watson?"

"Very much. Would I be correct in assuming you are enjoying yourself also?"

"I appreciate your subtlety Watson, but our friendship does not require it. I am enjoying the company of all – especially a lovely lady who continues to haunt my life. As I was remarking earlier today, I had held her, indeed all women, in what I intended as a place of respect. But, it was not so much respect, as distance. However, I have come to see Irene in a – a new light." He stopped. "I fear I am doing a poor job of explaining."

"On the contrary, you explain yourself exceptionally well."

The next morning found Holmes gathering his belongings. When I poked my head in his bedroom, he turned and approached.

"Watson, I must return to my cottage for a time. My files and library are there, and I am certain that, within that *mélange*, is valuable information about the Order of the Golden Dawn."

"I don't recall your having any encounters with them."

"Not as such, but I have voluminous materials on hermeticism, freemasonry, alchemy, astrology and the like. The Order of the Golden Dawn, I believe, has its origins in mediæval magic."

"So, you believe we may soon find ourselves in Merlin's cave?"

"Magic is often the means by which some people deal with what they cannot perceive or fully comprehend. The universe, after all, consists primarily of what we do not know. The greatest danger for man does not come from mere lack of knowledge, but rather from boldly and ignorantly stumbling into he does not know."

"And, you suspect that the Golden Dawn may be doing this?"

"I have no idea," Holmes said, "but I have learned, that secrecy is often the refuge of scoundrels."

"Malastier."

"Exactly, such as Mr. Malastier. Please stay in contact with Irene and apprise me of any significant happenings. I should be away no more than two or three days."

Holmes went off to Sussex; and, that afternoon, I settled down to chronologically plough through the pile of newspapers that had accumulated during this busy time. I was surprised, and disheartened, to learn that Emmeline Pankhurst, one of the guests at the Henley Royal Regatta gathering last July, was sentenced to three years penal servitude, for her role in recent violent actions by suffragettes. This would undoubtedly escalate this whole business to an unprecedented level, I thought. And indeed, the following week, the Nevill Ground cricket pavilion, in Kent, was set ablaze by militant feminists. Suffragette literature, and pictures of Emily Pankhurst, were scattered about the wreckage, sending a clear message that the movement had turned away from non-violence as its primary tool for reform.

I suspected that Miss Adler and her daughter were sympathetic to the cause and, as such, I was prompted to call on Miss Adler and Mrs. Dart.

I arrived at the Dart home to find that Irene was not there. Adaline was out of sorts. Over tea, I enquired as to what had upset her.

"This is a difficult time for mother and me, Dr. Watson. You are no doubt aware of the recent events concerning the suffragettes."

I nodded.

"Mother is becoming increasingly troubled. She feels that she has a role to play, but is uncertain as to what it might be. She comes and goes, which is not unusual, as she is her own person. However, her absences have become longer, and she refuses to tell me of her precise whereabouts. She says that it is for my own good that she does not share details of her 'ventures,' as she calls them."

"You are concerned, then, that she may be engaging in some dangerous activities?"

She reached out for my hand and clutched it tightly. "If I can share an incident with you..." She paused. "A gentleman, who would not give his name, came to our door yesterday enquiring after my mother. Our maid explained that neither of us was in. Becky reported that the gentleman had a 'very strange look about him.' It is not Becky's custom to comment on our callers. I am worried." She gave a deep sob.

"I see. How exactly might I be of help?"

"I don't know. I simply wish you, and Mr. Holmes, to know what's going on in the background of our lives. You have become our close friends."

I sent a message to Holmes, briefly sharing what little I had learnt about Irene's recent activities. The thought had occurred to me that it was not the suffragette cause that had preoccupied Miss Adler, but rather her efforts to infiltrate the Golden Dawn. That would also explain her reticence to share details with her daughter. More frightening yet, was the possibility that the strange gentleman caller might have been Malastier.

Holmes replied, stating that he was making progress in his research and would be unable to return for two days, but that I was to maintain close contact with Irene Adler. He suggested that I employ the irregulars in support.

Taking Holmes's advice, I sent word to our adolescent army, via the newsboy Archie, who maintains a post on south Sheen Lane. I asked that Miss Adler be located, and carefully observed. He was to report anything he felt was strange or menacing. I promised a handsome stipend.

Two evenings later, a knock came to my door. There stood Archie, cap in hand.

"We've done as you said, Doctor, and I've come as quick as I might."

I ushered the lad into my sitting room. He stood, stiff as a rod, inside the doorway.

"Please, sit down, Archie, and tell me what's happened."

The youngster took a dirty pamphlet from his pocket and handed it to me. It was crumpled and soiled – a church programme.

"This place, sir, is the church that stands next to an old

house where the lady comes and goes. We watched her regular sir, come and go each day. She made a visit this afternoon – about two o'clock it was, but she hasn't come out yet. It's late, sir, as you know."

"And, why does this alarm you, Archie?"

"Well, sir, my brother and I poked about a bit and – we found that building strange."

"How so?"

"Well, sir, there appears to be nothing – or no one – living there, despite many comings and goings." Archie fiddled with his cap as he struggled to give a proper report. "With my own eyes, I've seen gentlemen, and some ladies, come and go, including the fine lady, as I said, sir. And, this afternoon a score of gentlemen came."

"A score, you say?"

"Aye, maybe more, as many as three dozen, sir, and the lady as well. But, they didn't leave, and they ain't there now – at least not so far as we could see."

"Anything more?"

"Well, sir, we was poking around a bit more seriously, you might say, and we made our way inside – purely innocent, sir, I assure you."

"Go on."

"There were, indeed, strange goings-on, sir. Strange voices and a sweet smell like in a church, and then there was the hooded people, sir."

"Hooded people?"

"Yes, sir, the goings-on were below, sir, in a cellar. But several of these folks, in long gold and red coats, gathered in the kitchen from time to time."

"Do you know what was happening below?"

"No, sir, but it's not right. My heart says it's not right – and I fear for the lady."

"Can you take me there – inside?"

"Yes, sir, if that's what you wish."

"I do. You have done well." I handed Archie half-a-crown. "Wait for me."

I dressed warmly, for the approaching evening promised to be cool. I took my old service revolver, checking to ensure that it was clean and loaded.

The evening was dreary, with a heavy mist settling on the streets, and dripping off the leaves of the overhead trees. The weather added an ominous feeling to my growing panic, as I hurried to keep up with Archie. The street-lamps cast long shadows, and muffled sounds came from dark alleys. The smells from the gutters, and the nearby Thames, reminded me that we often walk in peril, after dark, in my fair city. I imagined that death itself was stalking these boulevards. My feelings were no doubt related to our destination, for Archie and I were only a few streets away from the bloody tower of London.

The neighbouring church, from which Archie had retrieved the pamphlet, was called All Hallows', but was known as All Hallows'-by-the-Tower. It is said to be the oldest church in London. Many renovations, carried out over the centuries, disguise its ancient history, which goes back to Roman times. Wrapped in the thick mist, the blackened stone edifice held its dreadful secrets. Long ago, beheaded victims of Tower executions had been sent there for temporary burial.

The stench of the Thames grew stronger, as we made our way toward the abandoned three-storey brick house that adjoined the churchyard. Despite evidence to the contrary, many insist that the heart of Richard I is buried somewhere in these grounds.

"There, sir," Archie said, shaking me out of my head, and pointing to the huge iron gate across the street.

I shivered, as a chill penetrated my dampened cape.

"I am going inside, Archie. I want you to return to Sheen Lane and wait for Mr. Holmes. If he arrives, you are to give him your report and tell him that I am searching this place for Miss Adler. He is to come at once."

"Take care, sir," was all that Archie said, with a nod of reassurance. "There is a window unlatched in the parlour." He pointed to the left. I returned his nod, and set off across the deserted street.

I made my way through the iron gates that were crowned with a shield baring a single letter H. I searched the street before I stepped onto the grounds. Not a soul was present. As I came to the stairs leading to the front door, I stepped quickly to my left and circled around through some shrubbery that stood before a succession of tall windows. I spied mud on the threshold of one window and, exerting pressure on the sides, felt it slide up.

I listened closely. Hearing nothing, I boosted myself over the sill. The clunk from the revolver in my pocket made me freeze for a moment, but nothing stirred.

The room was devoid of furnishings, and patches on the walls showed where paintings had once hung. I set out toward the rear of the house, where I supposed the kitchen to be located. As I passed the pantry, I saw a dim light flickering through a doorway ahead. I cautiously entered and there, on a huge pine table, found several bottles of brandy and wine, along with glasses. A low burning candle flickered, and the shadows from the surrounding bottles danced on the walls like witches around a cauldron. Then, hushed voices came from the pantry that I had just passed.

My retreat was cut off. I noticed, in the far corner, another door. I opened it, and found myself in a narrow servants' stairway. I tiptoed up past the first turn – and waited.

The voices became more distinct as men entered the kitchen. There were two or three of them. A bottle was dragged off the table, as one voice rose up.

"I'm asking your opinion of our neophyte, gentlemen. You've had an opportunity to be with her now for several days. Do you have any reservations about her?"

A throat was cleared, and a crusty voice piped up.

"I have been concerned, as you know, about the quality of our recent recruits, but I am very pleased that she will stand at our altar tonight."

Then a third voice: "On the whole, I agree with you, Edmund; but my endorsement of Miss Adler comes with some reservations."

Miss Adler was here… and in the clutches of these men! I thought.

"Go on, Ciarán," the first voice said.

"She seems most sincere, I would agree – possibly *too* sincere." A cough interrupted his reply and went on for some time. "Excuse me. I simply want to point out that there is desperation within her zeal."

"So, you are recommending – what exactly?" the first voice replied, "That she not be inducted?"

"No, no," was Malastier's reply. "It is too late to withdraw at this point. I simply feel that she needs to be overseen – and I intend to do that."

"Very well, then," the first man said. "I believe that everyone is assembled below."

There was the chink of the glasses.

"Cheers!"

I waited until the footsteps disappeared, descended the stairway, and opened the door carefully. Passing the table, I looked longingly at the brandy bottle wondering if I should brace myself with a swig.

I moved to the pantry. A faint glow revealed a raised

trap-door that opened onto wooden stairs. There were several bull's-eye lanterns and some matches on a nearby shelf. Shaking a lantern to ensure it held oil, I picked up some matches and prepared to follow the men below. I put my cap on the shelf as a possible sign for Holmes.

I waited several minutes before descending.

As I slipped down the stairs, I noticed a cloying smell that mingled with the musty air below. Two flights brought me to a foyer lit with large wrought iron candelabras. Before me was a brick cavern with a domed ceiling and, in the distance, a rusty iron gateway.

The gate was open, and candles along the dusty floor led into what was obviously a catacomb. There were niches on both sides of the passageway bearing small portraits, crests and family names covered with mould. This was most likely the burial-place for the early Christians who had worshipped at the ancient church nearby. Without the candles to light the way, I would have surely been lost in the passages that broke off left and right, creating a complex labyrinth beneath the house and churchyard.

A warm glow appeared as I turned a corner. A silhouetted figure stood in a huge arched doorway. With his back to me, I could see that the man was wearing a red robe and gold slippers. He stood just inside the portal clutching an unwieldy brass sceptre in his right hand.

A bell rang in the distance, and he stepped out into the chamber. I heard a loud rap and a piercing call from within:

"Hekas, hekas, este bebeloi!"

As I made my way toward the chamber, I noticed that, just before the entry, a narrow passage branched off, encircling the larger room. Light from the adjoining chamber filtered through smaller slots in this passageway, which had obviously been created for unobtrusive observation of the ceremonies held within. I made my way along for almost twenty feet, before it offered me the perfect vantage point from which to view the proceedings.

I was also aware, of course, that it was a perfect trap. I leaned back against the far wall so that I might not be seen from the chamber. However, I could observe the entire hall in which the meeting was taking place.

At the far end of the chamber stood six figures – five men and one woman. In front of them lay an ornate gold-leaf table bearing a red cross, white triangle, red lamp and, in a small vase, a single red rose. To one side of the table was a smaller one with several chalices and a pitcher.

Between those tables and me stood thirty or more people, of whom I could see only their backs. All were wearing floor-length golden robes with hoods. Along the far wall on my left stood Miss Adler in a white robe and gold slippers.

A strange ritual was unfolding before me. The five figures, at the far end of the room, wore similar dress – three in red robes, one in yellow, and one in blue. I recognized the man in the blue robe as Ciarán Malastier. He seemed to be leading the ceremony. "Fratres and Sorores of the Order of the Golden Dawn in the Outer, assist me to open the Hall of Neophytes of the Urania Temple."

The assembly clapped in unison.

The red robed man with the sceptre rapped it on the table.

"Father Kerux, see that the Temple is guarded."

A loud gong startled me.

Malastier responded: "Very honoured Hierophant, the hall is properly guarded."

The red-robed official proceeded: "Very honoured

Heireus, assure yourself that all present have witnessed the Golden Dawn."

With this, everyone in the room brought their right hand to their temple and lifted their left arm in a broad salute, causing Malastier to say: "Very honoured Hierophant, all present have been so honoured."

This was only the beginning of a complicated ritual, including a wide variety of invocations offered by members bearing ancient Greek titles – Hierophant, Stolistes, Kerux, and Hegemon.

At various times the men and women in the congregation stood, faced in various directions, and echoed responses to offerings from the leaders. The rite bore some similarities to many of the Christian traditions, including the offering of wine, water, and bread. I was growing tired. The ceremony droned on for more than an hour. Then, the congregation turned its attention to Miss Adler.

The red robed leader rapped three times on the table with his sceptre. "Fratres and Sorores of the order of the Golden Dawn in the Outer, I have received a dispensation from the greatly honoured Chiefs of the Second Order to admit Irene Adler to the Grade of Neophyte. Honoured Hegemon, instruct Irene Adler to hold herself in readiness for the ceremony of admission and superintend her preparation."

With this, a man stepped out of the congregation with a rope and hood. He placed a black velvet hood over her head and bound her around the waist with a golden cord. I cannot describe the helplessness I felt at this moment, watching this good lady hoodwinked and bound. This feeling in me was compounded when Malastier approached and, grabbing the rope around her waist, led her to the altar table.

Malastier then removed the hood, and the red-robed official stood before Miss Adler.

"Child of the earth, why dost thou request admission into this order?"

Prompted by Malastier, Irene replied: "My soul is wandering in darkness, seeking for the light of occult knowledge, and I believe that, in this order, the knowledge of that light may be obtained."

Then, the response came from Malastier: "Irene Adler, I hold in my hand your signed pledge to keep secret all relating to this order, but confirm it now to this assembly. Are you freely taking this sacred pledge?"

Malastier then took her right hand and placed it on the white triangle on the centre of the altar table.

"I am," Irene pledged.

The leader then handed her several pages to read. The acolyte, who had hoodwinked her earlier, held a candle close so that she could see. It was a lengthy proclamation, most of which outlined her obligations, but one section, at the end, elevated my mounting fears.

"I do swear secrecy, under awful penalty of voluntarily submitting myself to a deadly and hostile current of will set in motion by the Chiefs of the Order, by which I will fall slain and paralyzed from an invisible force, as if slain by lightening or suffocation."

What a horrible prospect! I thought. Irene was risking her very life.

Suddenly, Ciarán Malastier drew a sword from beneath his robe and placed the blade on the nape of Irene's neck. I gasped and, reaching for my revolver, knocked the lantern over on the floor. However, before I could act, Malastier withdrew the sword.

It seemed that, either no one heard my racket, or that they attributed it to another in the congregation. There was a furtive grin on Malastier's face as he returned his sword to its concealed scabbard.

The leader grasped Irene's shoulders and turned her to face him. He took a chalice in one hand, and the red lamp in the other. Raising them over her head he pronounced, "Soror Isis, I consecrate thee with fire and with water."

The leader then nodded to the acolyte who returned her to her original station.

As the ceremony drew to a conclusion, I relaxed and slumped against the back wall, knowing I would have to wait until everyone had left, before I could escape. As the last persons departed, the acolyte extinguished the candles.

I was left alone in the darkness to contemplate what had just occurred. My fear for Miss Adler grew, along with my disgust with myself for letting her participate in this escapade.

The quiet in this subterranean necropolis became oppressive. At times, I wanted to flee in a dead panic. I began to imagine the air getting thinner, and wondered if it were my imagination, or if the closed trap-door had cut off my supply of air. And, for the first time, I wondered about the trap-door itself. *Would it be locked?* I tried to recall how I dealt with fear during the Afghan campaign. *What was my special system? Ah, yes.* I began to imagine cleaning my service revolver. Strange, you might think, but there was comfort in reflecting on this familiar task that had, at one time, been so much a part of my life. Indeed, I have danced on the edge of death more than most, and knew that, someday soon, life's music would end. Indeed, my end could well come in a place such as this.

I waited a long while after the last sounds had faded. I opened the front of the lantern, struck a match, and put it to the wick. It flickered for a moment and began to glow, but almost immediately went out. A shake of the lantern confirmed my fear. When I had knocked over the lamp, the oil had spilled out. I would have to make my way with only a few remaining matches.

Although I knew my surroundings were cavernous, the walls seemed to close in on me. I paused for a moment to recreate a map in my mind. I felt my way down the narrow passageway that bordered the central chamber. I stepped through the arched doorway and stopped. *Which way now?* I reached into my coat pocket and counted the matches: three. It made sense to use one of them here to ensure that I was beginning in the right direction.

I struck one of my three matches on the nearby wall and held it above my head. I could see some footsteps in the dirt that led in several different directions. However, when I reflected upon my initial entry, it seemed as if the far left passageway was the right way. I followed the tracks, sheltering the fragile flame in my hands, as drafts licked at it from various directions.

The flame burned its last, and I decided to move on for a while without light. As I became accustomed to the blackness, I searched for some faint glow that might point the way. But, there was only blackness. Then, I heard vague sounds rumbling in the distance. A low-pitched vibration echoed, such as one might hear after a clapper struck a bell – a reverberation or echo. My instincts suggested that it emanated from the streets above.

I continued by sliding my feet out in front of me, with my arms outstretched, sweeping to and fro. The echoes seemed to get louder – *good!*

My other senses began to assist. My nose detected what appeared to be smoke mingled with the smell of black water. I was certain I was moving in the right direction, until my right foot slipped and I teetered on the edge of some kind of precipice.

Regaining my balance, I traced the sharp edge in front of me with my foot, poking around until I hit another ledge below – steps… steps that went down even deeper.

I pulled away, retrieved another match and struck it on the wall. It flared brightly to reveal a wide, long stairway descending. Before I could ascertain its distance, a breeze wafted up from below, extinguishing the match. I had learned enough to know that I had gone in the wrong direction and was, in all likelihood, lost.

I placed the burnt match in my pocket, thinking that it may become useful later. I turned about, and headed back in the direction I had come, feeling my way along the damp walls. My plan was to return to my original starting-point.

I encountered no turn-offs as I walked back, so I felt that I should be able to find my way, until I came upon what appeared to be a wide opening on my right. I stopped. *Was this where had I struck my first match?*

I took my handkerchief, twisted and knotted it into a thick wick, and dangled it in front of me. With the other hand, I took the last remaining match from my pocket. I wet my finger and felt for drafts. Feeling none, I struck the match, and carefully placed the flame under the scrap of cloth that had previously been my handkerchief. As it lighted, I held it before me, bending low to search for tracks in the dirt and dust. Again, there appeared to be trails in several directions, but one set of prints looked sharper and deeper. I had my direction now and briskly walked ahead in a race with the makeshift torch that I held between my fingers.

I came upon a large vestibule and recognized it by the extinguished candles along the edge of a wall. *Yes, this led to the ceremonial chamber*. I let out a large breath just before the wick burnt my fingers and dropped to the ground. As it smoldered on the floor, I quickly took several large strides forward.

I was, once again, in total darkness. I dropped to my knees and felt for the wall, brushing one of the candles that lined it. I do not know why I had not thought of this before.

I followed the candled wall to the large iron gate. It was closed. I rose to my feet and felt along the bars to the latch. I held my breath as I pulled on the bolt. *Thank heaven – it's not locked*. The hinges whined as the gate swung out. Recalling the orientation of the gate from my initial descent, I stumbled ahead in the darkness until my foot hit wood – *the pantry stairs*.

I crawled up the stairs on my hands and knees until my head bumped the trap door above. I crouched on the last steps to listen for voices. Hearing none, I put my back and shoulder to the door and pushed. Nothing. *Had it been latched above?* I did not recall seeing a lock, and wondered how to proceed. I pushed against the hatch again with the same sad result. I wondered if I should shoot through the latch or hinges with my pistol. But, as I did not know where these were located, such a plan was dubious at best. Moreover, if I did so, the wreckage would be discovered by the Order and that, in turn, might endanger Miss Adler.

Prudence suggested that I wait, at least for a while, before applying violent force. I settled into as comfortable a position as I might, on the wooden steps. I considered resting in the lower foyer, but feared that I might miss Holmes, or one of the irregulars – *if* they came.

I must have drifted off into a daze, because the next sounds that I recall were those of small feet padding on the floor above. Then a voice: "Not here, Mr. Holmes." It was Archie.

I began rapping on the trap door with the butt of my pistol.

"Holmes – Archie!"

Then, I heard what sounded like a huge object being dragged along the floor above. As the hatch opened, the light from a lantern dazzled my eyes momentarily. Slowly coming into focus came the familiar silhouette of my friend. He extended his hand, and I took it. I put the revolver back in my pocket and rose to climb out.

"Shooting your way out might have been a challenge," Holmes said, "as this door lay beneath a large crate loaded with porcelain."

"Then you saved me, Holmes – again."

"Archie," Holmes commanded, "see that the way is clear. The doctor and I are eager to return home."

As we made our way outside *via* the parlour window, Holmes collared Archie, handing him a few shillings and additional instructions.

We eventually found a hansom. When we settled into the coach, Holmes leaned forward, saying: "I expect you'll need some time to yourself, but I need to know if Irene is safe and well."

"I fear for her ultimate safety, but I believe she is in no danger for the time being."

"Very well. The irregulars will be our eyes and ears until we can determine our next steps."

With the kettle on, Holmes and I settled into a vigil.

"I have been able to glean some useful information from the files in my cottage; but, given your recent exploits, I suspect you have more to tell me."

Indeed I did, and I set about recalling the evening's events in as much detail as I could, including the awful and portentous vow that Miss Adler was forced to make during the ceremony.

"So, Watson, it appears that our dear lady has put herself in jeopardy."

"Yes, and it was not just the symbolic threat of death in the ceremony, Holmes. It was the look on Malastier's face as he placed his sword upon her neck. That, and the accusation that came from him prior to the initiation – the one that I overheard in the kitchen."

"And, what of *you*, my friend? You put yourself in jeopardy as well."

"Indeed, but my danger would have been less if I had not spilled my lantern. The most dreadful part of the whole ordeal was finding my way out of the unholy caverns. I nearly tumbled down stairs going even deeper into the darkness beneath the city."

"Undertown, I suspect," said Holmes. "There is another dark city that lies below our day-lit thoroughfares. I have only been to the edges of this shadow-city, but I know that it harbours the unseen poor who can afford neither house nor home, but only the sewers and hidden ruins below."

"Undertown. Thank heavens I did not stumble into that dismal municipality. The entire situation is becoming increasingly dangerous for us, as well as the lady."

"I concur with your assessment as to the danger, Watson, but I feel that the risks are justified. Ciarán Malastier is a sinister creature. He is up to worse mischief than baby-farming. Concerning Miss Adler, I can see no way to guarantee her safety, other than to ask her to leave the city."

"And, how would she respond to that?"

"She will not be eager to retreat, I agree. Indeed, I wonder as to her whereabouts at this moment. I hope that Archie will soon come with a report."

But, no report was immediately forthcoming. Indeed, Holmes and I had both nodded off in our chairs when, we were awakened by a knocking on glass. Archie had climbed up the drain-pipe and was rapping on my upstairs window.

I awoke first and opened the sash, whereupon Archie climbed inside.

Holmes chuckled. "Your parents must be worried, my boy."

"My parents?" Archie retorted, "No, indeed, sir, I'm at home in bed now – as you can see," he said, with a grin. "That's what's delayed me."

"So, is Miss Adler back at High Road?" Holmes asked.

"She is indeed, sir" Archie replied, "but, she didn't get home until late, sir – after midnight."

"That would be almost three hours after the ceremony," I observed.

"She has been up to something, but what it was we shall not find out until tomorrow," Holmes said; and then, to Archie: "I am putting Miss Adler in your charge. You and your brother are to keep watch over her at *all times*. Report anything unusual. Is that clear?"

"Yes, sir," Archie said with a salute, "me and mine will keep her close, as it were, sir." With that, Archie turned toward the window.

With a chuckle, I grabbed the boy's shoulder.

"I know windows are your preferred way of egress, my lad, but a passing copper might take a dim view of the proceedings. Why not use our front door?"

The next morning Holmes arose early and was fully dressed by the time I found my way to our drawing room.

"I say, Holmes, you seemed poised for a busy day."

He arose from the cloud of smoke that encircled his armchair. "Watson, I fear that Irene's induction may have served to heighten any suspicions which Malastier may have entertained. We must accelerate our efforts to learn what lies behind his carefully constructed professional and social facade."

"You have not told me what you have learned in *your* research."

"I have been gathering information on the Golden Dawn for some time, knowing that they, and some related factions, were gaining prominence, power and influence. The list of purported members is long and impressive – W.B. Yeats, Bram Stoker, Aleister Crowley, and so on. I would count Malastier as a minor character, except for the mysterious protection afforded him by the Secret Service. And, you yourself confirmed that he holds some high office within the order."

"It seems so, from the initiation ceremony, and the conversation that ensued with the leader of the temple. You believe that the Order of the Golden Dawn, then, has some illicit purpose?"

"Probably not," Holmes replied, "as most of the known members are artists, writers and actors – not troublemakers or revolutionaries, with the possible exception of Maud Gonne. However, this secret society would be the perfect cover for illegal or immoral activities. And, when one learns the roots from which the Golden Dawn has sprung, it offers further insight into what might attract Malastier, and others like him."

"What have you learned, then?"

"The temple on Byward Street is one of the first in Britain, established by a fellow named Westcott and others. William Wescott decoded a, heretofore, unknown document. It was written in English using the Trithemius cipher, but its origins can be found in another country. Do you care to guess which, Watson?"

"I would guess Egypt – Greece or Italy."

"And, you would be wrong, Watson. Look farther north."

"North, you say? Switzerland – Austria – Germany?"

"Yes, Germany. The cipher manuscript of the Golden Dawn, as it is called, emanated from Fräulein Anna Sprengel, in Bavaria. Her name and address is contained in the manuscript itself. When Wescott completed the decoding, he contacted Sprengel and was, as a consequence, anointed, and allowed to open a temple in London."

"Then you believe the German government may have some relationship with the Golden Dawn?"

"Probably not the government, Watson – most likely one of the nationalist groups. Nationalism is aflame in Germany at present – fueled by archaic ideas and ideologies – even pagan religions."

"Really?"

"Indeed, there have been several articles in recent Austrian publications, by a fellow named List, extolling the virtues of true German culture, which he says is rooted in priest-kings and pagan mysticism. The gist is that European politicians, and the Christian religion, have diluted the German culture. Buried within these notions is a more radical form of eugenics."

"And is the Golden Dawn part of this resurgence?"

"Possibly, Watson – at least with regard to the temple in Bavaria. And, throughout that country today,

Ario-Christian groups are sprouting up. These are based in Ariosophy, which goes back to sun-worship."

"You mean to say that people are worshipping the sun in this day and age?" I said, with a chuckle.

"Many religions, including Christianity, have their roots in sun-worship. The Egyptian religion is merely the best-known."

"Which would explain the Egyptian words and symbols within yesterday's ceremony."

"Quite right. The Golden Dawn does not discount other religions, but rather reinterprets them. Indeed, one of the runes that dominate Germanic pagan symbology is a twisted cross."

"All very interesting, Holmes, but where does it leave us with regard to Mr. Malastier?"

"In the middle of a mystery that may well be entangled with the destiny of our country. We know that Malastier has been, and possibly still is, putting eugenics into practice."

"The baby-farming you mean?"

"Exactly, Watson. There is no reason to believe that he has abandoned his dark quest. Moreover, he has a prominent position within the Golden Dawn. He may be one of the 'secret chiefs,' as they call them, who guide the activities of the temple. Such a position would appeal to his narcissistic nature, by allowing him to believe that he has a right to pass judgment on those whom he deems inferior."

"Which is probably everyone," I said, "including us."

~

After breakfast, we decided to meet with Miss Adler to learn what had transpired after the ceremony. Knowing that her home might be watched, we sent a message ahead requesting she meet us in Regent's Park, on the bridge near the small falls. It would not do for Malastier to learn that there was a connexion between Miss Adler and us.

It was a rather gloomy day, so the park was deserted, save for some ducks that had taken over the footpaths. As we made our way to the water-feature, we saw Miss Adler entering the park. We allowed her to move on alone in order to determine if she were being followed. Confident that she was not, we continued on to the meeting-place.

We saw the lady standing in the centre of the bridge as requested. She was wearing a violet cape and carrying an open yellow parasol that created the effect of a corona about her head. Holmes stopped in his tracks when he observed her.

"Would you mind if I went on ahead to speak with Miss Adler?"

"No, of course not, Holmes. I'll keep watch."

I found a bench where I could observe all comings and goings to the bridge. As I approached my sentry point, the lady noticed me and waved. I returned her greeting and watched as she turned to greet Holmes, who was mounting the bridge.

It made a dear picture, the two of them together atop the arched bridge. At one point, Holmes took her hand. He appeared to be pleading with her. When his pleas ended, she put her hand on his cheek, and laughed at something that he'd said. She then turned and began to walk slowly away. Holmes followed and caught up to her as she was leaving the bridge. I saw them strolling for some time before I lost them among the gardens.

I amused myself by watching the antics of the ducks nearby. It was nearly an hour before I saw the couple crossing the bridge again. They waved as they strolled to meet me.

Upon approaching me, Miss Adler opened her arms to welcome an embrace. We held locked arms and she proffered a small kiss on my cheek. "John – John – what are we to do with you? I want to thank you for your efforts to protect me at the temple. It was a brave thing to do."

"As was your initiation," I replied. "Although, I believe it was not a wise thing to do – for either of us."

She looked askance at me and smiled. "Now, I've been through all of that with Sherlock. I am duly admonished and warned – but not discouraged. Sherlock will tell you about our plans, and I must be getting back to my daughter who becomes anxious when I am away too long. Good-day, John."

She turned to Holmes and offered him her hand. His brow tightened.

"Your daughter and I share the same anxiety. Do not deride us. It is only that I... we, worry about you."

She did not reply but, once again, put her hand on his cheek in a small caress.

As the lady departed, Holmes remained in place, with some novel thoughts, undoubtedly, sweeping through his dusty mind.

We partook of a small meal at a restaurant near the park. I asked Holmes about what had passed between him and Irene, and, at first, he avoided answering me. Later, as we left the restaurant, he commented that some pieces were beginning to fall in place:

"Malastier invited the neophyte member of the Golden Dawn to a late supper," Holmes reported. "Miss Adler felt she could not refuse, as she saw it as an opportunity to learn more about the man.

"She reported that the dinner was mostly pleasant, except on two occasions: During the meal, Malastier had several bouts of coughing. You will recall, Watson, that he exhibited the same malady when he visited us. The other unpleasant occasion was when Malastier began pontificating about the prospects for war. He expressed grave concerns about the use of horrible weapons. This may give us a clue pertaining to his work in the War Department."

"But, exactly where does such a remark take us, Holmes?"

"It takes us to 'Blinker'."

"Blinker?"

"William Reginald Hall, Watson: the Assistant to the Controller of the Royal Navy, otherwise known as 'Blinker'."

"So, it's off to the Admiralty building."

"Yes."

On our way there, Holmes reminded me that, in the process of solving a case involving a vital naval treaty, he had made the acquaintance of Commander William Hall, who had assisted in our investigations. Filed away in some dark recess in Holmes's mind was the knowledge that, although "Blinker" might not know Mr. Malastier, he would, from his elevated position, definitely know *about* him.

"Watson, I should appreciate it if you would stay close to Miss Adler, and see that she arrived home safely. I believe that "Blinker" would prefer to see me alone, given the nature of my inquiry."

And so, we parted, to embark on separate missions until we should be reunited later that evening.

I had a grand bachelor's supper awaiting Holmes – asparagus soup, stottie cake, and a rich, blue-veined Stilton that I had come to enjoy.

Holmes was in good spirits when he returned; and, in the course of the meal, I was pleased to hear that "Blinker" had been helpful.

"I neglected to ask about Commander Hall's epithet," I enquired.

"Not an imaginative appellation, Watson. William Reginald Hall has a terrible tic, which causes one of his eyes to flash like a signal lamp. It is surprising how, after a few minutes with him, you find yourself accustomed to it."

"What did you learn between twitches?"

"More than I had dared hope. "Blinker" not only knew Mr. Malastier, but also the nature of his work."

"Which is?"

"Gas, Watson – poison gas. It seems that our intelligence service has intercepted communications from German spies here in Britain, to the effect that Germany is manufacturing and stockpiling poisonous gases – not only chlorine gas, but also a new one, of which we know little. Malastier's research involves developing similar weapons and counter-measures.

"I thought the Hague Convention..."

"Yes, well it appears that if there is to be war, it will not follow conventions," Holmes said.

"Gas... a cowardly form of warfare, Holmes."

"Our War Office agrees with you, but there are influential forces within our government who would have Britain create and use such horrible weapons of destruction."

"And, Ciarán Malastier is leading this effort?"

"It appears so; and, according to 'Blinker', his efforts

are at a crucial stage where new gases, and counter-measures, developed by a *cadre* of scientists, are about to be tested."

"What would be *our* connexion with all of that?"

"I am not certain, but I took 'Blinker' into my confidence and shared our concerns about Malastier – including his recent baby-farming crimes. 'Blinker' is sufficiently concerned to make further inquires."

"This is very good indeed, Holmes."

"Quite so, Watson. However, I know that there is a limit as to what 'Blinker' can, and will, share with us. We must continue to monitor the activities of Mr. Malastier as well."

In the days that followed, Holmes and I spent our time watching over Irene, while conducting research on gas weapons, and learning more about the Golden Dawn.

A few days later, "Blinker", William Reginald Hall himself, called upon us.

The Commander was not wearing his uniform, which I thought odd.

"I came *incognito,* Mr. Holmes," he said, blinking. "I dare not trust public messaging."

"Your business is urgent, then?" Holmes replied.

Our guest blinked at me. "I should prefer a private conversation, Mr. Holmes."

"Doctor Watson is my closest colleague, and is already in possession of all the known facts pertaining to this matter."

Commander Hall twitched several times in silence. "Very well! As I promised, I made enquiries regarding Mr. Malastier and his project. Indeed, I talked directly with him. I enquired as to –"

"I wish you had not made direct contact, Commander," Holmes interrupted. "Malastier is an intelligent and wary individual."

"I understand, Mr. Holmes, but in my current capacity, I expect that my enquiries did not raise undue alarm."

"I pray you are correct in this assessment," I interjected. My remark didn't merit a single blink.

"I came here because it appears Mr. Malastier seems poised to act – possibly to test various gases. And, I am uneasy."

"Uneasy? You yourself told me this was his charge," Holmes recalled.

"Yes, sir, this is true, but I – even I, with the highest clearance in the Admiralty – have been unable to obtain the details of his plans. He has evidently manufactured, or otherwise obtained, cylinders of various gases. I'm not sure of the exact amount."

"That would seem to be within his purview," I said.

"Quite so, doctor; but, only today I discovered a curious detail that alarmed me, and brought me here."

He had stopped blinking momentarily.

"Malastier has stockpiled this gas in a warehouse in the heart of London."

"Why are these materials in London?" Holmes asked.

"Why indeed? I made inquiries as best I could without raising alarm, but was told that Mr. Malastier was adamant about keeping the tests secret; and, because German spies are known to monitor our military installations, he plans to conduct tests well away from any military bases."

"Commander Hall," Holmes asked, "do you know the precise location of these materials?"

"Yes. They are in a warehouse that adjoins an abandoned wharf on Lower Thames Street."

"Really! Now *I* am alarmed. What comes to your mind, Watson, regarding a warehouse on Lower Thames Street?"

"It is near All Hallows' Church, and the temple of the Golden Dawn."

"Yes, indeed. The strands are coming together!" Holmes ejaculated. Our exchange seemed to puzzle "Blinker", who, nonetheless, continued:

"I am overstepping my authority, Mr. Holmes, when I come here now. You know this. I cannot guarantee your safety, nor provide any help or protection should you decide to intervene."

Holmes smiled and, turning to me, lifted his eyebrows in an enquiring manner.

I nodded and smiled in reply.

Holmes stood and walked to the hearth, and paused thoughtfully.

Commander Hall seemed restless, clearly eager to depart. "I have given you all the information which I have at this time. I only ask that you use the greatest discretion with regard to it."

"We will do so. I can see that you are anxious to take your leave. Thank you so much, Commander. I assure you that I – we – will justify your continued trust and faith."

With that, "Blinker" departed.

Holmes grabbed a pouch of shag from the mantle and, filling his pipe, sat in the large chair by the fireplace. The grand clockworks in his head began to grind. But, before I could muster up a cup of coffee, there came a knocking at our front door. I peered through the rain-streaked window to see a small boy.

Upon opening the door, there stood Archie, with no coat or cover, his cap in his hand. I ushered him in, brought him to the kitchen, and towelled him off quickly, before conveying him into the parlour.

Holmes was staring into the fire. "What is it, Archie – Miss Adler?"

"Yes, sir. A carriage pulled up to her house not more than half an hour ago. There was a man in the coach. Benjie and I followed him."

"How did you do that, Archie?" I enquired.

"We have our ways, sir."

"First, then," Holmes said, urging the lad on. "What did the man look like, Archie?"

"A proper gentleman. Fine clothes. Topper," the lad began. Holmes had trained the members of his diminutive platoon well. Their reporting was quick, sparse and clear. "A moustache, and those little glasses that perch on the nose."

"Malastier!" I exclaimed.

"Yes," Holmes said; and, turning to Archie again: "Where did they go?"

"That same place," Archie said, "the old place on Byward Street, where the lady was with all them gents in hoods."

"It could be a meeting of the Golden Dawn," I said.

"But, not like before, sir," Archie interjected. "When we got there, a tall dark-green lorry, all covered up, was in the street. But there was no coming and going like there was before. The lady and gentleman went inside alone."

Just then, another rap came on our door. I saw a messenger crouching in the doorway.

I retrieved the message, which was addressed simply "to Sherlock."

Recognizing the handwriting, Holmes reviewed the contents, and then showed the note to me:

Dear Sherlock,

I received an unexpected invitation from Mr. Malastier to attend a special meeting of the

Golden Dawn. He said only that he wanted to make sure I was included in his future plans. I see this as a grand opportunity to learn more about his intentions. I will make a report tomorrow.

I am sending this because I know that you are watching over me, and I do not wish you to be unduly concerned. I will be careful.

Give my best to John.

With affection,
Irene

"The lady is being *naïve,*" I said, "contrary to what she may believe."

"You are quite right." He grabbed the note again, and reread it aloud: "… he wanted to make sure that I was included in his future plans. Malastier would never include a novice in his planning. And, what *plan*?"

Holmes flung the note to the floor and turned to me with wild eyes.

"Watson, I fear that Blinker's enquiries, may have cast further suspicions on Irene, and caused this devil to act sooner than he might have planned. Whatever Malastier is planning, is going to happen tonight!"

We had almost forgotten about Archie, who was standing wide-eyed in silence. I took half-a-crown from my pocket and held it out. His eyes widened, as he held out his palm to receive the reward.

"Archie," I said, "you will go with us to retrieve your brother, but then it's home with you both. You've been a great help. On your way out, summon a hansom for us."

Holmes was already dashing to his room to dress. I did likewise.

"Bring your revolver, Watson, and some candles and

matches," he ordered from the hallway. He opened our linen chest and began tearing a bath towel into long strips, stuffing them into his pocket. "Do we have any bicarbonate, Watson?"

"In the cupboard, Holmes – on the top shelf."

He was already down the stairs when I finished dressing. Archie had a carriage waiting when Holmes opened the door. The lad was perched behind with the driver. The moment I swung into my seat Holmes yelled to the driver, "All Hallows-by-the-Tower." The reins snapped, and we were off.

Although we departed as quickly as possible, it had now been almost an hour since Irene and Malastier had arrived at the temple house. The lorry, of which Archie had spoken, was no longer there.

As soon as we stopped, Archie jumped down. His brother Benjie ran to us from the shadows.

"Archie – Archie!" Benjie called. "I thought you'd never get here. The lorry left some time ago with the men."

Holmes bent down and took Benjie by the shoulders. "Did the lady go with the lorry, Benjie?"

"No, sir, Mr. Holmes."

"Are the lady and gentleman inside?" I asked.

"Yes, sir."

Holmes stood up and gazed at the dark house. Not a light was to be seen. "Archie, take your brother home. Do not wait here. Do you understand?"

Archie stiffened and gave a small salute, "Right sir." And, turning to his little brother, "You did well, Benjie. Let's go." The boys hurried off.

The full moon lighted our way to the parlour window that had granted us access before.

"The centre casement, Holmes." I confirmed, as we approached the windowed area.

Holmes grabbed the frame of the window and began to push upward. Then, he stopped.

"What is it, Holmes – is it locked?"

"No, Watson; there is a letter on the sill."

"A letter?"

"Yes. Is that candle handy?"

We crouched down below the window. I fumbled for a candle and matches. Holmes had already opened the message by the time I made a flame. He read it aloud:

Holmes,

You are alive only because your death may have jeopardized my plans. Tonight the gloves come off. Tonight history is made.

Do not try again to send your minions, for they will suffer for your stupidity - as Irene will testify, if she is alive when you find her.

A few less feathers to pluck.

A black feather was threaded into the bottom of the paper – Malastier's signature.

"Damn, Watson!" Holmes cried, as he crushed the note in his hands. "We must hurry."

The window was opened, and we quickly made our way into the house and pantry. The crate, which had been on top of the trap-door, was now placed to the side, allowing easy access to the stairway below.

I grabbed two of the lanterns and lit them, handing one to Holmes. We dashed down the stairs. Upon reaching the ground, and the gated vestibule, we detected an odd scent.

"What's that smell, Holmes?"

He reached into his coat pocket and retrieved two pieces of torn towel. "Here, put your lantern down and hold these." He then took the bottle of bicarbonate from his pocket and poured it over the cloths in my hands. "Keep this one handy to cover your nose and mouth when the gas becomes more concentrated."

"Gas!" I exclaimed. "Gas here, Holmes?"

"Undertown," he said, enigmatically, "and Irene. Can you recall how to find the stairway that leads further below?"

Keeping our lanterns low, we could see where, just a short time before, someone had wheeled a trolley. As we continued, the chemical smell increased in intensity, and it became clear that at least one of the components of the gas was chlorine.

As we approached the wide stairway to Undertown, we could not see the bottom of the stairs because there was a grey-green cloud hovering only ten feet below us in the stairwell.

"Watson, I will wet my rag again and go below. You stay here; and, if I do not come back in five minutes, go for help."

"Holmes, you're being preposterous. You cannot go into that gas."

"The gas is heavy. The worst of it will be below me. Now, do as I request." With that, he wet his towel with bicarbonate, tied it around his face, and bounded down the stairs. I watched the gas swirl around him as the glow from his lantern dimmed into the gassy gloom.

I noted the time on my watch and waited. As the minutes wore on, I fully realized my dilemma. If I left for help, as Holmes had suggested, I should be abandoning him to a grisly fate. If I attempted rescue, I might well become another of Malastier's victims.

I had put but one foot on the first step, when I heard a shuffling below. I raised my lantern to see Holmes with a huge bundle lying over his shoulder. He was struggling to climb out of the treacherous green fog. I rushed down and grabbed him by the arm as he was about to collapse.

"Take her up, Watson," he gasped. His voice was raspy and muffled by the cloth covering his nose and mouth. "I can make it."

Just then a plume of gas vapour wafted upwards and stung my eyes and nostrils, so that I began to choke. I reached for my dampened rag, with which I wiped my eyes and covered my face. I regained enough composure to grab the slack figure, as it began to slide from Holmes's shoulder. It was a woman – I guessed Irene, but I could not see clearly, as there was a hood of some sort over her head.

I carried her up, moving some considerable distance away from the stairway, before I laid her down. There was a canvas helmet over her head that had eye-lenses. I unbuttoned and removed the hood.

I hurried back to the stairway, just as Holmes was crawling up the last few steps. I picked him up and walked him to where Irene was lying. He pulled the rag from his face and knelt down.

"Watson, help her, please."

I could see that her breathing was laboured and shallow. I bent close to her face and noticed an odd smell, like mouldy hay. Her eyes, which had been previously closed, fluttered.

"Irene," I pleaded. "Irene, it is John and Sherlock. Do you understand me?"

Her lips quivered and began to move. "John – Sher – lock." She was gasping for air between words.

"Don't try to speak," I said. Holmes was beginning to recover, and the shock of seeing Irene prostrate jolted his system. He let out a low plea: "No… please, no."

"We must get her to hospital, Holmes, and quickly. Help me carry her to the air above."

Our lanterns, which were now becoming dim for lack of oil, gave us just enough light to find our way out of the catacombs, and into the empty house.

I unlatched the front door, and we carried the lady to the edge of the deserted street.

"Cabby – cabby," I yelled. Just then, two tiny white faces poked out of the shadows across the street: Archie and Benjie. "Get a carriage, quickly."

The boys were off. I laid my jacket on the ground next to a tree, where we set the lady down. Holmes took off his jacket and covered her. Leaning closer he spoke:

"It's I, my lady. Help is coming."

Irene's eyes opened. "I knew you would come. I knew," she said.

"Save your breath," Holmes replied. "You are going to be fine."

Irene began to cough violently. Spittle poured from the corner of her mouth.

"It's the gas, Holmes. It has damaged her bronchial passages and lungs."

"She'll be fine though, I know it," Holmes declared.

The coughing continued and she was losing consciousness. I feared the worse, but said nothing.

The carriage finally came. I laid her head on Holmes's lap as we departed. Her convulsions and coughing became more violent. Holmes held her head in his hands and stroked her hair without uttering a word.

When we arrived at hospital, Holmes was reluctant to let two attendants take Irene from the carriage. However, we laid her on a stretcher, and followed close behind. I gave orders to a nurse who was hovering in the lobby.

Holmes wanted to follow, but the nurse sat him down in the waiting area.

Doctors were summoned, and within a minute, Irene

was headed for a treatment room. Again, Holmes tried to follow. I held him back as best I could, but he tore my arms away and burst into the room.

"Get that man out of here!" the older doctor shouted. "This woman needs…"

Before the good man could finish his sentence, Holmes had his coat in his fist, and leaned into his face.

"You must save her! Do you understand? Save her!" Holmes demanded.

When I pulled him away, he clasped my shoulders.

"Watson, will she be all right?"

I ushered him out of the room and seated him again. He stared at me, disoriented. I had no words for him.

Before I could speak again, a doctor came out and looked at Holmes.

"You are Sherlock, right? Come with me, she wants you."

Holmes sprang up and ran into the room. Another doctor, and the two nurses, pulled back as Holmes rushed to Irene's side.

Irene raised her arm and put a finger on his lips.

"Sherlock, my dear – Sherlock, listen – *listen* to me."

As she spoke, the doctors and nurses moved toward the door where I was waiting. I caught one of the doctors by the arm. He turned and shook his head.

Tears erupted from my eyes as this saddest of scenes unfolded.

"This is my – doing Sherlock," Irene began. "I have only one regret. That I will not have you… in this life. Perhaps though… perhaps in the next."

A deep sigh arose from within Holmes. *"My love!"*

"How I have waited – for those words." She touched his cheek. "My… love."

Those were her last words.

As Holmes clutched her lifeless hand in a daze, Irene's broken vow echoed in my mind – *I swear secrecy, under awful penalty by which I will fall slain and paralyzed from an invisible force, as if slain by lightening or suffocation*."

4

THE CURE THAT KILLS

Holmes pits himself against the Pinkerton Agency.

DURING IRENE ADLER'S funeral, the only outward expression of Holmes's feelings occurred when Irene's daughter, Adaline, asked him if he wished to pay his last respects before the coffin was closed.

Unobtrusively, Holmes removed the gold sovereign from his watch chain and placed it under Irene's cold, folded hands. Other than this outward symbol of his acceptance, Holmes's grief was expressed in a private and solitary manner. He sat quietly in my parlour for days after the requiem. I stayed near, but never encroached upon his vigil.

Five days after the interment, I was pouring steamy water into a waiting cup of a bracing mountain tippy tea that I have come to love, when Holmes approached.

"May I join you, Watson?"

"Bring a cup here, and try this exceptional brew."

"Yes, I noticed the Yu Ch'ien tea in your cupboard and looked forward to tasting it. It's harvested in the spring, you know, which accounts for its zesty tang."

"I only know that I look forward to this treat, which I

reserve for dreary afternoons such as this. It is a silly gift which I give myself."

"Silly, Watson, no. We solitary gentlemen need such small pleasures, do we not?"

This simple observation revealed a chink in Holmes's Spartan armour that, I believe, "the woman" had breached.

"I miss her also, Holmes. She had an enigmatic nature – completely feminine and, at the same time, warrior-like."

"Yes. And her passing reminds me, once again, that the fabric of fantasies often becomes a threadbare reality."

I twisted my chair around to face Holmes, who was staring into his cup. "Fantasies can be a response to a need, I believe."

"Yes – and, it is a little surprising, at my age, to discover some new aspect of my nature."

"A pleasant surprise?"

"Pleasant is not the word I might choose – unsettling, interesting at best."

"So, what does one do with new self-knowledge?"

Holmes grimaced and pulled back from the table, most likely signalling that I had ventured too far into his interior world. "What does one do, Watson? Channel it! Direct it toward something useful and meaningful."

He arose from the table and struck a pose of intended action. "I suggest that we pay a visit to my dear brother."

"Mycroft?"

"He has had enough time to rationalize the deaths of Irene and the hundreds of others."

"You're being cruel now, Holmes."

"Possibly. My brother and I share a latent flaw, and –"

"And, we must forgive ourselves – and others."

"Forgiveness awaits on the other side of justice – and I shall bring Ciarán Malastier to justice."

The next day, Holmes and I traveled to Mycroft's office in Whitehall.

When we were ushered into his office, we found Mycroft ensconced behind a massive carved oak desk in the corner of his vast book-lined chamber. Holmes strode across the office, and stood at the head of the desk. I trailed behind.

The silence grew with each passing moment, until it filled the room and pushed Mycroft from his chair. He arose and, steadying himself with one hand that trailed along the edge of the desk, walked the perimeter and came to stand face to face with his brother.

"Any apology which I might offer, Sherlock, could never communicate the deep regret that I feel for the disservice that I did to you and our country," Mycroft began. "I shall endeavour to compensate, knowing that it may never be enough."

Holmes stood silently. There was an imperceptible vibration working in his body, holding back deeper emotion.

Mycroft bowed his head. "I was wrong, Sherlock."

Those words broke the tension in Holmes's body and rippled out into the room.

"I, too," Holmes replied. "I had hereto elevated intellect above emotion, as the two seemed incompatible within my being. This tragedy is a condemnation of that philosophy. My intellect took me beyond reason – to a perilous audacity. My Promethean punishment is to be forever shackled to a deep regret from which I may never escape.

"Regrets come with life well lived, my brother."

Holmes grasped Mycroft's shoulders in both hands. "Let us, then, make the most of our regrets, my brother."

Watching Holmes and his brother reconcile restored

some of my faith in humanity, which had been damaged by recent events. As a physician, I have always been in awe of the capacity of human beings to heal even the most grievous wounds.

Stepping back, Mycroft motioned for Holmes and me to sit. He took a stitched file from his drawer and slid it across the desktop. As Holmes began to page through it, his brother retrieved a stack of photographs from the table behind, and spread them out before us.

My jaw dropped.

"My dear God," I mumbled. Holmes looked up from the file.

Mycroft narrated as Holmes and I poured over the grisly black and white scenes:

"Three hundred and thirteen dead at the last count, and scores more in a serious condition! However, these figures do not adequately represent the terrible result of Ciarán Malastier's atrocity. Over two hundred men, women, and children were blinded by the gas and will spend the rest of their lives like that."

We saw bodies stretched out in passageways, their faces contorted in a last agony as the gas burnt their lungs and eyes. Babes and children lay tangled in heaps – twisted in their death throes. Their eyes were frozen open in search of an invisible horror.

"As you can see," Mycroft continued, "children were especially vulnerable, as they were closer to the ground upon which the gases crept – heavier than air, you know."

"Then, there was more than chlorine gas," I noted.

"Yes," the elder Holmes replied. "There was an experimental mixture of phosgene and chlorine: a terrible combination that causes death to come slowly, sometimes taking as long as two days."

Holmes turned away from the images and closed the file. "Is he within reach?"

"No. He has fled. But, we are on his trail and will bring him to justice."

Holmes shook his head. "Let *me* find him. Allow me this, my brother."

"I shall share with you what little we know," Mycroft replied. "You have your methods; we have ours. We may not work in tandem, but I shall not keep you from the hunt."

Mycroft then pointed to the file. "Have you seen the note that Malastier left behind? It's near the back, in a torn envelope."

Holmes retrieved it and read aloud:

Dear sirs,

I fear that your catechized minds cannot fully comprehend the great service I have performed for our country. In one experiment, I tested our latest weapon, and rid future generations of the vermin that have been infiltrating, and propagating in the cesspools of our city. I pray this will serve as a call to arms to those who will no longer stand by and watch our noble seed being corrupted.

I have demonstrated the effectiveness of lethal gas in the trenches of war. I regret that time did not allow me to more completely test our deterrent - the LG-1 PH gas and smoke helmet. I am certain Mr. Holmes will be able to describe how effective - or possibly ineffective, this helmet might be.

What I did, I did for God and my fatherland.

Ciarán Malastier

Holmes looked up. "There is a postscript, Watson."

(P.S.) *Mr. Holmes I look forward to our next, and last, meeting.*

"What a diabolical creature he is!"

"The precise word, Watson; for, he is the most malevolent criminal ever to cross my path – and, that is saying a lot. I suspect Malastier will have me tracking him into the ninth circle of hell itself."

"Holmes, you have used an improper pronoun. Malastier will have *us* tracking him..."

"Another adventure then, Watson. Very well – with Dante as our probable guide, we shall bring this loathsome creature to justice."

Mycroft harrumphed. "By that, I hope you mean 'to trial.' There are many who have a grievous score to settle with this criminal. They deserve their day as well, and the people need to know that justice has been served."

"We shall do our best to accommodate you; but, as you see from the postscript, he anticipates a fight to the death."

"Please bear in mind, Sherlock, that you have my office, and that of Captain Cumming, at your disposal. If you apprehend him, I beg you to return him to us."

Holmes smiled in seeming supplication. "I shall do what I can to return Mr. Malastier to his fatherland."

Mycroft relaxed into a sly grin. "With that settled, let me share what little we currently know about the whereabouts of Ciarán Malastier."

Mycroft walked to the cork-covered wall next to his desk. It was dotted with notes and photographs, put together in a chronological arrangement.

"Malastier," said Mycroft, "fled his home in Brienheim with a Hartman steamer trunk. We know that the cabby took him to Waterloo Station. We lost his trail for a time, but have now discovered that he travelled to Southampton, where he boarded the R.M.S. *Olympic*, which arrived in New York City yesterday."

"He will easily vanish into a mass of five million," I predicted.

"We telegraphed the port authorities," Mycroft added, "and, I have sent two men over today."

"My dear brother, as Watson has noted, with thousands of immigrants streaming into that metropolis every day, Malastier can easily slip through any net. Furthermore, we cannot assume he will stay in New York. America is thirty times the size of Britain. To find Malastier, we must think like him."

"And, what does that conjure up?" Mycroft queried.

"We must turn his obsession to our advantage. He is on a crusade to pluck the black feathers from the white swan. Therefore, we shall seek out America's biggest and whitest swans."

Mycroft bobbed his head and chortled. "Good hunting, then!"

"Thank you. May I have a copy of Malastier's file – and, is it possible to gain entry to his home?"

Mycroft acquiesced to both requests and arranged for Holmes and me to visit Malastier's lodgings, which were currently under guard.

The next morning, I set about making plans to go to America.

"The first available ship is the *Imperator*, Holmes. However, I am not certain it is the best choice."

"Why – because she is German?"

"Yes, that – and, the fact that it will be her maiden voyage. She boasts that she is the biggest – that does not mean the best."

"I say she's the best for us. With every day, Malastier's trail grows colder."

"Then it is done. I shall book accommodation this afternoon and locate lodging in New York. I believe the Astor might be a good choice. The Imperator sails in two days."

We had a late breakfast and departed for Malastier's home in Brienheim. On the way over, Holmes expressed concern that clues were likely lost in the hurried search of Malastier's residence by agents of the Intelligence Bureau.

Upon our arrival, it was clear that the guard was expecting us. Holmes addressed him even before he could greet us: "Has anything been taken from this residence?"

"The contents from two desk drawers and a letter sitting on his desk, sir," the guard answered. "Oh, and – a package came this morning. I set it on the hall table."

The delivery was wrapped in brown paper, and bound with string. The label on it showed it was from Hawes and Curtis, an exclusive haberdasher on Jermyn Street. Holmes poked at it gently, and then opened it.

"Handkerchiefs, Watson, one dozen white linen handkerchiefs. What do you make of that?"

"Not much."

Holmes grimaced. "Would you please see if you can find anything of interest upstairs? I'm going to examine the parlour, his office, and the bins."

Bathrooms often have much to say about a person, and Malastier's bathroom was no exception. I found an empty bottle of heroin on the shelf. It is often prescribed for bad coughs, so I was not surprised. I brought the unfilled bottle of Bayer heroin down to Holmes, who greeted me holding a soiled handkerchief on the end of a pencil.

"What would you think if you found two blood-spattered handkerchiefs among the rubbish, Watson?"

"Pulmonary edema, tuberculosis, or something as serious."

I showed him the heroin bottle; and he nodded.

"Malastier is ill indeed. He will need to seek treatment, and that will help us to narrow our search. Watson, please search the kitchen and pay particular attention to foods that Malastier seems to prefer. I shall be in his office."

I found little of interest in the kitchen and went to find Holmes. He was staring at one of the bookshelves that lined the wall behind Malastier's desk.

"Nothing much in the kitchen, Holmes. A little stale soda bread and some lamb gone bad in the icebox. Anything here?"

"Possibly Watson – something that was here, at any rate. A book has been pulled from this shelf. See here where the dust on the edge of the shelf has been swept away by the binding. What book could be so important that, in a desperate rush to escape the county, he would take the time to retrieve it?"

"Something other than pleasure reading."

"Yes. To the left of the missing book, we find *Cardiovascular Diseases* by Thomas Jandrian, M.D. To the right, we find *The Doctor's Companion* by Andrew Millar."

"*The Doctor's Companion* is a diagnostic book, especially popular in America," I noted.

"It appears he has put books of special interest on this shelf here. See how these books and shelves have much less dust, while the others above and below haven't been touched in months or years. So, what is the missing book?"

Holmes pushed his fingers into the empty space and pressed it open. "Judging from the space, the missing book is nearly two inches in width. And, since it appears Malastier organizes his books alphabetically by author, the author of the missing book has a last name that begins with either J, K, L, or M."

"Any thoughts, Watson?"

"That narrows the possibilities down only a little, I'm afraid. We might have some luck at the Hunterian Library. Possibly Mr. Dart or Dr. Keith could be of assistance."

"Excellent idea, Watson! I'll take that advice. You have matters to attend to, so I shall go to the Hunterian Library and see what I may find. Let's sup at the Café Royal tonight. What do you say – about seven?"

"Jolly good," I said, as even then, my appetite was being stimulated in anticipation of the glorious meal that awaited me.

Holmes was late for dinner. The champagne that I ordered was growing tepid. But, he eventually sauntered in, carrying a book.

"Watson, I believe that I have found the book in question. What do you say to that?"

"Unless we can eat it, I suggest we order dinner and you can tell me about it over the roast duck that awaits me in the kitchen."

"And, Champagne too. What is the occasion?"

"A *bon voyage* celebration, since we sail the day after tomorrow."

The wine was opened and, after a sip or two, we settled into a pleasant evening.

"So, I take it that this book of yours is going to help us find Malastier amid a population of one hundred million."

"I believe so!" Holmes exclaimed, patting the dusty volume on the table. "Malastier has three goals: First, to escape; next, to treat his illness; and lastly, to further the cause of racial purity – in that order, I expect. Let us examine these in more detail."

"We shall have nearly six days at sea Holmes – but, go on."

"Thank you, Watson. I was somewhat surprised to find that our freedom-loving cousins in America have the dubious distinction of being one of the first countries in the world to sanction sterilization in the name of racial purity. Indeed, thirty-eight of the forty-eight states have laws preventing inter-racial marriage."

"It would seem that Lady Liberty is partial, to say the least," I quipped.

"Indeed. So, knowing that Malastier went to New York, I suspect that his first stop may be the Eugenics Record Office."

"In the city? I enquired."

"No, but close by, on Long Island. This noble institution is funded by the Harriman Railroad and the Carnegie Institution, and is under the leadership of the biologist Charles Davenport."

"So, that will be our first stop, then?"

"Yes. And, by the time we arrive, I shall undoubtedly have a more robust plan."

"And, the book?"

"Ah, yes," Holmes said. "Malastier is ill – seriously ill, we suspect. He will need to seek treatment, and that will aid our efforts." Holding up the brown, cloth covered volume, Holmes looked as if he were putting the clues together before my eyes. "All three of Malastier's goals converge on this book."

I squinted in the dim lighting to read the title – *Rational Hydrotherapy: The Physiological and Therapeutic Effects of Hydriatic Procedures, and the Technique of Their Application in the Treatment of Disease,* by John Harvey Kellogg.

"Is the author that American medical evangelist?"

"Indeed, Watson. And, buried deeply in the very heart of America, in the state of Michigan, in Battle Creek, lay the offices of Kellogg's Race Betterment Foundation *and* his sanitarium… which preaches the gospel of health."

"So, we're off to Battle Creek, in Michigan, as well?"

"I suspect so, but, as I say, this is but a skeleton of our plan."

"And, speaking of skeletons Holmes, our meal is arriving. Another glass of Champagne?"

We finished our packing the next day, and Holmes sent a telegram to Adaline Dart, Miss Adler's daughter, informing her of our planned crossing to New York City in pursuit of Malastier, and promising further news.

~

We were ready for our next adventure. And, on a crisp September morning in 1913, we found ourselves mounting the behemoth *Imperator* in Southampton.

We anticipated nothing more than a restful six-day voyage. However, our trip would turn out to be most memorable, as our paths would cross with those of a former U.S. president, and a remarkable magician.

I was not able to secure first-class accommodation due to the late booking. However, our second-class cabins, on B-deck, were Spartan, but satisfactory. My only criticism was that the undersized electric lamps on the walls were placed in precisely the wrong locations. As we should soon find, the cabin was dingy during the day, and cave-like in the evening. Like desperate moths, we would hover around two tiny square windows when dressing and reading.

As we were settling in, the ship's whistle bellowed thrice and cheers rose up from the passengers on deck and along the quay. The ocean-going vessel of 3,500 souls vibrated, as a swarm of tugs butted their heads against the *Imperator*'s hull.

Slipping into the channel, I could feel a low rumble, signalling that the engines had engaged, and we were under our own power. However, the tugs continued to mill around like dispirited natives watching their great god drift away into paradise.

I decided to explore our surroundings, while Holmes seemed content to stay in our cabin poring over Malastier's file, the Kellogg book, and countless volumes on the subject of eugenics.

Our cabin adjoined the promenade circumnavigating the ship, which made it convenient for walks. I returned from a detailed reconnoiter to see Holmes still hunched over Malastier's file.

"At this point, you must have that file committed to memory," I quipped.

"There are so many mysteries remaining about this man. What, or who, opened the door to the dark side of his nature?" Holmes wondered aloud.

"I suspect you may not find the answer in that portfolio. It seems to me that good and evil exist in all of us – or, at least, the potential for both. War taught me that; and I am grateful for the lesson. I believe that, when we are not aware of the seed of evil within us, it can sprout and grow in that ignorance."

"Well put, Watson!"

I took Holmes's coat from the closet. "Come, Holmes. Let us catch a glimpse of the last bit of the British Isles that we shall see for a while."

Holmes begrudgingly set his file down, donned his coat, and followed me to the rear of the ship. I noticed a barrel-chested gentleman, in a glistening white uniform, descending the ladder from the bridge. I guessed it was the captain who could now leave the wheel for his hosting duties.

Being the captain of a large ship requires an unusual amalgam of steadfastness, attentiveness, and appreciation for the social graces. The evidence for this came in an envelope to our cabin upon the first afternoon of our journey to America. Holmes and I were invited to attend a reception in the captain's lounge. Holmes was reticent to attend, but I cajoled him with the promise that we might learn something to our advantage, as we prepared to navigate in America.

The captain's lounge was an oval room of Baroque design. "Typical German vulgarity!" I remarked, *sotto voce,* as we entered the room. And, indeed, its opulence was startling to the point that it made one feel positively uneasy.

The brightly dressed guests were buzzing around the uniformed captain like bees about a flower. When we entered, several heads swivelled as we made our way to the captain through a crush of glittering ladies, and gentlemen in drab three-piece affairs. I noticed Holmes's brow rise slightly upon seeing one young man sporting a velvet jacket.

As we approached, a rather buxom woman, with diamonds draped across her ample bosom, was regaling the group with anecdotes of her adventures at sea. A ship's steward turned to us as we approached and whispered into the captain's ear. The steward's prompting shifted the group's unwelcome attention to us. The circle opened in expectation of our arrival.

"I am zo pleased zat you are able to attend my leetle festivity, chentlemen," he exclaimed, in a thick accent – which, for the convenience of my readers, I shall not attempt further to transcribe phonetically. "I am Captain Hoffman. Let may introduce you to your fellow-travellers."

My friend and I warily stepped into the ring.

"The *Imperator* is pleased and honoured to welcome

the distinguished Mr. Sherlock Holmes and Doctor Watson."

The how-do-you-do's resounded.

Our time in the social limelight, however, was short-lived, as Captain Hoffman then turned to welcome another arrival.

A great block of a man, with short-cropped hair and bushy moustache, stepped into the parlour, and surveyed the room as if it were his personal fiefdom. I recognized the fellow as once: it was Roosevelt – Theodore Roosevelt. He had a well-tanned, ruddy complexion, and sported gold-rimmed pince-nez. Without hesitation, he moved toward our gathering with resolute steps.

"President Roosevelt!" the captain exclaimed as the American approached. Eyebrows rose in unison, and conversation ceased, as the celebrity threw his arms wide as if to embrace us all.

"What a bully party!" the great man said. "When the invitation suggested formal wear, I was so fearful of a dreary afternoon – but look at you radiant people! Splendid – splendid!" With those words, Mr. Roosevelt captured the hearts of most of the guests.

One might have expected this gentleman's gregariousness to repel Holmes, but I could see, from the upturned corners of my comrade's mouth, that he was actually amused and barely able to contain a chuckle. I suppose it was a relief to the both of us that, once the intrepid former president came upon the scene, we could extricate ourselves without giving offence. Holmes glanced at the vestibule, no doubt contemplating escape, when another, vaguely familiar, gentleman entered.

In sharp contrast to the American President, this fellow was undersized, with dark, angular, and vivid features. He was smooth-shaven, with keen blue eyes, and thick, curly black hair tossed casually on his head. He looked familiar, but I knew we had never met. As I put my finger to my temple, in an effort to tap my memory, Holmes leaned in and whispered in my ear: "If I am not mistaken, that is Harry Houdini."

That was it! His face had been plastered on poles and trolley cars across Britain, to promote his European tour.

"The handcuff man," I said.

"Indeed."

"He's the fellow who escaped from handcuffs commissioned by the *Daily Mirror*. It took him an hour, but he did it." It was all coming back to me now. "Did he actually escape, or was it just a trick, do you think, Holmes?"

"He presents himself as the scourge of fake magicians and spiritualists, Watson. I expect he has skills that many of our adversaries would prize."

Mr. Houdini stood motionless for some time in the passageway. He possessed an imperious self-assurance, and commanding presence, that belied his size. As he took a breath, a smile formed upon his face with charming effect. He looked, for all the world, as though he were about to step onto a stage – and, so he was.

With an easy confidence the curly-haired man caught our eye; but, before I could extend a welcome, the ever-present Captain intervened.

"Excuse me ladies and gentlemen, our last guest has arrived. It is my pleasure to introduce Mr. Harry Houdini."

Gasps arose from several of the women.

Roosevelt adjusted his pince-nez and beamed. "Mr. Houdini," he exclaimed, "I've been looking forward to making your acquaintance for some time."

The pleasant-faced young man watched his hand disappear within the American's substantial grip. "Mr.

Roosevelt, I wonder if you might need a little magic to finish digging that ditch in Panama?"

The sturdy American bellowed with laughter, and slapped Houdini on the shoulder. "Do you think that it is possible, sir – is there any chance that you might share your rare gift with us this evening?"

A smattering of applause arose when the captain, no doubt seeking to rescue his passenger, stepped forward.

"Mr. Houdini is a guest, sir; like you, he no doubt –"

"Actually, Captain Hoffman," Houdini interrupted, "I should like to honour Mr. Roosevelt's request. Apparently, he was not able to attend one of my performances on the continent. So then, where have you been, sir?"

"Mr. Houdini," Roosevelt answered, "can you not read my mind?"

Houdini made a modest bow. "Mr. President, if it might please you, I believe I *could* disclose your hidden thoughts."

"A challenge sir, a challenge!" Roosevelt exclaimed. "Bully!"

With this, Mr. Houdini took the captain and steward aside for a conversation.

The party partook of liberal helpings of Champagne, caviar, canapés, and conversation until Captain Hoffman stepped into the centre of the room and begged attention with a few sharp claps of his hands.

"Ladies and gentlemen, the great Houdini has agreed to favour us with a display of his clairvoyant abilities."

The room buzzed with energy, as several stewards came in to arrange the chairs into a semi-circle. We were asked to take a seat, and Harry Houdini stepped into the centre of the gathering holding a piece of paper, a pencil, an envelope, and a book. As he spoke, the stewards placed a small chalkboard and table behind him.

"Ladies and gentlemen, President Roosevelt has graciously agreed to let me delve into his inner thoughts," Houdini began, nodding to Roosevelt.

"You may, indeed. But, no state secrets!" the former president jested, drawing chuckles from the guests.

"Mr. President, I am going to offer you a single piece of paper, an envelope, and a pencil – along with a book that you may use as a writing surface. When I do so, I should ask that you write a question pertaining to some event in your life that occurred during the past year. I will then delve into your mind and reveal your question. And… I will answer it," Houdini said, holding the paper and envelope next to his temple.

Roosevelt arose from his chair, and waited for the diminutive magician to pass the items on to him. "As you say!"

"Very well, sir,' Houdini said. I shall leave the room to give you more complete privacy. When you have completed the task, please seal your writing in the envelope supplied, and hand it to one of the stewards, who will place your envelope on this small table behind me. Only then shall I be escorted back into the room."

Houdini turned and walked out of the salon.

Roosevelt put the pencil to his chin and, almost instantly, began scribbling on the paper. He folded the paper, placed it in the envelope, and then held it up to the light – I presume to assess its transparency. Satisfied, he nodded to the waiting steward, who retrieved all the objects, placed the envelope on the table, and departed.

The room buzzed with whispers, until Houdini returned and walked to the table.

"May I examine the envelope, sir?" he asked Roosevelt.

"I should prefer if you did not pick it up, sir; but short of that, you may do what you will."

A few muffled murmurs rippled through the audience.

Houdini nodded and held his hands over the envelope, and then traced the border with his index finger. He pressed his fingers to his temples and closed his eyes. In that moment, complete silence embraced the room. A full minute passed in this manner until, suddenly, Houdini's eyes popped open in a blank stare. Slowly, a faint smile appeared on his lips. He looked Theodore Roosevelt in the eyes.

"You posed a question, sir?"

"I did, yes. What was it?"

Harry Houdini turned, made his way to the blackboard and picked up a piece of chalk. He tapped the chalk three times on the board before turning sharply to face us.

"Your question is: Where did I spend last Christmas?"

Roosevelt eyes widened, and his pince-nez fell from his nose.

"Amazing, sir; you are entirely correct!"

There was general applause.

"Do you know the answer?" Roosevelt asked.

Houdini went to the blackboard. "You were in South America," he said, as he drew an outline of that continent. Then he sketched what appeared to be a river winding its way from east to west. "You explored the Amazon River basin and," drawing a bold, jagged line, "an uncharted route called the 'River of Doubt."

Roosevelt, possibly for the first time in his life, was struck speechless. He arose, walked toward Houdini, and grasped the man's hand. As he did so, the audience gave a standing ovation.

Throughout this performance, Holmes remained in fixed concentration. I leaned closer. "Astounding, Holmes! How did he do it?"

"We'll talk later."

Needless to say, the remainder of the reception centred on Mr. Houdini, who graciously accepted the many compliments and stories that came his way. Holmes and I were able to make our exit without being noticed, save by one steward, who bade us good evening.

When we returned to our cabin, Holmes began to undress.

"Do not think that you are going off to bed before you tell me how Houdini did that trick!"

"I am uncertain as to how he garnered the information about Mr. Roosevelt's itinerary, but it is nearly impossible for an ex-president of the United States of America to travel anywhere *incognito*. As to how Mr. Houdini knew the specific question, I suspect it had something to do with the book used as a writing surface. As you recall, the steward retrieved the sealed envelope, *and* the book that the question was written upon. What happened to the book, Watson?"

"I don't recall."

"Exactly. All the attention was on the envelope – not the book. I suggest that the book found its way to Houdini. A little carbon dust blown across the surface of the fine leather cover would reveal what had been written," Holmes said.

"Simple, but clever!"

"Misdirection is the key to magic, and Mr. Houdini is a master. He has my respect because he lays claim to no supernatural abilities, but rejects mysticism and occultism. I found his performance thoroughly engaging."

~

Holmes seemed determined to spend the next four days in our cabin, leaving only to take meals, and an occasional pipe in the smoking room late in the evening. He studied

Malastier's file obsessively. I was curious to know what he was gleaning from it.

"Have you learned anything useful?"

Holmes tapped the file with his index finger. "Every scrap of information may prove useful. For example, Malastier was only eight years old when his father deserted the family. Such an event often creates a fear of abandonment, and a host of compensating behaviours. It likely accounts for his reputation for pleasing others."

"He pleases others, or attempts to, in order to avoid being abandoned?"

"Precisely, Watson. He no doubt resents having to do this – and thus develops a dislike for others. These feelings could possibly become twisted into a deep-seated hatred of mankind."

"Have you been reading Freud?"

"Actually, I have. You will find his *Zur Psychopathologie des Alltagslebens* on my shelf. The work is interesting to say the least – although he pays an inordinate amount of attention to matters venereal."

"No more than many, I fear."

I picked up my overcoat and walked to the door.

"I'm going to take some air. Why not join me in a brandy before we retire?"

"A brandy?"

"Yes, my sleep has been fitful aboard ship. A brandy might settle my nerves. It did the trick in my army days."

"My sleep suffers a little, too," Holmes confided. "It's the dreams. It is unusual for me to have recurring dreams, or any dreams, for that matter. Now, I have one frequently, and it is rather haunting."

"Haunting?" I enquired.

"In this dream I am sitting alone in a parlour. I feel that someone is standing behind me. I cannot see whom –

but I sense it is Irene Adler. A hand touches my shoulder, and I awaken with a start."

"That seems quite understandable after all that has happened."

"As you say, Watson. However, my reaction is as disturbing as the dream itself." He took on a bewildered expression. "I want to believe her spirit – ghost – call it what you will – is still here."

"There are more things in heaven and earth, Holmes. Come along, let us have that brandy."

Holmes closed the portfolio, and we walked out under the star-speckled firmament.

We strolled the deck silently for some time. It was after midnight when Holmes and I went to the smoking-room. As with the rest of the *Imperator*, it was grandiose. The smoking lounge was decorated like a late-renaissance Italian Palazzo, in deep reds and golds that glowed in the muted lighting. It seemed designed to appeal to the masculine taste; and, naturally, none of the fair sex was among those present.

There was one large gathering of gentlemen around a felt-topped gaming table in the centre of the room. As Holmes prepared his pipe, I made my way to the assemblage.

Seated there was Harry Houdini, with a deck of cards in hand. He was displaying the most amazing dexterity with a variety of one-handed shuffles. Then, he began scaling the cards: shooting them into the air in a perfect stream so that they arched, took flight, and landed in a waiting hand resting on the table. The laughter and applause eventually attracted Holmes, who I found grinning at my side.

Mr. Houdini glanced up. "Mr. Holmes – Dr. Watson! So good to see you both!"

Holmes nodded. "Do not let us distract you Mr. Houdini, we are here for a brandy and a pipe, respectively."

"May I join you?" he asked.

A collective groan arose from the small audience, who sensed that the show was over. But, so as not to disappoint, Houdini said:

"One last bit of fun, if you will assist me, Dr. Watson."

Houdini shuffled the deck of cards and set them on the table in front of him. He then retrieved a small rubber band from his vest pocket and put it around the deck of cards. Spreading the deck as wide as he could with the rubber band still around it, he addressed me.

"John – may I call you John? John, please pick a card and hold it above my head so that I cannot see it, but so that everyone else may. I shall close my eyes, too."

Doing as he bade, I drew the two of hearts and shared it with the gathering as instructed.

With his eyes still closed, Houdini stretched the deck open again and asked me to insert my card anywhere I wished. I did so.

Harry's eyes flashed open as he took the banded deck in both hands, and pulled it apart into two packs. Then he twisted and flipped over one of the packs exposing a card – the ten of clubs.

"That's not your card, is it, John?" he enquired.

"No, that is *not* my card."

Houdini then twisted the two decks several times, winding a knot in the rubber-band, and separating the two halves of the deck.

He then placed the knotted deck on the table. When he removed his hand, the rubber-band untwisted, turning the top half of the cards… and out popped the two of hearts.

"Your card, is it not?"

"Yes, indeed, sir!"

An ovation erupted as Mr. Houdini got up from the table, took his coat from the back of his chair, and joined us.

"You are a marvel, sir!" I said.

"Thank you, John," Harry replied; and then, turning to Holmes, he added: "I can see the wheels turning, Mr. Holmes. Can you deduce how the trick was done?"

"With some time, perhaps. However, I enjoyed it as it was intended – as a marvelous illusion."

"I believe you are a fellow magician, Sherlock, if you'll permit first names."

"It seems to be an American custom," Holmes said, "and, as we are headed there, I am bound by custom."

Harry shared but one brandy with us, during which time I learned little about the man himself. He was "all questions."

As he departed, Holmes remarked: "The man is a sponge Watson, having a voracious appetite for information. We have that in common."

"Indeed, and he's a handy fellow with playing cards as well. I am curious, though, Holmes – why did you not tell him of our intended mission?"

"That, I believe, is a private matter. I do not wish our business, or our grief, to be shared with others."

When we returned to our cabin we found a telegram on the floor by the door. It was from Adaline Dart, responding to Holmes's earlier message revealing our travel plans. Holmes read it aloud:

MR HOLMES

I AM HEARTENED BY YOUR HEROIC EFFORTS BUT FEAR FOR YOUR SAFETY AND THAT OF DR WATSON.

I HAVE CONTACTED FRIEND OF MOTHERS ELIZABETH BRICE. SHE HAS OFFERED TO ORIENT YOU TO NYC. AT NEW AMSTERDAM THEATRE FORTY-SECOND STREET.

PLEASE LET ME KNOW WHEN YOU ARE ONCE AGAIN SAFE.

ADALINE

"Elizabeth Brice" I said. "I trust her name conjures up different associations in America than it might in Britain."

"If you're referring to Lady Bryce, as a paramour of Henry VIII, it's my opinion that she never acquiesced to Henry's advances."

"And, that left her head in place, and very little else, as you may recall," I said.

"We might pay our respects to America's Miss Brice, but we cannot tarry too long. Malastier's tracks are vanishing as we speak."

"So, let us gather ourselves together. We make port tomorrow."

"I'll be back momentarily, Watson, but I should like to take a pipe on deck, as I missed that opportunity earlier. I have been enjoying the night skies at sea – a veritable star-bath!"

It was worth noting that, not long ago, the evening sky would have been little more to Holmes than a means by which to navigate. Now he saw the beauty of it.

~

The next morning, shrill blasts from the *Imperator*'s whistle alerted us to a swift cutter racing toward us from the waterfront skyline of New York City. Our vessel shuddered as the engines were reversed to bring us to a stop. The cutter pulled alongside, and a ladder was lowered, allowing a goodly party of men to board. No doubt these were the inspectors and immigration personnel who would assist the first- and second-class cabin passengers. All other passengers would be processed at Ellis Island.

As the cutter moved off, the engines hummed, and stewards bellowed into megaphones, requesting third class and steerage passengers to prepare for disembarkation. Cheers and shouts erupted from America's newest residents.

Holmes and I gathered our papers and reported to the dining room, where we presented our passports, and declared the purpose of our visit. I followed Holmes's lead and simply stated: "academic studies and research."

After completing the immigration process, we climbed to the top deck with others, who lined the rails to watch the vast metropolis swell into view. When we docked, we waited on board for a time to watch the hundreds upon hundreds of wayfarers transfer to ferries that would take them to Ellis Island. A Babellic clamour arose as Scandinavians, Dutch, Germans, French, Italians, Swiss, and other immigrants were bustled off to take their first steps into a new land, albeit and island initially.

There was something magnificent about this process. I could not help but wonder which of the passengers would be judged worthy, and which might not. If I had been the judge, I know that I should have been favourably disposed toward anyone with the sheer courage required to leave house and home behind, and start life in a strange country.

We eventually disembarked and arranged for the transport of our luggage, and found our way to the Hotel Astor. As it turned out, it was only blocks from the New Amsterdam Theatre, which we agreed would be our first call.

After a modest lunch in a splendid roof-top restaurant that overlooked Central Park, Holmes and I strolled to the New Amsterdam. The huge arched facade was draped in banners proclaiming the opening of "The Ziegfeld Follies of 1913," and stenciled along one side was Miss Brice's name, as one of the many stars appearing.

Although it took some doing, we found our way to Miss Brice's dressing room. The doorman asked us to wait as he went ahead to announce us. We were eventually led through a gauntlet of subterranean dressing rooms. At the far end of the hallway, I spied a lady waiting by the door. She raised her hand in greeting. When I responded, she retreated inside.

Belying the dusky grey enamel hallway, Miss Brice's quarters were painted in a periwinkle blue and awash with warm light. A battered piano was pushed into the far corner. The lady was waiting, seated in a large, red leather wing-back chair that was the focal point of a ring of furniture, set upon an Oriental carpet.

Elizabeth Brice wore a white silk robe with a turned-up collar that framed her face. A huge pile of auburn hair was fastened upon her head with black lacquer clips. Her lips were painted in a bright red bow. Her figure was beginning to wax matronly, and her once pale skin had grown roseate. But, her eyes – her eyes, and enticing smile – beckoned to the young man in me.

"Mr. Holmes – Doctor Watson – I so much appreciate your visit! Please, make yourselves comfortable," the performer said, gesturing toward the chairs. "I wish the circumstances of your visit were happier."

We removed our hats, and seated ourselves on either side of her. There was a momentary silence before anyone spoke again.

"Adaline may have told you that Irene and I were the

very best of friends. I know you were as well. She would be so pleased, I believe, to know we have met."

"We are but recent friends, madam," said I. "Did you and Miss Adler perform together?"

"We played on the same bill many times, but never in the same act. As to the nature of our friendship, you might be interested to know, Mr. Holmes, that Irene, on more than one occasion, related the story of her first encounter with you. I can assure you that she carried the thought of you with her for years before you actually came back into her life."

This revelation shook Holmes. His head tilted in disbelief.

"You must forgive me, madam –" Holmes replied.

"Liz – please call me Liz. All my friends do."

Asking Holmes to call a grown woman "Liz" was akin to requesting that he wear a "boater" to the opera.

"Well – Liz – I believe I did not fully appreciate the depths of Irene's feelings until..." Holmes stopped.

"She did bring out the best in us, did she not?" I intervened, in an attempt to look after my friend.

"Ah, yes," Liz added. "She was a ray of sunshine, was she not?"

Holmes nodded in deep reflection. "And, I had lived much of my life in shadows." His eyes grew glassy, and his body stiffened.

I shall break off my account of this meeting here, as it bears but little on our adventure. Suffice it to say that Miss Brice offered her assistance, along with two tickets for the next evening's performance.

We took breakfast early, if one can call it that. There was some resemblance to breakfast on my plates, which abounded with bacon and sausage of a sort, and not one, but several, fried eggs. It was accompanied by another platter bearing two waffles and fried potatoes. Nowhere to be found were beans, mushrooms, grilled tomatoes, or pan scones. What is more, I could barely finish my coffee, before the waiter swooped in to fill my cup to the brim. This Niagara of coffee had the effect of making it impossible for me to finish this gigantic breakfast, as my bladder would not permit it. But, this was all to the good, as Sherlock Holmes was champing at the bit – and not on the breakfast!

"Watson, are you attempting a new eating record? We must be off to Cold Spring Harbor."

We took a taxi to Pennsylvania Station. From there, a train took us around Long Island Sound. During the hour-long trip, Holmes and I developed a strategy that we felt might reveal the whereabouts of Ciarán Malastier.

We presented ourselves at the Eugenics Record Office, introducing ourselves as academics seeking to learn new strategies for implementing eugenics. This approach had the desired effect. After only a brief wait, we were ushered into the office of Doctor Henry Goddard, the partner of Charles Davenport, the organization's founder.

"Gentlemen, I'm Henry Goddard. You have come a long way, and it seems as though we might share a vision for a saner world."

"Indeed," Holmes replied. "Dr. Watson and I are on a cross-country excursion, as it were, to learn more about how you, in America, are dealing with the problem of the unfit."

At this Dr. Goddard's eyes widened and became almost lidless. "Well, this is an excellent place to begin. As the name implies, we primarily collect family pedigrees. These become useful in a wide variety of ways. Indeed, you no doubt came by way of Ellis Island, from which many of our records emanate."

Goddard continued, "Most people do not realize the enormous numbers of mentally disordered and morally delinquent persons in the United States, nor to how great an extent these classes are recruited from aliens and their children. Restriction is vitally necessary, if our American ideals and institutions are to persist, and if our inherited stock of 'good American manhood' is not to be depreciated."

I assure you, it took the greatest of restraint, and conscious control of our demeanour, to gain the trust and confidence of an individual whom we later learned was not a medical doctor, but a psychologist. And, while it felt to me as though Holmes's act bordered on the farcical, it was well received.

"I could not agree more," Holmes concurred. "Society must protect itself, and claim the right to annihilate the hideous serpent of hopelessly vicious protoplasm."

We continued on in this manner for some time before Holmes broached the question we came to ask: "Dr. Goddard, one of our colleagues, a Mr. Malastier, came on ahead of us, and we are having difficulty locating his whereabouts. I have reason to believe he visited here recently – possibly a week ago. Do you recall the gentleman?"

"Yes, I do, Mr. Holmes," came the welcome reply. "I myself did not have the honour of meeting with him, but my colleague, Charles Davenport, spent the better part of a day with him."

"Is Mr. Davenport available?" I asked.

"I am sorry to say that he is in Washington – Washington D.C., I mean. Advocating for our cause is an important part of our mission. Ultimately, our government must pass laws to protect future generations from the unfit."

Holmes ignored the comments and pursued his line of questioning. "Do you have any idea as to where our colleague, Mr. Malastier, might be, or whither he was bound?"

Goddard was most obliging. "I do not know, but let me make some enquiries among the staff. I recall that several from our office lunched with Mr. Davenport and Mr. Malastier." With that, he departed the office.

A secretary came with a tray of coffee. Holmes smiled at me.

"Not at the moment, thank you," I responded.

Dr. Goddard returned shortly, rubbing his hands together. "I think that I may have good news for you. One of our staff members recalls that Mr. Malastier was planning to visit the Race Betterment Foundation in Battle Creek, Michigan."

Once again, even after all our years together, Holmes managed to astound me. Not simply for his deductive powers, but his astounding instincts. What other person would be drawn to a gap in a bookshelf, in a manner that would compel him to spend the better part of a day finding the duplicate of a missing book – a book written by Dr. John Harvey Kellogg from Battle Creek? This realization occurred within the breath that Goddard drew between sentences.

"Dr. Kellogg's Foundation is an ally of ours, although his efforts are focused in a different manner. Indeed, you may know about his famous sanitarium, which he calls the 'temple of health.'"

"Only by reputation," I said. "Is he not an advocate of vegetarianism?"

Dr. Goddard laughed, "Yes, true enough, Dr. Watson,

but there is ever so much more to his work that that! John Harvey Kellogg is a pioneer in the arena of regaining and maintaining health."

Holmes intervened, "Then you believe that Mr. Malastier was bound for Battle Creek?"

"That is what I understand. You might return in two days, when Mr. Davenport is here. He may know more."

"No, thank you, Dr. Goddard. I am certain that we shall soon hear from our colleague. I suspect it is simply a matter of a wayward telegram. You have been most hospitable. Thank you."

With that, we departed. We took the waiting carriage back to the station and caught the next train to the city.

En route, I attempted to cajole Holmes into attending the Ziegfeld Follies, but I could not devise an appeal that could overcome his resistance. It was his indifference to faddish amusements, more than Victorian sensibilities, which precluded his attendance.

"Watson, when we stop in Manhattan, I believe I shall go on by myself. I have a little business in the neighbouring state of New Jersey. I shall join you sometime late in the evening. You will have to dine without me. And, please, please enjoy the city."

"Then, you will not tell me where you are bound?"

"I am going to do what all intelligent people do when they need help. I am going to engage a detective."

I was quizzical.

"I'll tell you later, Watson, if it works out as I hope. Enjoy the evening, please – go to the Follies!" he said, handing Miss Brice's tickets to me.

Being one who takes Holmes's advice, I found myself sitting in the centre-front mezzanine enjoying Elizabeth Brice singing *Let Me Stay And Live In Dixieland*. London had nothing like the Follies in terms of the shear spectacle.

Our girls are just as pretty, mind you, but they are more completely costumed!

When I returned to our room, I saw no sign of Holmes's return, and so elected to await his arrival on the roof garden. I took a brandy, and watched the clamorous streets below that seemed so American in their frenetic energy.

Holmes arrived just before eleven and found me, still, on the roof.

"Were you successful in your venture, Holmes?"

"Indeed, I went to Parsippany, New Jersey – to the offices of the Pinkerton Detective Agency."

"You were telling me the truth, then?"

"I always do, Watson. Malastier is expecting us, as you know. We must learn if his stated intention to go to Battle Creek was a red herring. If he is there, an American detective will be the best way to verify it. I hired the Pinks to locate Malastier. We shall await a report. If he is there, we shall quickly follow. The Pinkerton office will use Miss Brice as an intermediary when we travel."

"So, you expect the Pinkerton men will find him?"

"They have more operatives in the United States than there are soldiers in this country's army. I was assured that they would dispatch an agent from Chicago this very evening. Battle Creek is but a short trip thence – and that reminds me! Will you be so kind as to arrange the transport and lodging for us? I quite approve your choice of the Astor. Magnificent, isn't it?"

We both peered out beyond the glow of the "city that never sleeps" and speculated about what might await us in the dark and distant territory to the west.

~

In the intervening time, I did a little logistical research and learned what I could about Battle Creek, Michigan.

The most expeditious route seemed to be *via* Chicago, and then doubling back, shirting Lake Michigan eastward past Kalamazoo. I learned that Kalamazoo was an Indian word meaning "boiling pot" – an apt name in view of our mission!

Holmes was pleased when, after only a day, we received word from the Pinkerton Agency. A telegram, initially delivered to Miss Brice, quickly found its way to us, as we were returning from a walk in Central Park. Holmes read it to me:

SHERLOCK HOLMES

AGENT GERARD DISPATCHED TO BATTLE CREEK CONFIRMS MALASTIER VISITED KELLOGG FOUNDATION. NOW REGISTERED AT BATTLE CREEK SANITARIUM USING ALIAS GARDNER.

PINKERTON AGENCY

"Your faith in the Pinkertons was warranted. Ciarán Malastier is in Battle Creek, Michigan," I said.

"Let us hope he has not sniffed out the Pinkerton agent. He is probably taking treatments at the sanitarium for his condition – which must be serious enough for him to the risk a stay in hospital."

"It is not technically a hospital, Holmes."

"*A rose, by any other name*, eh, Watson! The Battle Creek Sanitarium treats people who are unwell."

"Good enough, then. But, I fear Malastier may be more dangerous in this situation – cornered, as it were."

"Yes, Watson. We may well be the only people standing between him and safety. He would like to put an end to us as quickly as possible," Holmes stated.

The next morning, we departed on a westbound train for Chicago, and beyond.

The magnitude of America is difficult for me to comprehend. Our trip from New York City to Chicago took an entire day of non-stop travel. There were huge expanses of farmland. Some farms akin to Scottish crofts, others covering leagues. The large cities between were few – Toledo, I can recall, and Cleveland, Ohio.

We didn't tarry in Chicago, but transferred to the first train to Kalamazoo and Battle Creek. Again, Holmes and I used our travel time to create a game plan.

Holmes began with a central supposition:

"Malastier will be expecting us. In that regard, we have lost the element of surprise. But, his heightened state of awareness brings with it a heightened anxiety, and that will deplete his energies, and possibly impair his reason. In this small way, time is on our side."

"So, what is next do you think, Holmes?"

"We know that Malastier strikes quickly, and without hesitation. If any pursuer comes close, he will strike – he will not run."

"Right, Holmes. For that reason, let me suggest a plan. You have been face to face with the man; I have not. If he has seen me at all, it has been from a distance. So, I believe that I should go on ahead and reconnoiter. I had arranged for accommodation in Battle Creek, but I now believe we should make camp in Kalamazoo."

"Excellent, Watson! I completely concur, and I believe you are in an enviable position with regard to your *entrée* to the sanitarium. As a physician, you could be consulting on behalf of a patient, who would benefit from their treatments. However, I suggest you take on a different name. Let us see – Moreau, Frankenstein, Jekyll –"

"Really, Holmes!"

"No, let us stay with something simple – Dr. John Steward. Then, you will be responsive to your first name."

"And, who, pray tell, is my patient?"

"Let me see," Holmes said, scratching his chin. "What about a simple-minded clergyman, Watson?" He paused.

"Holmes?"

"A clergyman, I think, would serve our purpose – a nondescript fellow who would blend into the woodwork of the sanitarium. We shall baptize him Father Joel Wiggins, an Episcopal priest, on a sabbatical for reasons of health?"

"What are his symptoms, Holmes?"

"You tell me, Watson – you're the doctor! Whatever is required to gain admittance as a resident of the sanitarium. I shall wait for you in Kalamazoo." He grinned. "Has a nice ring to it, Watson. I'll wait for *you* – in Kalama*zoo*."

"You are being silly, Holmes."

"Just getting into character, for I suspect that poor, unhealthy Father Wiggins is a little eccentric."

Our train pulled into what I had expected would be a lonely and forlorn station, but to the contrary, the platform at Kalamazoo was buzzing with hundreds of people.

Kalamazoo, it turns out, is where day-patients from the sanitarium usually seek shelter. Each morning, hundreds of health-seekers trek from Portage Station, where the interurban takes them to Battle Creek for their treatments.

While I was managing our bags, Holmes located the telegraph office to wire Elizabeth Brice regarding our whereabouts. When he returned, I was swimming against a tide of people seeking transport to hotels and restaurants.

"I say, Holmes, finding accommodation may be difficult."

"Not to worry, Watson, I have already made arrangements."

"Really?"

"While at the telegraph office, I had the good fortune to meet a gentleman who was suffering from ill fortune. He had just arrived to find that his business establishment in Chicago is on fire – or rather, *was* on fire."

"How dreadful!"

"Quite; but he is heading back to the 'Paris on the prairie' and will not require his accommodation here. I offered to make the cancellation for him – or rather, take his place. So Watson, you are Mr. George Maltby in Kalamazoo, and Dr. John Steward in Battle Creek. I trust you can you keep your multiple personalities in order."

And so, we clambered aboard a trolley-bus that took us to the Chenoweth Inn, a small country estate on the edge of the city. I signed the register as George Maltby, and Holmes and I were soon ensconced in a lovely dormered room overlooking the Kalamazoo River.

The Chenoweth had a decent kitchen, as it turned out, with many vegetarian and cereal-based dishes to accommodate the Battle Creek diets, which their patrons required. I myself was hopeful that I might find a decent cheese here in the heartland of America; and, while the selection was small, I was not disappointed by a white cheddar made at a nearby Amish creamery.

There were many pamphlets from the Battle Creek Sanitarium in the foyer. Holmes and I gathered them up before we returned to our room. A quick perusal suggested that Father Joel Wiggins would be suffering from a digestive disorder, and possibly afflicted with fits of constipation.

When I gave him his diagnosis, Holmes winced. "I fear you are dooming me to some rather unholy remedies. I shall not abide any invasive procedures."

"Very well; but, from what I have garnered from these

pamphlets and lecture bills, some cures can be worse than the malady."

"I believe I am detecting amusement on your part – at my expense."

"No, Holmes, at Father Wiggins's expense."

Holmes lips turned up only momentarily.

"And, here, I had long thought that you did not share the God-like tendencies of physicians."

Holmes was always droll; but this playful demeanour was something new. However, as we sat at our breakfast table the next morning, I noticed his mood was altered.

"There seems to be something weighing on you, Holmes."

"Doubt, Watson. I pray Bram Stoker is correct when he surmised that we learn mostly from failure, and not success. You are about to beard the lion, and I am sending you into his den."

"What nonsense," I exclaimed. "I go freely of my own choice. Would that I could engage this monster gauntlet to gauntlet, but such is not to be. We fight in clandestine combat, with our wits being our weapons."

"Spoken like a true soldier. Thank you, Watson. While you are away, I shall avail myself of the local library, pharmacy, and clothing shops. Please, please do not attempt to locate Malastier today. Ingratiate yourself with the doctors and staff. As the American idiom goes, get the 'lay of the land."

The local train carried me to a station adjacent to the Battle Creek Sanitarium. A sprawling six-storey limestone and brick edifice was strung out along the main thoroughfare. Sprouting out behind it, like spokes on a wheel, were three additional multi-storey buildings. The entry stood at the hub of this half-wheel, and rose in long vertical columns of a classical style.

Upon entering, I was greeted by a stoop-shouldered woman sitting behind a large circular desk in the centre of a marble gallery. The lobby of the Battle Creek Sanitarium was more akin to a cathedral than a hospital.

I introduced myself, was given a map, and asked to wait. Indeed, a map was necessary, as there were more than seventy offices, thirty diagnostic centres, two hundred treatment rooms and venues, four hundred guest-rooms, outdoor recreational sites, a creamery, and a vegetable garden. A massive food preparation facility sat atop the building – put there so that the smells, which rise, would not disturb the residents. It was the perfect melding of home, hospital and spa.

Within minutes, Dr. Thaddeus Macy, who was one of thirty physicians on staff greeted me. Dr. Macy was reserved, but congenial. He was also exceptionally short of stature, and seemed to compensate for this by wearing highly pomaded hair in a bulbous pompadour. With an outstretched hand, he approached. "Dr. Steward, I am so pleased to meet you. Your first visit – am I correct?"

"Indeed, you are, Doctor," I replied. "I hail from London, and have only recently taken up residence in Chicago. Your institution is well known, and I am currently treating a patient who may, I feel, benefit from your treatments."

The Battle Creek doctor craned his neck in a bird-like fashion, searching for my patient.

"No, no, Dr. Macy, he is not here. I thought it best to come on ahead to consult with you. You see my patient is a rather anxious fellow."

"Well, then – do you have time for a tour?"

"Certainly," I replied.

"Let us start at the beginning, then. The heart and soul of the Battle Creek Sanitarium is our assessment centre."

With that, I was on a whirling merry-go-round.

We visited the facility where patients spent as many as three days being poked, prodded, and probed. Every major organ, and system in their body, was tested – heart, lungs, liver, kidneys, stomach, brain, nerves – and especially intestines.

"Doctor Steward," Macy exclaimed, "the meaty diet of Americans is at the heart of many ailments. Meat putrefies in our intestines and discharges toxins that damage our organs."

I saw my chance to introduce Father Wiggins. "Dr. Macy, I am convinced that my patient, Father Joel Wiggins, will find what he needs here. Father Wiggins suffers from the most terrible range of digestive disorders and constipation, that I have ever encountered."

This news delighted Dr. Macy. For him, fecal matter was what *was* the matter. I could barely contain my mounting anticipation of the time when I might engage Holmes in a conversation about his bowel-movements.

The tour went on for several more hours, in which I was introduced to a vast multitude of therapies: hydrotherapy, phototherapy, thermotherapy, electrotherapy, &c. The underlying premise was that man is a product of nature, and that only the elemental forces of nature can restore his health. I must admit that, by the time the tour concluded, I was nearly a convert.

I was particularly taken with the attention paid to food, what the centre called the "bill of fare." Each guest, or patient, had his or her own "coefficient card" that detailed his or her unique diet. Chicken, lamb, beef and pork were on no one's menu.

As Dr. Macy concluded, he invited me to attend an afternoon lecture on "Biologic Living." I declined, saying that I had to return to Kalamazoo to meet my patient on his arrival. As I took my leave, I asked: "Do you think it is possible that you may be able to accommodate Father Wiggins as a resident?"

Dr. Macy took me in tow to the registration office that adjoined the gallery. He scanned the guest registry inscribed on blackboards that covered the walls of the room. Then, he conferred with a staff member sitting at a corner desk. The outcome was good.

"Dr. Steward, I am pleased to say that we shall be able to accommodate Father Wiggins, two days hence. In the meantime, he can call in daily to begin his assessment."

I studied the blackboard registry.

"Since all your patients are listed on these boards, shall I be able to know where my patient might be residing, who his supervising physician may be, and so on?"

"Yes, Doctor; but some of our patients do not use their real names. Father Wiggins, for example, may not wish any of his flock to know that he is taking treatments here."

"I see."

If the Pinkerton report were correct, Mr. Gardner's name should be found on this wall. I could not immediately find it; and, not wishing to call undue attention to myself, I made a mental note to investigate further tomorrow.

I returned to the Chenoweth Inn in time for supper. I entered our room to find a figure primping before the dresser mirror. There stood a stoop-shouldered gentleman sporting a broad-brimmed hat, baggy trousers, and threadbare cravat. As he turned, Holmes set a pair of wire-framed glasses on his nose and assumed a dim-witted smirk.

"Father Joel Wiggins. So pleased to meet you," he said, trying on a new, high-pitched voice. "I say, is it not a shame the condition people's souls are in? I mean s-o-u-l-s *and* s-o-l-e-s!"

"Perfection, Holmes," I retorted. "The theatre lost a great actor when you became a detective."

"Hardly, Watson. I fear I lack the necessary narcissistic traits."

"I think you are selling yourself short, Holmes."

"A-ha, Watson – you're a scoundrel!"

"Seriously, Holmes, well done! You will be pleased to learn that Father Wiggins will soon be glowing in renewed health."

I went on to describe my successful visit to the Battle Creek Sanitarium and confirmed my initial diagnosis for Father Wiggins: severe digestive disorder.

"I can tell this diagnosis pleases you – too much, it appears."

I then went on to describe the registration area and tomorrow's plan to confirm that Malastier, alias Gardner, was in residence.

"Keep in mind, that he has most likely done away with his moustache," Holmes noted. "However, his limp will be more difficult to conceal. Be watchful."

"What if he has fled?"

"It's possible, Watson, but doubtful. He wants us as badly as we want him. It comes down to whose trap is sprung first."

~

Holmes ate a hearty breakfast, knowing full well it might be among the last good meals he would have for some time. I had told him about the coefficient cards and the "bill of fare" which, for him, would not include meat or dairy of any kind.

I delivered Father Joel Wiggins to the waiting Dr. Macy as promised. Holmes became a living caricature of an affable, but dim-witted, priest. He acquired a shoulder tic in which his right shoulder twitched, and his chin moved in small sharp jolts, as he talked. His voice was elevated almost an octave and he spoke with a sibilant "S" and "C", that had had him pronounce Dr. Macy's name as Mathy.

As Holmes was escorted to the diagnostic centre, he turned to me with the look of a lost child. I wondered how much of that was acting.

I used my free time to explore the Battle Creek Sanitarium. A stethoscope wrapped about my neck became my pass to most anywhere I wished to go. Of course, I kept a wary eye open for Malastier, all the while.

I retrieved Holmes – Father Wiggins now – at the conclusion of the day, and was able to sit in on the consultation in Dr. Macy's office.

The doctor addressed Wiggins directly. "Father, our tests are not complete as of yet, but it will not surprise you to learn that your digestive processes are suffering and, as a consequence, *you* are suffering. You will receive your coefficient card at the conclusion of our diagnosis, but I can tell you now that your bill of fare, your recommended diet, will contain no animal protein whatsoever, and you must desist from smoking *immediately*."

Father Wiggins looked aghast. "Shmoking. Doctor Mathy?"

"There is no denying it, Father, your right thumb betrays you. You have a nasty habit of packing your pipe with your thumb – do you not?"

I could not resist. "An amazing *deduction*, isn't it, Father Wiggins? Why, Dr. Macy, you should have been a detective."

The next day we were told that the sanitarium would have an opening sooner than expected, and Father Wiggins would be able to take up residence later that afternoon. While Holmes continued his diagnostic process, I found my way to the registration office.

When the registrar engaged me in conversation, she naturally noticed my accent and remarked that the centre was hosting several of my fellow-countrymen. I saw my opening.

"So, some of my countrymen are guests here?"

"We have at least four others."

"That will be jolly good company for my patient. Might I know their names?" I said, with a wink.

"Oh, sir, we cannot share that information. I'm sorry."

"Of course," I said, as I scanned the names on the blackboard surrounding me. Suddenly, there it was: Gardner – *Mr. Patrick Gardner, room 433*. I turned to the registrar.

"Do you know, as yet, which room my patient, Father Wiggins, is to be assigned this afternoon?"

The lady thumbed through a ledger before her. "Yes, Dr. Steward. Father Wiggins will be in room 417."

Holmes will be deeper into the lion's den than he may wish.

I shared this development with Holmes as I settled him into his new accommodation, in the mid-afternoon. Given his proximity to Malastier's room, I asked that Father Wiggins's evening meal be taken to his room, and I returned to our lodgings in Kalamazoo.

Upon my arrival at the inn, I was given a telegram that had been relayed by Miss Brice.

HOLMES

PINKERTON AGENT GERARD MISSING TWO DAYS NOW. POSSIBLE FOUL PLAY. BE WARNED.

PLEASE ADVISE.

PINKERTON–CHICAGO

This was an alarming turn. It was a restless night for me, knowing that Holmes, even well disguised, was so close to Malastier, whom I now suspected of having the blood of the Pinkerton agent on his hands.

I dashed off a reply to the Pinkerton Agency in Chicago, whence the last message came, giving them the Chenoweth address, and noting that Holmes was in Battle Creek on Malastier's trail.

I caught the very first trolley to the sanitarium in the morning. Before I could make my way to the fourth floor to visit Father Wiggins, Dr. Macy intercepted me in the lobby.

"Doctor Steward, please," Macy called. "Please! Your patient refuses to leave his room either for treatments, or meals. I wish you would talk with him."

"I suspected something like this might happen, Dr. Macy. I am on my way up to his suite this very minute."

"He is in 417. I should like to accompany you, if I might," the doctor declared, in a matter-of-fact manner.

"Oh, doctor, please," I said, with one hand held out in delicate restraint. "I have treated Father Joel for some time. His digestive issues are exacerbated by a heightened state of anxiety. He has many phobias. I assure you that he simply requires a little time with someone whom he knows and trusts."

"Of course, Dr. Steward. Please, stop by to see me after you have visited your patient."

I made my way to the fourth floor, and cautiously walked to room 417, glancing into each room and hall along the way, fearing that I might see Malastier's angular face.

When I reached Holmes's room, I noticed several staff members were observing me from a distance.

"Father Wiggins," I said, with a gentle knock. "It is I, Dr. Steward." I heard the lock turn and the door crack open. A lone eye peered at me.

"Are you alone, Dr. Thteward?" came the sibilant reply from Father Wiggins.

"Yes, Father."

The door swung just wide enough for me to step inside. It then banged shut, and was quickly locked.

"Watson, I apologize for calling such attention to myself. It was the last thing I wished to do. But, two unexpected things have occurred, and I am not sure which is worse."

"Go on, Holmes."

"As you know, Malastier is down the hall in room 433. He was prowling the hallway late yesterday afternoon, and I was taken by surprise when I found him peering into my room just as my evening meal was being delivered. As I suspected, his mustache was gone – but it was he, to be sure. We nodded and exchanged smiles. I was fully costumed, but he may have seen though my disguise. He walked on, but –"

"Yes, yes, I see. And, I have something equally ominous to report." I went on to inform Holmes about the missing Pinkerton detective.

"What was the other matter that caused you to barricade yourself within, Holmes?"

"How do I say this, Watson? Well, in their words – they want to give me a – a 'G.I. cleanse!"

"You mean an enema?"

"Not just an enema – a *yoghourt enema*! I need you to change my treatment plan – today! And, secure another room for me, on a different floor. This move will only momentarily impede any of Malastier's efforts, but it may give us the time we need."

I immediately went to Dr. Macy's office to explain that Father Wiggins's anxiety did not allow for him to be on an upper floor, and that he needed to reside on a lower level. I also suggested that we should hold off on yoghourt enemas for the time being, and have Father Wiggins take his meals in his room, for a day or two.

I returned to the fourth floor and enquired of one of the staff, as to Mr. Gardner's whereabouts. I was informed that he was currently taking a gas-vapour treatment. I reported all of this to Holmes, whose mid-day meal had just arrived.

The meal, sitting on a nearby tray, was untouched. I could not resist a look. There was a co-efficient card on the tray that described the dinner in detail.

"Holmes, you must be famished. Here you have a lovely peanut cutlet, made entirely of raw ground peanuts and flax seed, a glass of soy milk and, what is this strange thing – a banana?"

"Give me the banana. You will, of course, provide me with something more edible later today?" Holmes peeled the fruit and devoured it as we talked.

"Watson, you must quickly ascertain Malastier's complete treatment schedule. He is most vulnerable during his treatments. With this information, we can strike."

"Obtaining his schedule will be a simple matter. I already know that he takes a vapour treatment this time of day."

"Wonderful. After you have done this, return to the Chenoweth to retrieve an item in my valise that is wrapped in brown paper and twine. And, bring any further word from the Pinkerton Agency."

"Very well, Holmes. I think it would be wise for me to stay nearby this evening, don't you?"

"Yes, I want you to come back, not only for protection, but to bring some edible food – peanut cutlets, indeed!"

After checking the hallway, I exited Father Wiggins's room, as a staff member was arriving to escort Holmes to his daily intake of fresh air. His revised treatment schedule now consisted solely of fresh air and physical culture.

As I surmised, it was a simple matter to learn Malastier's treatment schedule. I supplemented my stethoscope with a white coat which I found hanging in one of the treatment rooms. I knew that the registrar's office held the complete charts – diagnosis, treatments and diet for everyone at the sanitarium.

As I approached, the registrar greeted me. "Good afternoon, Doctor. May I help you?"

"Good afternoon. Yes, I need to see Mr. Gardner's portfolio – room 433, if I am not mistaken."

The filing system was excellent. Gardner's folder was in my hands in less than a minute. I retreated to peruse the file. The first section contained the diagnosis. I fully expected to discover a cardiovascular issue, but there, on the first page, was that terrifying six-letter word – cancer. Malastier had lung cancer. It was in the later stages. Most doctors in possession of these same medical facts would have entered "terminal" in the prognosis. However, this was the Battle Creek Sanitarium, where medical miracles were promised – even remission from cancer.

I went on to make notes regarding Malastier's treatment schedule. As I closed the portfolio and returned it, I wondered if, and how, this development might change our strategy. I was eager to report to Holmes, but felt this information could wait until I could return with his victuals. I left for Kalamazoo.

Returning to the Chenoweth Inn, I immediately went to the clerk to ask if there were any messages for Holmes.

The clerk shook his head. "However, sir, there is a gentleman waiting for him in the parlour. He has just arrived."

I asked the clerk to prepare a picnic hamper for Holmes and me, and went to greet the visitor.

There was only one gentleman in the lobby area. A hefty fellow, with the physiognomy of a pugilist, was seated in a skirted armchair in the corner. His disheveled tweed suit was stretched at the seams, and looked out of place on him.

As I approached, he stood up and nodded. "Mr. Holmes?"

"No, sir: his associate, Dr. John Watson."

He took my hand in a vice-like grip, held it, shook it once, and said: "Mike Swanson – Pinkerton Agency. Where can we talk?"

His hair had been tossed about, evidently in the course of his travels, which prompted me to make some enquiries.

"You are from the Chicago office, then?"

"Yes," was his sparse reply.

"The other agent?"

"Best wait 'til we're alone."

He grabbed his bowler and followed me to my room. When we got there, I pulled up two chairs and we sat down.

"The other agent, Mr. Swanson – any news?"

There was a long pause as he fingered the brim of the hat sitting in his lap.

"Killed – dead."

His bluntness added harshness to this revelation. This was Agent Swanson's manner: sharp, brief, and to the point.

I remained silent, partly in shock, and also because Holmes had, long ago, taught me the power of silence.

The Pinkerton agent went on: "His body was found on the river bank near Battle Creek. Strangled." There was a faraway look in his eyes as he spoke.

"You knew him, then?"

"Yes."

"I suspect it was Malastier. He's a killer," I said.

"He will pay, then."

"Yes, indeed. Holmes and I intend to bring him to justice. We have a plan to capture him. You could be most helpful in arranging for transport back to London."

"To London, you say. What of his crime here?"

I hadn't had time to consider that complication, so I demurred. "He will pay for all his crimes."

I then told the agent what we had learned – all except Malastier's fatal diagnosis. I thought it best to simply note he was ill. I told him I was planning to return to the sanitarium in a while.

"I'll be going with you, then," Agent Swanson stated.

"Well, I'm not sure that's necessary, but –"

He pointed his finger at me. "I *need* to go with you." His tone was on the edge of menacing.

"Very well. I have to gather a few things and pick up supper for Holmes. Have you eaten?"

"Time enough for that. I'll wait downstairs for you."

The man rose and walked out of the room. My instinct told me this fellow was trouble.

I found the package Holmes asked me to retrieve from his valise. It was a curious thing that I had never noticed the wrapped package before – some kind of clothing or fabric. *I'll know soon enough,* I thought.

The agent was waiting for me at the desk when I came downstairs. The clerk had placed a picnic hamper on the front desk for me.

"The next interurban doesn't come for another two hours," the agent said. "I have a carriage."

When we got to Battle Creek, we hitched the carriage and made our way to Holmes's new room. He was waiting, and initially surprised to see the new addition to our team.

"Holmes, this is Agent Swanson. He was waiting for me at the inn." Holmes looked wary. "He insisted upon coming, and hired a carriage for us."

Suddenly Holmes's countenance shifted. "Agent Swanson – you are here because of the missing –"

"Dead agent," the Pink interjected.

"Holmes, the previous agent was found strangled – by the river… near here."

"I am so sorry!" Holmes said to the agent. "Do you have any identification, sir?"

The agent pulled a silver badge fastened to a leather wallet. "Will this do?"

"Thank you," Holmes replied. "Please, have a seat. Dr. Watson and I are in an excellent position to take Mr. Malastier into custody."

The agent sat down. I opened the dinner basket and began to remove the victuals. Holmes waved off the meal, and gestured for me to join them.

The bulky agent crossed his legs. "I'd give him a wide berth if I was you," he warned.

Holmes leaned back in his chair, as if to gain a broader perspective on our guest. "You are from the Chicago office, I take it."

"Yep," the detective replied. "I set my course to Kalamazoo and got here a couple of hours ago."

"Indeed," Holmes replied. "You look a little worse for the trip. Have you had anything to eat on the train?"

"No. The food aboard trains is poor. Rest is what I need. I'm pooped."

"We shall appreciate your help, sir, but let us remember

that you are in our employ," Holmes began. "And, we feel that we have the situation in hand."

There was no reply from the agent.

The atmosphere was distinctly uncomfortable.

"Holmes, I explained to Agent Swanson that he might be most helpful in assisting in Malastier's return, once he is in custody."

"I think you may be underestimating Malastier – and me," the agent responded. "What's the plan, then?"

"I suggest that we talk tomorrow, after a good night's sleep," Holmes replied. Did you get a room in Kalamazoo, Mr. Swanson?"

"I wasn't planning on staying, but now – I suppose I shall," the Pinkerton replied. He pulled out his pocket-watch and popped open the cover. He leaned into the lamp next to Holmes to see. "Yes,... late, it's been a long day. I'll come along side tomorrow." Then, he turned to me, "Need a ride back to the inn Doctor?"

"No, thank you," I balked. "I'm having a spot of supper with my friend."

The man nodded and left without another word. When the door clicked, we both listened for his footsteps to fade.

"There is something worrying about that fellow," I said.

"Yes, he is not all that he claims," Holmes observed.

"But, his identification?"

"Oh, I believe him to be a Pinkerton. I simply do not believe that he is telling us everything. Indeed, Swanson may not be his name. Did you notice his watch?"

"No."

"You may not have been able to see, but his watch cover was engraved with the initials S. G."

"Why would he lie about his name? And, even so, the watch could be a family piece."

"Possibly. And, did you notice his shoes, Watson? They were damp. They have been recently wet, yet there is no rain about." Then, after a pause, "And, he said that he had arrived two hours ago. The trains from Chicago, as you may recall, arrive but twice daily – one at 8.12 in the morning, and the other at 12.32.

"He took a carriage, then."

"But, why lie? – and there is but a little dust on his clothing. Then, there is his speech: his vernacular seems out of place."

"The Americans have their own language, Holmes."

Holmes paused and shifted himself in his chair. "But, I digress. Tell me what you have learned about Malastier's treatment schedule as we have our supper."

I handed Holmes the picnic hamper and retrieved my notebook.

"I know why Malastier is here. He has terminal lung cancer."

Holmes's eyes widened. "Poetic justice, is it not? Malastier finds himself fighting a disease that will literally take his breath away. The lung cancer could be the result of his experimentation with gases. Mycroft's file shows that Malastier was personally involved in the research and development process and, at one point, was overcome by an experimental gas."

"Does this suggest a different stratagem, Holmes? He is obviously grasping at straws."

"And, what are these straws, Watson? What have you learned about Malastier's treatments?"

"He is receiving thermotherapy and phototherapy, but I believe it is his gas-vapour treatment that offers the best opportunity for us. He is alone in a booth for that, with only a single attendant present."

Holmes retrieved his pipe from his pocket and began filling it from a small leather pouch. "Gas-vapour treatment. How interesting! What can you tell me about it?"

"Dr. Macy explained the rather fantastic rationale for the carbon dioxide therapy that Malastier takes every day. As you know, Holmes, our bodies expel carbon dioxide when we exhale. The theory is, that if one breathes in a minor concentration of carbon dioxide, the body, attempting to expel it, increases the blood circulation to drive the unwanted gas out. In Malastier's case, his lungs will receive increased blood circulation and, theoretically, greater healing power."

"You said, 'a minor concentration of carbon dioxide,' Watson?"

"Less than ten percent, I should guess. Any more, and the patient might loose consciousness – and could die if the concentration were too high. Increased carbon dioxide creates a condition called hypercapnia, where the blood becomes acidic. At higher levels, carbon dioxide leads to a malfunctioning of the heart – including arrhythmia, and possibly a heart attack."

Holmes pointed his finger emphatically. "That's it, then! We have but to increase the concentration of carbon dioxide in Malastier's vapour therapy."

"It's an imperfect science. The line between loss of consciousness and death is a thin one. There are risks here."

Holmes was silent.

"We don't wish to kill him, Holmes,"

My friend turned away and walked to the window, cracked it open, and lit his pipe.

"I want us to be clear, Holmes. We promised Mycroft that we should do all in our power to bring Ciarán Malastier to London, and to justice."

Holmes swivelled and glared at me. His face was

incensed. "Justice, you say. Hanging – a short snap of the neck, after what he did to Irene and hundreds of other men, women and children?"

"We're both committed to a society where people's actions are not driven by wrath and whim, but rather reason and intellect."

"And, what about *heart*, Watson? Shouldn't justice come from the heart? After all, it is the heart that suffers the pain of a crime."

"Holmes, we have often danced on the line that separates the law from justice. I am not speaking of legalities here. It may not matter if Malastier dies on a gallows in Wandsworth, or a vapour booth in Battle Creek. I am thinking about you – what taking his life, in cold-blood, would do – to you."

He seemed numb to my words. He looked into my eyes and slumped into a chair.

"I recall what you said a while back," Holmes muttered, at last... "about acknowledging the dark seed inside us – and how that acknowledgement is what keeps that awful seed from sprouting and growing."

I nodded.

"So, Holmes – I shall learn all that I can about Malastier's gas-vapour treatment. In the meanwhile, you continue your own routine. A little physical culture will do you good."

Apparently recovered, he said, in more normal tones: "You might find a staff uniform in a size to fit me; and enquire of some of the locals concerning the nearest boat dock on Lake Michigan."

I spent a fitful night sleeping in the chair in Holmes's room. In the morning, I unknotted myself and prepared to meet the day.

Holmes had already risen and was stepping into the character of Father Wiggins in preparation for the attendant, who would escort him to his physical culture treatment.

"I think I shall take some breakfast," I said, "and make those enquiries you suggested regarding local docks. I shall join you in the gymnasium a little later. Malastier's vapour treatment is in the early afternoon. I shall want to reconnoiter before then."

Just then, the attendant came to the door, and Father Wiggins toddled off.

The sanitarium's dry cereal made a tolerable breakfast, but the surrogate coffee was akin to warm dishwater. I sat at a table with other staff members and made my enquiries. Afterwards, I donned my white jacket and headed for the hydrotherapy centre on the first floor. Passing the gymnasium, I decided to look in on Holmes.

"Father Wiggins – you are coming into full bloom," I remarked, as I approached.

Sweat dripped from Holmes's nose and chin. He spoke in sibilant huffs from atop a gyrating machine: "Doctor – tho good to thee – you. Yeth – yeth thith mechanical thtallion is ekthilarating – ekthilarating." And, as the attendant moved off, Holmes leaned in closer. "You will notice, Watson, that this electric pony does not have a head – more than symbolic of the overwhelming lack of horse-sense in this place."

The attendant returned with chart in hand. "Father Wiggins, it is time for your daily walk."

I waved my good-byes to Wiggins and continued on to the vapour therapy room. I found the therapist cleaning the booth in preparation for a treatment.

"Hello, there. I'm Dr. Steward, on orientation. It appears that I've missed the gas-vapour therapy session."

"Albert," the stout, uniformed youth replied, smiling and holding out a hand. "Al, actually. There's another session, in a while."

"Do you have a moment to explain the apparatus?"

"Yes, it's really quite simple. You can see that this booth is just large enough to seat the guest being treated. And there's a little window here, by the equipment, where I can keep an eye on the patient during their treatment."

"How does it all work, then?"

"The equipment does most of the work. I connect the gas canister to the vaporizer, adjust the volume here – usually five to ten percent, and turn it on. The warm water-vapour is already connected, you see. After that, I simply monitor the guest through the small window to ensure that they are comfortable. Some guests can be overcome, depending on their condition."

"Amazing. And, how long do these treatments last?"

"It varies, doctor: guests begin with ten-minute treatments and work their way up to thirty minutes."

"I should like to talk with a patient – a guest, I mean. I'm curious as to how they experience these treatments."

"It's not uncomfortable – a little strange perhaps – a tingling in the nose and such. Sometimes, lightheadedness."

"Thank you, I look forward to learning more. You said you had another session soon?

The callow young man walked to a schedule tacked on the wall. "Yes, I have a guest coming at one o'clock. One o'clock every day – Mr. Gardner."

"Thank you."

A little later, I found my way to the staff dressing rooms and found a set of whites for Holmes. I wrapped them in a piece of newspaper and took the package to Holmes's room, straight away.

When I entered Father Wiggins's room, the Pinkerton agent was waiting. "Getting the 'lay of the land,' Doctor?"

"Yes. Our plan is in place. We shall take Malastier tomorrow afternoon during a treatment," I answered.

Agent Swanson, or whoever he was, seemed pleased. Father Wiggins returned at that moment, surprising the Pinkerton agent with his disguise.

"You had me there, Mr. Holmes. I thought I was still groggy from my trip. Very sharp, indeed!"

Holmes untied his cravat and removed his shirt that had become soiled from his exercises. He went on to detail tomorrow's plan.

My task was to ensure that Dr. Macy was engaged and distracted during Malastier's one o'clock vapour treatment. Holmes, dressed as a staff member, would bring a false message to the attendant requesting that he go to Macy's office and wait. This would allow Holmes to administer the treatment and render Malastier unconscious. While the attendant was waiting in Macy's office, the agent and I should have the time needed to remove Malastier from the building.

On the way out, Holmes was to visit Malastier's room, to remove his belongings and leave a note. It must appear as though Mr. Gardner had decided to leave the sanitarium of his own accord. This would prevent any immediate alarm from being raised and give us time to escape.

"A good plan, Mr. Holmes," the detective agreed. "I suggest we use the back door, on the lee side of the building."

"Very good," Holmes said. "You have found lodgings, I take it?"

The agent nodded, "Aye, in Kalamazoo."

"Very good," Holmes cajoled. "It may be best if we take Malastier to your room, while we await the morning train. Also, it may be helpful to have some rope and several thick blankets at the ready tomorrow. Can I rely upon you to obtain those?"

The husky man nodded. "Are you going back to the inn, Doctor?"

"No, I think it best that I stay close by. I'll look for you about noon tomorrow," I replied. "It might be best if you were to wait outside the building – in back. I'll find you."

After the Pinkerton agent departed, Holmes shook his head. "Watson, please make sure that he is going to Kalamazoo, then return."

Upon my return, Holmes was pacing the room. "Were you able to learn anything about local docks?"

"The closest is in St. Joseph, about eighty miles."

"Yes, thank you," Holmes nodded.

We went over our plan again, in more detail. I should present myself in the gas-vapour therapy room just *after* Malastier arrives. Once Malastier is in the booth, Holmes would arrive to deliver the note requesting that the attendant, Al, see Dr. Macy. That would put Malastier in our hands.

"Where do the docks fit into this?" I asked.

"I need a bit more time to answer your question. Let me have until morning to finalize our arrangements."

Holmes gave me the bed that afforded a better night's rest. When I woke, Holmes, once again, disguised as Father Wiggins, was already off for his morning treatments. There was a note on his dresser saying that he would return at noon. I was to wait for the Pinkerton agent and confirm that he would wait outside the building for us, and learn where the agent's carriage had been hitched.

I waited in Holmes's room. As the time approached, I grew uneasy. It seemed as though this was all too easy.

Malastier did not seem to be in the hunt. *What if he were waiting for us?*

Holmes returned promptly at noon. Shedding Father Wiggins, he dressed in the white staff uniform I had obtained for him.

"I'm certain, now, that I know what the agent is up to," Holmes explained. "He is, or was, a sailor. Do you recall his nautical vernacular – 'come along side,' pooped,' 'lee side of the building."

"What does that tell us?"

"Remember, he lied about coming by train – and then there's his soggy shoes. We have a gentleman who came by water from Chicago, and didn't want us to know that."

"To what end?"

"He obviously intends to return that way – without us," Holmes said, with raised brows.

"Do you mean that he intends to abscond with Malastier?"

"Yes. He most likely used a false name. The agent killed may be a friend or relative of his. The Pinkerton Agency runs in families. It's highly inbred; and it has a reputation for taking care of its own. 'Kill a Pink, and you're red and dead,' that's how the saying goes."

"What do we do, Holmes?"

"A slight variation in plans, Watson. You will confirm that the agent waits outside the rear entrance. Then, just before one o'clock, you will find Dr. Macy and report a suspicious man lurking outside the facility. You will say that you saw him prowling inside the building, and you suspect he is up to no good. This will serve to keep Macy out of his office during Malastier's treatment, *and* distract the Pinkerton agent during our escape."

"What about transport?"

"The Pinkerton agent will not be needing his carriage, but you may have to move it to the front of the building.

"Then this is it, Holmes."

"Timing is crucial. You must check to ensure that our detective friend is in place, by the *rear* door, before you report him to Dr. Macy."

At 12.50, I confirmed that the agent was waiting, and asked him to stay close by. I then went on to raise the alarm with Dr. Macy, who called security personnel. In the hubbub, I made my way to the hydrotherapy centre.

I met Holmes just outside the gas-vapour treatment room. He was pushing a wheel-chair. His small brown-paper package was resting on the seat. He stationed the chair outside the treatment room, and motioned for us to retreat toward the window at the far end of the hallway.

We saw Malastier's reflection in the glass, as he made his way to the treatment room. As Holmes noted earlier, his moustache was absent and his hair was short-cropped now, but his telltale limp was there. We waited for a while after he entered the treatment room. Then, Holmes motioned for me to go on ahead. I entered as the attendant helped Malastier into the booth.

"Good afternoon, Albert," I said with a wave of the hand. "I'm running a little behind my time."

"Good-day, Dr. Steward. I'm just beginning the treatment."

As I approached, the attendant turned on the water-atomizer. "You see, this machine here creates a fine vapour. Look through this little window here and you can see the mist."

I took a quick glance at Malastier, sitting in profile, in the chamber.

"When the guest is comfortable I open the valve on this carbon-dioxide canister, and mix the gas with the water-vapour."

Al pointed to the valve. "You can see the concentration on this gauge. Ten percent is what we are looking for today – that's what Mr. Gardner here receives for fifteen minutes. If the guest gets tipsy, we reduce, or shut off the gas. That's all there is to it."

"Yes, simple, isn't it?"

When Al turned away, I waved Holmes into the room.

Holmes came with note in hand, carrying his package alongside. Al glanced at the note with some alarm, and then squinted at Holmes. "Thanks – I have to go. You're new here aren't you?"

Holmes nodded.

"I've got this guest over here just beginning his treatment. Can you handle it?"

In his best American accent, Holmes replied: "I sure can."

I piped up immediately, "I'll be here as well, Albert. Not to worry."

Al looked nervous. "O.K., then, but no more than fifteen minutes – ten percent."

As Al departed, Holmes approached the equipment adjacent to the gas-vapour booth and opened the valve on the canister of carbon dioxide until the gauge read ten. He stared at the gauge for some time. He then eased the valve open until it reached fifteen.

"That's enough Holmes," I whispered. "Any more might be fatal."

Holmes kept his hand on the valve – rigid – silent. I craned my head to see Malastier through the window, and noted the time on my watch.

After a few minutes, I could see Malastier began to bob and weave, as his eyes blinked rapidly.

"He's starting to go under, Holmes."

I heard paper rustle as Holmes unwrapped his package

and removed a ghastly object – the gas-helmet that had been placed on Miss Adler's head the evening she died in Undertown.

"He's beginning to lose consciousness," I reported.

Malastier shook his head and glanced at me through the window.

Holmes placed the helmet on his head and stepped before the window. Malastier turned and smiled. *He smiled.* I couldn't believe it. It was then I noticed the gauge on the canister. It read twenty percent.

Ciarán Malastier's face tightened, and his mouth hung open. He slumped over in his chair.

"Holmes, no! Please!"

I began to turn off the gas, but Holmes pushed me away and tightly grasped the valve-handle.

Then suddenly, his body relaxed – and he turned the gas down… and off.

"Holmes, hurry; we don't have much time."

He took off the gas-helmet and retrieved the wheelchair. We dragged the unconscious Malastier out of the booth and propped him up in the chair. We draped a towel over his head as a shroud, and tucked the gas helmet away.

"He won't stay unconscious long, Watson. Hurry; wheel him down to the front entrance, and I shall pack up his belongings. I have prepared a note explaining Mr. Gardner's departure. Quickly now!"

I hurried, but not so much as to raise the alarm. I made my way to the lobby. Holmes was close behind with Malastier's luggage. I left Malastier with Holmes in the lobby and retrieved the Pinkerton agent's carriage, imagining that the agent was still in a heated debate with Dr. Macy and several over-sized staff members.

It took little time to bring Malastier to the carriage.

The rope and blankets, that the agent had purchased, were waiting; but we drove some distance before we used them to bind up Ciarán Malastier, and wrap him in a blanket for the long carriage ride to Chicago.

Malastier regained consciousness well before we reached Chicago. When he fully regained his faculties he didn't speak at all, until Holmes addressed him:

"Glad to be alive, Malastier? *Surprised* might be a better word."

"What's all that about, Holmes?"

My friend swung back around in his seat and reached into Malastier's belongings. "When I gathered up his things, Watson, I found a letter on the table next to his bed. Let me read it to you:"

> *Mr. Holmes,*
> *If you are reading this, I am dead - murdered by you. You have done me a courtesy by giving me a painless death.*
>
> *You have taken it upon yourself to rid the world of a human being you judge to be unfit. My point is made.*
>
> *You are no better than I. Possibly worse because you claim to be a better man.*
>
> *Ciaran Malastier*

"He wanted us to kill him," I said, in amazement. "He expected it." I turned to my friend. "But, he was wrong. You *are* a better man."

Holmes shrugged his shoulders. "The strange thing is that, in a manner of speaking, it was Irene that saved me from becoming a murderer. With the helmet on, I could not help but think of her as the gas was overtaking Malastier. I thought of what she would do – what she would have me do. It was as if she were there."

"She is still in your thoughts – your life."

I let the soft silence pass to honour her memory.

As the chase drew to a close, we felt ourselves slipping out of the present moment and into an uncertain future.

Holmes wired Mycroft and requested that his agents in America rendezvous with us, and take responsibility for Malastier's return.

He sent two more telegrams: one was to Miss Brice, with the simple message that our mission was accomplished.

His last telegram was to Adaline Dart:

ADALINE

MALASTIER IS IN CUSTODY. HE IS RETURNING TO FACE JUSTICE.

YOUR MOTHER'S GOODNESS LINGERS WITHIN ALL OF US AND WE ARE THE BETTER FOR IT.

HOLMES

5

THE KONGO NKISI SPIRIT TRAIN

Holmes derails a plot to steal people's spirits.

"OUR FUTURE MAY be completely different from our past; but, it is *always* a consequence of the past." This commentary came from Sherlock Holmes, as he was dissecting a honeybee on his desk.

I believe it was his way of saying that, while he had accepted the loss of Irene Adler, he knew that, somehow, "the woman" would continue to influence his life.

After Malastier's trial and execution were behind us, Holmes withdrew to his retreat on the South coast. I suspected that he might appreciate my presence, and the bucolic seaside atmosphere afforded me the opportunity to reengage my writing, which I had neglected. Another in my series of British mythology tales was due within the month to *The Strand Magazine*.

When we arrived at Holmes's cottage, his first thoughts were of his bees. It was as if he sensed something was amiss. Before we crossed the threshold, he dashed into his back garden, where the hive boxes were stacked.

There, on the ground, lay hundreds of dead honeybees.

Dozens more were close to death, ambling in a twitchy manner like little clockwork toys – half dead, yet alive.

"What happened here, Holmes?" I enquired.

"I am not sure. I have had infestations from mites; and, of course, there is always the danger of temperature swings, but this is something else altogether."

Holmes opened the hive box nearest him, and removed the upper honey super, the top chamber that holds the comb and honey. Then he examined the brood super below it. "The entire hive is ravaged… the drones…" His voice trailed off.

He slowly gathered several deceased specimens, and carried them inside. He returned with a glass, and carefully retrieved a number of the creatures that still showed some life.

There was naught for me to do but to put our belongings within, and put the kettle on. It would be a long evening.

Holmes ignored the tea that I placed on his desk. He was peering into his microscope, silhouetted in the halo of his bench lamp.

"Look here, Watson," he said, pulling back to invite access to the lens. "Notice the strange contusion on the back of the head."

I peered through the lens at the hairy head of the honeybee, with its large vacant black eyes. Holmes said: "Look just between the head and the thorax, in front of the wings."

"Are you referring to the reddish-brown gash?"

"Something has attacked this bee, but what?"

He removed the bee from the slide and pinned it to his desktop. As he reached into the glass for one of the living drones, he stopped.

"They are dead, Watson. They're all dead. This is most curious."

Holmes's gift for understatement accentuated any feeling of anxiety I had in dreadful situations. If one believed in such things, these dead bees could be taken as a terrible omen.

My better days begin with a blank sheet of paper; and as Holmes continued his bee autopsies, I set out to begin my story about the "Mermaid of Zennor."

It seems that a number of Cornish fisherman, a fortnight earlier, had reported hearing an enchanting song arising from the sea as they set out, before dawn, for their daily catch. These reports served to revive a six hundred year-old myth of an alluring mermaid who had supposedly transformed a local boy, Mathew Trewhella, into a merman. For me, this was all to the good, as this story found its way to the pages of the *London Standard,* in turn, causing *The Strand Magazine* to suggest that the "Mermaid of Zennor" be the focus of my next article on British mythology.

When I mentioned these occurrences to Holmes, I received little encouragement. "I'll wager the enchanting song is a *catchy* tune, Watson."

His jibe put an end to our exchange. However, our day would take a singular turn with the arrival of a curious invitation. Indeed, I saw this change approaching in the form of a postman pedalling his bicycle up the road to the cottage. A missive was surely coming for us, as Holmes's rustic cottage was at the end of the coast road. Observing from the window, I alerted Holmes.

"I say, Holmes, mail today!"

"See to it, then, if you will."

I retrieved the letter and, when I saw it was addressed to both Holmes and me, opened it in the sunlight.

It seemed that, in her grief, Mrs. Dart had sought solace in Spiritualism – an unscrupulous practice, I thought. She appeared to be deep in the clutches of a medium called Margery. I came inside and risked interrupting Holmes's miniature investigation.

"It's a message from Adaline Dart."

There was no reply.

"Do you want me to read it?"

"If you will."

"As I say, it is from Adaline... she has taken up Spiritualism. Let me read it:"

Dear Mr. Holmes and Dr. Watson,

I have never thanked you properly for bringing mother's killer to justice. My grief had consumed me, and, for some time, there was room in my life for little else. Raymon was supportive, but I was inconsolable, until I made the acquaintance of a marvelous woman called Margery.

Margerey has exceptional gifts and is able to communicate with spirits beyond. I know you are highly rational men and may not share my beliefs, but I urge you to withhold judgment until you have the opportunity to witness what I have seen with my own eyes, and heard with my own ears. Such an opportunity is at hand, just up the road from you.

On Friday next, Margery will be holding a séance at the home of Sir Arthur Conan Doyle at Windlesham at nine. You are both invited. Know that Margery welcomes skeptics. She has many detractors, and has made believers out of most of them. I beseech you to come and see for yourself.

I have made contact with my mother and I know she would want to conjoin with you both.

In anticipation,
Adaline

Holmes sat up. "Our presence is requested?"

"Should we even consider accepting? Where is Harry Houdini when we need him?"

"We don't need the great Houdini. We are more than able to unmask this Margery."

"So, that would be your intention, then? Have you considered the situation?"

"Situation?"

"Adaline is grieving, Holmes. This is not the right time for sleuthing."

"Watson, you have a point, and I will not defrock this mystical mistress before the eyes of Mrs. Dart, or her guests. Margery has but to know that her trickery is found out, and she will likely slink away of her own volition."

"I believe that you credit her with more honour than she may possess."

~

Friday came, and we made ready for the séance. I had arranged for a trap to carry us the short distance to Windlesham, the Doyle family home. As we traveled, Holmes elucidated the methods of spirit mediums:

"Mediums are little more than backstreet magicians and, as such, they operate from the same rules and principles of any conjurer. The first rule is never to let the eye rest on the hand that is performing the sleight, but always somewhere else."

"Misdirection, you mean?"

"Precisely, Watson, and the methods of diverting the spectator's attention are various. There is the use of eyes, or the spoken word – where the medium tells the onlookers to observe a certain object or action. Indeed, the combined effect of the eyes and spoken word are generally irresistible."

"So, we mustn't look where we are told."

"Exactly; and the second rule is, never to let the audience know, beforehand, what is to be done – in this instance, what will happen during the séance."

"But I am sure Mrs. Dart will come with the intention of communicating with her mother – will she not?"

"She may well come with that expectation, but Margery will undoubtedly deliver something unexpected. You see, if the spectators knew what was forthcoming, they would be on the lookout, and might possibly detect the medium in the act of executing anticipated actions."

"I suppose that is why Houdini is so adept at unmasking these spirit mediums. He knows their ploys."

Holmes smiled. "Quite so. And, we may be just as effective, if we pay attention – especially to everything *but* what Margery asks us to observe… or we are able to directly observe."

"What do you mean, 'directly observe'?"

"We will no doubt be seated around a table, possibly locking hands. In that position, we are only able to see what is happening *above* the table. I suspect there may be much happening below, and in the dim distance away from our view."

"Are you proposing to dive below the table at some point?"

"That would be crude, would it not? You did not know, but for most of the afternoon, I have tightly bandaged both of my thighs just above my knee. It has proven to be more painful than I had anticipated."

I shook my head in astonishment. "Is blood still flowing to your appendages?"

"Enough. The effect, as you no doubt know, is to make my lower extremities unusually sensitive. I will be able to detect the slightest movements under the table."

"Holmes, I see that you have not ceased going to extreme measures to unravel a mystery."

"Extreme? Never. I simply do what reason suggests, and success requires."

As we approached Crowborough Common, the Doyle estate rose up on our left. It was a large two-storey affair with a gabled roof. Being entirely white, it glowed in the shimmering moonlight.

The driver brought us around to the main entrance. I noticed a bicycle leaning against the bushes at the entryway.

Our knock brought a young maid to the door, quickly followed by Jean Doyle, our hostess. Leaving our hats and coats, we were led into an immense room lined with chairs. A billiard table lay at the far end where a small collection of folks was gathered. Towering above this huddle was a hefty man, broad of chest and well mustached – Sir Arthur. Lady Doyle led us to the gathering and made introductions.

As Jean finished, Sir Arthur stepped toward us. "Mr. Holmes, we are honoured to have you as our guest. Long overdue, long overdue, as you are well nigh a neighbour. And, Dr. Watson… you are also most welcome."

Holmes nodded. "I tend to keep to myself, Sir Arthur, but I will look forward to future visits. My abode is modest, but know that you are always welcome. I noticed a bicycle as I came in. Possibly you take rides in the area?"

"No, I prefer walking. I believe the contraption on my

doorstep belongs to my friend, Robert Hunt, over there. He's the headman at the Beacon School, up the way."

We greeted Mr. Hunt and, of course, Adaline Dart who met us warmly:

"Mr. Holmes and Dr. Watson," Adaline gushed, "I am so happy you were able to come. I believe we can expect an amazing evening."

Indeed we were, for, at that moment, a gaunt gentleman approached from the room beyond. He was in sombre black dress, but sported a brilliant crimson tie. He glided into the gathering, just as Jean turned to take his hand.

"Ladies and gentlemen, let me introduce Mr. Henry Guppy, Margery's associate."

When introductions were complete, Mr. Guppy held his arms out in preparation for an announcement. "Ladies and gentlemen, as we are all present, Margery requests that we begin immediately. Please, enter the room quietly, and allow me to place you about the table."

Holmes's lips turned up slightly as he nodded in confirmation to himself. I suspected that Margery was about to meet her match.

We were escorted to a pitch-black drawing room that adjoined the large billiard room. The only light emanated from two candelabra set on either side of a large round table. As my eyes adjusted, I could also see a sharp dagger of moonlight cut across the table, from a curtained window. Margery stood at the head of the table where a three-sided Chinese screen was set behind her chair.

The self-proclaimed medium was young and pretty. Her blonde hair was in a *chignon* style and she wore a single sheer robe, *séance delicté,* which revealed much of her shapely anatomy. It appeared that voyeurism was part and parcel of a séance.

There was no preliminary ceremony. Guppy seated

us, putting Holmes on Margery's right side. I was placed next to Holmes, with Adaline on my right. The Doyles sat across from Margery, then Robert Hunt. As her assistant walked to his place on Margery's left, he leaned over Holmes's shoulder. "Mr. Holmes, you may note that there is a small wooden bell box at your feet. Some spirits find this instrument useful. You may feel it ring as some point."

Within moments of having found our chairs, an eerie whistling filled the room. As if on cue, the spirit of Walter, Margery's dead brother, whispered his arrival. Holmes's left shoulder flinched. Margery spoke. "Walter is making his presence known. Good evening, Walter."

A quiet, disembodied puckish voice replied, "Good evening, indeed, Margery."

The medium continued: "Walter, I can barely understand you. Please, speak so that all may hear you."

With that, a megaphone appeared, and levitated over Margery's head. Walter's voice spoke again. "Have Arthur tell me where to throw it."

"Toward me!" Sir Arthur replied, in a hushed exclamation. The megaphone flew through the air and crashed in front of him on the table.

Silence ensued then, until the medium stirred, sighed several times, and presumably went into a trance.

She spoke in a thin, solemn, far-away voice: "We are gathered here to bring back the spirit of a beloved woman who has passed into Summerland."

Holmes stirred and Margery responded: "Is there anyone here who has come in a spirit of antagonism?

The room remained in silence.

"I thank you. Let us pray."

The eight of us, speaking in unison, recited The Lord's Prayer.

The mistress of the séance continued: "I feel my psychic

power running high. From each and every one of you, I beg your help. Let your minds vibrate with me. Exclude other thoughts. Give your soul to the séance."

There was a long pause.

"Did Irene love the out-of-doors?" Margery enquired.

Adaline replied, "Yes, very much so."

"Then forgive me if I break the circle for a moment."

With a swift and graceful movement, Margery arose, spread the curtains, and threw open the window sash. The cool night air swept across the table and extinguished the candles around us.

"We will leave nothing between us and God's Heaven."

Silhouetted against the moonlit window, we could see Margery's well-formed figure through her flimsy gown. She took her seat again.

"Her soul is new, and she is not accustomed to man-made light."

Adaline spoke in a desperate whisper, "Are you there, Mother? I love you. I miss you dearly."

One end of the table began to rise and thump on the floor. Then, we heard a fluttering in a distant corner of the room, as if a bird were trapped within a box. The sound moved around the room, and something brushed my shoulder. A new voice came from the medium's lips, a sweet feminine tone – a distant voice. "It is so hard. It's terribly difficult."

Walter's voice arose suddenly. "Irene says it is difficult to come back. She is trying – struggling to find her way. However, her spirit is very near. She has a message for… for Sherlock."

There was a moment of silence before Margery murmured, "Yes… yes." Then, in a laconic voice, "Irene is offering a date… a year that has some meaning for her. I hear it. It is – eighteen eighty-seven… eighteen eighty-seven."

Holmes's hand squeezed my fingers.

Suddenly a luminescent form appeared over our heads. It drifted, haltingly, across the room and out of the window into the night.

There was a long sigh from the medium. Then, breaking the eerie silence, Margery's natural voice: "That's all I am getting."

Mr. Guppy's voice piped up. "I suggest that we withdraw for a time and reconvene a little later. Margery needs time to regenerate her psychic energies." He lit a candle on one of the candelabra, and guided us out of the drawing room.

Adaline grabbed Holmes's arm. "It was Mother's spirit Mr. Holmes. I felt it. But, I do not understand her message to you. What is the significance of the date eighteen eighty-seven?"

Holmes patted Adaline's hand as they strolled into the billiard room. "Adaline, I am not certain as to the meaning. I will share my frank assessment at a more opportune time."

Our host evidently overheard Holmes's remarks, for he intervened in the *tête-à-tête.*

"Mr. Holmes," Doyle said, "Do I detect skepticism within your remarks? I can understand your reticence, for there are, to be sure, many tricksters masquerading as spirit guides and mediums. But, it would be faulty reasoning to believe that, just because some mediums have been caught cheating, therefore all mediums are false."

"Sir Arthur," Holmes responded, "I fail to see how that argument can comfort advocates of Spiritualism – such as yourself, I assume."

Adaline stepped away as Holmes and Doyle stood toe to toe. Sir Arthur continued his appeal: "Judging by your reputation, I supposed that you were not one of those shallow fellows who imagine that they can explain any spiritual phenomenon as a parlour trick. I should have expected you to have a more receptive mind toward the mysteries which lie beyond this art."

"Like Diogenes, I am, above all, a seeker of truth. And, if it be possible to discover the truth that lies beyond the grave, I myself might expect to find it in deep reflection and lucid prayer, and not around an ill-lit table."

"Now you sound like my friend Houdini!" Doyle exclaimed.

"I have met the gentleman, Sir Arthur, and it surprises me that you have found common ground upon which a friendship might take root."

"I met Harry at the Brighton Hippodrome," our host said. "We were both appearing there. Later we struck up a correspondence around Spiritualism, which continues to this day. Indeed, the Houdinis have been guests in our home. Honest friendship is one of life's treasures, and I pride myself on thinking that Harry and I both hold that treasure sacred in every respect."

"I completely concur, Sir Arthur, and I trust that we too may have a frank conversation about Spiritualism. However, I fear this evening may not be the best time."

Doyle smiled and offered his hand. "I look forward to it."

Holmes shook his hand and offered apologies. "My friend and I must be getting home. We came, as you may know, at the behest of our friend Adaline Dart, and I realize now that I am not able to offer the kind of support that she requires. Not at this time."

Jean approached. "Gentlemen, please, will you take your conversation into the sitting room?"

Her husband responded before either of us could.

"Jean, it appears Mr. Holmes and Dr. Watson are going to make a short evening of it – but, they will be back," he said, turning to us. "I trust I am correct in that, gentlemen."

"Most assuredly, sir. I am Mr. Holmes's frequent guest."

"I'm pleased to hear that" Doyle said. "I have a strong feeling that exciting escapades may await us."

"I feel likewise, sir," Holmes echoed. "Please, offer our regrets to Margery. Please tell her, when you see her, that I was in a somewhat *fowl* mood… f-o-w-l."

Sir Arthur looked perplexed. "I… I will, sir."

With that, we made our way to the sitting area to take our leave. Holmes took Adaline by the arm and led her a short distance from the other guests.

"Adaline, I appreciate your invitation, and I am aware that there is something about Margery that is compelling and comforting for you. As your friend, I am asking you to be careful in your dealings with her."

Adaline bristled. "She has never asked me for a farthing."

Holmes wore a concerned look. With a deep breath he said, "I hold your friendship dear."

"And I, yours."

"Dr. Watson and I appreciate your invitation, and the opportunity to remain in your life in some small way. Please, call upon us at any time."

Adaline sighed. She reached out and, holding both our hands in hers, remarked: "You are the dearest of men, both of you. You will always have a place in my life, as you do in my heart. Promise me that you will visit when you are in London next."

We promised, and took our leave.

After donning our coats and hats, we found ourselves gazing at the evening firmament. *Somewhere in this vast universe there are answers to all the mysteries,* I thought.

"I suspect we might have an interesting walk home," I remarked.

"Interesting, only if you are not anticipating answers to *all* your questions."

"Then, you are reserving judgment on Margery?"

"She is a clever charlatan, Watson, but she may be more. Most of what happened this evening seems less mysterious if we realize that there were one, or more, accomplices – undoubtedly dressed in black, and most likely hidden behind the Chinese screen at Margery's back. An accomplice could easily gain entry, or depart, through the window when our attentions were misdirected, such as when the luminescent form appeared above the table. You recall that Margery created the need to open the window – an act which *also* extinguished the candles – darkness being the best blind."

"That may explain the whistle, Walter's voice, and the megaphone," I answered.

"And, the luminescent apparition," Holmes added.

"And what of the flapping sounds, and grazing touches that brushed my shoulder and head?"

"A tiny bird, Watson, possibly a blackened chickadee on a tether – released from a concealed cage. Look here." Holmes's held up a tiny grey bit of down. "I found this behind my chair."

"And, the accomplices shook the table, as well?"

Holmes chuckled. "No. The amazing Margery was able to lift the table by placing her head under the table's edge. My sensitive legs were able to detect this amazing feat despite the misdirection. You see, just before the séance commenced, Guppy had directed my attention to a bell-box at my feet in an attempt to keep my attentions focused there."

"And, what of the message… 'eighteen eighty-seven'?"

Holmes stopped in his tracks. "I don't know. I do not know how she knew that."

"Knew what, Holmes? What is the significance of that date?"

"I would have thought you might have guessed, Watson. My watch chain fob... my *former* fob."

"The gold sovereign! My god Holmes, you put your fob in..."

"In Irene's hand."

"It was buried with her. How could Margery know?"

"I cannot say," Holmes admitted. "Even if someone had seen it dangling from my chain, it was worn thin from rubbing. One could barely make out St. George, let alone the date below the tableau."

We hiked in silence until we reached the cottage. "I'm going to walk a little more, Watson. Please, don't wait up for me."

I watched my friend trudge down the road into the cobalt moonlight that bathed the fields beyond. I could not help but wonder where this new road was taking him.

~

In the following days, Holmes continued his enquiry into the mysterious deaths within his honeybee colony, and I got quite far along in my piece on the "Mermaid of Zennor." I was in search of an ending. I do not cater to superstition, yet I have learnt to keep the door to the unknown cracked open a little. Certainty can lead to arrogance – the stepsister of ignorance.

I had not considered the possibility of personally delivering my manuscript to the *Strand,* until a telegram came suggesting that I return to London, and that Holmes accompany me.

My housekeeper's message said that an "important gentleman," a Mr. Leander Starr Jameson, had made several enquiries after me, in an attempt to locate Holmes and myself. In his most recent communication, this visitor insisted that he was calling on behalf of the British people, and that it was imperative that every effort be made to contact us.

I shared this information with Holmes, who showed some curiosity – but not enough to stir. He asked me to send a telegram to his brother Mycroft's office in Whitehall, regarding Jameson. The gentleman's name was vaguely familiar to me, and particularly familiar to Holmes.

"Watson, no doubt, you may recall that Leander Starr Jameson played a role in the failed raid which he led before the last Boer War. He was the Administrator General for Matabeleland at the time. I am sure you recall the scandal, and trial, that followed. It seems that Jameson has returned home from Africa."

"Of course, Holmes, I recall now. The gentleman came from a gifted family. His father authored *Timoleon* and *Nimrod*. Indeed, I believe Jameson is a physician as well."

"Yes, you are correct. He primarily practiced in Africa, of course."

"And, are you not curious as to why this man seeks us out?"

"I am *most* curious. However, I am not eager to entangle myself in a hysterical, political escapade."

"And thus, your missive to Mycroft."

"Exactly so, Watson. The fact that Mycroft knows my whereabouts, suggests that Jameson's endeavours may not be officially sanctioned."

The following day we received Mycroft's reply, which confirmed Holmes's assessment:

SHERLOCK

JAMESON IS NOT EMPLOYED IN AN OFFICIAL CAPACITY. HOWEVER I URGE YOU TO HEAR HIM OUT. IT PERTAINS TO OUR INTERESTS IN AFRICA. I CANNOT SAY MORE.

MYCROFT

"Are we off to London, then?" I enquired.

Holmes grimaced. I understood that his reticence was not so much unwillingness to engage a new case, but rather to enter the seething cauldron that London was becoming. Our beloved Britain was in the clutches of labour and suffrage demonstrations, and increasing unrest in Ireland. Moreover, modernity was imposing its stamp on our way of life. It seemed that every household clamoured for a telephone, motorcycles screamed in the streets, and children were eating soup from tins. Despite these misgivings, Holmes and I departed for the city on the following day.

As we arrived at Victoria, the last bits of country-quiet vanished amid the shouts of the newsboys: "City visited by mystery air-ship! Defence committee baffled!"

The suffragettes would have to share the stage with an ultra-nationalistic caprice that was sweeping the continent. British lyricists, German nationalists, Italian socialists, Russian Bolsheviks, and others, were fervently waving flags. In the competition for headlines, some newspapers, like the *Daily Mail,* were scare-mongering about the future prospects of armed conflict. The new Trinity was God, King, and Country, and there was no shortage of jingoists to beat the drums of war. Many of the irregulars had joined the Boy's Brigade. Young men, particularly poorer ones, were imbued with idea that there was no greater virtue than to sacrifice oneself for one's country.

We made our way to my apartment that promised a meagre refuge. There we waited for Mr. Jameson to call. We did not wait long.

Leander Starr Jameson appeared on my doorstep on the day following our arrival. In physical form, he was an average man, of common stature, slightly balding, with a healthy mustache. He was faultless and fashionable in dress, and projected a tough-minded attitude, with a logical and sagacious temperament that was most pleasant. Indeed, Holmes and I felt the draw of his persuasive character, as he introduced himself in my parlour.

Jameson seated himself sideways, in a casual manner, on a desk chair near my hearth. "Mr. Holmes, and Dr. Watson, I thank you for seeing me today. I come to you as one of your countrymen, who has been the beneficiary of your extraordinary talents over these many years."

Holmes, who had included this fellow within his extensive files, replied: "Mr. Jameson, I can say the same for you. You have lived a life of duty and honour that you have brought to a wide sphere of work and achievements."

Jameson did not blush, or acknowledge these compliments in any manner. "I appreciate your generous nature, Mr. Holmes, but, as you well understand, it is only through impersonal aims that we become the fullest measure of a human being."

That statement provided the perfect means by which we could bypass further social niceties, and discover why the man was here.

"So then, Mr. Jameson," I replied, "do you come on behalf of someone else?"

"*Something else,*" the charming man replied. "I come as a patriot. The British Empire, all thirteen million square miles of it, represents one-quarter of the globe. I have spent most of my life serving our territories in South Africa. I come on behalf of all the people of Africa, especially those in our own colonies. Are you familiar with the Cape to Cairo Railway, gentlemen?"

"The dream of Cecil Rhodes, I believe," Holmes answered. "The objective being to build a continuous rail line from Cape Town, South Africa to Cairo, Egypt. Quite a stupendous undertaking."

"To say the least," Jameson replied. "Mr. Rhodes died more than a decade ago, but his vision lives on. The line is currently some 2,300 miles beyond the Cape, extending past Elisabethville in the Congo. And, from the north, the line has been pushed 1,400 miles southward to Khartoum, in the very heart of the Sudan."

"What remains is to connect the two," I observed.

"As you might imagine, Dr. Watson, that is proving to be challenging. The southern leg is 100 miles short of connecting with an upper tributary of the Nile, where goods and people might be transported northward by steamers. As you can imagine, this would be a great achievement."

"But, you find that further progress has been impeded," Holmes surmised.

"Yes, exactly, sir. The Cape to Cairo Railway has faced, and overcome, many obstacles over the last fifteen years – swamps, impenetrable jungle, the ravages of the white ants and termites, encounters with lions, elephants and other beasts, disease and unfriendly natives, to name a few. All of these have been overcome… until now."

I leaned forward in my chair. "What has put a stop to the progress now, Mr. Jameson?"

"The Kongo Nkisi. A native spirit-god."

Holmes cocked his head, as Jameson continued:

"To be honest, I do not wholly understand the African

religions or belief systems but, as I gather, the Kongo Nkisi is an incorporeal creature, or spirit, who can commune with human beings."

I was flummoxed. "Are you telling us that an African spirit has put a stop to the entire project?"

Jameson acknowledged my bewilderment. "I assure you that I am rational man – not prone to superstition or other clap-trap. In all my years in Africa, I have never known anything like it. I cannot explain it in any logical or reasonable way. It is a mystery."

"Exactly what has the Kongo Nkisi done?" Holmes asked.

"Well, at first, it merely threatened workers. As you may know, there is a shortage of African labour. In our naïveté, we instituted a poll tax and hut tax to force the natives to work 'more productively' – shall we say. Working for the colonists, you see, is the primary way they can earn the money needed to pay their taxes. This has not proved to be an altogether effective strategy. However, working with native chiefs, and with the more recent influx of Asian-Indian immigrants, the railway obtained much of the labour it required."

"But, the Kongo Nkisi frightened these already scarce workers away," I said. "How was this done?"

"As I say, initially through warnings. The native workers would find a Kongo Nkisi fetish in their hut, or in the tool room. The fetish, called *zumbi* by the natives, is a warning from a witch – a witch that has engaged the power of the Kongo Nkisi. The belief is that, using the power of the Kongo Nkisi, a witch can tear out, and devour, the spirit from a person's body."

"A necromancer," Holmes added. "And, *all* of the workers were frightened in this way?"

"No, not all were frightened away... at first." Jameson

looked at both of us sheepishly. "Some natives continued to work, and many of the immigrant workers – non-believers, if you will – continued working for a time."

Jameson paused before delivering his next statement. "You must understand, gentlemen, that there are things in Africa which no white man has seen. Unbelievable things." He hesitated again. "Workers – those that remained – began to disappear from the rail camps. Within a month, more than one hundred disappeared, and many more since. A few have returned... but they were not the same. They came back as altered people. They breathe. They walk and move about – but in a deathlike trance. They do not speak or interact with others... they can function, but only at a primitive level. They are more dead than alive."

"So, the natives believe that a witch has used the power of the Kongo Nkisi to remove the souls from these people?" Holmes asked.

"Fantastic, Mr. Jameson!" I exclaimed. "Have you seen these victims yourself?"

"I have not, but my colleagues have sent detailed reports. It seems that medical science does not offer a ready explanation. In part, I suppose, it is because the symptoms that these poor folk exhibit appear to be as much psychological, as physical."

"Are you speaking of their dull demeanour?" I asked.

"Dull, mostly," Jameson replied. "However, loud noises, bright light, and other stimuli, can cause violent behaviour – ranting and screaming. If you confront them, they attack you, and bite you – literally tearing flesh from your body."

I was stunned.

Holmes pushed on. "Yes, amazing. So, the railway now has few, if any, workers."

Jameson nodded, "The labourers are all but disappeared, along with some engineers, a station master, and a few others associated with the project. And… most recently… a train has vanished."

Holmes's eyes lit up with an eager energy that overtook his manner. "A *train* disappeared, you say? Quite a feat!"

"Exactly so," replied our guest. "The natives believe that the Kongo Nkisi witch, using the spiritless slaves which he has created, rides this spirit train through the jungle, looking for new souls to eat. Indeed, it is reported that, on a quiet night, when the wind is right, one can hear the whistle of the Kongo Nkisi spirit train in the far-off jungle."

Holmes rose and retrieved his pipe from the mantel. "What do *you* believe is going on, Mr. Jameson?"

"I have no immediate explanation. I have been asked to come to you. My associates and I hope that you will be able to unravel this mystery, as you have so many others."

"So, you wish us to go to Africa?" I asked.

"I am an emissary sent on behalf of our country and colonies in Africa – colonies rich in resources that we need, especially if war is in the offing."

I looked at Holmes with some trepidation. He was thoroughly engaged in the problem.

Holmes caught my eye and nodded.

"Dr. Watson and I have much to consider," Holmes said coolly. "If we decide to take your case, we shall need more information; but, for now, we have what is required. Can you give us some time to consider your request?"

"Most certainly. My home is in Hyde Park. I will leave my card. When you have made a decision, please send word to my residence."

"One last question, Mr. Jameson," Holmes said. "Can I assume that you are not acting as an official agent of our government?"

"Not officially," he said, taking his hat and coat from the table. "However, you can imagine that there is considerable interest in Whitehall. Your commission would come from the Prime Minster of the Cape Colony, and the managing director of the railway." And then he added, "Money is no object, of course."

It will not be surprising to learn that, within the week, Holmes and I found ourselves boarding the R.M.S. *Alaunia* in Liverpool. Leander Starr Jameson had arranged passage for us, and himself, on the very day we accepted the case.

The *Alaunia* was a second-class ship, but more than comfortable. The twelve-day journey afforded us time to plan, prepare and relax. Regarding the latter, I found myself thoroughly engaged in a new pastime – word-cross games. Holmes found such amusements nonsensical.

"Holmes, what is a four-letter word for an aromatic plant?"

He paused. "Nard, sage, mint, chia… will those do?"

And that is how it went. When one has Sherlock Holmes as a companion, word-cross games are not challenging at all.

The best part of the voyage was the ship's menu – which was varied, and quite delightful. Indeed, between meals, a cold buffet was always available in the dining room. This accommodated Holmes's propensity for hiding away in our cabin, pouring over the small library, and laboratory equipment, that he managed to bring on board.

Holmes showed unusual delight, one day, as he came upon me during my morning ablutions. "Watson, I have discovered what it is that has attacked my honeybee colony."

"Wonderful, Holmes! What was it?"

"Apocephalus borealis – a fly that lays eggs *inside* bee workers. Its grubs eventually eat the bee from the inside out. The infected workers abandon their hives to die. The larvæ, laid within the bee, migrate to the head and devour the tissue inside. The brainless bee wanders aimlessly for days before the larvae dissolve the connection between the bee's head and body. The head falls off, and an adult fly emerge from it."

"A gruesome business, Holmes! I trust these flies are harmless to human beings."

"Our heads are still attached. That can only be a good sign."

I left Holmes to his studies and decided to spend some time with Jameson. I was particularly curious about his medical practice in South Africa. I found him standing at the prow of the ship, the wind in his face, and his eyes cast upon the distant horizon.

"Mr. Jameson, would you be amenable to some companionship?"

"Thank you, Dr. Watson, and you must call me Lanner."

"Very well. And, I am John. I must admit that you have a singular name – most memorable!"

The lanky gentleman smiled. "There is a story there, if you wish to hear it."

"Please."

"On the very morning of my birth, my mother had sent my father out walking to prevent his complicating the birthing process. He walked along a nearby canal that had unusually steep banks, and fell in. Fortunately, he was rescued from drowning by an American traveller who fished him out of the canal."

Jameson leaned in. "Well, my father dragged the kindly stranger home, and appointed him my godfather. His name was Leander Starr."

"What a delightful story, Lanner."

We chatted for nearly an hour, as Jameson gratified my curiosity about his medical practice.

"My career, of course, began in London. It was a budding practice that quickly drove me to overwork. My health broke down. At the urging of friends, I moved to Kimberley. I practiced on and off, in Africa, for more than two decades."

"I imagine you encountered diseases that were not to be found in our textbooks."

"There are some rare diseases to be sure, such as tunglasis or nigua, caused by the bite of a particular flea. There are, also, all the diseases of the modern world. Indeed, my reputation as a medical man brought the Matabele Chief Lobengula to me. He had a dreadful case of the gout. I was able to cure him, and he was extraordinarily grateful. I was given the post of *inDuna*, advisor or commander, in the Matabele King's favourite regiment. It is a great honour that afforded me access to the Zulu, and other tribes, in the region. My position allowed me to negotiate with Chief Lobengula, who granted concessions to the agents of Cecil Rhodes, to form what is now the British South Africa Company."

"So, that is how you met Rhodes, and began your association with the Cape to Cairo railway project?"

"Yes, John, that was the start of a long and fruitful relationship with the colossus known as Cecil Rhodes."

"Rhodes was an extraordinary man – at least by reputation."

"And, in life as well, John. Rhodes held sway over most everything that happened in South Africa. He was the epitome of a British colonist. He believed that the Anglo-Saxon race was destined for greatness. Unfortunately, his attitudes were reflected in his poor treatment of the native population. He saw the Africans as inferior.

"How were you able to maintain a relationship with Rhodes," I enquired, "knowing that your sympathies lay elsewhere?"

"Yes, well... I am my father's son in that regard. As you may know, my father was a reformer, who led the fight against slavery, nearly seventy years ago. But, despite Rhodes's beliefs, I was able to see the good that he was accomplishing – which was immense. And, being a model of pragmatism, he saw that I could help him achieve is vision."

"You can be rightfully proud of your accomplishments in Africa. But, do you no longer have a home in Kimberley?"

"I moved back to London last year. Robert Williams, the managing director of the railway, asked me to enlist your aid, and that of Mr. Holmes."

"Your confidence in Holmes is more than justified," I concurred. "I am a mere acolyte."

Jameson held a glint in his eye. "I know better, John. You do what any good colleague does, and provide something that Mr. Holmes needs, even if he may not fully comprehend it."

"I cannot imagine what that would be."

"Certainly, a shared journey is richer, and more meaningful. You make that richness available to one another. But also, much of Mr. Holmes's life is lived within his lofty intellect. You provide the tether that ties him to humanity, and grounds him in the world."

"I had never thought of our relationship in that particular manner."

"What is more, Mr. Holmes is a craftsman, an artisan. His craft is unique; but, like all craftsmen, his work must be seen and appreciated. As the master storyteller, you bring his craft to the world."

"Mr. Jameson... Lanner... your sagacity and discernment are much appreciated. You hold up a mirror into which I seldom peer. Thank you."

I could easily see what inspires the devotion that Jameson receives from his contemporaries. Whatever one felt about Leander Starr Jameson, or his projects, in the abstract, when one met the man, one could not help liking him. He has a singular ability to clearly perceive things as they are. This was reassuring, as Holmes and I were about to join our fortunes with his.

Lanner and I lunched together; and, afterwards, he suggested that I acquaint myself with the equipment and supplies that he had gathered for our use in South Africa. A steward showed us to the cargo bay, and helped us to open two of the crates.

Jameson's supplies included everything from compasses to citronella. However, he seemed particularly eager to retrieve two long walnut cases. "These are the rifles I have selected for you both. I urge you to carry them with you, at all times, when we are in the bush."

He opened one of the cases. An exquisite Verney-Carron .577 Nitro Express lay swathed in lavender velvet. The walnut butt was hand-carved and chequered. The two barrels stood apart, large, thick, and menacing.

"This rifle can kill most any game at sixty yards with one shot," Jameson noted. "That is important, as you will only have one shot most of the time."

"If Holmes takes up a rifle, it would be a rare thing," I explained. "However, I am comfortable with firearms – although this one seems more robust than my old Enfield."

"You will be surprised how little recoil this weapon delivers, John. I suggest you do a little shooting off the stern before we reach Cape Town. I'll leave you to familiarize yourself with the remainder of the gear."

After Jameson left, I decided to don my poplin bush jacket and trousers. I topped off my outfit with a pith helmet, and went to the cabin to find a mirror.

As I entered our cabin Holmes, leaned back in his chair to take in my uniform. "Dr. Watson, I presume," he said, with delight.

I gave the appropriate response: "Yes, and I feel thankful that I am here to welcome you."

We both chuckled.

It was interesting to note that Stanley and Livingston's remarkable meeting in central Africa was more than forty years ago. Holmes and I would soon be on our own incredible journey into the hidden reaches of that vast continent.

~

The R.M.S. *Alaunia* made port at Cape Town on the 27th of October, 1913. The docks were bustling with cargo going from and into ships. Jameson had evidently telegraphed ahead regarding our arrival, as a large welcoming party was waiting at the end of the gangway.

The weather was surprisingly pleasant, a comfortable seventy degrees. "It's not so hot as I had expected," I exclaimed, as we disembarked.

Jameson concurred. "On the coast, this time of year, it is heaven. In the interior, where we are headed, you will find that the temperature, and especially the humidity, will climb to heights that you may never have experienced."

We were given rooms at Robert William's estate that was located in an area called Claremont, just south of the city. As we rode in his open automobile, I was amused to find the city streets bore the names of explorers, British towns, and even American presidents. There was little evidence of the African culture until we passed number of small huts just outside the estate.

You might have thought that we had gone on holiday. During our first two days in Africa, we were given grand tours of the locale, and were guests at two dinner parties. A ball was even held in our honour. Little was said about trains, soulless labourers, or the Kongo Nkisi spirit. However, on the third day, Jameson, Holmes and I rode with Robert Williams to his office in Cape Town.

In a four-storey building, that looked more a presidential residence than an office building, we met Mr. Henry Birchenough, Director of the British South Africa Company, and Dr. A. Abdurahman, the newly elected president of the Cape Colony. Holmes and I suddenly found ourselves sitting with the three most powerful men in South Africa.

Holmes, of course, had knowledge of all of these gentlemen. As he was introduced to Dr. Abdurahman he remarked, "Congratulations on your recent victory, sir."

"Thank you, Mr. Holmes," the stately man replied. It was interesting to note that Dr. Abdurahman was a man of colour – Cape Malay, I believe. It also struck me that he was very young to be holding such a weighty post.

When introductions were complete, Mr. Williams took charge. "Gentlemen, I believe we are all aware of the situation in which we find ourselves. We have exhausted local resources, and so have reached out for your expertise, Mr. Holmes and Dr. Watson."

"I am curious as to what caused you to seek us, in particular?" Holmes enquired.

The railway director smiled. "You are a well known consultant, an accomplished detective, and a recognized patriot. I must admit, however, that your name first came to mind when I read an article in the *Manawatu Standard*. There was a report on the Kongo Nkisi affair – as it has come to be called, in which the writer described it as 'a mystery that only the great Sherlock Holmes could solve.' Obviously, I agreed."

"I should like to see that editorial, if possible," Holmes remarked.

"That can be arranged, Mr. Holmes," Williams answered. "Jameson here will assist in any way. He is thoroughly familiar with the facts of the case, but I thought that you might have questions, or requests, for us. We want to impress upon you the fact that we are – all of us – united in your support."

Holmes glanced at me and tapped his breast pocket. This was his way of asking me to make notes. I retrieved my notebook, and Holmes commenced his enquiry. "I suppose the most obvious question is: Who benefits from the stoppage of work? Who does not want the Cape to Cairo Railway to be completed?"

There was a momentary silence. Finally, Dr. Abdurahman began: "Just as Esau and Jacob fought over Canaan, so Britain, Belgium, France, Germany, and other European countries have set upon Africa like a pack of hyænas. And, while claims and territories have been established for some time, the struggle for control continues. The balance of power is fragile. The Cape to Cairo Railway would solidify Britain's dominance in Africa, allowing Britain to control its far-flung colonies, and export natural resources on a scale hereto unimagined."

"So, you believe that one or more foreign governments are at work here?" I asked.

Jameson squirmed in his seat. "Dr. Watson, we must

be cautious with conjecture. As you know, the tensions on the European continent are high. A casual opinion, or brash accusation, could create a political firestorm. What Dr. Abdurahman says is true, but we have not found any evidence of foul play by any political agent. And, I should be remiss if I did not point out that there are many tribes who are in opposition to the railway."

"Then is it fair to say, that all of you reject a supernatural explanation of the Kongo Nkisi business?" Holmes asked, pointedly.

Dr. Abdurahman, once again, rose to the enquiry. "We are educated, rational men, Mr. Holmes; but I can say, being a son of South Africa, that there are true mysteries here. The spiritless workers are real. I have seen them myself. What changed them, and who changed them, we do not know."

Jameson stepped in again. "If one or more of the tribes were attempting to stop the railway, they might turn to a *n'anga* or *mungoma* – a medicine man. However, the *mungoma* are healers. I have never known one to use their knowledge to intentionally harm people."

"This would not seem to be the case with regard to the spiritless workers," I observed. "I should like to see one of these poor souls, if I might."

Mr. Williams looked askance at Henry Birchenough "I wish we could accommodate you, Dr. Watson, but they are all dead."

"What?" Jameson said, aghast.

"Yes, it appears that they can only live in their state for four or five weeks, at best," Williams stated. "Our last report to you was sent before the full effect of their affliction had manifested."

"What was the cause of death?" I asked.

"It varied," Birchenough said. "With some, their heart

gave out. Others, we are told, died from gastrointestinal bleeding."

"A horrible death," I said.

Jameson pulled back in his chair. "I have never known anything like this in all my years here. *Mungoma* are often ineffective, but I have never seen them intentionally inflict pain or suffering on others. I do not believe that the natives are behind this."

"You have always given the natives more credit than they are due," Williams said. And then, turning to us, "Mr. Holmes – Dr. Watson, I think it best that you investigate and draw your own conclusions… and, the sooner you start, the better. I have put one of my foremen, Mr. Murdoch, at your disposal. He will see to your transportation, housing and protection. Jameson has agreed to accompany you as well. If you need anything more, you have but to ask either of them."

Sensing that our meeting was coming to an end, Henry Birchenough, Director of the British South Africa Company, made it clear where most of the power in this triumvirate lay. "The B.S.A.C. has a large stake in the Cape to Cairo Railway. You are here because you possess extraordinary *investigative* skills. If, and when, you discover the culprits behind this fiasco, I ask that you immediately report to me… to us. We are in the best position to take action. A militia is standing by. I am sure you understand."

Holmes nodded. "You want answers from us, not action."

"Precisely," Birchenough said. "Best of luck, gentlemen."

With that pointed orientation, our search for the Kongo Nkisi spirit train began.

Lucas Murdoch was waiting for us as we departed from the railroad headquarters.

Leaning against a brilliant green Crosley, his smile reveled an almost full set of pearly teeth. There was a hole where his right cuspid had once resided. His hairless face was slightly bruised to match his knuckles. He wore a red tartan shirt with canvas trousers.

"G'day Dr. Lanner," he exclaimed, as he spied Jameson. "Still cavorting with the tall poppies, I see. Couldn't stay away, mate?"

"Could not *get* away," Jameson responded. "Lucas, meet Mr. Sherlock Holmes and Dr. John Watson. Gentlemen, meet the finest foreman on the railway, Lucas Murdoch."

As we shook hands, Holmes remarked, "How do you find your first year away from Australia's citizen army?"

Murdoch's eyes lit up. "And, how would ya know I was a soldier... and out less than a year, no less?"

Holmes pointed to a pistol holstered on Murdoch's hip. "The Steyr-Hahn self-loading pistol, Australian made, became available in 1912... only a recent army issue."

"Fair dinkum!" the Australian acknowledged. "Yes, sir, Mr. Holmes, I'm an ex-soldier, ex-sheepherder, ex-alcoholic and, right now, ex-tremely hungry. How about you gentlemen? I'm your guide, your bodyguard, and," as he opened the door of the motorcar, "your driver."

Lucas Murdoch drove us north of the city to a rail yard. There, lined up along more than a dozen tracks, were as many locomotives, with brass plates bolted to their noses. Behind many of them was line after line of railway cars. I noticed the supply crates from the *Alaunia* had been delivered, and were waiting nearby.

A short drive put us outside a large clapboard building, sorely needing paint – our African headquarters. It served as a bunkhouse for the railway crews, as well as engineers and foremen working on the Cape to Cairo project. It was now mostly empty. The only other inhabitant in the two-storey domicile seemed to be an Indian cook, at work over a wood stove.

Holmes and I were given a private room, as most of the beds were sprawled out in dormitory fashion. Jameson was staying close by, at the home of a friend. He took his leave, saying that he would be back for dinner. As he left, Holmes asked him where the offices of the *Manawatu Standard* could be found.

I was famished and something smelled wonderful. However, Holmes cut off my planned inspection of the kitchen.

"Watson, please go to the offices of the *Manawatu Standard* and find the editorial that included my name. If you are able, learn the author, and make their acquaintance." I grimaced a little before Holmes added, "the mutton curry will still be here when you return."

My route to the newspaper office took me past an Edwardian edifice, built with honey-coloured limestone. This imposing City Hall building was a visual declaration that Cape Town had taken its place on the world stage. Further down, on the Grand Parade, was the office of the *Manawatu Standard*. There wasn't much to distinguish it from the other shops and commercial buildings, save for a motto emblazoned across the front window: "Serving the Children of Mother City." "Mother City" is the name that the locals had given to Cape Town – some jest, because it takes nine months to get anything done here.

Upon entering, I was confronted by a long counter that ran the breadth of the office. Behind it, sat two men pecking away at typewriters. As I approached the counter, a young woman suddenly materialized.

"May I help you, sir?"

"I am interested in a past edition. In particular, the report about the Kongo Nkisi affair."

"That was a while back, nearly a month," she said.

"So, can you provide a copy for me?

"Certainly, sir." The pretty lady smiled and walked back to several tall stacks of newspapers on a nearby table.

When she brought the newspaper to me, I made another enquiry. "Do you happen to know the individual who wrote the Kongo Nkisi story?

"Tenpence," she said, sliding the paper over the counter. "Mr. Arbuckle, over yonder, is your man."

"May I speak with him?"

The lady pursed her lips, and made her way to a shaggy-haired man, who had just torn a page from his typewriter. As she whispered in his ear, his eyes caught mine. He shrugged his shoulders, and made his way forward.

"Lucy tells me you are an admirer of my work," the reporter said.

"Exactly, Mr. Arbuckle. I much appreciated your story on the Kongo Nkisi affair, and wondered if you were still following the story."

"Nothing new to report, as far as I know. But, if there is news, the *Standard* will have it."

I opened the paper to the find the column in question. "I was curious about your reference to... who was it... Sherlock Holmes."

"Yes," the newspaperman said. "An afterthought. My investigations took me to a coffee shop in Elisabethville – *Tasse de Café*. It's popular with expatriates, and the place to go if you want the latest news – official and unofficial. The proprietor, a woman they call May, latched onto me when she learned I was visiting from Cape Town. She's the one… she said it was a case for Sherlock Holmes. It stuck."

"Interesting," I noted. "Thank you so much for your time, sir… and your excellent work."

I hurried off, eager to share my information, but also, in keen anticipation of a dinner that I suspected would include some of the best Asian cuisine to be had since I left India.

Dinner was waiting as I arrived, and I was able to make my report to Holmes, who had little comment. After the plates were removed, Lanner and Lucas spread a large map on the table.

"We leave the day after tomorrow," Jameson said. "Here's the railway's route," he added, tracing a line on the map with his finger. "What do you wish to see first, Mr. Holmes?"

"Dr. Watson and I will want to go to where the train disappeared – where it was last seen."

"Not to worry! That'd be about thirty-eight miles north of Elisabethville – at the end of the line," Murdoch said. "More than two days from here by train. I'll make arrangements."

"Thank you, Mr. Murdoch," Holmes said. "And, Jameson, do you have other maps, something with more detail of the Congo region?"

"I can obtain them."

"Do, please," Holmes requested. "And, Watson, you may wish to acquire some medical instruments and supplies in the event we encounter some spiritless workers. That is all the planning we need do at the moment."

As we had our coffee, Holmes quizzed Murdoch, who was the only member of our troupe present during all the events surrounding the Kongo Nkisi affair.

"Lucas," Holmes enquired, "how can a train disappear?"

Lucas laughed. "Now, that would be a question for you – no?"

"Surely, you have an opinion," I cajoled.

"Well… it was Engine 112. Supply trains come and go from the Cape bringin' materials and supplies to the crews at the end of the line. One-one-two made its delivery, and was initially delayed in its return by a mechanical problem – eventually fixed. We saw it leave for Cape Town; but it was never seen again."

"When did you discover it was missing? I asked.

"Not for another five days, when another supply train brought the news. The driver was put on the lookout for Engine 112. He thought he would find it broken down along the way. But, it wasn't there."

Jameson joined in. "Are there other spurs along the route?"

"I reckon… I checked every one of 'em," Murdoch insisted. "Ya can't hide a fifty-ton engine behind a bush."

"No indeed Mr. Murdoch," Holmes agreed, "you could only hide it in plain sight."

Murdoch was struck dumb. "That would be a beaut of a trick."

"Yes, a trick", Holmes echoed.

~

Upon our last morning in Cape Town, Holmes and I walked the railway yard, hoping to enjoy the bracing morning air. We came to a line of locomotives, and Holmes asked me to record the engine numbers as we encountered them.

"Are you expecting to find Engine 112?" I queried.

"The engine, possibly, but not the number."

Holmes stood in front of each engine, staring at the number emblazoned on the brass plaque bolted on the front. He did this to all of them, in turn, at times retrieving his magnifying glass to inspect the plate. At one point, he came to number 161. He smiled. "Put a star by this number, Watson, if you please."

He then retrieved his glass, and stepped up on the plow. He brushed the head of several of the bolts with his finger.

"What do you see, Holmes?"

"I believe I see 'old' 112," he replied. "Notice how this plate is shiny and new, but the bolts are corroded."

"Did someone exchange the number-plate on this engine, then?"

"Exactly, Watson, simple sleight-of-hand... misdirection. Everyone was looking for a *number*, when what they should have been looking for, was the engine."

"But surely, the station master would have discovered a new number – a new engine as it were?"

"Yes, you would think so. What will you wager that the station master is one of the sad souls who were spirited away?"

Holmes was, of course, correct. Our enquiry revealed that the stationmaster, a Punjabi named Gilkar Mahal, was one of the afflicted workers. He died shortly after wandering back into Cape Town.

Further investigation took us to the logbook in the maintenance shed. Running his finger down the list of locomotives, Holmes's finger rested on 161. He retrieved his glass to focus on that entry.

"Making 112 disappear was as easy as replacing a number on a page, and a brass plaque."

Holmes had thus solved part of the Kongo Nkisi mystery, before we had even departed for Elisabethville.

"Holmes, what made you suspect that the missing train was here?"

"It was the only plausible solution. The fifty-ton engine could not be moved without rails, so it had to be 'an accounting error' – so to speak. Of course, the perpetrator had to select a new and different number. And, as most people do, when asked to generate a random number, the perpetrator selected one that had some relevance for them. Unconsciously, people invariably select a number that comes from their past experience."

"That is what you were pondering as we perused the engine numbers, I understand. But, what is the significance of 1-6-1?"

"It's called the Golden Number – Phi, which is written as one-dot-six-one. To the Greeks it was the dividing line in the extreme and mean ratio. For Renaissance artists, it represented 'the Divine proportion'."

"So the perpetrator is an artist?"

"Possibly, or a mathematician. If I didn't know better, I would say that Professor Moriarty were involved."

"Perish the thought, Holmes! We know better, do we not?"

"As you say, reason suggests that Moriarty cannot be a factor… unless he has reached beyond the grave."

Mr. Williams, as you can imagine, was pleased with Holmes's discovery.

"Ha!" he said, when he received Holmes's report. "Spirit train, indeed! But, wait a moment, what is it then, that people hear in the distant jungle?"

"That, we shall discover soon," Holmes promised.

We kept to our schedule and, the next morning, Holmes and I found ourselves in a plush passenger car with

Jameson and Murdoch. The walls of the car were paneled in oak, and decorated in gold velvet. The lilac carpeting was as deep as heather on a hill.

"This is Mr. William's personal car. The sleeping quarters are just as spiffy," Murdoch explained. "And, I happen to know, there is more than one bottle of exceptional Scotch in the cupboard."

"I thought you were an ex-alcoholic, Lucas?" I enquired.

"Oh I *am,* Doctor, but is there another bloke on earth who knows better where the booze is hid than an *ex*-alcoholic?"

"What, in particular, caused you to give up the drink?"

"Now that's a story I will save for a rainy evening, Doctor."

"What is it brought you to Africa, then?"

"The war. I served here, and stayed on afterwards. Like every young lad from Kalgoorlie, I dreamed of being a grazier, and tried to make a go of it here."

"How did you fare?"

Murdoch wore a distant look. "I had sheep brought here. When I put them on my station, my Bantu neighbours pointed at the fuzzy white animals saying *chakula cha jioni*. It means 'big dinner or feast.'"

"So, they were looking forward to a mutton supper?"

"No, Doctor. They were referring to other dinner guests – the leopards and cheetahs that roam my valley."

We had a good laugh. Indeed, Murdoch, Jameson and I passed much of the journey in jolly conversation. Holmes would drift in and out, but spent much of his time in a comfy chair stationed next to one of the large floor-to-ceiling windows in our carriage. These windows made one feel as though they were flying over the vibrant African countryside.

Even without seeing the landscape change, we were all aware that we had left the cooler coast, and were heading into the jungle. With each mile, the temperature and humidity seemed to increase by several degrees. By the time we reached Kimberley, we were in shirtsleeves.

The closest Holmes or I had, hereto, come to Kimberley, was when we had retrieved the Countess of Morcar's blue carbuncle from a goose's throat. However, Kimberley had been Jameson's home for nearly twenty years.

We stopped for lunch in order to confer with Nkosinathi, a Matabele regimental commander, and close friend of Jameson's. When we arrived at the station, Nkosinathi, or Nathi as Lanner called him, was waiting in full warrior dress, complete with assegai spear. A large entourage stood alongside.

The warrior was tall, and broad-chested. His appearance seemed anachronistic. While Nathi's hair was beginning to turn silver, his body was that of a young man – well muscled and firm. His smile broadened, as his friend stepped off the train.

As Jameson approached, Nkosinathi spread his arms wide and gripped his friend by the shoulders.

"Nathi, *unjani*!" Jameson said, in greeting. The two friends clasped arms and continued to chat. At one point Nathi slapped Jameson's left arm hard. Jameson smiled and rolled up his sleeve to reveal a scar-tattoo of a deer-like animal. The welted tattoo on Jameson's arm was tinted with brown and black. I would later learn that it was acquired during an initiation ceremony. Nathi pointed to the okapi tattoo and said something in his own language, laughing heartily. Jameson translated: "Nathi says that they did not need to use white pigments when they carved the totem tattoo into my arm."

After introductions, we made our way to an area

known as Greenpoint, the coloured quarter of the city. It was apparent that modernity had spread its tentacles into the heart of Africa. The main thoroughfares were paved, and lined with electric lighting.

Our luncheon was served in an open-air restaurant. Breezes wafted in wonderful smells from the outdoor kitchen. After we were seated around a massive bamboo table, the servers carried in something called ba-boor-tea, a delicious mixture of curried mutton and fruit, with a creamy golden topping. It was exquisite. Murdoch made a joke. "So, this is where my sheep disappeared!"

Jameson explained the jest to Nathi, who howled and slapped our Aussie comrade on the back.

Nathi spoke some English, but drifted back and forth between languages, as we discussed our mission. At one point, Holmes nudged Jameson and asked if it he might ask a question. Evidently, Nathi understood.

"Mista Holmes," Nathi began, "you are an onad guest. Ef I can help you, dat would be good."

Holmes nodded in appreciation. "Nathi, what do you know about the Kongo Nkisi spirit?"

"Kongo Nkisi make bad magic."

With the help of Jameson's translations, Nathi went on to explain that Kongo Nkisi is a spirit, or magical energy, that witches can harness in order to bewitch or charm others.

"Called *umthakathi* among the Zulu, and *moloi* among the Sotho, these witches are often unaware of their malevolent power," Jameson explained. "They do not learn their craft, but are perceived to be born with magical ability."

"So, these *umthakathi* are using the power of Kongo Nkisi to make the soulless people we have heard about?" I asked.

Nathi nodded, and pointed a finger at me. "Yes."

"Can you give us any help or advice?" Holmes requested.

Nathi turned to a woman who had been standing behind him throughout the luncheon – one of his entourage. She had not taken lunch with us, but stood completely still and silent – until now. "Welile," he called.

As the stocky woman came forward, Jameson leaned to my ear, whispering: "Her name means 'those who have crossed over.' I believe she is a witch hunter."

And, such was the case.

Welile was dressed in beautiful lynx skins, folded over and over from waist to knee. The upper part of her body was covered in strings of teeth, fangs, and beads. Lynx tails hung like lappets on each side of her face. Her hair, greased and dyed red, hung as a fringe covering her eyes. Her arms were folded, and she held a ceremonial whisk in her right hand, from which long animal hairs bristled.

The Matabele warrior explained that Welile was a renowned witch hunter, and that he had asked her to use her powers to help us.

I thought that Holmes might have reservations, but I was mistaken.

"We are grateful for her help," Holmes answered, and went to welcome Welile. As he shook her hand, she froze. Then, she spoke in a low rasping voice. I asked Jameson what she said.

"She is telling Holmes that there is a spirit that follows him," Lanner explained.

"Is she saying Holmes has a strong spirit?"

"No, no: she is saying that she can see a spirit following him."

"More mumbo-jumbo."

"I think not," was all that Jameson said in reply.

We took our leave of Nathi, and our expedition, richer by one, boarded the train for the last leg of the trip to Elisabethville, and beyond.

Welile was wary when boarding the train, swatting the carriage doorway with her whisk and chanting, as she entered. A boy followed close behind her, carrying her belongings in a bundle, tied up within gaily-coloured cloth. As she took a place on the floor near the rear of the car, I wondered what this witch hunter would bring into our lives.

As we made our way north, somewhere near Gweio, we heard a shrill whistle and squeaking brakes. As we lurched to a stop, I stuck my head out of the window to see a full-grown lion stretched across the line, basking peacefully in the sun. In reply to the piercing whistle, the brute looked up lazily, but did not attempt to move. The efforts of the engineer and stoker, to drive him off with billets of wood, were no better rewarded. The driver then re-engaged the wheels, and the train creaked forward. Suddenly the lion lunged at the engine, then swaggered away, thoroughly frustrated by the huge black, tough-skinned beast that fed on fire, and bellowed as it ran.

The remainder of the journey was uneventful. I was dozing as Jameson shook me to attention. "We have just crossed into the Belgian Congo. We should be in Elisabethville within the hour. You might wish to make use of some of this train's amenities before we arrive."

Our train did not pull into the station, but was sent off on a spur. When we came to a stop, a flatbed truck pulled up to the boxcar in front of us. As Murdoch jumped out, he shouted. "I'll see to your luggage and supplies. See ya at the hotel. Jameson knows where."

Welile stepped off the train and wandered off without a word. I pointed her out to Jameson. "Don't worry," he said, "she knows where we are going. She will find her way."

As we gathered our belongings, something that resembled an automobile, pulled next to our carriage. It was an oddly-narrow, boat-like vehicle – a kind of canoe mounted on four wire wheels. Holmes, Jameson and I piled in, tandem style, for there was barely room for two abreast.

"Strange vehicle," I commented.

"A Renault. Only the French could design something this bizarre," Jameson replied.

Fortunately, it was a short trip to the hotel, because the penetrating heat was at its peak. The rainy season was just beginning, and the air was thick. I sweated through my shirt within minutes.

Elisabethville was large by comparison to Kimberley, which puzzled me. "I am quite surprised by the level of commerce here," I observed.

"Elisabethville is built on mining," Holmes replied. "Copper is king, but you can find cobalt, tin and gold, as well as semi-precious stones. It is regions such as this that lie at the heart of the colonial tug-of-war."

"And this is Belgian territory?" I asked.

"Yes, Watson. The city was named in honour of their beloved queen, just three years ago. She has proven to be a good ally."

"Yes, thankfully," Jameson agreed. "The Cape to Cairo Railway might otherwise be impossible, as the French on the west, and the Germans on the east, would not likely allow passage."

Jameson swung around in his seat. "Gentlemen, I have taken the liberty of changing our hotel in order to accommodate Welile. Only whites are allowed in the city centre. I know an excellent hotel in the *cité indigene* to the south. It is quite comfortable."

The Hotel Bougain was simple, clean and quiet. Neither Holmes nor I slept well aboard the train, and we took to bed early. The next morning Holmes, as usual, was up and dressed before me. "Come along, Watson, are you up for a stroll and a cup of coffee?"

I certainly was, and, in short order, we were off. We strolled silently through the city for some time before Holmes spoke, "What was the name of that café, which the Cape Town newsman, Arbuckle, frequented?"

I retrieved my notebook. "*Tasse de Café*," I said.

Within ten minutes, we had found our way there. Though early, the establishment was bustling. As we entered, a well-kept middle-aged woman behind the counter straightened up, as if in recognition. "That would, no doubt, be May," Holmes said.

I consulted my notes to see that he had remembered correctly. We sat at the counter. May approached. "Coffee for you, gentlemen?"

"Yes, please," I replied.

She returned with the two cups of brew. "You're not from these parts?" Her ample assets were on display below the deep-necked white blouse she wore. Her hair was pulled back from her face and fastened tightly behind her head with a red scarf. There were no adornments, save her own, and a bulky necklace bearing a heavy ornament.

"Nor, are you," Holmes replied.

"English" she surmised. "London. Am I right, then?""Yes," I replied.

Holmes put a finger to his chin. "And you, young lady, are from West Yorkshire. Am I correct?" And, after a pause, "Do I detect a… yes, you hail from Leeds."

This brought on a look of confusion on the woman's face. "You're a clever fella, are you not?"

"Mr. Arbuckle, in Cape Town, recommended your café," Holmes said, taking back the conversation.

"Well, I'm certainly pleased you're here," May replied. "Pleased, indeed."

As she walked away, I reacted to her strange, forward manner. "She's a little odd, Holmes."

Holmes sat silently and watched as the proprietor moved from patron to patron, chatting in a variety of languages – French, German, and Dutch. She occasionally glanced back at us and smiled.

"Does she remind you of someone, Watson?"

"No," I replied. "She does you, I conjecture."

"Yes, an old, old acquaintance. Did you notice her necklace?"

"Do you mean that circle with the letter 'I?"

"It is the Greek symbol for Phi. What does that conjure up, Watson?"

"The missing locomotive 161."

"Yes. I am again in need of your investigative skills. See what you can discover about the pretty proprietor of the *Tasse de Café*. If we must, we can delay our excursion into the bush for a day. I believe I require another cup of coffee."

"Very well, Holmes. I'll do what I can, of course."

I made my way to the city hall to check on licencing, then, went on to several nearby pubs – always the best source for local information.

Holmes was gone when I returned, but I had a bite to eat at a small tavern, across the street from the *Tasse de Café*. At one point, a Mercedes town car pulled up in front. The late-morning sun danced on the brass fittings of this plush crimson and gold motorcar. It seemed out of place, as did the café proprietor who climbed aboard, now wearing a duster and pith helmet. I could not follow the car, but I noted that it turned to the east at the end of the thoroughfare.

I reported all this to Holmes, and when I shared May's full name, his face grew grim. "Maeve Murtagh, you say."

"Yes, and she only *recently* purchased the coffee shop," I added. "I'm told she comes and goes from the establishment often – sometimes for days a time. From her dress today, I'd say she was headed into the jungle."

"Moriarty may, indeed, be reaching beyond the grave… in a manner of speaking."

"You mean, Maeve?"

"Murtagh is a variant of the old Irish Ó Muircheartaigh, as is Moriarty."

"A relation, then?"

"Yes, a close one, I suspect."

"But, why is she here in the heart of Africa?"

Holmes handed me a small piece of torn paper with lettering upon it.

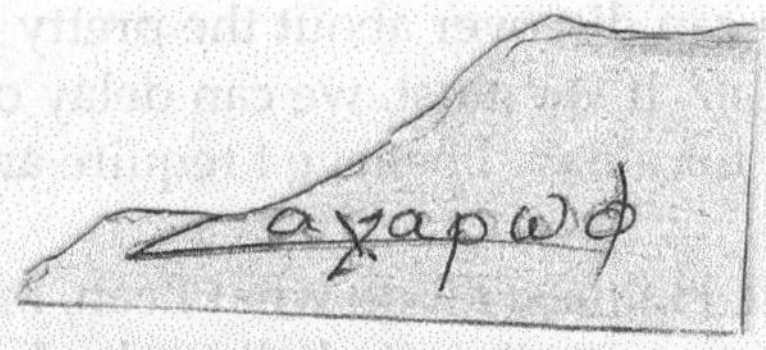

"Greek?"

"Yes, a word that begins with zeta or sigma… probably zeta – a Z. My Greek is not what it should be. After you left the café, a man came in and delivered a note to May… Maeve. She read it; and then torn it into small pieces and stuffed the bits into the pocket of her apron. One of the pieces fell on the floor – that piece."

"What do you make of it?"

From the manner in which it is written, and the placement on the paper, it's probably a signature. It could be something of interest, given her furtive manner. Then again, Maeve may have intentionally left this scrap of paper for me."

"You, Holmes?"

"Maeve may have inherited the profane playfulness of her father."

"Her father? How can you be sure?"

"Ears are one of the corporal signs of primogeniture," Holmes answered. "Maeve has Moriarty's ears. The professor would have kept her existence a secret, of course."

"So, she is after revenge?"

"Possibly, but I suspect I may simply be the 'icing on the cake.' Maeve Moriarty is after much more."

~

At Holmes's request, Lucas Murdoch engaged a stout fellow to watch the *Tasse de Café*, and Maeve Murtagh. With that provision in place, we moved out.

The driver and stoker of our train were not eager to make the journey to the end of the line. Holmes gave them the Verney-Carron express rifle Jameson had meant for him, as a token of comfort. I, however, kept mine close at hand.

The brief journey was uneventful.

When we reached the end of the line, the stoker banked the coals, and shut the engine down. Holmes, now outfitted in khakis, stepped out of our car and walked to where the rails stopped. He then went on, following a pathway to the north. The rest of us trailed behind. Welile remained in the car.

Holmes examined the cut brush and turf as we followed silently. We had hiked nearly a mile before he stopped and turned back to Murdoch. "How far ahead do you clear the way for the rail bed?"

Murdoch shrugged his shoulders. "No hard'n fast rule. My man seldom clears more than a mile out, as the jungle quickly overtakes any clearing."

"Just one man does the clearing, then?"

"Yes. Usually, in small brush like this, Mr. Holmes."

"Very good. We have gone about a mile to here." Holmes picked up the end of a limb from a tall bush nearby. "See here how this limb was cut by a right-handed person – as the cut terminates down, at this angle. The lower part of the blade was sharper than the upper part."

Holmes then walked forward several paces and picked up another branch. "This bush was hacked back by a left-handed person, and the blade was entirely sharp."

"Ain't you a corker?" Murdoch mumbled.

"Two different people cleared this path," Holmes asserted. "My guess is that we will find that the person, who cleared the path from this point forward, was *not* a member of your crew."

Murdoch slapped Holmes's back. "Cunning as a dunny rat, you are."

We had trudged on only a short distance before the trail suddenly widened.

Holmes went to his knees and rummaged through the broken brush. "Notice, as the trail opens up, the brush is no longer cut, but rather crushed and broken by something… something rather large."

A little further up the trail, we crossed under a canopy of large trees. Holmes inspected the turf again. "Here, where the soil is moist, you can see where wheels have made an impression."

We all gathered around. "Clearly some type of transport," Jameson observed. "Something able to negotiate the jungle terrain."

I pointed to a blackened spot on the ground ahead. "Look there!"

Murdoch touched the blacken stain and brought his fingers to his nose. "Oil. It's a bloody machine, gentlemen."

"The Kongo Nkisi spirit train." Holmes stated. "Onward."

Jameson hesitated. "I too am as eager to move on Mr. Holmes, but I suggest we make camp at the train tonight, and set out early tomorrow. By the time we are outfitted today, we will have lost most of the light."

It was agreed. When we returned to the rail bed, we found Welile standing in front of the engine with her arms spread wide, eyes closed, and chanting. Jameson put his arm out to stop our entry. We waited for nearly five minutes before the witch hunter lowered her head and ceased her chanting.

As we made our way to our car, Welile seemed to pay particular attention to Holmes. After we passed, she beckoned Jameson. We moved on, while Lanner and Welile chatted in hushed tones.

Murdoch had enlisted the aid of the driver and stoker to help him unload the supplies and materials from the adjoining boxcar. I pitched in, helping to uncrate our equipment. The driver offered to use the heat of the boiler to cook our dinner, as the rest of us set about erecting tents and collecting wood for a fire.

Darkness comes quickly in the jungle, due to the height and density of the trees. After dinner, we all sat about the fire, which cast dancing shadows on the surrounding curtain of greenery. The effect suggested phantoms were lurching just outside the circle of light. In the darkness beyond, alien animal calls prompted me to check the breech of my rifle.

Jameson lit his pipe and made his way to Holmes and me. "I thought you might be interested in the conversation I had with Welile earlier."

"She holds herself a little apart," I noted.

Jameson nodded. "She lives in the place between the physical and the supernatural, in touch with both realms, belonging to neither." Jameson cleared his throat. "Mr. Holmes... how would you describe your relationship with the metaphysical realm – spirits, and the like?"

Holmes replied: "Modern man is increasingly afflicted with the notion that, if he does not know or understand something, it either does not exist, or it is unimportant. I do not share those convictions." He took a long drag on his pipe. "On the other side, archaic superstitions, and outrageous magical ideas, are not a substitute for reason, or scientific exploration. I suppose then, that puts me somewhere between a believer and a total skeptic, Mr. Jameson."

Our guide tapped his pipe on a rock. "I was in a similar place, Mr. Holmes... until I came to Africa. Here I experienced things that I can only describe as 'magic.' The human mind has untapped power – more than the ability to think and perceive. Certainly, you would agree that human creativity *begins* in the mind – with an idea. I am convinced that our mind's creative power does not end with ideas. I believe that the mind can manifest things."

I watched Holmes's expression shift and change as he considered Jameson's assertions. I can say, sitting in this primitive locale, watching the fire dance on Welile's inscrutable face, that Jameson's conjectures carried more veracity than they might otherwise have done.

Jameson leaned closer. "Welile said that a witch has traveled on the very trail we were on today. She sensed that he had a powerful magic, possibly the Kongo Nkisi spirit. She said the Kongo Nkisi dislikes the white man's intrusion, and is particularly angry at the railway. That is what is behind the Kongo Nkisi's alliance with the witch."

"None of this is particularly helpful, is it?" I said.

"On the contrary," Holmes interrupted. "Welile validates our plan to follow the trail we discovered; and confirms that black magic and superstition are being used to stop the railway project. What is more, the revelation that some kind of modern mechanical vehicle is involved tells us that someone, *in addition* to the witch, is at work here. I am very hopeful."

Just then... a shrill blare sounded in the distance. Heads turned in unison. Again it sounded. The driver of our train was the first to speak. "A steam engine."

Welile bolted up and spread her arms as if to embrace the night. "Kongo Nkisi."

"Or... a steam whistle," Holmes countered.

"Holmes, it is possible that the vehicle that travels the trail ahead is steam powered?" I proposed.

Murdoch turned to me. "Makes sense, Doctor, not much petrol out here... plenty of wood." The brawny Aussie gathered up the coffee cups around the fire. "Brekkie comes early gentlemen. G'night."

As Holmes and I rose to follow Murdoch, Jameson caught Holmes's arm. "One more thing Holmes. Welile... once again, told me that she sees a spirit following you. She believes it is the spirit of a woman. I understand this is not logical, but does it make any sense to you?"

"It is not logical, but, in a way, it makes sense."

"A wise perspective. You are in Africa now. Goodnight."

The driver and stoker stood the first two watches bearing the rifle Holmes had given them. Murdoch evidently stood the remaining watches, for he had coffee waiting when I was awakened by a cacophony of jungle birds.

As we finished a rather Spartan breakfast, Holmes wrote a brief report and asked the driver, who knew Morse code, to send it on to Mr. Williams in Cape Town. As the driver perused the message, he enquired, "When might you return from the bush?"

"We are uncertain, but Jameson will wait here. If we do not return within four days, he will go for help."

Lucas glanced at me reassuringly. "I think that's a bloody good idea, Mr. Holmes."

With that, we took up our packs and began retracing yesterday's trail. The first day's march was slow going, despite the fact that the trail was partially cleared by the strange vehicle, in whose tracks we followed. Murdoch estimated we had traveled about ten miles in all.

As the sun set, we found a good campsite, near a stream. It took all the remaining energy I had to pitch our tent. We made a fire for protection, and ate a cold dinner of tinned meat and beans. We refilled our canteens and sought our bedrolls, with little campfire conversation.

I arose a little more slowly the following day. The trail did not have the same allure it did as when we began. My eagerness seemed to wane in proportion to the loss of creature comforts. However, no one complained, least of all Welile, who always seemed serene.

As we set out, Murdoch noticed animal sign crossing the trail. He bent over the prints in the turf. As he endeavoured to distinguish them, Welile leaned over his shoulder and offered a word, "*Ncobo.*"

Murdoch translated. "She said it is a duiker."

"A duiker?" I asked.

"A small bush antelope. Bloody good eating. These tracks are fresh and I'm thinking that I will bag some bush meat for dinner tonight... that is, if you are willing to move on without me. I'll catch up."

Holmes, Welile, and I continued on.

As the sun touched the treetops, I was growing concerned that Lucas had not yet returned. "Maybe we should set up camp a little early?" I suggested. "It seems the duiker led him on a merry chase."

Holmes disagreed. "He knows the jungle, Watson. The trail is clear. It is best to keep to our plan."

As the shadows overtook the trail, we prepared to make camp against a cliff wall. The terrain here was drier, more rugged, and rockier. I was gaining respect for the vehicle that seemingly had the power to move with ease through this harsh terrain. No sooner had this thought occurred to me, when the sharp screeching of a steam whistle shattered the quiet of the jungle, scattering the birds from the trees above. A few moments later, it blasted again, obviously getting closer.

"It is coming," I said.

Holmes hurried us along as we gathered up our gear and scampered toward some large rocks that would provide cover.

We waited.

Eventually, we could hear the rhythmic whine of an engine. Before long, a metal monster appeared on the trail. Preceding it were two bare-chested natives – trotting – spears in hand. They had short-cropped hair and beards and glistened with sweat. Welile whispered, "*Bad Abantu*."

Holmes remarked, "Yes, they bear all the markings of Bantu."

We slid quietly behind the rocks and waited for them to pass. I released the safety on my rifle.

Suddenly the metal machine released a gush of steam and came to a stop near our hiding place. We froze. Waited.

We were taken by surprise by native chatter above us. I looked up to see another Bantu warrior standing atop the cliff overhead. He was pointing down with his spear. Then another voice broke through:

"Meester Holmes and Doctor Votson, ve know you are zare behind ze rocks. I fear zat zare is no escape. Please come out. Do not make me keel you."

I raised my rifle, but Holmes pushed it down.

At the behest of the German voice, we showed ourselves. The two Bantu guides were waiting on the other side of our rocky cover. Just behind them were two white militiamen with rifles raised and pointed. They wore khaki uniforms.

On the trail beyond was a strange machine, similar to a Sentinel steam truck. It had large knobby wheels and a large metal cabin sitting high atop the huge front wheels. Standing within the cabin was a slender man in a field-grey uniform and pith helmet. His hands were propped upon hips as if scolding a naughty child. "Ve haf been vaiting for you."

"Have we stumbled into German territory, Holmes?"

"No, Watson, it seems they have invaded Belgium's."

"Quiet, please," the German ordered. "I had saught zat your capture vas an on-necessary complication. Boot now, I see eat as poetic. The English must learn that causalities are part of vor."

"War!" I exclaimed. "We are not at war."

"Not yet," our captor hissed.

The German in command nodded, and the two white militiamen took my rifle and escorted us out. It was then that I noticed that Welile was no longer with us. What was more amazing, no one seemed to be aware of this fact. It was if they had never seen her.

Our hands were bound behind our backs, and we were blindfolded and thrust into the jungle-buggy (for such it was). Within minutes, the vehicle turned around and headed back from whence it came.

The air inside the steel cabin, exacerbated by the heat from the steam engine beneath, was stifling. The cacophony of the engine was such that conversation was futile.

Hours passed, and the vibrations absorbed by my body dulled my senses. I overheard the German leader shouting orders. I understood little, but I knew Holmes had a good knowledge of the language.

It was nightfall when the eerie steam-whistle blew again, announcing our arrival at a camp. When our blindfolds were removed, a dazzling ring of torches blinded me. Behind each one was a militiaman, bearing a rifle.

We were given water and marched into a two-storey metal-clad building. The upper floors were ablaze with light, but as we entered, we found the lower area completely dark. One of our two well-armed escorts lighted a lantern. Nearby, something or someone stirred, and made a growling sound. The devil behind me poked with his rifle barrel and nudged me forward.

As we entered the huge room, a terrible racket arose – people writhing in pain. My blood ran cold, as the clamour rose to a crescendo. One guard bellowed an order. He raised the lantern, and swept it back and forth. As he was doing so, my eyes, now becoming accustomed to the dimness, revealed large cages ringing the perimeter. And, something was moving within those cells.

Huddled against the far walls of the cages were men.

Natives… their hands covering their eyes. Hundreds of them. Not a word was spoken, just increscent moaning and caterwauling.

"*Halt!*" The tall guard said, and gave another order.

"Stop," Holmes translated for me, "so that they may remove our bindings."

We were shoved inside a separate cell, and the door clanged shut.

As the guards left, the light did also. However, blue-white moonlight filtered through tiny vents set high along the perimeter walls. As our eyes adjusted to the light, our surroundings took on a terrifying spectre.

Most immediately apparent was the fetid smell of excreta that permeated the sultry air. The earbashing had ceased, and only a few sobs and sighs could be heard now.

"Hello," I called. "Who are you?"

My entreaties only served to precipitate a few howls and laments from our fellow prisoners. We sat silently for a long while. Eventually, exhausted, I drifted off to sleep.

As the dawn came, spikes of sunlight pierced the chamber revealing a ghastly presence. Hundreds of men were packed into dozens of cells ringing the chamber. Eyes vacant, starring… bodies slack and unresponsive… hair tangled, clumped and patchy. Tattered clothing, coated thick with grim, clung to their frail frames. Most stood quietly, shallow breathing their only movement. Others fell prey to what seemed to be uncontrollable spastic gyrations.

"Holmes, the spiritless people."

"Yes, and I fear, we may soon join their ranks."

Dread and panic swept over me. "To what end, Holmes?"

But, before Holmes could reply, an earsplitting steam

whistle sounded, bringing the enchanted assemblage to the bars. The steel entry doors slammed open. A dozen guards swarmed inside with rifles and whips. Cell doors clanged open, and the soulless troupe was driven out like a herd of wild beasts. Some, who clawed at the guards, were beaten back into line with whips. They trudged forward in silence.

Shortly afterwards, Holmes and I were bound and taken from our cell and escorted toward a large open-sided hut of bamboo and reed construction.

As we plodded onward, the last of our fellow inmates, now bearing shovels and picks, was marching, single-file, toward a large mound in the distance. Small-gauge rails, which criss-crossed the area, fed into a large tin-covered building, from which smoke belched.

As we entered the reed hut, the commander, who had captured us the day before, was sitting at his desk.

"Ah, Meester Holmes and Doctor Votson. "Please escuse my English. I trust you passed a peaceful night."

"What kind of illicit mining is going on here?" Holmes asked.

"Vot arrogance! I do not sink you are in any position to make demands, sir. But... I vill tell you." He arose and grabbed a tin can and dumped a pile of silver-grey gravel on his desktop.

"Silver." I instinctively blurted out.

"Nein, Doctor Votson, somesing much more valuable."

"Cobalt," Holmes replied.

"Yes, yes. Cobalt."

Holmes walked to the table, and ran his fingers through the granular substance. "A critical alloy... resistant to corrosion and wear... essential for aircraft engines, large guns, and underwater craft."

"You are a fountain of knowledge, Meester Holmes,"

the acerbic commander jested. "Yes, ve need it. And, unfortunately, von of the vorld's richest sources is here. And... ve must have it. Ve stopped ze train, and get ze ore."

"Even if you have to drug, enslave and murder hundreds of poor souls," Holmes accused.

"Zay are inconsequential – inferior beings," the commandant said, with a shrug. "Zey are poor verkers, but ze price is right," he said, with a forced laugh. "But zey are not drugged. I geeve zem to the vitch-doctor. Vitch ees vare you are going *jetzt*. Za crazy black man do his, how do you say, mumbo-jumbo, and zay become zittle verker bees."

"But, why us?" I asked. "Why have you brought us here?"

"Two reasons. *Erste*, you ar in de vay. *Zweite*, eet ees a, how du you zay, a contactual arrangement mit a colleague."

"The colleague's name?" Holmes enquired.

"I em not certain zey vould appreciate my telling you. No more questions. You must be going. Za pit avaits." With that he waved his hand, and our two escorts, who were waiting behind, marched us toward a thatched hut nearby.

A gruesome native, whose body was decorated head to foot in vivid magenta and indigo designs, was waiting. His face was painted white, giving his head the appearance of a skull. He wore a breastplate made of black shells.

"Holmes, what did he mean by 'a contractual arrangement with a colleague'?"

"Quiet!" came a shout from our guard. And then... a warbling scream came from the nearby bushes. Appearing amidst a tall plume of blue-green smoke stood Welile.

Our guards raised their rifles just as Welile flung a red

brown powder that stuck in our throats and blinded everyone. I felt a hand, Welile's hand, on mine; and I grabbed Holmes's hand as the witch hunter pulled us into the bush.

Suddenly, water was splashed on my face. Welile cut our bonds, nodded, smiled, and pointed to a trail. "Must go quickly," she said, trotting off, with us following.

Shouts emanated from the camp. The steam whistle blew in short, sharp blasts. Our captors would be close behind. We stayed with the trail for some distance, before Welile stopped and pointed to the left. "Holmes and Doctor go there. Welile here." We were separating, in the hopes of throwing our pursuers off the scent.

The whistle continued to bellow as Germanic shouts came ever closer.

We ran. Twisting. Turning. Each step a struggle in the tangled brush.

I gulped the air, my breathing becoming deeper, but ever less effective. Holmes pushed ahead, clearing the way for us. His face and hands were flecked with blood from the vines and brambles.

Holmes yelped, and tumbled to the ground. He reached for his left leg. The shouts in the background grew louder. They were close now.

"Holmes, your leg!"

"Twisted." I helped him up, but his leg folded. I could not hold him up. "Holmes, get on my shoulders."

"No, go, Watson. Bring help. Go."

I hesitated, disoriented. "Holmes..."

He grabbed my arm. Pulled me close. "You, only you, can stop this. Go now!" He released my arm, and pushed me away.

A nearby whoop sent me scurrying. I ripped at the vines and brush. My arms became leaden. I pushed on...

and on. I fell and, for a moment, lay on the cool earth to catch my breath. I thought of the duiker that Murdoch had hunted. It must have cringed in the bushes, tired and frightened, like me.

A loud Germanic clamour arose from the trail behind me, telling me our hunters had come upon Holmes.

I cannot recall how long I toiled, tearing my way through the undergrowth before it opened up into a clearing. As I straightened up I saw our angel, Welile. Her tawny skin was shiny with perspiration, but otherwise she was not disheveled at all. Her initial smile quickly dimmed as she saw that I was alone.

She guided me to a small rivulet, where I drank deeply. She mopped my brow and washed my face with cool water. However, we did not tarry. "We must hurry to get help," I barked.

Welile pointed, and we soon found what I suspected was the original trail that took us to the German mining camp. It was broad and easy to navigate. We had only gone about a mile before we heard other voices… shouts: "Holmes! Watson! Welile!"

And, there he stood, Murdoch. "Watson, Watson," he sang, as he swung his rifle over his shoulder and rushed to me. Close behind him were more than two-dozen armed men, including Jameson.

Jameson conferred with Welile before he greeted me. "Where is Holmes?" I pointed behind me. Welile was already beckoning for the others to follow her to retrace our previous steps. "You rest here, Doctor," Jameson said.

"Never!"

Two men with machetes cleared the way, and the rest of us followed at a brisk pace. Murdoch explained that he had lost his way hunting the duiker. He caught up with us just as we were taken captive. Seeing our captors were well armed, he decided go for help.

"This Maeve gal is mad as a meat-axe," Murdoch said. "The bloke I posted to watch her passed on a detailed message from her, telling us exactly where to find you. She walked up behind my man one afternoon, and handed him a message with a map. Of course, knowing we were headed into an armed camp, I gathered up some of my mates in Elisabethville... and here we are."

It was not long before we came upon the spot where Holmes went down. As rain began to fall, one of the machete-swinging trail-breakers turned and raised his hands to hush us.

Murdoch and I crept forward in the mud. We could see smoke in the distance.

Jameson suggested we wait until it was dark, but I insisted that we go in immediately. Holmes was, no doubt, in the clutches of the witch whom we had eluded earlier. Murdoch agreed and handed me his Steyr-Hahn pistol and a handful of bullets.

Jameson pulled me aside. "John, Welile says that Holmes is with the witch. She is afraid that, if we attack, Holmes's life will be in jeopardy."

"We have to go in," I begged.

"Yes, yes of course, but I believe it best if we let Welile guide us to Holmes, *before* the others attack."

And so, we agreed that Welile, Jameson, and I should go in first. Once Holmes was safe, we would signal the others to attack.

Welile began to chant in a low, droning manner. She swatted our shoulders with her whisk.

Jameson whispered: "She's protecting us with her magic."

It took no time to work our way around behind the

witch's hut. When we were in position, Welile held up one finger, asking us to wait. She then stood up, and casually walked into the hut. It was if she were invisible.

Then, a beastly shriek arose from inside the hut, splitting our ears.

"I think we should go," Jameson said.

We raced into the hut.

There huddled on the floor, before Welile, was the witch. He was hunched over on his knees. Her whisk was resting on his back. He was bleeding from his ears and nose, and his entire body shuttered.

"Holmes, where is Holmes?" I demanded.

Welile pointed to a wooden coffin-like box that was set against the far wall of the hut.

And there lay Holmes, as if in death.

My body lurched as Jameson's rifle fired to signal the attack. I noticed that Holmes did not react. His eyes were without animation.

"Holmes!" I shouted, shaking his shoulders. He did not see or recognize me.

Shots rang out from every direction now, as the skirmish around us ensued. English and German shouts mingled in an angry *melée*.

Jameson approached Holmes and felt for a pulse. "He's alive. We must get him into care quickly. Wait here, I'll be back."

I examined Holmes as best I could in the dim light. His pulse was weak. Breathing slow. Breath fetid. His wounds were minor, save for a nasty cut on his upper right arm.

I pulled him from the box and laid him on the floor. Welile hissed something in her own tongue to the witch. It must have been convincing because the man rattled on and on, incoherently. I looked on, desperate for understanding. Welile held up a finger and the witch stopped chattering. She turned to me and offered one terrible word:

"Venom."

I opened Holmes's shirt to put my head to his chest. Suddenly he jerked up, staring straight ahead.

"Holmes, thank god, I thought you were..."

There was no reply. No recognition of me... of anything. He was a spiritless slave, like those that worked the mines... like those that had wandered into Elisabethville... like those that had died a horrible death.

The battle ensued outside the hut, but the gunshots became less frequent, and the shouting faded.

Welile stood over the witch, who had now rolled into a whimpering ball. I could not fathom what power the witch hunter held over him. Welile lifted his head in her hands. She asked a stern, insistent question in her native tongue.

The witch pointed to a table in the corner. Welile went to the corner and picked up two wooden bowls with powders in them. She brought them to me, just as Jameson returned.

"They're on the run," Lanner said. Then, glancing at Holmes stretched out on the dirt floor, "Are we too late?"

"No," I replied. "Welile said something about 'venom'. I think it's the powders here that put Holmes in this state. Welile got them from the witch.

Jameson dipped his finger into the first bowl and rubbed the reddish powder in his fingers – then brought it to his nose. "I know this one. The natives call it 'powder strike.' It is a neurotoxin found in the flesh of the puffer fish." He then poked his finger in the bowl of grey powder, "I believe the other one is..."

Jameson turned to Welile to ask a question, to which she replied in her own language.

"I'm right," Jameson said, "Welile calls it 'the devil's snare', but you and I know it as Jimson weed."

"That's a medicinal plant, used to treat influenza, asthma and nerve diseases."

Jameson nodded, "Yes, but too much produces hallucinations."

"The two together would bring about a death-like state and strange behaviour, would they not?" I surmised. "Ask Welile about an antidote or cure."

Welile clutched the witch's face in her hands and interrogated him as Jameson fed her the questions. In due course, Jameson had some answers.

"The powders are introduced directly into the blood stream through a cut. Look there on his arm. You can still see some of the residue from the powders. We must wash out as much as we can." Jameson paused. "There is no antidote. It has to work through his system."

"Or not," I said.

Murdoch poked his head inside the hut. "It's a rip-snorter. We creamed 'em. Most fled into the jungle, but we got that blighter of a Commander. How's Holmes?"

"We must get him to hospital, as soon as possible," I said.

"Reckon!" Murdoch replied. "I'll leave my men here and get you back to the train. What about you, Jameson?"

"I'll stay here, with Welile, to see to the poor souls in the mine… if you don't mind, Watson. He can do no better than to be in your care. I will follow on as soon as I can."

Murdoch ducked out. I turned to see Welile washing Holmes's wound. I had come to trust her completely. She held a rare measure of power, courage, and wisdom.

Within a few minutes Murdoch returned, with two men carrying a makeshift stretcher. We placed Holmes on it, and headed south to the waiting train.

Initially, the only response from Holmes was a mild delirium – his head rocking back and forth. Later his eyes popped open, and he tried to sit up. I laid him down. "Holmes, you are fine," I said, wondering why I had lied.

As we approached the end of the trail, Murdoch fired a rifle shot to signal our arrival. "That engineer bloke is likely to go off like a frog in a sock," the Aussie noted. "Don't want 'em shooting at us." Then glancing at Holmes, "Sorry, I forgot about the patient."

"He never heard you."

We carried Holmes into the car. As we began to lay him on a couch, he became violent, broke away, and stood up. He attempted to walk and talk, but his movements were shuddering and erratic, as were his vocalizations – not speech at all.

"Maybe we should tie him down," Murdoch said. "He's wiry."

Yes, he still has his strength, I thought. *That is a good sign.*

I decided to take Murdoch's advice and fetter Holmes. Even travelling non-stop, at full speed, it would take more than an hour to get to Elisabethville, and I would be without help.

Murdoch and his men waved off and left for the mining camp. The train shuttered and clanged as it went into reverse and headed south, picking up speed quickly. The click and clack of the cars on the rail became a metronome, counting time that was now more precious than ever. Holmes had wrestled with death many times, and had always been victorious. Now, as he struggled with his bindings, grunting and struggling goggle-eyed, I prayed that his remarkable constitution would come to his aid, once again.

Caught in my thoughts for some time, I barely noticed that Holmes had stopped thrashing. His breathing was less forced, and serenity had overtaken him. Even his eyes relaxed and began to blink in a normal fashion.

He began to mumble, and I leaned closer to hear. "Um, yes... where... are we?" he said. And after a pause, "But I want to... be... with you."

He was in some delirium, but a calm one, a harmless one... a fine one, it seemed.

Holmes remained in this peaceful state, talking, mumbling, and even smiling. I noticed, too, that his breathing had become strong and regular. His limbs had lost their rigidity. This was bewildering because it was too soon for the poisons to have worked their way through his system.

With this improvement, I felt I could leave his side to get a drink of water and freshen up. I was gone no more than three or four minutes. When I returned, I saw Holmes was no longer on the couch. He had broken his bindings and was standing before one of the large windows, staring out into the passing jungle.

I approached cautiously. "Holmes, it's me, Watson."

He turned and cocked his head, as if conjuring up a memory. His face lit up in a soft smile. "Watson. I've been asleep."

"Indeed, and very ill."

"I had a dream... an amazing dream. Irene was there. She said that she knew she would be needed. She stood in the bright sunlight. I could not see her face. Then... she had to go. She told me she would not be far... and we would see each other again."

"What a lovely dream."

"Yes... a dream." He raised a clenched fist, and held it out between us. Slowly his fingers opened.

There sitting in the palm of his hand was a gold sovereign. It was worn and old, with a hole pierced in it for a waiting watch chain.

I picked it up and held it to the light. "Eighteen eighty-seven" it read. *Eighteen eighty-seven*. "How can this be?" I mumbled, as I looked up at Holmes.

He just smiled, retrieved the coin, gripped it tightly in his hand, and turned his gaze to the window and beyond.

Holmes's recovery was rapid. Jameson, Welile and Murdoch returned with long faces, expecting the worst when they came to the hospital. When Holmes greeted them with a smile, they nearly fainted.

"Holy dooley!" Murdoch exclaimed. "Here you are grinning like a shot fox. Why you'll soon be as fit as a Mallee bull."

Welile, however, just said a few quiet words in her language.

Jameson looked puzzled. "Welile said something about a woman saving Holmes. Who was that?"

Holmes smiled. "Another time. Tell me about the German camp, and Maeve."

Murdoch patted Jameson on the shoulder. "The German camp is finished, and the commander's in the nick."

"The Belgian authorities have moved in now to secure the area," Jameson added.

"What of the poor souls?" I asked.

"Sad business, that!" Jameson said. "They're under care now. Some may come around… it's too early to tell."

"Watson told me that it was Maeve who led you to the mining camp," Holmes said.

"She even drew a map," Murdoch replied. "She may have saved your life, Mr. Holmes."

"I suspect the opposite."

"All very confusing, Holmes," I said. "Maeve worked

with the German mining company, conspired to kill you, and then betrayed them? To what end?"

"She hoped the German intrusion into Belgian territory would trigger a response by Belgium's close ally – Britain. And our murder would provide a *casus belli*."

"She wanted to start a war? But, why?"

"Do you recall the Greek word on the piece of paper I showed you? It *was* a name, as I thought – Zaharoff… Basil Zaharoff."

"The merchant of death," I replied.

"Yes – industrialist, philanthropist… and arms dealer," Holmes explained. "The acorn does not fall far from the tree. Our little Maeve Moriarty has grown up to peddle death, destruction, and depravity on a scale that her vile father never imagined. I fear that we have not seen the last of her."

ABOUT THE AUTHOR

KIM KRISCO, author of three books on leadership, now follows in the footsteps of the master storyteller Sir Arthur Conan Doyle by adding five new, and exciting, Sherlock Holmes adventures to the canon. He captures the voice and style of Doyle, as Holmes and Watson find themselves unraveling mysteries in, and around, pre-WWI London that, as Holmes puts it, "appears to have taken on an unsavory European influence."

Meticulously researched, all of Krisco's stories read as mini historical novels. His attention to detail includes on-location research such as his recent trip to Aviemore Scotland, and Ben Macdui Mountain, so that he could better capture the authentic feel of the setting for *The Bonnie Bag of Bones* – the first of Holmes's and Watson's post-retirement adventures.

In *Sherlock Holmes – The Golden Years*, Kim Krisco breathes new life into the beloved "odd couple," revealing deeper insights into Holmes's and Watson's protean friendship that has become richer with age... and a bit "puckish."

Kim lives in the Rocky Mountains of Colorado in a straw-bale home he and Sara Rose built themselves.

JAICO PUBLISHING HOUSE

Elevate Your Life. Transform Your World.

ESTABLISHED IN 1946, Jaico Publishing House is home to world-transforming authors such as Sri Sri Paramahansa Yogananda, Osho, the Dalai Lama, Sri Sri Ravi Shankar, Sadhguru, Robin Sharma, Deepak Chopra, Jack Canfield, Eknath Easwaran, Devdutt Pattanaik, Khushwant Singh, John Maxwell, Brian Tracy, and Stephen Hawking.

Our late founder Mr. Jaman Shah first established Jaico as a book distribution company. Sensing that independence was around the corner, he aptly named his company Jaico ('Jai' means victory in Hindi). In order to service the significant demand for affordable books in a developing nation, Mr. Shah initiated Jaico's own publications. Jaico was India's first publisher of paperback books in the English language.

While self-help, religion and philosophy, mind/body/spirit, and business titles form the cornerstone of our non-fiction list, we publish an exciting range of travel, current affairs, biography, and popular science books as well. Our renewed focus on popular fiction is evident in our new titles by a host of fresh young talent from India and abroad. Jaico's recently established translations division translates selected English content into nine regional languages.

Jaico distributes its own titles. With its headquarters in Mumbai, Jaico has branches in Ahmedabad, Bangalore, Chennai, Delhi, Hyderabad, and Kolkata.

SINCE 1946